i

Whose Land is it Anyway

Benjamin Sibangani Sibanda

Benjamin Pages PBC
36 Audley Street, Cranbourne
HARARE, ZIMBABWE

ISBN 978 1 779205-40-7
EAN 9781779205407

Dedication

This book is dedicated to the people of Zimbabwe, most of whose dreams remain unfulfilled.

Chapter 1

Even by Zimbabwean standards, this was a particularly spectacular sunset. The sun, what was left of it, was a fiery, bright orange circle that peeped over the horizon from behind the line of indigenous Msasa trees in the distance, turning the strips of light clouds above it into a kaleidoscope of colour; red, orange, purple, yellow and even some pink. Between the manmade lake at the end of the manicured lawn and the Msasa trees, the tall savannah grasses, green in early February because of the recent rains, but soon to turn golden brown with the onset of the dry season, swayed as a light breeze had come up, a welcome relief from the suffocating heat earlier in the day. The whole scene was then exaggerated by its own reflection in the lake just below Jacques Venter's farmhouse. It was like a painting on a very large canvas, except the painting kept changing as though it were alive. As the sun sunk lower, the colours changed; the clouds nearer the horizon took on a darker, almost brooding appearance, while those higher up, still benefitting from the reflection of the sun as it rounded the earth's curvature, took on the brighter colours, though with less intensity.

Then there were the birds. Drawn to the lakeside by their need to be in close proximity to water and, for some, by the reeds and other waterside plants that were ideal for their nesting, the variety was stunning and the cacophony of noise that characterised the early evenings around the Venter homestead as the birds prepared to settle down for the night was breath-taking. Soon, the frogs would join in, adding their own brand of song to nature's orchestra.

"This is God's own country, heh," he said, almost to himself.

"It is, isn't it," his guest responded, regarding the same scene with awe. "I have just been sitting here thinking how blessed we are to be living in such a picturesque part of this beautiful country."

"Pity about the *munts,* heh. They seem determined to fuck it up for us… err, sorry vicar, but you know what I mean."

"I don't, actually," Pastor Jones feigned ignorance.

This was one of those visits the pastor did not look forward to. Jacques Venter was crude; crude of dress, crude of manner, crude of language. Pastor Jones watched his host, who was leaning against the balustrade of his veranda, holding a beer – his favourite end of day drink. He was dressed like many white farmers in these parts, almost like it was part of some uniform; khaki shirt and shorts and *veldt scoens* of the same colour on his oversize feet. It was clear from his rather ample girth that Jacques Venter ate well and consumed copious amounts of alcohol. He was one of about a dozen white farmers in the Macheke commercial farming community that Pastor Jones ministered to, and, as such, had to be visited regularly by the pastor.

"Well," Jacques Venter appeared to enjoy riling the pastor, "twenty years ago, they inherited from us a country that had one of the best run and most progressive economies in Africa. In twenty short years, they have fucked it up completely. We are now the bane of all jokes

2

about Africa!"

Pastor Jones said nothing for a few minutes. He regarded his host in the darkening gloom of an early evening that always seemed to close in so quickly. Although he ministered to the predominantly white commercial farming community, he spent a lot of time with their workers who, quite frankly, needed his services more. He had gained their trust and he had been hearing and sensing some discontent with the government's slow pace of land distribution. In fact, it seemed to have disappeared from the ruling party's agenda for a while. But recently, a new opposition party, the Movement for Democracy (MFD) was ruffling their feathers and the land question was being looked at again, with more urgency, by the ruling Zimbabwe Patriotic Alliance (ZIPA). There was even talk of the government considering forcibly removing white commercial farmers and redistributing the land to black peasant farmers – who, in Pastor Jones' opinion, needed and deserved more land. They were crammed into what were called African Reserves – then Tribal Trust Lands – before independence and had now been sanitised by being renamed "Communal Lands." Their land was overpopulated, over cultivated, overgrazed and had hardly any trees as wood was not only the main fuel but was also the major building material, while the likes of Jacques Venter enjoyed the ownership of about a thousand hectares of land, most of which was, in his view, idle.

"You know, of course that the land question has not really been addressed adequately since independence. It has been twenty years and the people must surely be getting rest…,"

"What land question? These people got what they wanted; mansions in bloody Borrowdale and fancy Mercedes Benzes. They have no interest in farming whatsoever."

"You are talking about a small minority of the ruling elite. The vast majority of the people of this country need more land…"

"To do what with?" Jacques asked sneeringly. "The vast majority of our blacks are very happy to be working for us. They have always been. It's the trouble makers in your so called ruling elite who keep talking about wanting more land. Have you seen what they have done with the farms that they acquired?"

"Well, they are ruling and…"

"More like ruining than ruling." He laughed heartily at his own joke.

"…and they could take the land by force, if needs be."

"These people? Come on pastor, do me a favour. These bods could not organise a piss up in a pub if they tried. Anyway, how are they going to do that? We have title deeds, which mean that we have legal title to this land. Even your "ruling elite" can understand that, surely?"

"Be that as it may, what would you do if they decided to take the land by force?"

"Let them try. Do you know how many guns are in the hands of farmers?" Jacques Venter held up his arms as though he was pointing a rifle, "Pow! Pow! Pow! It would be like target practice. I can just see their black faces exploding into red…"

Pastor Jones was horrified. "Those are human beings you are talking about…!"

"Oh, sorry vicar, I forgot that you church types have this funny belief that all men are created equal!"

"Of course everyone is equal in God's eyes…"

"They are not!" Jacques was almost shouting, "Look at what they have done to this country in twenty years and tell me that they are equal to us. Even your bible says so. You know, after the flood, when whatshisname got drunk…"

"Noah," Pastor Jones interrupted.

"Yes, him, when he was running around naked after taking some wine – which you keep telling me is a sin – didn't one of his sons laugh at him and God, Himself, said that his descendants would be the servants blah, blah, blah…"

"I must give you a bible study one day," the pastor tried to change the subject.

"There is nothing you can teach me about the Bible. God, my friend, is white. Isn't that right, Jonas?"

"Yes sir," Jonas, the garden boy was working way past the government stipulated working hours and had not really been paying attention to the conversation that had been taking place above him as he finished tending the lawn in the gloom. He had been thinking about what was happening to the country; about independence and how excited he had been that there was now a black government that would understand the needs of people like himself. Yet as he saw things now, it seemed to him that nothing much had changed. In fact, things appeared to have gotten worse. He had worked for the Venters for some years, starting before the country's independence. He had seen them appear to prosper even more after independence and they seemed more confident about their position. There had been a time, just after independence, when they had seemed to treat him with more respect, but as the years had gone by, they seemed to revert to their old ways, and they ignored whatever new laws that had been put in place with regards to minimum wage and working hours. He found himself thinking about a conversation he had had with his son, Chenjerai, a few days earlier.

"Dad," his son had said quietly, "How long do you think you will carry on working for the Venters?"

"I have not really thought about it son. I will work for as long as my body can work…"

"For the Venters?"

"Well, yes. They have been good to me and your mother and we have built ourselves a nice home in Murewa Communal lands. By the time I am ready to retire, I will have a few cows, a few goats and we can spend the rest of our days happily looking after our livestock and homestead."

"Have you thought about retiring now?"

"Why would I want to do that?" Jonas could not believe his son, "I am still strong enough to work. Besides, I need to put together a nest egg so that when I retire…"

"You will have nothing," Chenjerai had interrupted. "You are, what, forty-five now? You have worked for the Venters for twenty six years, since you were nineteen. What have you to show for it?"

"As I said, I have a beautiful home in Murewa and I have educated you, with the help of Mr Venter, I might add. You are now at University; your two brothers are almost out of high school. What more do I need?"

"A decent retirement," Chenjerai had replied. "A retirement that would allow you and mum to enjoy your latter years and have an income that will sustain you. Look, dad, you have worked all these years, have you ever gone on holiday? Yet Mr Venter takes his family on holiday two, three times a year and every few years they even go overseas! You, on the other hand, can't even enjoy the simple pleasure of co-habiting with your wife! You have to wait for when you retire, and then you will not really retire because you will have to continue eking out a living from that piece of land that gets less and less fertile every year." He was quiet for a few minutes, and then carried on, much more forcefully.

"It seems to me, dad that you will only enjoy the kind of pleasures that the Venters of this world take for granted now, in heaven, but as we all know, even that is not guaranteed, so you could live a life of no pleasure here, and then end up in hell anyway!"

"Son, there are things you do not understand. Mr Venter is a good man; a good employer. He has been good to me and has helped me in so many ways, even paid some of you and your brothers' education…"

"But you should have been able to earn enough to educate us without his help, not that I am not grateful…"

Jonas had laughed, "You think I could have sent you to University on a garden boy's wages?"

"JONAS!!!!"

He had been so lost in thought that he had not heard his employer's first two calls.

"Why are you ignoring me?"

"Sorry sir, I was thinking…"

"Well don't think in the time I pay for. Fetch me another beer. A very cold one."

Jacques roared with laughter after Jonas had left.

"He was thinking, was he? What has he got to think about? I look after all his needs; I pay his children's school fees. I own the man! I own his fucking wife! Well, I did anyway," he said more quietly. He looked pensive for a short while then went on. "She was a pretty little thing when she was younger. If the wife had not caught on, who knows, there might be a couple of *goffle pikinins* running around the old farm, hey?"

He stopped as Jonas walked in with his beer and a tray of tea and biscuits that Mrs Venter had sent for the pastor. He started to pour the tea but was stopped by the pastor who preferred his tea to steep for a while. He went on to pour his employer's beer, just as he liked it, with hardly any head.

"Is your man alright?" Pastor Jones asked after Jonas left. He had seemed angry as he poured his employer's drink. Could he have overheard what Jacques had been saying?

"My man?" Jacques was looking into the distance.

"Jonas, he looked rather, thoughtful."

"Oh he's probably thinking of his dead mother or something. You never can tell with these people."

Indeed Jonas had caught the end of what his employer had been saying and he was livid. As he walked down the stairs, he could not believe what he had just heard. His wife had slept with Mr Venter, had she?

He did not bother to cook that night, but when he went to bed, he could not sleep either. Sekai, his wife, had been the only woman in his life. He remembered how, as a young nineteen year old school dropout who had spent the last three or four years trying to get work in the factories in the then Salisbury, he had ended up at the Venters because they did not ask for any qualifications. Mrs Venter needed someone to look after her garden of green grass and flowers. When he had been told that he was going to work in the garden, he had assumed that he was going to be growing vegetables! What did these white people need grass for? It had to be cut and watered and weeded, just so they could enjoy looking at it? It had seemed strange to Jonas, but it meant an income every month so he would do whatever they wanted.

Everyone at the workers' compound congratulated him for getting the job at the big house, partly because it was thought to be easier than the fields, but mainly because Sekai, who every young man that worked there lusted after, worked in the house. He had seen her for the first time on his second day there and had immediately decided that she was way beyond him. She was the prettiest girl he had ever seen, yet she seemed so superior, throwing whatever food she had been instructed to give to Jonas by the madam at him with the air of one having to deal with, well, only a garden boy. Although he had found

9

this strangely endearing, he had also decided that she was way out of his league. His only other interaction with her was when she came to relay instructions from the madam, Mrs Venter. Then one day, he was called by Mr Venter and asked to sit down on one of the easy chairs in the veranda.

"No, sir," he had said, "I'll stand." He had never been allowed to sit down in one of his employer's chairs before and he had started to worry that he may have done something to offend his employer.

"Sit down, Jonas!" Mrs Venter had said with finality.

He sat on the edge of the chair, now totally convinced that he was about to lose his job. Mrs Venter had always seemed so distant and unwilling to speak to the black workers and he had generally only caught glimpses of her as she did whatever it was she did in the house, and occasionally, when she went out in the car. Why was she here?

"Jonas," Mr Venter had started hesitantly, "how would you feel about marrying Sekai?"

He had stood up without knowing why. How could Mr Venter be asking him this? Sekai was not even his girlfriend. She surely had a boyfriend with all the suitors on the farm and beyond. He had even seen someone who had a car come to visit her on weekends.

"Sit down, Jonas!" Mrs Venter seemed impatient, "You like her don't you?"

"Yes," he said absentmindedly, "No, NO!...."

"You don't like Sekai? I think she likes you."

"I don't mean that I don't like her," where was this going and why was Mr Venter not saying anything. It was as if he was afraid of his wife. "But she is not my girlfriend. I think she has a boyfriend…"

"She does not," Mrs Venter sounded sure of herself. "I will speak to her and I am sure that she will see the wisdom of marrying someone like you."

Mr Venter still said nothing and seemed too embarrassed even look Jonas in the eye. He even looked smaller than the bellowing giant that always shouted at him whenever he had done something wrong.

For a few months Sekai and Jonas had been encouraged, it seemed to Jonas, to see each other at every opportunity. The first few meetings were quite awkward as Jonas was unsure what to say to the lovely Sekai. Their meetings had gradually become less uncomfortable and they talked about their backgrounds and their dreams, but he still said nothing to indicate that he liked her as Mrs Venter had indicated. She, on the other hand was getting desperate. Mrs Venter had made it clear that her job was in danger unless she found herself a boyfriend, and Jonas seemed to be Mrs Venter's preferred candidate. He was not so bad looking, she thought and he seemed to have quite ambitious thoughts about his own future and the futures of any children he might have. She could do worse. Sekai decided to take matters into her own hands.

"So, Jonas," she said suddenly one Sunday afternoon as they sat together besides the dam across from the Venter's house, "have you thought about who you might marry?"

He had stood up almost as though he wanted to run away. Why was she asking him this? For months, he had been trying to find a way to introduce the subject to her and could not find the right words, or the right opportunity. Now she was spoiling everything. Good girls did not introduce the subject of marriage without being asked – at least that was what he had always thought.

"I," he started, and then went quiet for a while.

"Sit, Jonas," Sekai offered her hand to encourage him to sit down. He took it and sat down heavily as his legs seemed to buckle at her touch.

"I love you," he blurted out.

Sekai threw her head back and laughed. His awkwardness was so… sweet, she thought.

Jonas stood up again. He had blown it. How was he ever going to look at her again? He sat down again, slowly this time and felt depressed.

She never told him that she loved him back, but somehow, their relationship seemed to take on a new lease of life. He had found himself laughing with her without knowing why; their meetings became less awkward and without really talking about it, they had become a couple. With a timely "loan" from the Venters, Jonas had been able to marry Sekai and within a few months, she had become pregnant. He had been surprised that she had not been a virgin but decided not to ask, preferring to assume that some unscrupulous man had taken advantage of an innocent young girl. He had not wanted to know who that man might be. Now he knew and wished he did not.

When her time came, Sekai had gone to her mother's to give birth as was tradition. She was never to return to work for the Venters, her temporary replacement was Antonio, a Mozambican who had worked at another homestead, being preferred by Mrs Venter.

Sometime in the early hours of the morning, sleep finally overtook Jonas. He had finally decided that whatever had happened between his employer and Sekai was because Mr Venter had taken advantage of an employee who had few if any rights under Rhodesian Law. Perhaps those who were advocating that land be taken back from the whites had a point, he thought.

In the big house's master bedroom, Jacques Venter made love to his wife more passionately than he had done in a long time, all the time thinking of Sekai. A young, voluptuous and willing Sekai.

Chapter 2

P ASTOR Patrick Jones had a routine. He had been invited by the white farmers of the Macheke Commercial farming area to minister to the small and dwindling congregation in what had started as a Dutch Reformed Church congregation but was now a non-denominational community chapel. It was built on land donated by Jacques Venter's grandfather when he first bought the farm that Jacques now farmed. It sat on a rocky outcrop of granite stones which meant that it was elevated and overlooked the vast savannah plains where Jacques Venter's cattle grazed. Across the plain, one could see the double-storied Venter residence in the distance; its picture postcard beauty of green lawn, colourful flowers and a shimmering lake, particularly in the dry season, starkly contrasting with the brown dryness all around it. In the rainy season, it merged into the natural flora around it as if it was put there at creation. Besides the chapel, separated from it by a bougainvillea hedge, stood a two-bedroom stone bungalow that was the pastor's residence. He had lost his wife of many years in a tragic road accident and his only son had moved back to Wales from where the good pastor originally hailed, so the accommodation was more than adequate for his needs.

On Sundays, the pastor was in church, after which he would generally be invited to one of the farmers' homes for lunch. On Mondays, he visited five of the farms in his area. This generally took him all day because of the distances involved as the farms were quite large. On Tuesdays, he visited what he liked to call the larger half of the population he ministered to – the farmers' workers and their families and even the people in the nearby Nhowe Communal Lands. The need here was great and he found it more fulfilling to be able to support and provide where he could, even though he knew that whatever he did was inadequate. On Wednesdays, the farmers and their wives went to Marondera, some thirty or so kilometres to the west, towards Harare, seventy-five kilometres further. Marondera was the nearest biggish town to them – although there was Macheke town, which was closer, but did not have all the supplies that the farmers needed. In Marondera, the women would shop in the morning, have lunch at Marondera Hotel and then have their hair done in the afternoon at the one salons that catered for Caucasian hair. The men would play golf in the morning at the Marondera Golf Club where they would have lunch and then spend the afternoon drinking while they waited for their wives. The late afternoon or early evening drives back to their farms were therefore, not without incident.

Pastor Jones took advantage of the absence of the farmers on Wednesdays to do what he called his administrative work, which involved telephoning or writing to donor organisations on behalf of his larger constituency to get funding. On Thursdays, he visited the other six white farmers, on Fridays, he prepared his sermon for Sunday and on Saturdays, he went fishing.

It had rained most of the day this Wednesday and the pastor had, after finishing with his administrative work, had nothing much to do so he sat and watched the rain. He thought of the irony of the situation with this season's rains. There had been no rain when it was needed to germinate, grow and mature the crop. Now that most of the crops had failed and there would be little to harvest, the rains had come, finally, to destroy whatever had survived the drought. There was going to be massive crop failure and there would be need for food aid. Yet Zimbabwe was being hailed as the bread basket of the region because the few white farmers, well financed, highly mechanised and skilled were making it so; but their immediate neighbours were starving because they did not have enough land to grow enough even for their own consumption! Surely there was some middle point where the two farming models could co-exist, and be able to create a more equitable food supply.

He thought again about the rumours that he had been hearing that there may be trouble brewing with regards to land. It needed to be addressed, clearly, but Pastor Jones was not sure that the government of the ruling Zimbabwe Patriotic Alliance (ZIPA) was serious about tackling it. They kept reminding people about how they won the war, which was fine as far as it went, "but it does not provide food for the people," he said out loud to himself. He smiled as he remembered a conversation he had had with a twenty-three year old a few days earlier.

"Pastor Jones," young David had asked, "I keep hearing that ZIPA won the war and brought independence to Zimbabwe?"

"Well, David," he had answered, "they did!"

"But why is that such a big deal?"

"They had to go to war to fight a recalcitrant, racist government that would not even consider giving the indigenous people of this country the same rights as the whites; would not even allow blacks the basic right to elect their own rulers. It was a big deal!"

"But there were about six million of us against two hundred and fifty thousand whites. We were bound to win. Why do they make such a big deal about a war that was so heavily stacked in our favour? We couldn't lose!"

"It wasn't as simple as that, David."

David would have been three when the war ended. Could he even understand that eighty percent of the Rhodesian army was black? According to the government's own statistics, more than half the population of Zimbabwe was under thirty and the war of liberation meant little to them. Why were they continuing to talk about a war that meant nothing to most of the active members of the population? "It's because they have nothing else to offer," he said aloud to himself again. In the early years of independence, they had been Socialists, but as the opulence that came with power took hold, they had all but dumped that ideology, but what had they put in its place? The past glories of winning the war were not going to help the people. They needed something that the people could look forward to... "That's it!" He sat up suddenly. It occurred to him then, as clearly as daylight, ZIPA was looking for a current, more relevant war to offer to the people in response to the threat posed by the MFD!

The rain had relented. He looked out through the window at the scene below him. It always took his breath away, particularly after it had been raining; the air seemed somehow cleaner and the smell of the wet grass made everything seem fresh. He remembered then that he needed a few supplies – some candles and matches in case the power went out as it seemed to with more frequency these days. Most of his basic supplies were supplied by members of his congregation and he knew that after the visit to Marondera, there would be parcels arriving the next morning. He would take advantage of the lull in the rain to take a walk to the Mberi Trading Store about half a kilometre down the road in the Nhowe Communal Lands, which bordered the Macheke Commercial Farming Area.

The Mberi Trading Store stood on the side of a dirt road that formed the approximate border between the commercial farms and the communal lands. It was the only building left that was still operating at what was still known as Manhowe Township as all the other stores on either side of it had closed and only the fading, rusted advertising boards – for soft drinks, beer, cigarettes, pain killers, cough syrups and condoms - on the buildings gave an indication of what they once had been; a bottle store, a 'butchery', another Trading Store and a grinding mill – which was the only one with a hand painted *chigayo* on the wall. Peter Mberi, the owner of Mberi Trading Store had survived longer than the others and now as the only one left, provided the services that all the others had been providing, under the same roof. It was, thus the place where the people from the Communal lands and the farm labourers came to socialise and have a drink, and where Pastor Jones occasionally came to catch up with some local gossip.

On a late Wednesday afternoon, on a rainy day, there were not many people there. Themba Ndlovu, the war veteran was there though. Pastor Jones had a love-hate relationship with Themba. When he was sober, they could have quite lucid discussions about his war years and the situation in the country. When he was drunk, as he seemed to be now, the pastor would avoid him like the plague. And he tried to avoid him.

"*M'fundisi,*" Themba's sharp eyes were always on the lookout for anyone that might be able to buy him his favourite drink, "I am soooo happy to see you," he shouted with some relish. Pastor Jones realised that there was no way of avoiding him, so he stopped and regarded him with a mixture of pity and disgust at the way he looked. He had been a handsome young man. Pastor Jones remembered the first time he saw this strapping young man who had just been demobilised from the army when the former freedom fighters and their antagonists in the Rhodesian army had been merged into The Zimbabwean National Army. The numbers were just too high and there had been those like Themba, who had been paid what were, to most of them, very large amounts and put out to pasture. Themba had come home a hero. He was tall, he was handsome and he had some money, a good prospect for any girl of marriageable age. And there were many who would do anything to be seen with Themba, the war vet; young teenage girls who had dropped out of school, single mothers who were the unspoken victims of the war as they had mothered babies sired by the freedom fighters – or by Rhodesian soldiers, depending on who got there first - and even school girls at the nearby secondary school seemed to understand that Themba was the man to be seen with.

"I can't help it if they want me," he would explain to anyone who said anything about his philandering and the obvious danger he was putting himself in, particularly as HIV/AIDS was affecting so many people. "In any case, I have to make up for my comrades who died in the war. There are too few of us left to look after all these girls."

It did not take long for the money and the friends to desert him.

"Hello, Themba." Pastor Jones said, as politely as he could master. Themba's clothes looked like they had been on his unwashed back for many days and there was a pong around him. His hair was matted and unkempt, which made it look like he had tried to twist it into dreadlocks and then changed his mind; his shoeless feet were dry and cracked. He looked like anything but a conquering hero!

"Please make me a *scud,* M'fundisi," he was almost pleading. The scud was the name given to the brown plastic container that had become the trademark for a traditional African beer which, ironically, was now brewed by a major transnational corporation. It came from the Scud Missile, which had gained notoriety during the Iraqi invasion of Kuwait a few years earlier. Pastor Jones had never quite worked out how a rocket missile had become synonymous with an African beer container.

He felt sorry for Themba. It was not as if the man had not tried. He remembered a conversation he had had with the war veteran during one of their more lucid conversations.

"You know, M'fundisi, when we were taken from that school by the freedom fighters, we were excited…"

"You were abducted, weren't you?" Pastor Jones had interrupted.

"No, that's just what the newspapers and the radio said. We were excited because we thought that we were going on a short adventure; we thought that we would be back at school within a couple of days, but that for those couple of days, there would be no teachers to tell us what to do. They told us that we were going on an important mission to liberate our country; that our parents would be very proud of us when we came back, and, of course that we could have any girls we wanted when we did – which was most exciting to our seventeen year old minds. By the time we got to the base in Mozambique, we had walked for a long time and the excitement had worn off. We wished we had stayed behind with the few who refused to come or had been left because they were too young, or were just not in the right place when the freedom fighters came."

He had stopped for a few minutes almost as if he was reluctant to continue, then went on in a sombre tone.

"You know, they told us that those who stayed behind were sell outs and cowards who were missing out on the opportunity to do something great for their nation; that when our country was liberated, there would be no place for them. We hated them almost as much as we hated the Rhodesian soldiers." Themba had laughed without humour.

"You know what I found out when I went job seeking in Harare? Those same selfish cowards who stayed on at school, finished their secondary education and went on to University are now the managers of companies, the senior civil servants and the directors of parastatals!" He had shaken his head ruefully.

"'Mr Moyo can't see you today, he is in meetings all day; what was it you wanted to see him about?' The pretty secretaries would ask, looking down their noses at you. 'Do you have "O" levels?' They would ask. 'I was in the war of liberation, they did not teach "O" levels there', I wanted to say to them, but I did not. I just walked out and tried the next place.

Once I made it into the boss's office.

'You are Themba aren't you? Themba Ndlovu! How are you'? I did not recognise the man, but I was encouraged. He even shook my hands with what felt like genuine warmth. 'You don't recognise me, do you? It's Garikai; Garikai Mhlanga, from Mount Selinda Mission. You were in form three when we were in form one. What happened to you? The headmaster was always talking about what a great future you had; we all looked up to you…'

'I went to fight in the war of liberation', I said quietly.

'Oh, the war', he sounded as if he was mocking. 'Why?'

'Why, what?' I was puzzled.

"Why did you go to war? Why did you not stay and finish school? You could have been anything now; a doctor, an engineer, anything."

I wanted to wring his pompous neck! What was it he did not understand about the war? He made it sound like going to war was the most stupid thing that one could have done!"

Themba stopped abruptly, as if something had just occurred to him.

"Come to think of it, it was stupid, wasn't it, M'fundisi? I went to war and what do I have to show for it? Mr Garikai Mhlanga (most of my friends call me Gary, now) was right!" Themba looked like he was close to tears. "Anyway, at least he offered me a job – as a cleaner in his offices. I wish I had taken it now but I was a war hero; I had put my life on the line so that 'Gary' could sit behind the large desk that he was looking down at me from; so that he could send his children

22

to any school of his choice and all he could offer me was a job as a cleaner? Because, in his own words: 'I can't offer you anything else, you don't have "O" levels'."

"The scud, M'fundisi," Themba was saying in the present.

"Come," Pastor Jones said as he went into the shop, "Give the man a scud," he said to Mr Mberi, "and a box of matches and some candles for me."

"Why do you bother yourself with Themba?" Mr Mberi asked after he had given Themba his drink and the latter had gone outside to enjoy it.

"Well, he is our only real life hero, isn't he?"

"But the war ended years ago. He should get over it."

Pastor Jones found himself getting angry. He liked Peter Mberi with whom he had a very good rapport. But Peter was also the District Chairman for the ruling ZIPA.

"Peter," he said with feeling, "the war ended twenty years ago. Have you in ZIPA got over it?"

"That's politics, pastor, it's different…"

"It's Themba's life!" He interrupted, "do you know that Themba is as much a victim of the war as the thousands who died? The many girls who are now looking after children whose fathers they do not know? Do you know that while you are playing your… your politics, Themba has an all day, every day nightmare about the war of liberation and how it changed his life? I am surprised at you, Peter. I thought you were a better man than that!"

23

"All I am saying," Peter Mberi was surprised by the onslaught from the pastor, "is that Themba is not the only one who went to war. There are many of his erstwhile comrades who have got on with life, put themselves through school and are now gainfully employed or running successful businesses. They have got over it…"

"Have they?" The pastor interrupted, "or are they just better at disguising their pain?"

"I don't know, M'fundisi. Who is the better person, one who sits around my store hoping to bum a drink off someone, anyone, or one who disguises his pain, but gets on with life?"

"We are not all constituted the same," Pastor Jones was regretting having lost his temper. It was not a good thing for one looked up to by so many to lose control of his feelings. He decided to change the subject.

"Peter," he was not sure how to broach this subject without causing more offence, "is there any truth in the story that I hear that you guys are considering forcibly taking land from the whites for resettlement?"

Peter laughed out loud, relieved that the moment of awkwardness had passed. He was a gentle, kindly man and Pastor Jones decided that he really liked him.

"You know you whites are strange people. You seem to believe that we have no intelligence whatsoever. Land redistribution is an important part of what ZIPA is all about. The war, after all, was largely about the unfairness of your system of government, and the unfair land distribution. I'm sure even you would agree that this current situation where a handful of whites controls large tracts of land while the majority of our people are crammed into the unproductive communal lands is unfair and needs to be addressed."

"Obviously," Pastor Jones agreed.

"We need to move away from the current situation where, even though we are a major food producer, the majority of our people still have to rely on handouts from people like you, however well-meaning you are." He paused as if to allow the pastor to appreciate his reasoning, and then went on, "But unlike you guys, we think long term. We realise that there are things in our history that we cannot change; that if we are to go forward, we need to let 'bygones be bygones' and accept that, for now, we are a major food producer because of our white farmers – who, after all, are as much Zimbabwean as I am. We will find a solution to the land question, but it will not be one that will harm our economy, or our food security. So the answer to your question is no, we will not take land away forcibly, even though your forefathers did that to us, excuse me."

Peter went across to serve a customer who had come into the shop, an elderly lady. He spent quite a while with her as she counted her coins, with his help, to make sure that she had enough for what she needed. They then spent some time discussing the late rain and what effects it was going to have on the harvest. When he came back, he resumed.

"You know what I find funny is that the white farmers do not seem to realise that it is in their best interests to engage the government constructively on this. They need to come up with suggestions on a way forward. Instead, they sit smugly on their farms as if they believe that they have the upper hand…"

"All they want is a fair compensation for the land that they bought and for the infrastructure that they have put into those farms," the pastor interrupted.

"Our Government does not have the resources to compensate the farmers. There are so many areas that need resources and compensating farmers for land that was taken away from our people for free is not high on our list of priorities. A lot of the land on the farms is idle. Why do the farmers not, for example, give up some of that land and offer it to government?"

"But Peter, the British government did pay for some land. What happened to it? It was given to politicians and their cronies rather than to the peasants who need it most!"

"Ah! The British," Peter sounded sceptical, "they have reneged on their promise to pay for the land, and now they are supporting the opposition. They still want to have a say in how we run our country even though we are now an independent, sovereign state."

"Well, they are using money that is from their tax payers. Surely you understand that they cannot just continue to give it even when they can see that it is being abused."

"So, in your opinion, all the land should be given only to peasant farmers. There is no room for commercial farming in the new dispensation. Giving the land to politicians, who don't have it, is abuse?"

"I don't mean it like that, Peter; look at what they have done to the farms that they have taken. They have run them down and now they are not as productive as they used to be. Some of them are now completely unproductive."

"We have to go through a period of readjustment. They are still learning, and they don't have the Capital that their white counterparts have."

Pastor Jones was not convinced. In his mind, politicians had selfishly taken the land for themselves out of pure greed. They saw the infrastructure on the farms, the houses, the dams, and the equipment and they thought that it would be good to have it all. Many of them seemed to have no interest in farming whatsoever and the farms were just weekend getaways until they were so run down that it was no longer fun to go there, and then they would just abandon them. He was not even sure that his friend Peter, was high enough in the organisation of ZIPA to be able to enunciate government policy on land. He was thus not convinced that Peter's assurance was worth anything.

"Anyway, I must go before it gets too dark," he said at length, "and the rain looks like it wants to come back."

"Go well, M'fundisi, but remember the war ended twenty years ago and those fatherless children are now grown up and probably looking after their mothers," he said, referring to the pastor's earlier outburst.

"That is also true," the pastor responded good naturedly.

They parted on good terms.

Chapter 3

The sun was relentless, beating down on the small crowd that had gathered at the Manhowe Township with a ferocity that typically preceded the onset of a tropical storm. But the storm was a few hours away yet. They had been gathering since eight in the morning with the active encouragement of the ruling party's youth wing who had been going door to door with their own particular brand of encouragement. Most of the villagers dared not heed the call, but, then again, there was nothing much to do this Sunday morning and going to listen to a government minister was probably the only entertainment they were likely to see for a while. They might, after all, come away with some handouts from government as the usual thing was that ruling party officials – or government officials; they were never sure which hat they would be wearing – would give away 'goodies' which could be anything from fertilisers, seed, chemicals and even beer. But the minister was late. He had been expected at ten o'clock and it was nearly midday! The crowd was getting restless, and so was Peter Mberi, the District Party Chairman who had closed his Trading Store business to accommodate the minister's speechifying. It would not do for there to be a rival attraction while the Minister was addressing the people.

He looked at his watch again and again; he looked towards the direction from which the minister was expected. There was no sign of any vehicle. He took his new acquisition, a cellular telephone, out of his pocket and glared at it as if it was responsible for his problems. It had no signal; it never had signal when he was at his home base and only worked when he was away from home, closer to Marondera or Harare. Sometimes, however, if he stood on higher ground, he would get a weak signal, but this morning, even this did not work.

"They are late again," he said to no one in particular.

"They will be here," George Magaya, the enthusiastic ZIPA District Youth Chairman said with conviction.

"I just wish they wouldn't take people so much for granted. These people have been here for hours, in the hot sun..." He shook his head as he scanned the crowd, "No wonder the MFD are gaining so much ground on us, they..."

"The MFD are a bunch of Western puppets that have nothing to offer the people! The people know that our party is the revolutionary party that brought independence; that freed us from the yoke of British imperialism. There is no way the people of Zimbabwe will abandon us. They are currently just excited by a new kid on the block and want to try something new."

"I hope you are right," Peter was not impressed by the enthusiasm shown by his younger colleague. He felt that the party was not doing enough to respond to the new reality; that the MFD was not doing anything spectacular, just capitalising on the mistakes being made by ZIPA. He looked around at the crowd. A few more had come in since he last looked. They were clustered in small groups as they tried the best they could to shield themselves from the sun. At midday, the sun was overhead and the buildings offered little shade. The one big tree that did offer shade had been reserved for the expected dignitaries and a table covered with a cloth that was once white and the most comfortable chairs were in place. Most of the women held up umbrellas, while some of the men held old newspapers over their heads and others had old towels, handkerchiefs, jackets; anything that could reduce the effects of the sun on their heads.

"These people are not serious; do they think that we will continue to vote for them like before when they treat us so badly." Tongai Chibamu was a foreman at one of the white commercial farms in the area. He had a reasonable education and was looked up to by many people.

"We will if they keep giving us inputs for our crops," Robson Chemhanza was a ZIPA member who worked at one of the other farms, where he was the Village chairman. "And with the drought this year, they will not only give us food aid, they will give us inputs for the next season as well."

"But is that what they should be doing?" Tongai was not convinced, "I think that they should be spending their money on developing infrastructure like dams and irrigation systems. That way, we would be able to grow enough for ourselves even in drought years like this one. Giving us handouts does not help us to help ourselves. Do you know that some of those inputs end up on the black market, being sold to the highest bidder? Guess who the highest bidders are? The white farmers. How does that help us improve our agricultural production?"

"I never sell my inputs," Robson insisted, "and those who sell should not get any the next time round!"

30

"Robson, you sold me a bag of fertiliser last year," Paul Chikwama, a farmer from the nearby Chimbwanda African Purchase Area – smaller scale commercial farms that the Rhodesian government had sold to black farmers that were deemed to be reasonably competent – "should you not get some this time round?"

"That was different; I was short of school fees for my daughter. Most of these people sell so that they can buy beer."

"That's because we cannot afford to buy beer otherwise. My point is, if the government built the infrastructure that I am talking about, we would be able to grow enough, not just to feed ourselves, but also to be able to send some of it to market. That way, we can send our children to school without having to sell our fertilisers and to buy ourselves a beer or two when we are relaxing, like the whites do. What is wrong with that?"

"Where is the government going to get that money?" George Magaya had overheard the conversation when he was passing. "The government has many other areas that need its attention…"

"Like buying fancy cars for ministers and going on overseas trips with large delegations…"

"No! You farm workers spend too much time with whites and you are beginning to sound just like them. Our government needs to spend on important areas like health, and education. It is every child's right to get a decent education…"

"With all the will in the world, your government does not have the resources to do all that you say they need to do. All I am saying is that if, for example, instead of using all that money to buy inputs for people, they channel it instead to developing irrigation systems, in the long run, the people would be self-sufficient and would not need handouts."

"And in the meantime, what will the people eat? What is the point of developing irrigation while people are starving?"

"Well, if your government was not fighting against the rest of the world, we would probably get…"

"Aid? Is that what this is all about? That we should be going to our erstwhile colonisers with begging bowls to ask for help? Do you know what conditions that so-called aid comes with? I am surprised that somebody with your level of ed…" he stopped suddenly, "Oh, I see. You are another one of the MFD supporters! You think that all our problems will go away if we ask for aid from the West, from Britain? Is that why you keep referring to the government as 'my' government…?"

"I have always voted ZIPA," Tongai found himself on the back foot, "but tell me this, George, is our country better off now than it was twenty years ago?"

"The Minister is here!" Someone shouted before George could answer. He had wanted to tell the MFD sell out that the country had to necessarily go through some difficulties if it was to be revolutionised; that this was the nature of revolutions and that unless the country went through such pain, they would never enjoy true independence. Instead, he went to join the other party officials in welcoming the Minister.

The Minister arrived in a convoy of three vehicles, all spanking brand new Japanese four-wheel drives. Many of the people there had never seen such cars. Itai Mugwazo, Minister for Agriculture, did not want to be here. He did not want to spend his Sunday in some God forsaken backwater addressing people who had no appreciation of matters of state. But the President had insisted that his ministers should stay close to the people, especially now that there was an opposition party that seemed to be gaining ground.

"We need to go out there where the people are and remind them of the revolutionary pedigree of this great party. We don't want the MFD upstarts to continue misinforming our people," the President had said.

Itai Mugwazo looked around disdainfully at the crowd. Did these people really care about the politics of the country or were they just there to hear what handouts the Government was going to give out this year, he wondered. But he also realised that something was different. Normally, they would have been a lot of singing, ululating and clapping to welcome this important visitor from Harare. Instead, they were all standing around watching him, almost as if they expected him to break into song and dance or something. Their faces inscrutable, they held their hands up to shield their eyes from the sun following his every move and noticing just how well dressed he was in his Hong Kong-made 'bespoke' suit and shiny crocodile skin shoes. With pretty secretary in tow, he headed straight for the VIP seats in the shade, absentmindedly shaking the hands of the fawning party officials who had formed a line in his honour. His burly bodyguards followed close behind, making sure that no one got too close. As he sat down, he noticed a vaguely familiar face sitting apart from the rest of the crowd watching the goings on with what seemed like feigned disinterest. He decided that whoever the man was, he could not possibly know anyone so badly dressed.

Meanwhile, Mr Mberi was doing his best to whip up the crowd's enthusiasm with party slogans and the traditional raised fist. The responses he was getting were mainly from those that held positions in the party and a few others. The rest looked and sounded like they would rather have been somewhere else. Itai Mugwazo was not overly concerned. He knew exactly what to say to get the crowd going. He would give his speech, get the crowd into a frenzy and then leave to spend the rest of the afternoon with his secretary. He wished Peter Mberi would hurry up.

"And now," the District Chairman was concluding, "it gives me great pleasure to introduce to you our special guest. A son of this district who did us all proud when he went to fight in the war of liberation, and who is now doing a sterling job in government as Minister of Agriculture. Let's give him a big hand."

The response was better than it had been up to this point, but was still less than what both the minister and the district chairman would have expected. Minister Mugwazo stood up and scanned the crowd before a lengthy spell of sloganeering where, with raised fists, the virtues of the leader of the party and President of the country were extolled and the heroics of those who went to fight in the war of liberation were reiterated. Finally, the vices of the opposition MFD were denigrated as the fists were brought down to emphasise the "down with the MFD" slogan that, by now, everyone was shouting.

"Fellow Zimbabweans," Minister Mugwazo started, "it gives me great pleasure to come and address you, the people of this district; a district which bore the brunt of the atrocities of the Smith regime's soldiers during the liberation war. Your party will never forget you." For the next hour, he gave a history of the armed struggle in the area, which was somewhat superfluous as most of the people here had experienced first hand that period and could have told the minister a more accurate account. As he spoke, he could sense that the people were bored and some were beginning to drift away in search of shadier positions. This speech was not going as well as he had anticipated. He needed something to capture their attention.

"The war we fought," he went on, "was mostly about our land; the land that was stolen from our forefathers and is now in the hands of white farmers." The mood swing was palpable. The people's faces brightened, those who were walking away stopped in their tracks, and the levels of attention seemed higher. Minister Mugwazo was encouraged.

"We are tired," he went on, "of continuing to scratch a living from the crowded, infertile Communal Lands while our oppressors of old continue to enjoy the best farming land, the land where there is plenty of water."

The applause that followed surprised even the Minister himself.

"Who won the war?" He asked the crowd.

"WE DID!" they responded in unison.

"Who led the heroic people of Zimbabwe to victory?"

"ZIPA," they shouted with raised fists.

"Who wants total liberation for the people of Zimbabwe?"

"ZIPA!"

"Who has our land?"

"Foreigners!"

Minister Mugwazo paused for a while. He was on a high, but was what he was about to ask these people the correct party position? Could there be any ramifications from it? As government, they had, for years, been assuring the white farmers that they were important to the economy and that their tenure on the land was secure. He decided that as he was addressing a group of peasant farmers with little education, there was little chance that this would go very far. By the next day, he would be in faraway Harare and these people would have gone back to doing whatever it was they did when they were not attending political rallies. They would probably have forgotten about the minister and his visit. He lowered his voice.

"So, what are we going to do about the land that is in the hands of foreigners?"

"TAKE IT BACK," the crowd roared.

"What are we going to do?"

"TAKE IT ALL Back!"

A distance away from the excited crowd, Themba watched the Minister perform and shook his head. He was hung over from the night before and wished the speechifying would end so he could get a drink. There were many more people here today and there was bound to be someone willing to buy him a scud.

"Same old shit," he said to himself. He was remembering how they had been told the same slogans when they were in Mozambique, being prepared to go to the battle front. They were going to take the land from the whites; they were going to move into the palatial mansions in Harare's Northern suburbs; they were going to drive the fanciest cars. They were going to be rich. Period!

He looked down at his cracked shoeless feet, his smelly, dirty clothes that had not been washed for as long as Themba had not bathed. He looked again at the minister's attire, the pure wool suit and silk tie, the shoes; the gold watch on his wrist, even his socks looked like they were specially imported. It was difficult to equate this confident, pompous government minister with the scared young boy he had first met in Mozambique.

Young Itai Mugwazo had arrived about a month after Themba's own group. By this time, members of Themba's group were virtual veterans who were almost ready for battle. He remembered how sorry he felt for the young boys. Did they really know what it was they were in for? This was no place for children and Itai looked particularly vulnerable. Themba had felt pity for him and taken him under his wing so that even when Itai went on his first excursion into the battle field, Themba had made sure that he stayed close to him and protected him as much as he could. At the end of their first engagement, Themba had looked around for his protégé who had become detached in the heat of battle. The young man had been found cowering behind a large rock, in tears with a strong smell of excrement around him. They had had to dunk him in the nearby Mazoe River, notwithstanding its crocodile infestation, before they could go back to base. He had never been able to live that one down, but that was also his first and last battle of the war.

Young Itai seemed particularly adept at ingratiating himself with the hierarchy and in no time, he had become some sort of runner whose main task, it had seemed to Themba, was to relay messages from the top echelons of the party to the rest. Themba had watched the young man become part of the hierarchy, all be it at a very junior level, but high enough for him to give instructions to the likes of Themba. There had been persistent rumours that Themba was never able to confirm, that the young man was giving sexual favours to some of the senior party officials who had acquired the alternative sexual orientation during their long years of political detention! For a little while, Themba considered the possibility of going over to introduce himself, but quickly discarded that notion. There was no way Minister Mugwazo would recognise Themba, and even if he did, would he want to be associated with a vagabond like him? There were, of course, the body-guards as well.

The minister was ready to leave. He shook the hands of those closest to him and while the crowd sang and danced, he got into his car and the convoy left. Minister Mugwazo felt satisfied that he had fulfilled his duty relatively painlessly and he could report a successful rally to the President.

At Manhowe Township, Peter Mberi had opened his shop and scuds were flowing. Themba still sat apart from the crowd and wondered what all the excitement was about. The Minister had made it clear, earlier in his speech, that government did not have the money to continue giving away handouts. They were going to only give to the neediest of cases. He had blamed the country's problems on the Western world, particularly the British, who were advocating sanctions against a small, defenceless country and were refusing to help the government pay for more land as they had promised. There was going to have to be some belt tightening, he had said. Yet the people seemed to have quickly forgotten that part of his speech, only remembering the last bit about taking back the land from whites. How was the government going to do this? He wondered. He decided that the Minister had just made more empty promises to a gullible electorate.

"Hello, Themba, can I get you a drink?" Jonas, whose Sunday off had been delayed because his employer was entertaining, had just arrived to enjoy a couple of drinks after a long day serving his master and his friends. He could not understand what all the excitement was about and as Themba seemed the only one not caught up in the moment, he would try and find out from him what had happened to cause such joy. Jonas was one of very few people who still saw Themba as a hero who had fallen on hard times. He was quite happy to share a scud with him whenever he could.

"You are a good man, Jonas," Themba's eyes lit up and he was almost drooling. "I'll have a Castle please."

Jonas laughed. Themba was always trying to get people to buy him the Western clear beer that most people in places such as Manhowe could not afford, except perhaps at month end when they got paid.

"Have you looked at the calendar lately? Where do you think I am going to get the money to buy you a Castle at this time of the month? I am not a government employee, you know!"

They both laughed as Jonas stood to go and buy the scud from the shop. Themba watched him go and thought how lucky this man was to still be employed by a white farmer. He was well dressed and always had a bit of money for a drink whenever he came to Manhowe.

When he returned, Jonas was smiling to himself.

"What are you so pleased about?" Themba asked.

"Well, my friend, I have paid for a pint of Castle that Mr Mberi has set aside for us. We can drink it at the end to wash down this mud," he said, referring to the traditional beer, which had the colour of mud. "Anyway," he went on, "we might as well enjoy it. Do you know that there was a time when we were not allowed to buy or drink the white man's beer?"

"Really?" Themba knew what was coming, but did not want to disappoint his benefactor who liked to tell this story.

"Well, many years ago, when my father worked at The Grand Hotel in Salisbury, he stole a pint and brought it home to Murewa. He invited all his friends in the village to come and sample what he told them was his favourite drink when he was in Salisbury. There was a lot of excitement and it was decided that this special beer was to be drunk last after they had finished the home brewed traditional beer that my mother had made to welcome her husband home." Jonas was quiet for a while as he thought about the similarity between his life and his father's life. They both had to live away from their wives in order to earn a decent living.

"Anyway," he went on after a while, "when the traditional brew was finished, and one of my father's friends had made a long speech about how proud they were of their friend who worked in Salisbury and rubbed shoulders with white people every day and how, now, he had afforded them the privilege of tasting the beer that was only reserved for white people, the bottle was opened. It was warm, of course, as they had no fridges. My uncle, my father's elder brother was given the honour of taking the first sip. He took a very large swig, then promptly sprayed everyone with the beer as he spat it out.

'It's urine'!" He shouted accusingly, 'my brother has made me drink his urine!' My uncle was very angry. They all took turns to smell it and confirmed that it was, indeed, urine. My father, who had lied that he drank it all the time, also confirmed that it was urine, although it was in fact beer; they just had not expected it to taste like that! At the time, he assumed that one of the patrons at the hotel had urinated into an empty bottle and closed it.

Anyway, the incident was soon forgotten although my father had to apologise by giving a goat to his elder brother. The bottle was discarded and no one thought any more about it. Then one day, a white policeman on a motor bike was riding through our village and found the empty bottle. All the men in the village were rounded up and interrogated about where the bottle had come from. They all protested that they knew nothing about it, but after he took them one at a time and gave them a thorough beating, some of them must have confessed that it was my father who had brought it and that he worked at the Grand Hotel. My father lost his job as a result!"

They both laughed heartily, but Themba was thinking that the story seemed to get better and longer each time his friend told it.

"What is all the excitement?" Jonas asked after a while, "Did someone win the lottery?"

"The Minister was here," Themba said, "I am not sure what it was he said that caused such excitement."

"Were you not here for the speech?"

"I was, but I still don't know what is causing such excitement. He said something about taking the land back from the white people."

"Oh, that," Jonas was sceptical. "How many times have they made such statements; and people still believe them?"

"They seem to. Look at them, they are having a party."

For a while, the two of them sat side by side and watched the revelry. The singing got louder and more boisterous as the alcohol took effect, and the dancing got more vigorous and lewdly suggestive.

"So, when they have taken the farms, who are they going to give them to?" Jonas asked.

"He did not give that much detail. In fact, he did not even say how they are going to take back the land."

"We will just walk in and take it," George Magaya, the District Youth Chairman had overhead the conversation as he passed to go and re-plenish his drink. "They took it from our forefathers and we will take it from them."

"And I suppose they will just stand aside and say, 'here, take it. I don't need it anymore', will they?"

"This is a revolution," the young man was slurring his words, but looked quite convinced by what he was saying. "We need to transform this economy and give power back to the people. After the land, we will go for the companies…"

He could not finish as both Jonas and Themba burst out laughing.

"George, you don't even own a bicycle," Jonas said almost in tears, "and now you want to own a company?"

"I don't know why I waste my time with you old people. You have been so, so…" he could not find the word he was looking for, "…colonised," he said finally, "you don't know your rights anymore."

George walked away, swaying to the beat of the drums that had somehow found their way into the township and were adding to the rhythm.

"I don't know what is getting into these young people," Jonas said wiping his mouth after another sip from the scud, "my son is also talking this kind of nonsense."

"Chenjerai?" Themba wanted to confirm the name, "He is at the university, is he not? He is highly educated surely and can get any job in an office like the white people."

"I don't know about 'any' job, but he certainly can get a good job. Perhaps he can then start to look after his mother and I and I can retire to Murewa."

"He'll soon have a family of his own to think about, you know, and may not be able to look after you…"

"I sent him to school! I have struggled all my life to try and get him a better life than mine. How could he not be able to look after his parents?"

"The world is changing my friend. With higher levels of education, children are adopting more and more of the white man's ways. Many young men these days are ruled by their wives. They talk about equality and other nonsense like that. Do you know, I have a cousin in Harare who cooks for his wife, while she sits and watches television? His explanation is that she also goes out to work and she is tired. Can you believe that?"

"Chenjerai better not marry someone like that! His mother and I will never accept such a daughter in law!"

"You cannot arrange marriages for your children anymore. These days they talk about love and they ignore the long believed counsel that people should marry from among their own people, whose traditions and ways they understand. Now they can bring you a girl from anywhere; they'll soon be marrying white girls even!"

"They have started already," Jonas confirmed. "A young man in our village brought one home from England. I never met her, but I believe she really tried to fit in and be like one of us, but she looked different and there was the language barrier with the rest of the family. She had to go back to England, taking her husband with her. I think we have lost that one to England."

For a few minutes, the two friends sat side by side watching the increasingly boisterous revelry without speaking; just taking turns to drink from the common scud.

"I wonder what they look like, you know, down there," Themba said after a while, crossing his legs as he spoke.

"Down where?" Jonas did not immediately understand.

"You know," Themba looked around to see if anyone could hear them. No one was within ear shot. "I mean down where babies are made."

Jonas roared. "Apart from the pale skin," he said, "they must look like our women, surely?"

"I don't know, they say the Chinese women's… err… womanhood sits sideways rather than up and down like our women."

Jonas's shoulders heaved as he laughed at his friend's display of naivety. "Who has ever been with a China woman to know that? All people are the same except for the skin colour and hair texture."

"Exactly!" Themba exclaimed, "White people's hair is a lot longer than ours," he hesitated, "You don't think that it would be as long, down there?"

"I see what you mean. But if it were that long, it would surely stick out below those short skirts they like to wear; then again, I suppose they can always cut it."

"You and I, my friend," Themba said crossing and uncrossing his legs, "will never know."

Neither of them noticed the beautiful colours in the sky as the sun set to end another day at Manhowe Township. Even if they had, it would not have made an impression. Sunsets like these were common place and they assumed that everyone around the world saw them.

The rhythm of the drums went on late into the evening.

Chapter 4

Peter Lawrence had never known his father. In the nineteen thirties, his mother had gone to work for a white farmer whose land was adjacent to the Mhondoro African Reserve where her parents had just settled in after they were moved from an area to the east of Mhondoro because it had been designated a white area under the Land Apportionment Act of 1930 whose purpose was to allocate land between the Native blacks and the white people who had settled in the then Southern Rhodesia. The only name by which the farmer was known was *Chikwepa,* the Shona word for a tobacco pipe, because he seemed to always have one in his mouth, lit or unlit, almost as if it was part of his natural anatomy. She had come home pregnant, but would not disclose who the man was that was responsible for the pregnancy. The family was very upset, not least because she had, during her absence while she worked for Chikwepa, adopted the English sounding name of *Loveness,* instead of *Rudo,* the name she had been given by her parents at birth. She also had acquired a reputation for being somewhat liberal with her charms.

When the child was born, the traditional midwife that facilitated the birth came out of the hut looking very sad. She shook her head as she approached Loveness's mother, who was waiting anxiously outside the hut. She had heard the distinct cry of a baby thus could not understand her friend's apparent sadness.

"What is it?" She asked, her anxiety making her voice sound squeaky.

The midwife shook her head again. She was not sure how to break the news to her friend because it could mean the death of the baby, as tradition dictated.

"I think your daughter has given birth to an albino," she said finally.

"No!" Kubvoruno, Rudo's mother shouted as she ran into the hut, where she found her daughter cuddling her baby with such tenderness that she involuntarily started weeping. The midwife joined them and the three women sat in silence for some time before any of them spoke.

"What are we going to do?" Mai Muchaneta, the midwife asked finally.

"What do you mean 'what are we going to do'? What do people normally do with babies?" Loveness was puzzled.

"Well, my daughter," Kubvoruno said quietly, "Your son looks different. He is an albino and in our tradition, such children were killed. We do not believe that anymore, but we are not sure what your uncles will have to say about this." Both older women had joined a Christian church and did not believe in some of the traditional beliefs, particularly where human life was concerned.

Loveness looked closely at her baby for the first time. She immediately knew that her baby was not an albino, but she also knew, as quickly, who the father of the baby was. How would her parents take it?

"My son is not an albino!" She shouted vehemently. "He is white. My son is white."

The two older women looked at each other without understanding. The poor child was obviously upset at the thought of losing her baby, but they were each in their own minds, thinking of ways to disguise the baby so that the rest of the family could not see that he was different. Loveness's mother was particularly disturbed by her daughter's behaviour. Did she think that by working for a white man…

"What do you mean your son is white?" She asked although she was beginning to understand, even though what she thought she was beginning to understand did not make sense to her. Surely white people did not sleep with their servants?

Mai Muchaneta, the midwife, was also beginning to understand.

"You mean, this is Chikwepa's son?"

"I think so," Loveness answered timidly.

"What do you mean, you THINK so?" Both women spoke together. "You mean you slept with more than one white man?" Kubvoruno could not believe what she thought her daughter was saying.

"Sometimes," Loveness said, "Chikwepa would ask me to sleep with his friend, whose name I do not know. He was always drunk and it never lasted that long."

The two older women sighed together, after which there was a lengthy silence.

The uncles seemed to be more understanding than the women had predicted and Rudo, also known as Loveness, was allowed to keep her baby, although the baby was not seen in public too often. By the time he was three, the family had accepted the child as one of their own and he had a relatively happy early childhood, doing everything that any boy of his age would do in rural Mhondoro – looking after the family's cattle and goats and, as he grew, helping out in the fields. Peter, as his mother had named him, proved to be very good at the many fist fights that were an integral part of herding cattle and this meant that although he looked different, no one dared make fun of him. At seven, he started going to the local school where he, once again, proved his mettle at fist fights although he did not particularly excel at school work. But he was happy.

Then one day, he came home from school to find a strange looking white woman talking to his grandparents. She was dressed all in black with a frock that went all the way down to her ankles. There were white bits of cloth around her head and face. For some reason, she made Peter think of witches, even though he had never seen one.

"He is a handsome boy," the woman said in a strange sounding Shona, looking directly at Peter, "just like his mother said. I'm sure he will be very happy where I am going to take him" – her Shona made it sound like 'I am sure it will be happy where I will take it'. Peter had no idea what she was talking about and was sure that whatever she was saying had nothing to do with him; but how did she know his mother, who, by this time worked in faraway Salisbury but came home every few weeks, always with presents for the family, but with the best presents of toys and sweets for Peter? And what was it she wanted to take away.

"There you are, Peter," his grandfather said cheerfully, "Sister Concillia here has some good news for you. Sit down and I will tell you all about it."

Peter went and sat cross legged on the ground, as far away from 'the witch', as he thought of her, as possible. What good news could she possibly bring?

"Peter," the witch said, "I am here to take you away, to a better school."

Peter was not sure what to say. What did she mean by 'a better school'? He liked the school he was going to and saw no need to go to another one. He did not particularly relish the thought of being taken away by this woman.

"Will Taurai come too?" He was very fond of his cousin, Taurai and if he was to come along, then perhaps things would not be so bad. After all, it would only be during the day and they would come home in the evening.

"No, Peter," his grandfather said, "Taurai cannot come with you. This is a special school only for your kind…"

"Then I am not going… what do you mean by my kind? Is Taurai not my kind? You have always said that we are like brothers…"

"Yes, Peter, but you must know that you are different and people like you are not supposed to live in Reserves like this. You deserve better."

Peter thought about what his grandfather had said. He remembered how the other children in the community and at school seemed to treat him differently when they first met him, feeling his skin and touching his hair. This had never really bothered him as it never really lasted that long and he was quickly assimilated as one of the boys. As he sat there looking at his grandmother with pleading eyes, he remembered two occurrences that had never meant much to him, but now seemed to confirm what his grandparents were saying.

The first time he went swimming with the other boys, they had been gasps of surprise when he took his clothes off. His skin was so pale that the other boys thought that he had no skin at all. For a while, they would not allow him to get in the water because they were not sure what would happen when his body got wet! Starting with his feet, Peter had gradually got himself wet and soon swam with the others without incident.

Then, one day, when they were out watering the cattle at the river, a white policeman on a motor cycle approached them wanting to ask for directions. Ignoring all the other boys, he addressed Peter directly, in English. Peter of course spoke Shona like the rest of the boys and had no idea what this man was saying; but the man seemed convinced that this boy, who looked almost white, should have been able to communicate with him. In the end, he was shouting at Peter as though he thought that the only way the boy could not understand him was because he was deaf. Peter had run away because he could not understand why this man seemed to be getting angry with him. There had been, of course the incident with the boy who was visiting from Salisbury. He had called Peter a *Chigure,* after some traditional dancers who originated from Nyasaland and who always wore masks that looked like white people during their performances. Peter had dealt with him the only way he knew how; with his fists. The boy had never been back to visit since!

"… when you come back, you will speak English like white people and you will be able to get better jobs," his grandfather was saying. "We will all be able to ride in your car?"

Peter could see that he had no support even from his grandmother, whom he loved dearly. It had also become clear to him that this was not just another school in the area. He was being taken away to a school far away from everyone he had ever known and loved; and he was going to go and live there!

"What about my mother?" He shouted tearfully, "How is my mother going to find me?"

"It approached us," the nun appeared to be saying. "It wants a better life for its only child."

"You are lying! My mother would never allow you to take me away!"

"Don't be rude, Peter. You know that you should never tell an adult that they are lying," his grandfather chided gently. "I hope that you will not let us down and will always remember the good manners that we have taught you,"

Peter had looked around at all the faces around him. The only one that was smiling was the witch. Everyone else looked sad but determined that Peter should go. Just like that, he was leaving the only home he had ever known; the only friends and family he had ever known. It was probably the saddest day, by far, of his young life. Sadder even, than the day his mother left him with her parents so that she could go and find work in Salisbury.

They arrived at the new "better" school three days later, having travelled first by a donkey drawn cart into Salisbury where he slept in a place full of women dressed exactly the same as the witch, who by now was his only friend. The following evening, they travelled by train to Bulawayo, which he had heard about, but had always thought of as being as far away as heaven or some of the places from the Bible that his grandmother had told him about. They had spent another day in Bulawayo where his only diet was a very sweet drink accompanied by buns. He had enjoyed this at first, but now wanted home-cooked *sadza,* the maize meal staple that they ate every day at home. In the evening, they had taken another train to a place called Plum Tree, which Peter had never heard about. They arrived there in the middle of the night and had to wait at the station until daylight. Peter was very tired but found himself having to walk, most of the day, to the school. They arrived just after sunset and Peter was taken to a bed in a room full of other boys of roughly the same his age. Many of them had hair of similar texture to Peter's, but some were darker than Peter. He was thus not sure why these people, who did not look exactly the same, were his kind. The room, called a dormitory, or dorm as everyone seemed to call it, was to be his bedroom for the rest of the year. He had his own bed – the first time he had slept in one – in which he slept alone, unlike at his grandparents' where he shared blankets with two other boys, Taurai and Promise, his other cousin. How he missed them just then!

He had no time to dwell on that as he was soon caught up in the routine of boarding school life, which he hated. There was not the freedom he was used to when he was out herding cattle. Here, everything was done in a certain way at certain times. You ate at a set time, you slept at a certain time, you showered at a certain time. Peter found it difficult to keep up with all the rules and often got into trouble. Of course it did not help that the other boys all spoke English – or a version of it as he later found out – and he only spoke Shona, which seemed to amuse the other children. He was, he found out, part of a race called Coloureds and they were not supposed to speak Shona. They were supposed to speak English like their white fathers.

Peter found this particularly hard to understand because as he got to know the other boys, he found out that most of them had similar backgrounds to his own. Many, not all, had no idea who their fathers were and had been brought up by their mothers who all spoke Shona or Sindebele. Why were they expected to speak the language of fathers they had never met? But the nuns insisted and Peter gradually learnt how to speak English as spoken by Coloureds. He missed his mother and his grandparents terribly, but found out that he could only visit them during school holidays.

The other thing he found he had to change was his surname. Thus far, he had used his mother's surname of Chimuti. That was not acceptable for a Coloured. No one had ever told him who his father was and, to this point it had not mattered to him. Forced into having to find a suitable surname, he decided to adopt one of his uncles' names, thus he became Peter Lawrence. Those who had any idea who their fathers were simply took on those names which were, in some cases, first names, others just translated their vernacular names into English – Eric *Nyoni* (Sindebele for bird) became Eric Bird. Others used the month in which they arrived at the school as their family names: John January, Joseph August and so on. Having all but lost their identities, they became each other's brothers and sisters and formed a community of Coloureds that, to their understanding, was superior to black Africans, but inferior to the whites. Peter still found it difficult to accept that members of his family were inferior to anyone.

Over the years, Peter's visits to Mhondoro became less and less frequent although he was very fond of his mother and members of her family. But his new status as a Coloured meant that he could not be seen to be mixing with Africans.

On one such visit, he had asked his grandmother the one question that was beginning to bother him.

"Who is my father?" He had decided to ask the question outright and not embellish it in any way.

"Chikwepa," his grandmother had not expected the question and blurted out an answer before she had had time to think.

"You are not serious," he had responded incredulously, "Chikwepa from Little Fountain Farm?" He found it difficult to believe that the white man with whom he had had so many run ins as a little boy was his father. Many times, they had evaded the man when he caught them grazing their cattle on his land. They easily outran him and would hear him cursing and calling them little kaffir bastards and other not so complimentary terms.

"He cannot be my father," Peter had made up his mind. Chikwepa was so stupid, how could he possibly be his father? By this time Peter, of course had some idea how babies were made and he could not see his mother with that ugly white man.

"Well," his grandmother said, "why don't you ask your mother? She will know for sure."

"You mean you don't?"

"I don't what?"

"You just said that my mother will know for sure. Does that mean you don't know for sure?"

"You keep saying that you don't believe that Chikwepa is your father. What am I supposed to tell you?"

"I just meant that it does not seem possible. Is he still at the farm, by the way?"

"No," his grandmother sounded relieved, "he sold the farm and moved away. The last I had he had died."

Peter never asked about his father again.

At sixteen, it became clear to the nuns that Peter would never excel at school. It was therefore decided that he was old enough to go into apprenticeship, which he did with great success, starting as a bricklayer and graduating to metalwork and carpentry. He seemed naturally good at doing anything with his hands and he soon had many Africans working under him. He really enjoyed the deference with which he was treated by the Africans; almost as if he was white, but he knew that white people still looked down on him with disdain. While many of his friends in the Coloured community took to drinking, smoking, drugs and girls, Peter had one burning ambition. He wanted to buy a farm, like the one his uncle Lawrence had managed to buy in what were called Native Purchase Areas, where Africans (the natives) were allowed to buy land in terms of the Land Apportionment Act. The main reason he wanted the farm was, apart from that it would give him the independence of his childhood years, that he wanted to take his mother out of the Reserve and live with her on a farm that he owned.

In 1973, at the age of forty, he had saved enough money to be able to buy a farm, so he went to the District Commissioner's office to inquire on the availability of farms in the nearby Muda Native Purchase Area. The District Commissioner's messenger, looking all self-important in his khaki shirt and shorts, and a wide brimmed hat that was turned up on one side, made him fill in a form which he did with some difficulty as English and spelling were not his strong points.

"You want a farm in Muda, hey?" The messenger asked.

"Muda would be good, but I will take one anywhere in this country to be honest."

"But the farms in Muda are for Africans. You cannot buy a farm there…"

"What do you mean I cannot buy a farm there?"

"I mean that you are a Coloured, and Coloureds are not allowed to buy land in areas reserved for Africans."

"But I am an African," he insisted.

"No sir, you are not," the messenger was equally determined.

Peter had to summon all his self-control to stop himself punching the messenger's smug face. How could the idiot be looking so pleased about making such a stupid and irrational statement. He tried again.

"Where was I born?"

The messenger looked through his form until he came to the right section.

"It says here that you were born in Mhondoro,"

"Where is Mhondoro?"

"If you come outside, I can show you the road that will take you to the road that leads to Mhondoro."

"I know how to get to Mhondoro, I was born there remember? What I am asking you is which country is Mhondoro in?"

"In this country, of course…"

"And is this country not in Africa?"

"It is, of course…"

"Then why on earth am I not an African?" Peter's face was turning red with anger.

The messenger picked up Peter's form, turned it round so that Peter could read it and pointed to the section that said 'RACE'.

"Do you see what you filled in under RACE? You had three choices; European, Coloured/Asian and African. Which one did you put a tick on?"

Peter looked down at the form. He could see that he had ticked over Coloured/Asian. That is what he had been told he was for the last few years. He was not an African, yet he was born in Africa. All he wanted was a farm. Why did it matter what race he was?

"Do you agree now, my friend that you are not an African? Otherwise you would have ticked here," he pointed to the right spot, "where it says 'African'."

"I am not your friend," he said as he started to walk out, then had another idea. There must be someone more senior, surely? He went back to the messenger's desk.

"Is the District Commissioner in?" He asked hopefully.

"He is here, but he is very busy. Let me call someone for you... *Sekuru!*" He shouted looking towards an inner office. Peter's spirits sank. If the senior person was being addressed as uncle, what were the chances that he would have a different decision?

The young man that came in surprised Peter. He was tastefully dressed in a pair of navy blue trousers, blue and white striped shirt and a blue tie. Peter suddenly felt the stifling heat in the office. How could this young man be wearing a tie in this heat? He did not know it, but those were the regulations. A tie and jacket were compulsory for all civil servants! He looked around the office and noticed for the first time, how sparsely furnished it was. There was a table behind which the messenger sat and two chairs that had lost their backs over the years and had never been repaired. Against the wall, near the door, was a bench that could sit six, but probably housed ten people when the office was busy. It stood empty at this time. Most of the window panes were broken and Peter could not decide whether the ceiling fan was broken or whether it had just not been switched on.

"What seems to be the problem," the District Commissioner's clerk, a Business Administration graduate from the University of Rhodesia was very well spoken.

"This *Mukaradhi* man wants to buy a farm in the Muda Native Purchase Area."

Peter hated the way that Africans pronounced the name of his race. "I am a Coloured, not a Mukaradhi," he corrected.

"I am very sorry, sir," the clerk spoke and behaved like a white man, Peter thought, although he was not sure if the apology was for the messenger's mispronunciation of the name of his race.

"I am sure that Garikai here," he pointed to the messenger, "has already explained to you that you cannot buy a farm in Muda."

"Why ever not?"

"Because," the clerk was being very patient, "those farms are only reserved for Africans, and you, sir, are not an African."

"What seems to be the problem?" No one had heard the District Commissioner come in; 'he looks hung over', Peter thought to himself, as he looked at the young white man dressed in a safari suit, a more appropriate attire than the shirt and tie that the young African was wearing

"I am trying to buy a farm" he addressed the District Commissioner directly, "and these people are telling me that I am not an African!"

"I think they are right," The Commissioner said, dismissively, "You look Coloured to me." He was looking at Peter through red bleary eyes.

"All I want is to buy a farm," Peter was pleading, and "I just want to go farming."

"What do you want with a farm? You Coloureds aren't farmers. Don't you have an apprenticeship of some sort? Anyway, you cannot farm in

Muda. That area is for Africans," he walked back into his office.

For the second time since coming into this office, Peter had to exercise self-restraint.

He went and consulted his friend Ronald, who first angered him by asking him why he wanted a farm.

"We Coloureds are not farmers," he said looking puzzled. "Why do you want to farm? It is such a hard life!"

Ronald soon realised that his friend was very serious about this.

"Why don't you buy one of these farms that whites are selling? There are farms being advertised in the newspapers every day."

"Aren't those reserved for Europeans?"

Peter had never thought about the farms that were owned by whites as ones that he could acquire. They were much larger and much more developed than the African Purchase Area farms and he had always assumed that only whites could buy these farms.

"I have never seen one that says, 'only Europeans need apply'," Ronald said.

"Do you think, then, that even Africans can buy these farms?" Peter wanted to know.

"Of course not! Africans would never be allowed into these areas. But you, Peter, are not an African; you are a Coloured."

Peter almost laughed out loud at the irony, but decided that his friend was probably right and he would try and acquire one of these farms.

61

For the next two years, he bought the Rhodesia Herald every day and scanned the 'Farms for Sale' column in the classifieds. He telephoned for appointments to view and it seemed to him that the farmers were quite happy to speak to him and show him their farms until they saw him. Then their stories would change.

'We have promised it to someone already', or 'my wife thinks I am charging too little and we need to review the price', or simply, 'we have decided not to sell'.

Surprisingly, when he looked in the papers the following days and weeks, the farms were still being advertised. He realised after a while that it was his race that was the problem. Some of the farmers would recognise his accent immediately on the telephone and ask outright, "Are you a Coloured?" He decided that he preferred these because he did not waste his time and money driving sometimes quite long distances to view farms that he had no chance of ever purchasing. But he kept looking anyway.

"Are you a Coloured," the man on the other end of the line asked, without sounding hostile.

Peter's spirits sank. "Yes I am, is that a problem?"

"No, no. Please come over and we can discuss."

Douglas Philips, it turned out, was a Coloured himself even though he looked as white as any white man. Peter found it hard to believe that the man in front of him had any black blood in him.

"I don't look coloured, do I? Well, I am. My great, great, great grand-mother was a Xhosa woman from the Cape in South Africa who married my great, great, great grandfather, an Englishman who had come to the Cape to seek his fortune and ended up living among the Xhosa people, much to the annoyance of the other whites in that country. My Xhosa ancestor had a very light complexion so that the children of that union could easily pass for Southern Europeans like Italians and Portuguese. Several generations later, who can tell the difference?" He concluded with a chuckle.

In 1975, Peter Lawrence got his farm at last and Douglas Philips moved to South Africa as a white man, with a white wife. Peter was probably the only man in the world that knew Douglas's real 'race'.

The other whites in the Machete area where Peter had got his farm were put out by the fact that one of their own had sold to a non-white, and Peter found himself completely isolated. He did not visit them and they did not visit him even though among themselves, they were a very tight community. Peter was never invited to the many social functions that they were always organising and his wife had to homeschool their children as they were not accepted at the local whites only school. It did not matter to Peter. He had his farm; he could bring his mother to live with him and he would show them that he was as good a farmer as they.

Five years after he got his farm, Rhodesia became Zimbabwe and Peter felt confident that things could only change for the better. They did not. The new government, it seemed to Peter, was concerned with appeasing white farmers who they said were very important to the agro-based economy of Zimbabwe. Government ministers were always surprised when they met Peter at the many farmers' meetings that were held at that time.

"I didn't know we had Coloured farmers," Minister Mugwazo had said to him at one such meeting. "I thought you guys were only interested in being motor mechanics, train drivers and so on. I could never have visualised a Coloured as a farmer."

Peter had felt mildly annoyed but thought that the minister was as much a victim of the Rhodesian propaganda machine as anyone so he could be forgiven. As far as he was concerned, he was an African and he hoped that the term Coloured would be removed in the new dispensation. He was wrong, of course.

Chapter 5

Peter sat on his king-size bed and looked at his naked body in the full length mirror on his dressing table. For a sixty seven year old, he thought, he did not look too bad. Independence, twenty years earlier, had not brought the changes that he had expected and he was disappointed that Coloureds were still marginalised, although it did not help, in his view, that many of them preferred to talk about their white heritage even though they knew little about it and almost completely ignored the African side of their families. But things had gone well for him, personally and his farm was doing well. His herd of cattle numbered nearly two thousand and he grew large crops of maize and tobacco. The only sadness he felt was that his mother had died of old age a few years after independence, still complaining about the stupidity of giving the country to blacks – who, according to her, had no idea how to run a country. His wife of many years had succumbed to cancer a few years later and his children had all left the country and gone to South Africa and England claiming that they saw no future for themselves in independent Zimbabwe. The farmers around him were more accepting although he still felt like he was an outsider.

The invitation to join the other farmers for lunch at the Venters had thus come as a complete surprise. He was not sure how to take it. Were they finally accepting him as one of them, or did they feel an obligation to embrace a non-white? It had taken him some time to make the decision but now that he had decided to accept the invitation, he was not sure what to wear for the occasion. At times like these, he missed his wife, Sheila, terribly. She was from a more affluent Coloured family who were better acquainted with the ways of the white man and she would have known exactly what he needed to wear. Eventually deciding to be semi formal, he chose a pair of khaki long trousers, a brown short-sleeved shirt, brown socks and a pair of veldt scoens. He regarded himself in the mirror again and thought that he looked good – like a successful, moneyed farmer.

As soon as he walked into the Venter homestead, he felt overdressed. All the men, who were sitting around the large swimming pool were dressed in boxer shorts and were mainly without shirts. It looked like some of them had been swimming but were now concentrating on the large selection of alcohol that was on offer on a table placed strategically within easy reach. The homestead itself, with manicured lawns and a wide variety of plants and flowers was probably the most impressive private residence he had ever been to. For what seemed like an age, he stood beside his pick-up truck, not quite sure where to go. It did not help his cause that all conversation seemed to die down as soon as he appeared.

"There you are, Peter," his host said, walking towards him, "what took you so long? I thought you had decided to snub us. Guys this is Peter Lawrence," he addressed the other guests. "He bought Dougie Philips's old place, oh, five or so years ago…"

"Twenty-five years ago, actually," Peter corrected.

"It's been as long as that, hey? How time flies. I thought it was time we got to know him, you know, us farmers need to stick together, hey," Jacques seemed at pains to justify to the other guests his decision to invite an outsider into their midst.

"Hello, Peter," they all greeted, not quite in unison.

"What's your poison," Jacques asked the newest arrival.

"Poison?" Peter was not sure what he was being asked.

"What will you have to drink? We have beer, whiskey, brandy, wine…"

"I'll have a beer please," he decided that it was better to stick to what he knew. He had heard of occasions where people had ordered drinks they were not used to only because they thought that they would enhance their images as sophisticated socialites. Of course the opposite happened because they would end up consuming too much and embarrassing themselves – and their hosts.

"Grab yourself a seat, anywhere," Jacques waved his arm expansively, almost as if he was saying that his guest could find a seat anywhere on the entire farm.

Peter found a seat on a bench, not too far removed from the others. There was an awkward silence as all the others were not sure how to proceed. Some of the jokes they had been telling were suddenly not so appropriate in the presence of the new arrival. Peter was still looking around the homestead. The massive double storey house was in the style of what was commonly called Cape Dutch, although Peter was not quite sure what that was. The swimming pool area was clearly designed for entertaining with a large number of garden chairs casually strewn around the pool and the obligatory braai (barbecue) stand in one corner. The houseboy was roasting an obscenely large quantity of meat on it. In the other corner were two refrigerators, both well stocked with beers and besides them, was a bar that could fit into any medium sized drinking establishment. Through the gate in the wall that separated the homestead from the rest of the farm, Peter could see what appeared to be a large lake at the bottom of the garden. He wished he had seen this earlier, before he had finished planning his own homestead.

He could just imagine it. Sitting with his Coloured friends around a swimming pool just like this one and eating and drinking like this – better than this. His black relatives on the other side of the house enjoying their own party drinking traditional brew and roasting the offals from a cow he would have slaughtered. Perfect, he thought.

"Lunch is served," Mrs Venter came out of the house leading a procession of black servants who were carrying trays that they carefully set on the prepared tables. The lady of the house then spent a few minutes making sure that everything was in place before calling everyone to help themselves. The meat from the braai was added to the selection.

Peter was surprised to see that the African staple, sadza, was among the dishes and that the whites seemed to eat it without embarrassment. Many in his own Coloured community seemed to think that it was demeaning to eat sadza and often found themselves having to hide it when visitors arrived unexpectedly during meals.

The discussion soon turned to things agricultural, or rather, agro political.

"So, Peter, what do you think of the MFD?" Jack van Breda was quite drunk and had lost all inhibition. Most farmers would not have dared raise this subject with someone they hardly knew.

"I don't really involve myself in politics," Peter was also being careful with his answer. "I am a farmer and that is all that interests me. I leave politics to politicians."

"That is exactly the problem. Politics is too important to be left to politicians." Jack was not sure where he had heard that. "You see, Peter, the way I see it, we would be better off with the MFD. They seem to understand the needs of the farmer a lot better than our friends in ZIPA."

"Jack, Jack, Jack," Jacques Venter came into the conversation, "you don't seem to understand that these people are all the same. They have no idea what they are doing. As far as I am concerned, we are fucked whichever one of them is in power. Fucked with a capital bloody F. F A C K E D, Fucked…"

"F U," Peter corrected.

"There is no need for that hey, we are all friends here," Jacques said testily.

"I mean that fucked is spelt F U C K E D not F A like you said," Peter responded quietly.

"Whatever." Jacques was not great at spelling and disliked being corrected, particularly by a non-white. "Anyway," he went on, "I don't believe we are any better off with any of them. The worst thing that Ian Smith did was agree to negotiate with these people. We should have carried on with the war…"

"And you would probably be dead by now," Dudley White was a relative newcomer into Zimbabwe having arrived from England and bought a farm just before independence, hoping to be part of the new dispensation. "I think that accepting that the majority should be allowed to vote was the right thing to do."

"You, my Pommie friend, don't know what you are talking about. You have no idea of the history of this country and until you do, I suggest you keep your bloody opinions to yourself," Jacques hated these liberal immigrants who thought they knew all the answers to the country's problems.

"By history of this country, you mean the history that started with the arrival of the 'civilised' Europeans, of course," Dudley White was being sarcastic.

"Of course," Jacques agreed, "there is no history before then."

"That is not true. The African peoples have a long history and culture that we could learn a lot from…"

The others all burst out laughing, "What history and culture? These people were killing each other like there was no tomorrow. Had it not been for our intervention, there would still be killing and eating each other even now!" Jack said with conviction.

"And the country would still be nothing but wasteland," Jacques added. "We have brought in education, health and development. If these people had a long history and culture as you say, how come they have adopted everything European? They dress like us, want to live like us and even speak our language better than us. Why are they abandoning their long history and culture?"

"Well," Dudley responded, "what would you do if someone came into your country with superior fire power and told you that your way of doing things is primitive? These people were forced into accepting the European ways…"

"You don't really understand Africa and its people do you, Dud? If you did…"

"My name is Dudley and I would appreciate it if you did not shorten it."

"As I was saying, Dud," Jacques said defiantly, "African politicians are all the same. They never mean anything they say. All they are interested in is holding on to power and fuck everyone else…"

"Politicians all over the world never mean what they say and, I dare say, they also want to hold on to power at all costs"

"Oh Please, Dudley, don't come with your liberal views and tell us that we did wrong. Why did you leave England? Is it not because you have allowed the Communists to take over your country…?"

"Communists?"

"Yes, they masquerade as the bloody Labour Party…"

"The Labour party is not a Communist party. That's the problem with you people; you have been so insulated in this racist 'paradise' as you call it, and the world has moved on and left you behind."

"Look at all the countries in Africa that got their independence. Look how far they have regressed. As soon as the white man leaves them to their own devices, they revert to their 'long history and culture' of no

71

planning, no organisation. They just loot whatever is in the country's coffers as left by the white man, marry many wives and repress their own people to make sure that they are not accountable."

"That is a stupid argument," Dudley was not giving up, "You guys came here, introduced a different system of administration, and left the local people out of the loop. You treated them like children."

"Did you just call me stupid?" Jacques was advancing menacingly towards Dudley, who stood his ground and refused to be intimidated. For a few seconds, the two men stood face to face, neither of them giving in. It looked as though they were ready for a fist fight.

"I did not call you stupid. What I said is that your argument is stupid."

"Come on guys," Paul Jones, who up to this stage, had not had much to say, came between the two men, "there is no need for that. We have had a very pleasant afternoon. Let's not spoil it."

Peter was surprised. Whites had always seemed so united and 'civilised' and he had never thought that they could get to the point where, it seemed to Peter, fists would fly. It seemed to him that the two men loathed each other.

"That was fun – almost," Jack van Breda broke the silence that followed. "So, Peter," he went on, "what are they saying on the other side?"

"The other side?"

"The blacks. You have black relatives, surely?"

"My mother was black," Peter said quietly. "Is that a problem?"

"Of course not. That gives you an insight into how they think."

Peter found himself getting angry.

"My father," he said, "was white. I never met him. As far as I know, he died without ever knowing that he had sired a bastard child. There are many out there like me – whose mothers were made pregnant by men like you (and I am sure that some of you have slept with your servants) and, like me, abandoned to be cared for by their black African mothers. I don't know whether sex with our mothers was not as much fun as it is with your wives. All I know is that when they got pregnant, they were sent away to confront their families on their own. In many cases, this meant that they were ostracised because, as far as the families and friends were concerned, they had been whoring with white men and no self-respecting black man would marry a confirmed whore. So they brought us up the best way they could, and when they saw what they thought was a good opportunity for us, they sent us away to schools that formed us into what we are today; a race called 'Coloureds'. Our white fathers have never acknowledged us. Come to think of it, I could be a brother, cousin or even uncle to some of you, but you would not want to know that, would you?"

Peter spoke quietly, but the pent up rage in his voice was frightening.

"Who is on my side then? The white father that I don't know or the black mother that was there for me and brought me up against many odds?"

"I was just saying…," Jack van Breda was too drunk to realise just how angry Peter was.

"…that my mother is somehow on the other side from me? How dare

73

you?" Peter was surprised at his anger. Like many in his community, he had so wanted to be white; wanted to be accepted by the whites as being closer to them than the blacks. But the suggestion that his mother was from a different side from him, coming from one who probably had fathered his own coloured children and not acknowledged them infuriated him. He looked at all of them and could just imagine them sneaking into their servants' quarters to have sex with women that they dared not be seen in public with. They probably did not even talk about it among themselves! And he had so wanted to be like them!

"I am sorry, Peter," Jacques tried to pacify him; "our friend Jack has had a bit too much to drink. Come and lie down Jack," he took Jack into the house.

'Bravo, Peter', Dudley White was thinking. 'It's about time someone told these bastards the truth about themselves'.

Peter was the first one to leave. He could not stay much longer after his outburst and the atmosphere had become awkward.

Jacques felt he had to say something to his guest before he left.

"Are you coming to the Commercial Farmers Association meeting on Thursday? The President of the Association is bringing the Minister of Agriculture to address us. It should be of interest to all of us."

"I'll see," Peter said as he got into his car. He had no intention of going to spend more time with these people.

Chapter 6

In the leafy suburb of Borrowdale, in Northern Harare, Minister Itai Mugwazo was entertaining other ministers and business colleagues. They had just finished eating an unnecessarily large meal and most of the men around the unnecessarily large pool around which they sat, were dozing. None of them could swim, although their bulging stomachs suggested an ability to float. It was a week after the Minister's excursion to Manhowe Township. For most of that week, he had been thinking about the people's reaction to the land issue. He had not realized just how strongly the people felt about their need for more land, but he was not sure whether to bring his observations to the attention of the President, who, after all, had been assuring the white farmers that their farms were safe under ZIPA. Yet Itai Mugwazo had also become aware that the emergence of the Movement for Democracy had eroded the people's support for ZIPA.

"Did I tell you," he started, "that I went to Macheke last Sunday to address the people...?"

"We all know," George Moyo, a businessman whose success was due to the many government supply tenders that he was involved in did not appreciate his siesta being interrupted, "that you go on these trips as an excuse to be with that secretary of yours. Do you want to brag now?"

"George, I am being serious. The people were very unresponsive until I mentioned the issue of land. It seems to me that we need to address this matter urgently."

"What do they want more land for? Let's face it, Itai, the white farmers are much better at what they do than us. The reason that we are so successful as a country and can boast of our food security is because of these white farmers. You cannot take land away from them to give it to people who will probably turn it into semi desert. Look what they have done to the Communal lands."

"The Communal lands are the way they are because people are overcrowded in them. All I'm saying is that unless we address this matter, we will lose the people's support."

"And just how are you going to address the matter. The farmers bought the land. They hold Title deeds to it. They have a legal right to be on that land and one of the successes of this government has been in upholding the rule of law."

"But unless we do something to appease the people, we are going to lose to the MFD."

"What can they do? Forcibly take the land? Look, the MFD are being supported by the West and they will not do anything that will adversely affect that relationship." Paul Gwaze, the Minister for Industry and Commerce saw no point to this discussion. "Our economy," he went on, "is agro-based. Tamper with agriculture and you destroy the economy. As it is, our colleagues in Economic Planning are doing all they can to attract foreign direct investment. Their efforts will be futile if we are seen to not respect private property…"

"We don't have to take it away forcibly; we can compensate them," Itai Mugwazo started, "I can ask Finance to allow for funds for this purpose in the next budget…"

George Moyo burst out laughing, his ample stomach pulsating, "What country are you living in, Itai?" He asked sneeringly. "You people have been spending money like it comes out of a tap. Where do you think Minister Mangwiro at Finance will get the money from?"

"Perhaps we can reengage the British. They did promise to let us have money to compensate the farmers and we can try to make them live up to their promise."

"You think the British government will talk to you after all the insults that your president has hurled at them? I don't think so. In any case, they can see that their baby, the MFD are gaining ground and will hold on to their money until such time as their protégés are in power, then they will release it."

"Do we have to compensate the farmers?" David Chitende, Permanent Secretary for Education, had dozed off but had been part following the conversation. He was fully awake now.

"Of course we have to compensate the farmers. What kind of stupid question is that? We just have to find the money somehow…"

"Why?" David asked quietly.

"Why what?" Itai was confused.

"Why do we have to compensate them?"

"Because," Itai could not believe that they were having this conversation, he was very proud of the portfolio he held in government and he knew that agriculture would always look good, making him look good in the eyes of the President – and of the nation – as long as they kept the white farmers happy and productive. "Because they own the land; they bought it fairly on the open market and in this country we have good laws that protect private property."

"They bought it fairly? Are you sure about that? Not so long ago, the laws of this country prevented us, the natives of this land, from owning such farms! Yet they took it away from our forefathers without compensation…"

"That was a long time ago, David…"

"Ah, that makes it alright then. It was a long time ago, so it does not matter," there was heavy sarcasm in David's voice.

"Look, David," Itai was getting irritated by the civil servant who seemed to believe that he knew better than the politicians, "we cannot keep harping on about what happened a long time ago. This is a new, civilised Zimbabwe that has taken its place in the community of nations. Let us let bygones be bygones…"

"How can we let bygones be bygones when we have not addressed the unfair distribution of land that resulted from those 'bygones'? The settlers came and refused to respect our laws and traditions and somehow believed that they had a right to take our land because, to them, it had no value to us…"

"It had no value to us," George Moyo interrupted, "What were we doing with it?"

"It does not matter what we were doing with it. The fact is; it was our land, period!"

"How can we say it was our land?" Minister Mugwazo asked. "There were no laws about ownership…"

"There were laws about ownership! Land was owned communally and traditional chiefs had the role of allocating it."

"Come on, David, you cannot define what we had as laws; they were not written or tabulated in any way and could be changed at the whim of the chief."

"Let me remind you of our history, which some of you appear to have forgotten," David was on the edge of his chair, "the Kingdom of *Mwenemutapa* was a vast empire, which spanned virtually the whole of Zimbabwe and even took in parts of what are now neighbouring countries. Do you think that such an empire could be run without any laws? Do you think that Great Zimbabwe, that iconic symbol of our nationhood could have been built by an uncivilised people with no laws? I don't think so. You know what your problem is? You have accepted the myopic European view of our history and swallowed it hook line and sinker." David paused and looked around at his audience. His words did not seem to make any impression. He tried something else.

"What about the armies of the *Ndebele* people? How organised were they?"

"They were only organised to raid the Shona people," Itai Mugwazo did not hate the Ndebeles, but he was so convinced of their culpability in this regard that he never missed an opportunity to mention it.

"That is not what David is saying," Patrick Ndlela, Minister for Social Services was Ndebele and did not like this subject raised, particularly given the very recent history of what the national army had done to his people in the name of fighting dissidents.

"History tells us," David went on as if Patrick had not spoken, "that at any given time, there are ethnic groups that will dominate other ethnic groups. It happened in Europe and in any other part of the world you can think of. It is happening in Europe even now. But their wars are civilised because they use civilised, sophisticated weaponry and ours are primitive and unnecessary."

"Should we then seize land from a productive commercial farming community on the grounds of their ethnicity?" Itai Mugwazo still wanted to defend his Ministry.

"No," David answered, "we should redistribute the land because it is the right thing to do. But because we do not have the resources to compensate the whites, let us look for other ways."

"There are no other ways within our laws. Are you suggesting we ignore our own laws?"

"You guys seem to have an obsession with the law, which, after all, is enacted by human beings. Does it not bother you that the laws that governed the current distribution of land were imposed on us without any input from us? Should we not, perhaps be looking at amending the law so that we can, 'within our laws' correct the imbalances created by those past laws?"

"Look, David," George did not like this kind of talk. It was not good for business. "The past is gone. The part of our history that started with the arrival of the white man is a reality and we need to recognise that, whether we like it or not, they have fast tracked us into a civilised, modern society with good laws that are written and tabulated, unlike the laws of our forefathers that were only in the heads of the ruling elite…"

"The British Constitution is unwritten. In whose head is it? Who defines its breach?"

"I did not know that…" George started.

"That is because, like most Zimbabweans, you have no interest in History, particularly the history of our country. We have all decided to adopt the white man's ways and our children can't even speak our languages properly because it is more civilised to adopt the white man's language."

"We live in a global world, my friend. What are our children going to do with Shona, or Sindebele?"

"Our culture and our language are what define us as a people. We lose that, we lose our identity. That is all I am saying. As for the land question, well, Itai, you are the Minister of Agriculture and, as you say yourself, it is clear that the people want more land. What are you going to do about it?"

"Nothing, for now," Itai was looking thoughtful, "I cannot see any clear alternatives to what we have now. Perhaps we should be looking at a gradual process, which will not adversely affect our economy. But we should have a clear land policy that says in, say, ten years, so much of the land will be in the hands of blacks and so on."

"The people of Manhowe –and others – may not be willing to wait ten years," David said as he stood up to go. "Anyway, thank you very much Itai. This has been a most pleasant – and enlightening – afternoon. But tomorrow is Monday and some of us have work to do. After all, you politicians rely on us to tell you how to run the country."

There were handshakes all round as David took his leave.

"Do you think he has political ambitions?" George asked Itai when the latter returned from seeing David off.

"Who has political ambitions, David? He is just an academic with no war credentials. You know how academics like to talk. This is his pet subject for now; he'll soon find another."

The gathering broke up soon after this with everyone getting into their cars and going their separate ways; some to their homes, some to other social gatherings where alcohol was consumed, and others to their girlfriends and concubines, then home.

At lunch on the following day, David met up with other senior civil servants at a popular hotel in the Harare Central Business District.

"I had lunch with your ZIPA Ministers yesterday. It's amazing how we are ruled by people who are so ignorant," he said to laughter from the others.

"They won the war," Dr Mbodza, Managing Director of a major food processing Company in the City, held a degree in Agricultural Economics.

"They may have won the war, but can you believe that they have no idea what to do about land redistribution? Minister for Agriculture Mugwazo wants to leave things as they are because white farmers are important to the economy!"

"He may have a point. Agriculture is more than just the farmers and their workers, important though that is; it is a major earner of foreign currency, which we are woefully short of, and supplies significant quantities of raw materials to companies such as ours. If Agriculture sneezes, the whole country will catch a cold."

"Let's face it," Agriculture Ministry Permanent Secretary Giles Kamba had just been reading a study carried out by a department in his ministry, "if we interfere with agriculture now, it will take years before our people are able to reach the level of production that is currently achieved by our white farmers. If there is one thing that all politicians are afraid of, it is the sceptre of being confronted by a hungry populace."

"Are you suggesting, Giles, that giving land to the majority will necessarily lead to hunger?"

"Yes. How would we be able to feed ourselves if our production levels drop significantly?"

"So, in your view, only white farmers can produce at these levels..."

"Our peasant farmers' yields are, generally, a tenth of what the commercial farmers can achieve. You do the math."

"Could you, yourself not achieve the levels of production that the whites are achieving? Surely any of us can match these levels of production?"

"David, we are not farmers. We are professionals with work to do in our chosen fields of expertise. We have farmers who are doing a good job. If we all go farming, who is going to run the civil service, who is going to run the companies that need our level of education?"

David felt deflated somewhat. Why did everyone else not see what seemed so clear to him? Many of the white farmers did not possess even a fraction of the qualifications that most of the people round this table had. Yet they were, some of them, millionaires and lived in the laps of luxury while these academics were mortgaged to the hilt in order to enjoy only part of what the white farmers enjoyed. He looked round the table. These people had grown up in abject poverty, not believing that they could live the kind of lives they now enjoyed. Now, they believed that they had arrived because their children went to schools that they did not have the privilege to go to, they drove fancy cars that they did not own and they lived in parts of the city that hitherto had been reserved for whites.

"You know what I think?" He said finally, "I think that we should redistribute the land in a manner that allows our peasant farmers to at least feed themselves, then give commercial farms to people like you and I, who can use them efficiently and maintain the levels of production that we currently enjoy..."

"But we are not farmers, David..." Dr Mbodza started to say.

"Were these whites born farmers or did they learn? Why can we not learn also? Our problem is that we do not have a plan. The whites had a plan. Their government put in policies that encouraged them to stay on the land and work it; they provided them with financial incentives and they supported them in every way possible!"

"Suppose we go with your plan, David," said the Doctor, "where would we get the land to give to these new professional farmers, most of whom do not have the means to purchase such land? Some of us are struggling to pay off our mortgages and we have children in school who still need to go to University. We cannot afford to start investing in ventures that we know little about."

"Somehow," David argued, "Government has to find a way to get us onto the land. Leaving out food security in the hands of the white farmers means that they can blackmail us into doing what they want, at the expense of the majority."

"I don't know about the others, but I don't want to go farming," Giles Kamba said matter-of-factly.

David could see that he was getting nowhere. He decided to drop the subject - sort of.

"I have been reading about the history of how the whites got to own so much land. You will be amazed." He said as he took out some notes from the inside pocket of his jacket.

"Did you know," David said, "that land has always been important to the whites; that it was in fact the main reason they colonised our country?"

"What has that got to do with anything?" Ivan Mbodza was getting tired of this conversation.

"Listen," David said patiently, "you might even learn something!"

He ruffled through his notes.

"Even before the country was occupied, the British South Africa Company – the occupying vehicle that the British used – had, through something called the Lippert Concession – in 1889 – acquired permission for would be settlers to acquire land rights from the indigenous peoples. They did this by buying land concessions from the British Monarch…"

"The British Monarch?" Giles was astonished, "how do they come into the equation?"

"Search me," David said before going on, "but they bought the concessions and the revenue accrued was repatriated to the United Kingdom!"

"In 1898," David went on, "they created The Native Reserves Order in Council, which created Native Reserves for blacks only and paved the way for blacks to be forcibly moved from their lands in order to create vacant land for whites to expropriate. They said," David was sounding quite amused although his face looked angry, "that the native reserves were being created to prevent the extinction of the indigenous people, while at the same time guaranteeing that the settlers got the lion's share of fertile land…"

"How did Reserves guarantee that we would not be extinct?" Giles was puzzled.

"The reserves were generally, in low potential, low rainfall areas," Ivan Mbodza proffered, "what could we do there except breed!" He had expected laughter, but everyone seemed to have lost their collective sense of humour.

"After a period of consolidation, which included a period of forced labour for blacks, the whites were ready to formalise the separation of land between the two main races," David was getting quite emotional, "having, in 1925 set up something called the Carter Commission – led by a Morris Carter – and made up of only white people, which made the recommendations for such separation." He looked into the distance, unable to speak for a few minutes.

"In 1930," David said in a calm even voice, "they enacted The Land Apportionment Act for that purpose and all the high rainfall areas were set aside for large scale, privately owned white farms."

As nobody said anything in response, David went on. "Do you know how the land was shared?" He asked before consulting his notes, "29 000 acres were set aside for native reserves; 8 000 acres for what were called Native Purchase Areas for what were called "progressive" black farmers – making a total of 37 000 acres for blacks whose population then was estimated at just over one million – and 49 000 acres were reserved for 'Europeans' who were at the time, a mere 50 000!"

"How did these people, in such a short time, manage to convince our people to accept a secondary role in their own country?" Dr Mbodza had never really thought about how the process of colonisation had worked.

"I don't know," David said, earnestly, "I think that when the whites first came, the locals were quite accommodating because, I don't know, perhaps there was the novelty of people who looked different, dressed different and came from lands that we had never even heard of."

"But surely, they must have realised quite quickly that these newcomers were up to no good..." Giles started to say.

"They did," David looked and sounded frustrated by his friends' apparent lack of interest in their history. "That is why you had the rebellions in the 1890's – the history we were taught called them the Matebele and the Mashona rebellions; we call them the first *Chimurenga!*

But, let's face it, the whites had far superior fire power – guns against spears and sticks – and they were motivated by the thought of untold wealth which they believed was theirs to take. The so called rebellions were ruthlessly put down with methods that, quite honestly, bordered on genocide!"

For a few moments, no one spoke. They all regarded their respective plates of food rather intently, not quite sure what to say.

"Then of course there was the technology..." David started.

"Technology?" Giles was not sure what his friend was saying.

"Can you imagine what our ancestors thought when they first saw... a train for example. They had not even discovered the wheel yet and here was a monster with thousands of them! What kind of humans were these that could make such a large, self-propelled vehicle? It must have seemed to them that these were a little more than human beings – gods almost!"

"So what you are saying is that, fairly early on, we accepted that we are inferior to these people?" Giles was beginning to understand.

"That's how I see it anyway," said David. "In many ways, we still accept that even today..."

"I don't," Ivan protested.

David wanted to argue the point; to tell his friend that it was because they accepted the White man's inherent superiority that they would not even consider farming because the white man was naturally better at it. But he decided to let it go.

"Anyway," David went on, "So important was land to the settlers that they continued to enact laws to entrench their position. Of course one of the laws they put in place, The Land Husbandry Act of 1951, may have accelerated Nationalistic politics when they sought to enforce private ownership of land, destocking and conservation practices on black smallholder farmers. It was resisted so much that it was scrapped in 1961!"

David looked round the table again. His friends looked impressed, but there was still no emotion there. It seemed to him that nothing he had said had made any of them feel as strongly as he did on the issue of land.

"Then, of course, after Ian Smith and his cronies declared independence from Britain, unilaterally, they enacted, in 1969, the now infamous Land Tenure Act." He ruffled through his notes again.

"Listen to this: *'The purpose of the Land Tenure Act',*" he read from his notes, "*'is to ensure that each race shall have its own area.... Neither race shall own or occupy land in the area of the other race'.*" He paused and looked round the table. "Do you know how they went on to divide the land?" He looked at his notes again.

"'In implementation of the above, the 96 million acres of land in Rhodesia have been divided into 6 million acres of national land and 45

89

million acres each for the African and European areas'. Can you believe that? At independence in 1980, whites formed about 4 percent of the population of this country. Even assuming that the ratio was the same in 1969 when this piece of legislation was enacted, 4 percent of the population was given 50 percent of the available land with the remaining 96 percent – the Africans – getting the other 50 percent! It even goes on to say, *'this division, with an allowance for a 2 percent variation, IS FIXED FOR ALL TIME'!"*

Giles whistled softly, "They really thought they were here for good, didn't they?"

"Ian Smith did say that there would be no majority rule in this country for another thousand years," Dr Mbodza reminded the others.

"What fascinated me about all this, is how the races were defined in the Act," David went on and paged through his notes until he found the right page and read. "'*For the purposes of the Act, an African is defined as 'any member of the Aboriginal tribes or races in Africa and the islands adjacent thereto including Madagascar and Zanzibar, or any person who has the blood of such tribes or races and who lives as a member of an Aboriginal native community'. A European is defined as 'a person who is not an African'.*"

Doctor Mbodza was the first to recover from the laughter that followed.

"So," he said, laughter still in his voice, "according to those definitions everybody who is not European is an African, and everybody who is not African is a European."

"Pretty much," David concurred, "But take the case of Coloureds for

90

example, they have the blood of Africans but will only be defined as African if they live within a Native community. Does that mean that if they live outside of a native community, as they do now, they become European?"

"What about the Asians - The Indians and Chinese? According to this definition, they are European."

"By that definition, Australian Aborigines would have been right to come here and claim to be European!" Kuda Mudimu, Permanent Secretary for Foreign Affairs had been reading the paper and now joined in the conversation, "do you think that they would have been accepted as such?"

"They obviously, at some point, realised the absurdity of their definition, and then created a third race of Coloureds and Asians. I don't know if at that point, they were allocated a share of the country; the Coloureds and Asians, that is. I have not gone that far yet."

"Where do you get all this information?" Giles Kamba was hearing some of this information for the first time. He knew about the Land Apportionment Act and the Land Tenure Act, which was enacted in 1969 to fine tune the provisions of the earlier land Act, but he had never bothered to read up on them. As far as he was concerned, they were to be consigned to the dust bin of history and no one needed to waste their time studying them.

"You will be amazed how much of this information is freely available. All you have to do is know where to look."

"Interesting though all this is, I still do not see the need to disrupt a vibrant sector in the economy just to settle historical scores." Dr

Mbodza was still not convinced. "In any case," he went on, "how can you take seriously people who could enact such a bad law?"

"I agree," said Giles Kamba, "I think that we should just forget whatever injustices there have been and concentrate on building a future for our children. History is interesting but that is all it is; history. It is not going to help us out of the economic mess that our country seems to be getting into. A vibrant agricultural sector will."

"I am finding all of this very interesting and am actually considering enrolling for a Doctorate at the University of Zimbabwe to try and unravel some of our history. It may help us understand what mistakes have been made and how not to repeat them." David was looking thoughtful.

"It seems to me, that one of the major mistakes made when the legislation you have just been talking about was enacted was to look at the short term view," Doctor Mbodza said getting up, "let us not repeat that. In the short term, it may seem to be the right thing to disrupt agriculture, but in the longer term, how is that going to affect the whole economy?"

"On the other hand," David Chitende said, shaking his friend's hand and looking directly at him, "doing nothing now to redress the imbalances of the past is, in my opinion, the short term view. Imagine what future generations will say about this generation. They will call us the generation that went to war to liberate the country from colonialism, and forgot about the land!"

The three men parted to go back to their respective offices. Each one of them deep in thought about the discussion they had just had.

Chapter 7

Peter Lawrence decided to go to the CFA meeting after all. However disagreeable his neighbours were on the issues of race, he was, first and foremost, a farmer and it was important for him to know what was happening and what the government's plans were for the future of this sector. All the people from the lunch at the Venters' were there and while they did not exactly hug Peter with displays of unbridled joy, they seemed to look at him with a new respect.

"Hello, Peter. Glad you could make it," was repeated to him almost as if it had been rehearsed by all the farmers. Everyone in the large hall at the Marondera Country Club that was the venue for the meeting seemed to be speaking in whispers. It had been decided that the bar would remain closed until after the minister had spoken. Although this had not gone down well with most of the audience who had had their usual weekly excursions into Marondera on the previous day thus were suffering the effects of the overindulgence thereof, everyone had complied in deference to the expected guest.

"I wish they would get on with it. I am dying of thirst here," Jacques said aloud.

"Get some water," Dudley White said, jokingly.

"Water will not quench his kind of thirst. Come to think of it, I don't think that beer will, either. What you need my friend is a stiff shot of brandy…"

There was sudden commotion at the entrance and the Minister and his entourage came in. As usual, Itai Mugwazo was impeccably turned out in a suit that looked completely out of place among the casually clad farmers. Even the President of the CFA was in semi formal clothes. There was no mistaking which one was the Minister. The burly body guards only confirmed what was clearly apparent.

After a few minutes of sloganeering and air punching, made difficult by the fact that the audience were not as familiar with the slogans as the Minister's usual audiences, the Minister was ready to speak.

He stood up and scanned his listeners; the sea of expectant mostly white faces watching him with what looked like wariness, but could have been boredom. For a brief moment, he felt his own importance. These were people that he had grown up worshipping and idealising; people that would not have given him the time of day until he and others took up arms. Now they were hanging on his every word, wanting to know what he, Itai Mugwazo, was going to say about them and their future. He wanted to tell them how unfair their system of government had been; how privileged they had been while his parents had had to make all sorts of sacrifices just to get him a basic education. He wanted to tell them that things had changed in Zimbabwe and that their privileges had to come to an end. Instead, he said, "I come to you as a friend," and was rewarded with tentative smiles.

"I come to you as a friend who understands the important role that you play in our economy. I and my whole ministry understand just how much easier our work is because of the sterling work you are putting in on the farms. The whole country is indebted to you because, not only are you one of the major earners of foreign currency for the country through your exports of tobacco, cotton, coffee, and now, increasingly, fresh produce and flowers, you provide employment to millions of Zimbabweans. We therefore consider you as partners in our efforts to develop the country…"

Peter Lawrence found his mind wondering. It seemed to him that the Minister always said the same message to the farmers. There was no substance to this message. Peter wanted to hear the Minister address the many challenges that were facing farmers, like the chronic short-age of foreign currency which meant that they were still using old and obsolete equipment; the minimum wage that government was insist-ing that they pay the workers regardless of the profitability – or lack of it – of their farms. He wanted to hear how the government was going to deal with the current drought and whether the issue of land redistribution was still on the agenda. He knew many black farmers who needed more land – who deserved more land – but were unable to acquire it because they did not have the money to pay the prices being asked for.

Instead, the minister seemed to be going to great pains to assure the white farmers that the status quo would remain; that government would only acquire land on the basis of the "willing buyer, willing seller" principle that they kept talking about. Yet it was becoming clear that the government did not have the resources to buy any land, particularly as their priorities seemed to lie elsewhere – building more schools with no teachers and building more rural health centres that remained closed for lack of staff and drugs. It occurred to Peter that even equipping the army was getting higher priority from government than equipping black farmers with more land.

"The president," he heard the minister say, "is aware though, that in spite of the smart partnership that government has been building with the farmers over the last twenty years, some of you are supporting the opposition MFD. Indeed, some of you are funding the activities of this new opposition party whose only agenda is to return this country to the dark old days of British imperialism. Perhaps some of you prefer to go back to those days. Perhaps some of you believe that the hand of reconciliation proffered by my Party and government is a sign of weakness." He paused and looked around the room, almost as if he was expecting someone to respond and tell him that the farmers were fully behind ZIPA and behind the government. There was some uncomfortable shuffling in the audience. This was not what they had come to hear. After all, government had been reassuring them and the world that Zimbabwe was a democracy where people were free to elect leaders of their choice.

"Zimbabwe is a democracy," he seemed to read their minds, "and anyone is free to vote for candidates of their choice. It is up to you to make wise decisions in the interests of the country and in your own interests. Do you really want to take on the revolutionary Zimbabwe Patriotic Alliance? Do you really want to go back to the days of war?" He paused again and took a good look around the room.

"Let me make something clear to you," there was a hard edge to the minister's voice that had not been there before; "Zimbabwe will never be a colony again. The freedom that so much blood was shed for, will not be compromised because you want to retain the unfair privileges that you continue to enjoy." He looked around the room again. Most of the faces were looking down at the ground, avoiding looking into the minister's eyes. Only the coloured man seemed pleased with what the minister had said. Was he a farmer? Itai Mugwazo asked himself.

"The President is extremely disappointed that the friendship that he has been fostering between government and the white farming community is being spurned like this. I and my ministry feel betrayed by the actions of some among you. Let me tell you this, the hand of reconciliation that has been extended thus far can easily turn into a fist." He held up his fist and brought it down violently, "A fist that will crush the MFD and anyone else who sympathises with them. Do not be caught in the crossfire."

He scanned the room again. The farmers were looking unsure of themselves. He almost felt sorry for them as they stood around regarding the ground with some intensity.

"The president," he went on, his voice softening "is keenly aware that it is only a minority among you who have been misled by the MFD. We know that the majority of you have Zimbabwe's best interests at heart and that you will not do anything to jeopardise what we have been building over the last twenty years. When I get back to the President, what message do you want me to give him? Do you want me to tell him that the farmers of this area are selling out to the opposition? Do you want me to tell the President, that the farmers of Marondera/ Macheke do not appreciate what his party and government have done for the farmers over the last twenty years?"

"We are with ZIPA and the government," Peter Johnston, President of the Commercial farmers Association spoke up. "Our members know

98

what is important for Zimbabwe and if there are those who may have misunderstood what it is that is expected of us, we apologise and can assure you, Minister, that the commercial farming sector understands its responsibility."

"I shall tell the President," he had stayed longer than he had intended, "that he has nothing to worry about. I will let him know that you wish him a long life because you know the important role that His Excellency still has to play in the development of this country." He stood up and raised his right fist. The farmers followed suit without really knowing why.

"*Pamberi ne* ZIPA!" (Forward with ZIPA), he shouted.

"*Pamberi!,*" the farmers shouted back as one.

"*Pamberi Mberi ne* ZIPA!"

"Pamberi!"

"*Pasi ne* MFD" (down with the MFD), he said as he lowered his fist

"Pasi," the farmers threw down their fists.

The minister walked out to much cheering and ululating.

"What was that all about?" The bar had just been opened and the farmers were gathered in small groups, beers in hand, discussing the Minister's just ended speech. Jack van Breda was the first to speak.

"I think we have just been told that we can vote for whoever we want as long as they belong to ZIPA," Paul Jones responded.

"The man did say that the president knows how important farmers are

99

to the economy of the country. I don't think that ZIPA will do anything to disrupt farming. It is the one sector that they can point out as a success." Dudley White was seeing positives in the Minister's speech.

"I'll drink to that. Waiter, give us another round."

Having lost much of the day waiting for the minister's speech, the farmers decided to spend the rest of the day drinking. In the end, it looked like they were celebrating although none could say quite what it was they were celebrating. Such minor details were never allowed to get in the way of a good party!

Chapter 8

Cynthia Venter watched her sleeping husband and sighed loud-ly. He had woken her up with his snoring and she had not been able to go back to sleep. She wondered what had happened at the meeting with the minister the day before. When her husband had left in the morning, he had expressed some apprehension over what the minister was likely to say. When he came back late in the evening, he was in a particularly jovial mood and it was clear that much alcohol had been consumed. He had come home singing what she liked to call the white farmers' unofficial anthem, "Rhodesians never die" and had even made drunken amorous advances when he got into bed. In spite of the fact that she never really enjoyed making love to him when he was in this state, she had found her body responding because the last time – the night after Pastor Jones' last visit – had been particularly good. But she had been disappointed. He had, after some awkward fumbling at her night clothes and a crude exploratory hand up her skirt, turned over, lifted the blanket, and while still lying down, emp-tied the contents of his bladder into the corner of the bedroom with pin point accuracy – how was that even possible? Within seconds, it seemed to Cynthia, he was snoring.

She looked again at the lump of humanity lying beside her and con-tinuing to produce a rumbling sound from its mouth, punctuated by other sporadic rumbling sounds from its rear and wondered how she had ended up in this place. He had been handsome once, she told herself. Or was it that her well-bred English personality had been attracted by the crude rugby playing Afrikaner boy whose manners were even worse than those of the African staff that her parents, successful industrialists, in what she still referred to as Salisbury even though the name had been changed to Harare almost a decade earlier, employed? Her thoughts turned to James Sweeney, a lanky, acne-infested teenager who she had been dating when Jacques Venter came into her life. So taken had she been with Jacques that she immediately broke off her relationship with James. Her parents had been mortified, of course. The Sweeney's were good, long standing friends of the Carringtons and they were English. It had always been assumed that the James and Cynthia would end up as husband and wife.

But James had seemed so boring in comparison to Jacques, even though he was an A stream student who had gone on to become a successful, world famous heart surgeon in the United States of America. For a few moments, she fantasised about how different her life might have been and felt herself getting quite depressed.

"Never mind," she said aloud to herself as she got out of bed.

"Never mind what?"

She had not been aware that her husband was awake and was startled when he spoke.

"Oh, I did not realise you were up. I thought you were taking a load to the floors today?" It was tobacco selling season and he had been planning a trip to the tobacco auction floors all week.

102

"It's Friday and I'm bloody hung over! The bloody auction floors will still be there on Monday, please fetch me some water to drink, doll." He obviously thought that addressing her as 'doll' was romantic. She hated it but in spite of her protesting, he continued to use it.

She felt herself getting more depressed. She had hoped to go with him and spend some time at her parents' home with her mother while he was at the floors. If the prices were good, she had been sure that her husband would have got drunk and not been able to drive back to the farm which would have meant spending the weekend in Harare, going shopping with her mother and maybe even catching a movie. Life on the farm was alright but, from time to time she needed to go back to the life she once knew.

"Bring me some aspirin as well," her husband shouted after her.

"Okay, dear," she said whispering mockingly; "shall I go to the toilet for you as well?"

"I heard that!" He had not heard what she said but knew that she would have been mocking him. He tried to remember how he had got home the night before, but could not. He vaguely remembered how happy everyone had been at the club after the minister left but could not quite understand why they all got so happy. The minister's speech was no different from what government had been saying all along, so, how was it that this time, they all seemed to think that he had made and earth-shattering announcement?

"You seemed very happy when you got home last night. What did the minister have to say for himself?" Cynthia had decided that perhaps if she became less disagreeable with her husband, he might change his

103

mind about the auction floors.

"Funny thing," he was holding his throbbing head, "he did not say anything new, but somehow, it seemed to make us all happy."

"Well, you have been anticipating that he was going to say something about land redistribution. I presume that he did not?"

"No, he did not. Although he made some not-so-veiled threat about our supporting the opposition."

"I don't think that they can afford to upset the farmers at this stage. Agriculture is about the only sector that is still running properly."

"Aghman," he said getting out of bed, "these people are so unpredictable you don't really know what they are thinking at any time. I suppose I have to see what the workers are doing outside. Maybe we should bale more tobacco and I can take a bigger load on Monday. What's that on the floor?" He had just noticed the puddle of what he thought was water in the corner of the bedroom.

"I'm not sure. Antonio probably spilt some water and forgot to clean it up. I'll tell him to do it now." She did not dare mention his drunken advances the night before, in case he got funny ideas in his head.

Cynthia watched her husband's wobbling stomach transfer itself from the bed to the en suite bathroom and felt herself cringe inside. He was not going to change his mind about the auction floors, she realised.

Having cleaned himself up and brushed his teeth, Jacques was feeling a little better when he left his bedroom to go out and give instructions to his workers. He had decided that he would have a meeting with his foreman to give him new instructions as his not going to the auction floors that morning meant that the priorities had changed. His two-way radio was crackling. Most of the commercial farmers in the area were connected by radio because it was felt, particularly during the war of liberation, that farmers were vulnerable as most of them were very isolated. He listened, expecting to hear someone making a joke about how drunk they all got the night before. Ten minutes later, he was still listening, not quite believing what he was hearing. When Cynthia came into the room to tell him that Wonder, the foreman, was waiting for him, he motioned for her to be quiet and together, they listened to the radio.

"What could this mean?" She asked after some time.

"I don't know. Probably some trouble makers. The police should be able to deal with it," he said although he did not believe that himself.

George Nicholson, a farmer in the Hwedza Commercial Farming Area, not far from Macheke, had had an eventful morning. With his wife, Mildred, they had bought the farm some forty years earlier and had developed it from what was just over a thousand hectares of grass and trees, into a modern, well equipped farm that grew three hundred hectares of tobacco, a similar hectarage of maize and, his latest project that he was particularly proud of, a sizeable and growing orchard of oranges that he was exporting. He had got up nice and early as usual to do his morning rounds making sure that everything was alright around the farm and to give instructions to his farm manager, a bright young man called Never, whom he had groomed and sent to Agricultural College, and who now ran the farm with great enthusiasm and knowledge. George had decided that, as his only son had moved to South Africa where, after completing his Law degree, he had joined a large firm of lawyers there and had no interest in the farm, he was going to sub divide the farm and let Never have two or three hundred hectares for himself.

Although he had not yet told Never this news, he was very proud of his decision and felt that when he finally made the announcement, government would be very happy with him because he not only would have played his part in the redistribution of land, he had also provided the country with a competent farmer who could ensure the continued viability of agriculture in the country.

The scene was peaceful and idyllic. The workers were busy doing their various chores, Mildred had just finished feeding her dogs and was supervising Cornelia, the maid, in feeding the free range chickens that she kept, more as pets than a source of meat. She was coming back into the house to make breakfast for George, who was sitting on the veranda, engrossed in the latest edition of "Farmers Weekly," a South African Farmers' magazine that he had brought from Marondera the previous day. He had come back to the farm straight after the minister's speech because he had a lot of work to catch up on and he did not drink. It was cooler than it had been of late although George knew, from his experience of many years in the area, that it was bound to get hotter as the day wore on. He looked up as his wife walked past him and took a moment to admire his labour of the last forty years.

Everything looked just right; from the lush green lawn that surrounded his large house, and the straight lines of orange trees that went down as far as his eyes could see from where he was sitting. He knew that beyond the orchard was the new dam that he had finished building just before the rains. It had not filled up because the rains had been erratic, but he believed there was enough water to irrigate his orchard, which he planned to expand. He exhaled a sigh of satisfaction and smiled to himself.

"What are you so pleased about?" His wife asked as she passed. She was a beautiful and hardworking woman with whom he had built the farm. He was very proud of the fact that for forty years, they had worked together to build what they had.

"I love you, Mrs Nicholson," George was at peace with the world.

Mildred started to laugh and then stopped as if she was listening to something. She was.

"George," she said wiping her hands on the apron that she had on, "Am I hearing things or is that din coming towards us?"

George listened for a while then went back to reading his magazine.

"It's probably some ritual or other at the Chief's compound." Their farm was adjacent to the Juru Communal lands. The Nicholsons had lived alongside the Juru people for the forty years that they had been on the farm and although they lived completely separate lives, there was a tacit peace between them and the Juru community. Their paths hardly crossed although, from time to time, the community would ask for assistance from the Nicholsons; assistance which the latter were quite willing to give as it did not cost them much and created some goodwill. Just a year earlier, the Nicholsons had been guests of honour at the investiture of the new Chief Juru and they had donated a whole cow for the festivities. While the new, younger, more educated chief

Juru was different from his late uncle – the previous chief Juru – the relationship had seemed to carry on as usual, although Mildred Nicholson was always telling her husband that she did not trust the new chief.

"You don't trust anyone, do you?" George would ask his wife.

"I trust you, George Nicholson," she would respond good naturedly, "but I think our new chief has delusions of grandeur. He believes that he is better than he actually is."

"He is the chief, you know. In fact, to his people, he is a King!"

"It looks like your 'King' has decided to pay us a visit," Mildred was looking down the long driveway that led to the farm gate on the main road to Marondera.

George stood up and looked in the direction that his wife was looking. The chief, easily identifiable even at that distance because of his 'regal' attire of pith helmet, red gown and shiny chain and plate that he wore on his chest was heading towards the Nicholson homestead leading a group of spear wielding villagers who seemed quite animated. It was not unusual for the chief to visit the Nicholsons and although this was the first visit by the new chief, and indeed it was the first time that the chief was accompanied by such a large retinue of villagers, George was quite relaxed as he watched the approaching group.

"They probably need some help with something - money perhaps - do we have any money in the house? You know how these people expect you to have money any time they ask for it."

"No, George, I don't really have significant amounts of money in the house, but you are taking a load of tobacco to Harare this morning, are you not?"

"Yes I am. We'll have to ask them to come back in the morning."

The chief and his followers were, by now, entering the gate to the main homestead. The people carried spears, sticks, axes and a whole assortment of other crude weapons. Two of the men carried traditional drums on which they were beating a high tempo rhythm that sounded quite aggressive. They looked like they were ready for war, their faces determined. Although George observed all this, he felt no threat towards him and his wife. He had lived among these people and he knew them. There was mutual respect and he really believed that he was one of them – the old chief had, in fact always called him "Mhofu," one of the commonest, but respectable totems among the Juru people.

"Changamire," George walked confidently towards the chief, arms outstretched before him in a show of deference, addressing the chief in the traditional Shona greeting for a chief.

The chief did not move. His arms stayed in the position they had been since his arrival – one hanging loosely on his side and the other holding a spear, which pointed upwards. He was not smiling, but George was unperturbed.

"What brings you here so early in the morning, Changamire?"

"We have come to take back our land." The chief spoke with a quiet authority.

"YOUR land?" George was uncomprehending.

"Yes," the chief said, simply. "This land that you call your farm, belongs to the Juru people and has done so for centuries."

George laughed nervously, "I bought this land, Changamire. I own it and I have owned it for forty years!"

"As I said," the chief was still speaking with an even voice, "this land has been the property of the Juru people for many, many years…"

"I bought it, Changamire," George was still not sure how serious the chief was, "I can show you Title Deeds that will confirm that I am the legally registered owner of this land…"

"I can show you the remains of my great, great grandfather's homestead; I can show you the graves of my ancestors who lived on this land until it was taken away from us, I can show you where my ancestors used to plough their fields…"

"Yes, but then I bought it chief. I paid a lot of money for it…"

"Did you pay that money to the Juru people…?"

"No," he said throwing up his arms in frustration, "I bought it from the government who…"

"…stole it from my people," the chief finished George's sentence for him, "now we have come to take it back. We have waited for twenty years, thinking that the new government would address this situation. They have not, so we have decided to act."

"This is stupid! We have laws in this country. You cannot just walk in here and say you will take my farm simply because you have some notion that your ancestors once lived here," George was getting angry, "they lived on this land – if what you are saying is true – they did not own it."

"Did you just call me stupid?" For the first time since his arrival, the chief raised his voice.

"I am sorry, Changamire." George retreated, "I did not mean that you are stupid. I meant that the idea that you can claim the land based on folk lore, is stupid. The law is quite clear…"

"Ah, the law," chief Juru advanced towards George, who took a step back, "is it not your law that states quite clearly, that a thief cannot transfer ownership of what he has stolen because it does not belong to him?"

"Yes, but…"

"Your government stole this land from us. How do they have a right to sell it to you?" He paused and looked around the homestead then went on. "Here is what we are going to do. We realise that you have lived here for many years and that this is your home. We will therefore give you seven days to pack your things and vacate this land…"

"I cannot do that," George was determined not to show any weakness, "and I don't believe that the government will stand for it either."

Chief Juru turned around and nodded to his people and all hell broke loose. The attacks were random and senseless. They fanned out in all directions and set about breaking anything that looked breakable; Mrs Nicholson's flower pots were the most obvious targets, followed by the windows to the house, which shattered as rocks, bricks and pieces of pottery from the flower pots were thrown at them.

111

"Wait, WAIT!" George Nicholson shouted desperately, "Surely we can discuss this chief?"

Chief Juru heard him but decided to ignore him for a while. He was going to teach him a lesson or two before they discussed anything further.

Meanwhile, his wife was on the radio, broadcasting to the other farmers – having first spoken to the police in Marondera who advised that they would come as soon as one of the two serviceable vehicles at their disposal became available.

"There is some nonsense here with that chief Juru," she said into the radio, "he is here with a group of his people saying something about his ancestors owning this land, can you believe it?"

"Are you alright though?" A voice she did not recognise asked.

"Of course we are all right. I've been telling George all along that that new chief is trouble, but you know George, he believes there is good in everyone, even Africans."

"Where is George now?" She recognised Jacques Venter's voice and accent.

"Oh, he's outside trying to negotiate with the man, but they are trashing my garden. Can you believe that they have broken all my flower pots?"

"Can you get out though, Mildred?" Cynthia Venter's voice was concerned.

"Of course we can get out. But why would we want to get... gosh!

112

They are hurling rocks at us!" Mildred ducked as a rock landed on the table in front of her, having just missed her head. "What nonsense is this?" She shouted into the radio as she pulled the table away from the window. "I don't know what has got into these people."

Outside, things were quietening down. Chief Juru, having decided that their point had been made, gave the signal to stop and all went quiet, the chief's followers taking positions behind their leader.

"You see, Mr Nicholson, we are not interested in your property; your grass and flowers. We are not even interested in your house. All we want is our land."

George Nicholson chuckled and looked straight at the chief. "You cannot take the land without taking everything that's on it. Anyway, I don't know why we are having this discussion. This is my farm, and that is all there is to it." There was a note of finality in his voice. But George was worried. In all the time he had lived on the farm, his black neighbours had always been respectful and generally looked up to him and his wife. He could not understand what it was that had got into a people that were considered the friendliest blacks in Africa. He could not decide whether the new bravado they appeared to be showing was a result of agitation from a few individuals or if it was something encouraged by a desperate ZIPA. But only the day before, Minister Mugwazo had been reassuring the farmers that their land was safe. He decided that the chief and his people were working on their own.

"Look, Changamire," his voice took a softer, more conciliatory tone, "we have lived side by side for many years without any trouble. I understand that there may be some frustration at the slow pace of land reform, but surely there are official channels through which you can

bring your plight to the attention of government? I don't think that trying to take over my farm by force is going to achieve what you want.
As it is, the police are on their way..."

Mention of the police reminded him of his wife. He had not seen or
heard from her since she went into the house to call the police.

"Where is my wife?" He shouted frantically and turned to run into the
house without waiting for the chief's response.

"The police cannot stop us," he heard the chief say behind him, "this
land belongs to us and we have every right to take it!"

He found Mildred cowering in the passage, still clutching the radio,
although she was neither speaking into it nor listening to the commu-
nications that were going on between the other farmers. For some reason, George thought she looked very beautiful then. They embraced
without speaking, their closeness giving them all the comfort they
needed then.

"What is going to happen to us?" Mildred verbalised the thoughts they
had both been having.

"Shhh," George wanted to reassure his wife with an assurance he did
not feel, "We'll be alright. The police are on their way."

"What can they do?" Mildred had no respect for the Zimbabwe Republic Police (ZRP), whose growing reputation for corruption and
incompetence infuriated her, "they will probably want the farm for
themselves?" She did not believe that, but thought it would bring
some humour into their situation.

"You think they will arrest us instead? Then keep us here to work the land for them. They certainly would not be able to do anything with it."

"I don't know," it was becoming some kind of game between them; "this house is in better shape than most of their police stations. Perhaps they will just move in here, and turn it into one of those hovels they seem to like living in!"

"And we can move into our apartment in Harare. What a clever investment that was!" George was being sarcastic. They had bought a block of flats in Harare as an investment five years earlier, after a particularly profitable tobacco season and given it to an estate agent to manage for them. As black Zimbabweans moved into the formerly whites only flats, with their large families and not particularly high standards of hygiene and property maintenance, the flats were in a bad state of repair, in part because the Estate agent was not really doing his job properly. They had, in fact, been thinking of putting it on the market. If this situation deteriorated any further, perhaps they could just clean up one of the flats for themselves, George was thinking. But things seemed still quiet outside. Perhaps the chief had made his point and was preparing to lea....

"Mr Nicholson," the chief's booming voice interrupted his thoughts, "we mean you or your wife no harm. But we are very serious about this. Please pack your things and leave."

George stood up, over Mildred's protestations, and looked out through the window. The chief stood in exactly the same spot that he had been when he left although now there was someone holding an umbrella over him to shield him from the scorching sun. The other people were scattered over his grounds finding shade where they could – under trees, next to tractors and other vehicles and even on the side of the main house. He had not looked at the level of destruction that had taken place and was surprised that so much damage could have been inflicted on his life's work in such a short time. He decided to walk out and confront the chief. He barely heard his wife's whispered "be careful" behind him.

Chief Juru was surprised to see George emerge out of his house. He had assumed that the farmer had taken shelter inside the house and would not come out until the police arrived. He found himself grudgingly admiring the man. 'The man has balls', he thought to himself wondering if he could have had the guts to come out and confront such a mob. Then again, whites believed they had a God-given right to be superior, so perhaps it was not so surprising after all.

George was fighting hard to disguise his fear. Clearly these people meant business, but he was not going to let them know how terrified he was. He had spent forty years of his life building this place up and he was not going to give it up just like that. At his appearance, there was a stir as the villagers scrambled to get up and look menacing. The initial excitement at coming onto what had hitherto, been forbidden space, had worn off as the reality of what it was they had done sank in. Many of them liked Mr Nicholson and had rather hoped that he would have just left when asked to.

"Changamire," George said with a lightness he did not feel, "I see you guys have been having some fun."

A woven flower basket hanging from the veranda fell besides George, startling him. He looked at it, remembering how much time Mildred had spent tending the orchid in it. 'This year it should flower', he remembered her saying just a few days earlier. Now, as it lay on the ground beside him, it seemed to summarise how, in a few minutes, their lives had changed. Would the orchid flower this year? If it did, would they be here to enjoy it?

"There was no need for this," the chief spoke with a quiet authority. "We will have this land whether you like it or not. We can agree to do this the easy way or there will be more unnecessary destruction of property."

"The police might have something to say about that." The statement was made in hope rather than conviction. He was not so sure that the police were equipped to handle such a situation.

"Policemen want land too, you know. They will probably be pleased at what we have done."

George took some time to digest this. It seemed to him that the chief might be right. If this was what the Africans of Zimbabwe wanted, the police would be among those who would want land. Yet, and it was a big yet, these people had always seemed so agreeable, so willing to defer to the white men. Apart from the small minority of Soviet-inspired agitators who went to fight in the so called war of liberation, the vast majority of what George and his colleagues liked to call 'their' Africans were quite happy with the status quo. They had seen, by what happened in their Eastern and Northern neighbours, how countries could be ruined by wanting to change things too quickly. And Minister Mugwazo had assured the farmers, only the day before, that their land was safe. The rule of law, he continued reasoning this out, was respected in Zimbabwe – by and large – and he had Title deeds which proved that he legally owned the land. There was no way that the government would stand for such lawlessness! He felt emboldened.

"Look Chief," he took a step towards his adversary, "you can destroy as much of the farm as you want, but nothing will change. I built this farm from nothing and I can do so again. All these things that you are throwing about," he waved his arms in the air to emphasise the point, "are insured. I will put in a claim and the insurance company will pay me out and I will replace all these things. This time next year, I will be inviting you round for a drink." George was feeling quite confident now.

"This time next year," the chief spoke with equal conviction, "I *may* invite you for a meal at my house on this land. We will be neighbours, you see; because we have no interest in your house, we will build our own and we will plough our own fields…"

"That, my chief," George interrupted, "will not happen. I own this land, and I shall not give it up. I will die first."

"Should we harvest his oranges, Changamire?" One of the villagers asked the chief in his native Shona.

The chief shook his head slowly, his eyes fixed on George's face. "No, Mseyamwa," he spoke deliberately. "Mr Nicholson here still thinks that this is a joke. Let us see how long he can stay cooped up in his house with his wife. Go on, chief," his voice went up a notch, "back into the house…"

"You can't order me about," George started, "this is my…"

"I can and I am," the chief raised his spear, held it up for a few seconds, then pushed it into the ground with a force that surprised George, and diluted his resolve. He turned quietly and went back into the house.

"What did he say?" Mildred asked anxiously even before George sat down.

"I think," George said, throwing himself into an easy chair, "that this could take a while."

"What do they want? Money?"

"No, I don't think that they are after money. I think that chief Juru genuinely believes that his ancestors owned this land and that he is entitled to it."

"Have you offered it to them?"

"Offered what, to them?" George was genuinely puzzled.

"Money, of course. These people are always short of money and I am sure that if we go into our savings and investments, we can raise enough to buy them off. It's that young chief. He has seen an opportunity and he is going for it. It will probably cost us less than a season's tobacco proceeds."

George looked at his wife with what could have been compassion but was, in fact, pity. For years he had tried to tell her that this day might come; that the Africans would not always be docile and pliable. He had looked into the chief's eyes and he knew that the chief and his followers were serious about this. What he could not work out was whether the government would stand for it. Yes, they had been making the right noises, but now they were under pressure from the MFD, and there was no telling how they would react to something like this. Could his wife understand that this was the beginning of the end of their very elevated way of life? George did not think so. She still saw this as 'a bit of nonsense' as she would probably call it that would soon go away and they would get back to business as usual.

"There are things," he addressed his wife, "that even money cannot buy."

At the Venter's homestead, the troops were gathering. Word had gone round the small farming communities of Macheke and Hwedza that one of their number was under attack. The Venter's residents seemed a natural choice for a meeting venue, not because it was conveniently close for everyone, but because of the famed Venter hospitality. Once they had dealt with the little disturbance at the Nicholsons, they would get back to Jacques Venter's for some well-earned refreshments and some well-cooked home food. Mrs Venter knew how to put together an impromptu meal to satisfy any of them.

"We need to go out there urgently," Jack van Breda said as he got out of his pickup truck. "It sounds like those two are in real trouble."

"Yes, but we have no idea what is happening. My wife and I spoke to Mildred briefly but now they seem to have gone silent..."

"Didn't you say that the last time you spoke to Mildred, she said that George was outside negotiating with the chief?" Dudley White interrupted Jacques.

"That's the last we heard and then, nothing. It's as if they have switched off their radio."

"So what is it we are hoping to achieve by going there? Should we not let the police handle this?" Dudley was being cautious. He did not feel the adrenalin rush that everyone else seemed to be feeling.

"The police cannot handle this. You seem to forget that we are in the minority here and we have always survived by supporting each other." Jack, who was looking very excited, stopped and regarded Dudley sneeringly. "Then again, what do you Poms know about surviving in Africa? You were not even engaged in the bush war. Just came to enjoy the spoils."

"There is no need for that, Jack. Right now, we need to all pull together against a common enemy…"

"But, they are not the enemy! They are fellow citizens of this country and all they want is …"

"Who cares what they want? They cannot have our farms. Period." Jacques was getting tired of this discussion. "While we are arguing about what our African friends want, do we know what is happening to George and Mildred?"

"I think that Dudley is right. We need to let the police handle this. However, our presence there would boost the Nicholsons' morale. I certainly would like to know that the rest of you guys would come if anything like this happened to us." Cynthia Venter spoke up even though this was a man's discussion. She had been serving them coffees and felt compelled to come to the aid of Dudley who, like her, was English.

"You know of course that you cannot come with us, Cindy?" Jacques was annoyed that his wife had joined in the conversation and called her by the shortened version of her name that he knew she hated.

"Why ever not?" She ignored the intended slight, "Mildred will need some female company."

"At this point, we don't know what is happening at the Nicholsons and I am not so sure that it would be prudent to take a woman into the fray. Why don't the men go first, assess the situation, then we can decide how to approach it."

It was finally agreed that the men would go in a convoy of four cars and see what exactly was happening at New Bristol Farm – so named because the Nicholsons had originally come from Bristol in England. There was some argument over whether they would carry arms or not, with Dudley, once again being the lone voice for caution. They thus left armed with whatever weapons had been collected from the farmers.

Chapter 9

Itai Mugwazo was upset. Word had just got to him that villagers in Hwedza, led by their traditional chief, had occupied a commercial farm claiming that it was their ancestral land. How dare they? He was in charge of probably the most successful department in government because the commercial farmers were successful. He had heard the villagers of Manhowe express the desire to take back the land during the rally that he had addressed, but had not really taken it seriously. He was going to call the Minister for Home Affairs to make sure that this problem was nipped in the bud. There was no telling how other villagers would react once they heard what had happened in Hwedza.

"And why did they have to go and do this on a Friday?" He said aloud to himself. He had plans to take his new girlfriend to the holiday resort of Lake Kariba for the weekend.

"Who did what on a Friday?"

He had not heard his secretary, Felistus, come into his office. He looked up at her. She had put on weight lately and was not as attractive as she was when he first employed her, and then went on to have a stormy relationship with her. He regretted that and was now thinking about the warnings he had been given about relationships in the office.

"After a while, they begin to think that they own you," George Moyo had counselled. "You are better off with someone away from your work. Secretaries are dangerous. They can even challenge your wife!"

He thought about the truthfulness of that statement now as he remembered the last encounter between Felistus and his wife. It was the day after their trip to Macheke and his wife had come into the office to talk to him about something. Felistus would not let her in on the pretext that he was busy.

"Mr Mugwazo left very strict instructions that he is not to be disturbed. I can take a message…"

"I'm his wife and I can see my husband any time I want."

"I know who you are, but Itai, eh… Mr Mugwazo left instructions that under no circumstances is he to be disturbed. He is writing a report for the President."

"I don't care if he is writing a report to the Secretary General of the United Nations, I need to see my husband now!" Chipo was getting angry. She had for a while now, suspected that her husband's relationship with this bimbo was more than met the eye and of late she had felt that every time she called, Felistus would make it as difficult for her as possible to speak to her husband.

Felistus had busied herself moving files from one end of the desk to the other while whistling a tuneless melody. Chipo had watched her, wondering about her fuller figure. Was she pregnant? Was it Itai's if indeed she was pregnant. Without warning, she had stood up and barged into her husband's office before the secretary could react. She was in time to hear the end of his telephone conversation. There was nothing on the desk except his feet, which he quickly removed as his wife came in.

"…. am looking forward to Kariba this weekend. Eh, yes your excellency. I will make sure that it is done your excellency." Itai hung up hurriedly even though there seemed to be conversation still coming out of the phone. His excellency, she thought, sounded very much like a woman.

"I tried to stop her," Felistus was saying behind her, " she just barged…"

Itai waved her away dismissively. "It's alright. My wife can come in any time." Felistus had stood there for a few seconds, her eyes pleading with Itai, then she withdrew back into her office.

" I thought you had an important report you were writing?"

"A report?" Itai was bewildered.

"For the President. Your secretary just said that I could not come in because…"

"Oh, that? She must have misunderstood. I said I needed time to speak to the President. That's who I was concluding with as you came in."

"Perfect timing then," Chipo was now convinced that she had been lied to and that there was more to the relationship between her husband and his secretary. "Tell me," she went on, her voice not giving away her thoughts, "is the President suffering from a cold?"

"No! Of course not. Whatever gives you that impression?"

"Nothing. Just wondered," she said thoughtfully before changing the subject and moving on to the reason for her visit, which was that she needed some foreign currency in order to travel to South Africa to buy the family's monthly groceries. That evening, of course she confronted him with her suspicions and would not let go of the subject until he confessed and promised that it would never happen again. He had also promised his wife that he would get rid of Felistus.

Now, he was looking at her and wondering what thoughts were going through her mind. 'Hell hath no fury like a woman scorned' he was thinking. He had spoken to her about moving to another government department and working for someone else explaining to her that their continuing to work at such close proximity was not healthy for their relationship and that sooner or later, his wife was going to find out. She was no fool, of course and she knew exactly what was happening. Her beauty and novelty were waning and he wanted to move on to someone newer and younger, like the Lillian that had become a regular caller. But she was going to get as much as she could out of this. By the time they finished their discussion, she had managed to get herself in line for a diplomatic posting, as secretary to one of the country's ambassadors abroad.

"You were saying something about someone doing something on a Friday?"

"Oh yes," he came out of his reverie, "some chief in Hwedza has led his people on to a commercial farm, asking the farmer to leave because the lands belong to his ancestors."

"Do they?"

"Do they what?" She could be thick sometimes.

126

"Do they belong to his ancestors?"

"What has that got to do with anything? The farmer bought the land legally and has legal title to it. We cannot keep going back to the time when there were no land laws and try to unravel who owned what. Can you imagine what a can of worms we would open? Everyone would be claiming that this land and that land belongs to their ancestors. Where would it all end?"

"But, if this chief can show that the land belonged to his ancestors, surely he cannot be denied. I know that in Lower Gweru where I come from, in the Midlands, my great grandparents had to move from Somabula to make way for white farmers. What is the meaning of our independence if we cannot undo those injustices that were perpetrated on our forefathers?"

This was new. Itai Mugwazo had never seen his secretary as one with any depth besides where her next meal, her next perfume, her next designer dress, her next manicure was coming from. Any man who could provide would do and for a while, he had been that man. He had never seen her as one with any political views whatsoever.

"Matters of state are complicated," he said after a long pause, "we are now part of the international community and there are certain minimum standards expected of us as a member of the community of nations."

"I don't see what is complicated about taking back what belongs to us. When the whites were in government, they took land from our ancestors, there was nothing complicated about that. Now that we are in government, why is it suddenly complicated?"

"There are laws to be followed…"

"Your party, comrade Minister, has a more than two thirds majority in Parliament. Surely you can make the necessary laws?"

"I wish it were that simple," Minister Mugwazo threw up his arms and walked back into his office, banging the door behind him.

He was livid. Who did she think she was? Did she think that just because she had slept with a government minister, she could now understand how to run a government? It took him about fifteen minutes to get over what his secretary had said, by which time, he found himself thinking that there was some sense in what she was saying.

"But what does she know? She is nothing but a glorified typist!" He said to himself out loud.

"Get me the Minister for Home Affairs," he barked the instruction to his secretary over the phone. Everything was falling apart. He had his weekend planned to the minutest detail. This girl had been giving him the run around for a long time and now that she had accepted his proposal, he wanted to show her what kind of man he was. If he could speak to Dennis at Home Affairs, maybe he could salvage his weekend after all.

There was no love lost between Itai Mugwazo and Dennis Mangwiro, the Minister for Home Affairs. Their feud was fuelled mainly by the competition for the President's approval that characterised the ZIPA cabinet. Itai felt that he was superior in the President's eyes because his department, Agriculture, was being hailed internationally as a great success, while Dennis, who thought that Itai's department was too reliant on white farmers, felt he controlled the more critical department that had such institutions as the police under it.

Denis knew about the invasion, of course, having been briefed by the Commissioner of Police himself. He was not sure what he felt about what had just happened in Hwedza. He had been told many stories by his grandfather, of how they had had to move from the area known as Chikomba district to Mhondoro African Reserve to make way for white farmers.

'It used to be called *VuHera,* were the Hera people lived', his grandfather would say, longingly. 'Then the white man came and decided to call it Buhera. I was very young, of course, but I remember us being packed into lorries with our belongings and moving here...'

"What is it you want, Itai?" He asked after exchanging a few awkward pleasantries with his colleague, "I have already given instructions that the police must remove those people from that farm as quickly as possible. I'm just waiting for the report that says that my instructions have been carried out."

"Please keep me updated on developments. As you know, we cannot afford to disrupt agriculture like this!"

Itai was almost pleading and Denis was surprised. The little twerp was always so full of himself and he always gave the instructions. This time, his voice sounded almost as if he was begging.

"I know how important your portfolio is, Itai," he put as much sarcasm in his voice as he could master, "but please leave the professionals to handle this. We know what we are doing."

"I know you do..."

"You KNOW? What has got into you, Itai? For you to acknowledge that there are other departments that actually work and have as important a role as agriculture, no, in this case, that can save agriculture, must be rather painful."

"Denis please," Felistus walked in at this point, "how many times have I told you not to come into my office while I am talking to other ministers…"

"His Excellency is on the line," she whispered.

"Who?" He had heard but could not quite believe it. He had hoped that by the time he spoke to the President, the little problem at the Nicholsons would have been resolved. He had, in fact, hoped that he would have called the president to tell him how his ministry had dealt with a troublesome crowd of villagers.

"The President…"

"I heard you the first time!" He snapped at her, "Denis, let me call you back," he said into the telephone and hung up.

"Your Excellency," he said fawningly, "it is so good of you to call…"

"Cut the crap," the President was, clearly, in no mood for small talk. But the President also never used such language. "What are you doing about Hwedza?"

"We err," he started, "the Minister of Home Affairs and I are working closely to ensure that the problem is resolved as quickly as possible."

"And your solution is….?" The President left the question hanging.

"Our solution, your Excellency, is that those villagers must be removed from the Nicholsons Farm as soon as possible."

"Why?"

The question was totally unexpected.

"Why, what, sir?" Itai Mugwazo was bemused.

"Why must they be removed?"

"Because, sir, they are occupying private land, an action that is against the law. Because they are disrupting an important sector of our economy."

"I have told Denis at Home Affairs to halt the evictions, for now. I am calling a Cabinet meeting in the morning to discuss a way forward."

"Tomorrow morning, sir?"

"Of course, tomorrow morning…"

"Your Excellency, it is Saturday tomorrow!"

"I know what day it is tomorrow. Do you think that matters of government go to sleep because it is the weekend?"

"Err, no, Your Excellency, I just thought…"

"Good. Ten o'clock tomorrow, then." He hung up.

Itai was desperate. Why did these things happen only to him? Of all the days, of all the weekends available to them, why did Chief Juru and his people choose this one to make whatever point they thought they were making. Surely they knew that they could not succeed in what they were trying to do. The Nicholsons had title to that land and were very productive. They were part of the reason that Zimbabwe was being called the bread basket of the region. No one in their right minds would want to destroy that, surely?

But then, why was the President calling a Cabinet meeting? What was there to discuss? How does a whole Cabinet meet to discuss the fact that people had broken the law? The police are there to handle such things and if they cannot, the army could always be called in.

His thoughts turned to Lillian. She still lived with her parents and had told them some story about going away for the weekend with work colleagues – as he had told his wife about a business retreat with some of his Cabinet colleagues. He could explain to his wife about the Cabinet meeting, but how was Lillian going to explain to her parents that she was not going after all? And she probably would not be able to lie successfully about the trip being postponed to the following weekend. Perhaps the meeting would be short and sweet and they could still go on Saturday afternoon, which meant that he would have to find Lillian somewhere to sleep for one night – not a problem, she could be booked into a hotel; but could he trust her to be in a hotel room on her own while he was home with the wife? That was a worry, but meanwhile, he had to call the Lodge and tell them that he would only come on Saturday, not Friday, cancel the sunset cruise on the lake and a dinner booking for that evening at the Cutty Sark, rebooking both for Saturday evening. He would then have to decide which hotel to book Lillian in for the night, and perhaps spend a couple of hours with her before going home, so it would have to be somewhere discreet. The only problem with all this was that he would have to do all this himself

– he could not ask Felistus to do this for him.

'She'd probably phone my wife as soon as the bookings are done to give her all the details', he thought to himself, 'better get started'. For the next couple of hours, which included his lunch time, he was on the phone and by two thirty, he had done everything except make the booking for Lillian. He had not even told her about the postponement.

At three o'clock, as was his custom on a Friday, he left his office for the week and headed to the exclusive, aptly named Moonlight Bar in the Sheraton hotel to meet with his friends. He would discreetly speak to the Manager about a room for Lillian so that by the time he went to pick her up, that would all be sorted out and he could then explain about the postponement on the way, but be in a position to tell her that their weekend together would start in Harare, not at Kariba. He was pleased with himself and was whistling contentedly as he walked into the Sheraton. If the news of the farm invasion in Hwedza entered his mind that afternoon, he quickly dismissed it as a minor irritation that would soon go away. It was nothing to worry about. He should have been worried.

In Hwedza, the Nicholsons were watching the goings on outside with growing despair. Two police officers had arrived in a pickup truck that, although it was probably a couple of years old, looked like it had been around for a couple of decades. George Nicholsons watched the two constables arrive and was thinking how badly the police looked after their vehicles. 'No wonder they don't have enough transport when you need them', he thought to himself. The body language of the policemen did not offer much encouragement. They were being overly deferential to the chief and seemed ill at ease as they spoke to him.

They did not exude any authority at all.

"Look at them, Mildred," he said to his wife, "they look like they are asking for permission to do their job!"

"Well, what did you expect? He is their chief too, you know."

"The chief is not above the law! They should just arrest him and take him away."

"Two of them, you say," Mildred was knitting sitting on the sofa with her back to the window. She could not bear to look at what her yard was looking like. "How do you expect two policemen to deal with a mob this size? I told them: told them George, that we were being attacked by a mob, and they send two cops. I don't suppose the life of a white person is worth much in this country these days."

"You are right there. Anyway, here comes the cavalry," George's spirits were raised by the sight of a convoy of pickup trucks' some of which he recognised as belonging to farmers from the area. "It looks like Pet van Zyl and the others. Perhaps they can knock some sense into these people."

"Are they armed?" Mildred asked hopefully.

"I don't see any arms, but I don't think arms would do much good in this situation. Things could only escalate at the sight of arms."

"Do you think they can get any worse?"

"Of course they can get worse. People might get killed!"

"That chief Juru deserves to be shot," Mildred was feeling quite belligerent.

"You do realise," George said quietly, "that we are prisoners inside our house. If the situation were to escalate, do you think that we would be safe? We would be hostages in our own home."

"Do you think they might kill us?" For the first time, Mildred showed signs of being worried. George sought to reassure his wife.

"No, I don't think they are after any bloodshed. I think they are just rattling their sabres a bit with the hope that we will flee in panic. The police are here, our friends are here, I do not think anything will happen to us. Not today, anyway."

"And tomorrow?"

"One day at a time, my dear; one day at a time."

Outside, the police and a delegation of farmers were consulting with the chief. The police, who had got there earlier, had been asking the chief to leave peacefully, while the farmers wanted access into the house to see if their friends were alright. The two constables were somewhat confused with the instructions that they had been given. First, a large contingent had been assembled with instructions to remove the chief and his people by whatever means. As this group was made up mainly of the notorious black boots, whose claim to fame was their ability to touch offenders with their batons at high speed with great force, there was no doubt as to what the 'whatever means' meant. They were in the two lorries that were to take them to Hwedza, psyching themselves up for the task ahead by singing revolutionary songs (which in actual fact were dirty songs whose lyrics were not for the faint hearted), and banging their batons onto the floor of the lorry in unison and in rhythm with the singing, when new instructions came. Harare, the Minister of Home Affairs himself, had instructed that the Public Relations Department of the force was to be sent to try to negotiate with the chief and ask him to leave peacefully. Under no circumstances was force to be used and if they refused, the police were only to stay there as observers.

"It's been twenty years," the chief was saying, "twenty years since we got our independence, and what have we got to show for it? I support ZIPA, and I have faith in this government, but if it means I go to jail for this, then handcuff me now," he proffered his hands.

"No, Changamire," constable Muchena, the senior of the two was feeling quite awkward talking to his chief like this, "we are not here to arrest you, but do you see the disruption you are causing? We have been given this message for you, government is aware of your plight and frustration, but these things take time. The President has called a Cabinet meeting for tomorrow to discuss the land question and to deal specifically with you and your people."

"Then we will wait it out. We are not interested in land, just any land, we want this land, the land where the bones of our ancestors lie."

Pete van Zyl and Jacques Venter had been seconded by the other farmers to go in and see if they would be allowed to talk to the Nicholsons. The convoy from Macheke had, as had been arranged over the radio, driven to the Hwedza Country club, where they met up with the farmers from Hwedza, so that by the time they got to the Nicholsons, their convoy was made up of ten vehicles. The destruction that they found sobered them up and disabused them of any notions that they had that they could, by show of force, drive out the offending chief and his

136

people. They parked on the road, some distance from the main home-stead and came out of their cars and huddled for consultation. Jack van Breda, who had disembarked carrying his rifle was quickly told to put it back in the car.

"This is no time for bravado," Pete said. "Let us first see what we have here before we decide on a way forward."

They surveyed the scene quietly for a few minutes and while they sympathised with the Nicholsons, most of them were thinking of their own farms and wondering how they would react if something like this happened to them, wondering, in fact at the likelihood that what had happened here could spread and start to affect other farms in the area. The African, to their European minds, liked to mimic what others did and they could see workers on their own farms downing tools and try-ing to emulate what Chief Juru and his people had done.

"We need to find out what the situation is with the Nicholsons," Jacques said looking around at the others, "but it is important that we get back to our own farms as quickly as possible. We need to make sure that this thing doesn't spread any further. Let's try not to speak to our workers about this until we know what government's reaction is."

It was thus decided that Jacques and Pete be sent in to speak to the police and the chief and, if possible speak to the Nicholsons and offer to take them away if they would be allowed to.

They had never seen Chief Juru before, at least not to their recollec-tions, but he knew Pete van Zyl well, having spent a lot of his child-hood working on Mr van Zyl's farm during school holidays and week-ends to supplement his school fees. He remembered him as a hard task master who was quick to use the whip on those he thought were slackening in their work. He also used a lot of what Chief Juru had since found out, was foul, insulting language. At the time, they knew no better and phrases like 'facken Bastet' and words like 'shiti' had become part of their lingo.

"Good afternoon chief, officer," Pete nodded at the chief and the constable in turn as he greeted them. He could see that the policeman was a mere constable, but thought that addressing him with the respect that a higher rank conferred on the policeman would be good PR at this time.

"Good afternoon sirs," constable Muchena replied politely while the chief, who stood erect and proud, remained silent.

"What have we here?" Jacques asked, trying to sound unaffected by what was around them, "this place looks like it has been hit by a bomb."

"If Mr Nicholson had agreed to our demands," the chief spoke, "we would not have done this. We would have allowed him to take as much time as he liked to remove his property from here without causing any damage. All we want is our land!" He lifted his spear and drove it into the ground with such force that almost half the shaft went into the admittedly soft ground due to recent rains.

"Are the Nicholsons alright?" Pete van Zyl was anxious to know.

"I was about to go in and see them," constable Muchena said, "if it is alright with the chief."

"We are not savages as you people seem to think," the chief cut in, almost smiling as he was amused by the deference that the white farmers were showing, "they have not been harmed and are safe inside their home, for now. Of course you can go in and seen them, take one of the whites with you."

Constable Muchena was relieved that he was not having to go in alone. He was not sure what he would find and how the Nicholsons would react to the news that the police were not here to remove the invaders.

They did not take it well, at least Mildred did not. She stood up and paced the floor of the rather large lounge.

"Are you telling me, that even though we have title deeds to this land, even though we have lived here forty years and built this place to what it is, the police cannot protect us; the law cannot protect us? What kind of country is this?"

"Ma'am, the President has called a Cabinet meeting tomorrow morning to discuss this very issue..."

"People break the law and the President calls a Cabinet meeting! What is there to discuss? George!" She glared at her husband, "don't just sit there! Can you hear what this man is saying?"

"What can I do?" George suddenly felt very old and very tired, "if the Cabinet..."

"Tell him... Tell him that this is not acceptable!"

"Constable, this is not acceptable..."

"Tell him like you mean it, George!"

"Perhaps," Pete spoke up for the first time, "it would be prudent for you to pack a few things and come and spend the night with us. Things will look a lot easier after a good night's rest…"

"NO!" Mildred was emphatic, "we are not leaving our home."

No amount of persuasion would move Mildred from that position and, in the end, it was agreed that they could stay and the others would check on them in the morning.

"Please stay in touch on the radio and the police are here if there is any nonsense."

It was very lonely when they watched their friends drive away. But they were still in their home and they were safe. It had been a long day. They said a prayer, huddled together and tried to sleep, but sleep would not come.

"I suppose it is only a farm," George said quietly in the early hours of the morning. They had both been awake, lost in their thoughts, each one being quiet because they did not want to disturb the other.

"It is our farm, George," Mildred replied, equally quietly.

"Do you think that they would let us go into town?" George asked after another lengthy silence, "we need to replenish our supplies. We could be here for a while."

"That would depend on whether they see us as hostages or not."

"I'll ask the chief in the morning." There was another long silence.

George awoke with a start, surprised that he had actually fallen asleep. Mildred was in the kitchen making breakfast.

"Good morning sunshine," she said cheerfully, giving her husband a peck on the cheek, "did you sleep well?"

"I did, my dear," he responded equally cheerfully, "what's for breakfast?"

"Hmmm, let me see now, we have stale bread, eggs, margarine, coffee and some oranges from our own orchard!"

They continued the charade of cheerful banter through breakfast, after which they went to bath and dressed in readiness for going to town.

"Right," George was feeling anxious, "I'll go and ask the chief if we can go, and if he will allow us back."

"OK George. Go tell him!"

"Right." George said again.

He walked out into the bright sunshine and felt vulnerable. The chaos that he found himself standing in surprised him once again. He looked around. Some traditional beer had somehow come into the yard and the empty containers were all over what used to be the Nicholsons' lawn. Those who had been drinking were lying around in various stages of sobriety, on the lawn, in Mrs Nicholson's car, in Mr Nicholson's truck, on the tractors and their trailers, anywhere that offered some sort of bedding and shelter for the night.

"Good morning, Mr Nicholson, did you sleep well?" George was not sure if the chief was joking.

"Good morning Changamire. It's good of you to ask."

They whole scene looked and felt surreal. The chief stood there in the middle of the chaos, dressed in his official regalia which looked ridiculous at the best of times, but now looked completely idiotic, speaking to a white man who had just bathed and shaved and looked like one going to play golf, which George did on Saturday mornings and was half hoping that if he was allowed to go, he might get in at least nine holes. They chatted for a while, George being surprised at the chief's command of the English language and even at his general knowledge. They had never before, spoken as equals thus George had only judged the man on assumptions.

Finally, George felt confident that he could ask what he needed to.

"Changamire," he started hesitantly, " my wife and I were wondering if we could go into town, you know, buy a few supplies…"

"Are you asking for my permission?" The chief seemed amused.

"Well, I thought… I suppose I am, yes."

The chief laughed suddenly. A booming laugh that seemed to come from deep within him. It was not a nasty cruel laugh.

"George," he addressed him by his first name for the first time, "this is your home. Until such time as you have officially vacated, you can do what you bloody well please. You can even go and not come back, but if you do come back, we will in no way stop you from living your life."

"We can leave," he told Mildred when he got back into the house.

"The chief says we are free to do what we want until such time as we officially," he made inverted comas in the air with his hands, "vacate"

"Does that mean we have to feed them?"

They drove out to much cheering and ululating from those who were not close enough to the chief to understand what the arrangement was. They thought the Nicholsons were leaving for good and the cheering was because they thought the house was now free for them to go into. They were soon disabused of that notion.

George was surprisingly cheerful as they drove out. He felt a sense of freedom he had not felt in a long time. He was going to go shopping with his wife, something that he normally would not do as he found her lengthy decision making about what she wanted to buy quite tiring, then they would have lunch together at the Marondera Hotel after which he was going to play his round of golf and Mildred would have her hair done. They were going to have fun before coming home in the evening to confront whatever it was that would be awaiting them. It could not get any worse! Or could it? He looked at his house in the rear view mirror as it receded from view. Was he ever coming back here? He wondered.

Chapter 10

Jonas sat under the big *Muhacha* tree and stared into the distance. It was a hot morning and although he had been up for a few hours looking for something to fix around his rural homestead, he had found everything in good order and even though he was pleased that his wife was such a good homemaker, he felt as though he was not needed. Yet this was not the first time he had found his home in perfect condition; it was one of the reasons he loved Sekai so much. He spent his working life doing back-breaking work at the Venters and it was always a relief to find that his weekends off were a time to rest and recuperate; to sit and have lengthy conversations with his wife about their children, their home and his pending retirement.

Something was different this morning though. Sekai had been busy with her household chores since before sunrise and seemed to be doing her best to avoid him; their conversation polite, but distant. He looked around at the well swept yard; the small patch of lawn that his wife so lovingly kept in front of the main structure in their home: a four-roomed farm brick under asbestos sheets bungalow that had become something of a landmark in the area. "Get off the bus near the large house," people would advise friends and family where to get off the bus when they were visiting from Harare. Compared to the huts around it, Jonas's bungalow was indeed large. Jonas was very proud of his rural homestead and he was particularly pleased with the flowers that his wife had added since his last visit.

"I like the flowers," he said cheerfully, trying to draw his wife into conversation.

His wife grunted and carried on polishing the floor without looking up.

She seemed angry with him, but was not saying why, although he had an idea what her anger was about. For the first time since they were married, he had been unable to make love to his wife. Every time he tried, he could just see his wife with Mr Venter. It must have been consensual, he reasoned. Otherwise she would have told him; and if it was consensual, she must have enjoyed it, which meant that she was probably thinking of Mr Venter when they made love! Then she went along with the Venters when they decided that they no longer needed her and wanted some mug to take her over. Yet when he looked at her this morning, he saw a wise, loving wife who had given him three wonderful children and a good home. But why was she angry with him? She was the one who slept with the boss and kept it away from him.

He stood up and went to the edge of his allotted piece of land. There was a good crop of maize in spite of the erratic rains and they were going to be alright. When he looked at his neighbours' fields, he found himself feeling sorry for them. Their fields had been ploughed over and over again and had lost what fertility they may have had. Thanks to his employers, who would make sure that he had fertilisers, and to his hard working wife, his fields still produced reasonable yields. Perhaps, he thought, that is why there is so much talk of taking land from white farmers. He thought about the last twenty four hours and how he had found himself with an unexpected weekend off.

The day had started normally, like any other Friday, except that Mr Venter had been late coming out of the house. This had not surprised Jonas because he had had to open the gate for his boss when he had come in the night before, looking, smelling and sounding like he had had quite a lot to drink. There had been some confusion because some of the workers had expected to go to Harare with the boss when he took his tobacco to the auction floors, but had found out that he was not going to the tobacco auctions after all. When Mr Venter finally emerged, it was not to bark instructions to the workers about what work needed to be done on that day. Other farmers came and there was a lot of animated talking and arguing. Finally, a convoy of the vehicles with all the farmers left to go somewhere although none of the workers could understand what was happening.

Once the bosses had gone, very little work was done and workers were to be seen in small groups discussing the happenings of the morning. There was a lot of wild speculation, but the most popular story, which, by the end of the day had been accepted as fact, was that workers on a nearby farm had gone on strike demanding higher wages. This was popular because the workers hoped that if the striking workers got their way, they would also benefit and get higher wages.

In the late afternoon, the bosses came back and after another meeting, they dispersed, after which the workers at Ventersburg Farm were called together and advised that they were all being given the weekend off except for key staff like the supervisors (also known as 'boss boys') and, Antonio, the house boy. The workers did not know this, but the employers had decided that it would be safer to remove all the

146

workers from the farms lest they decide to copy what had happened at the Nicholsons. The consensus was that by the end of the weekend, the police would have dealt with the little problem in Hwedza and everything would be back to normal.

Jonas had been excited, of course because it had been several weeks since he had seen his wife. They would have the weekend all to themselves because their youngest son had just started secondary school and had gone to boarding school.

On the bus, there had been more wild stories about a farm in Hwedza that had been taken over and depending on who was telling the story, the white farmer had been taken prisoner; had been chased away and in extreme cases, had been killed. Most of the people on the bus were agreed that this was not a clever move because "we cannot farm like the whites." One or two people argued that the whites were good farmers because they had been given advantages that black farmers did not have.

"If we were given the same advantages, like money, tractors, fertilisers... We could produce as well as the whites," one of them had argued to loud laughter.

"All you will do with the money is marry another wife and make many children. The tractor will then become your transport to ferry your large family to..."

"And when the girls see you driving a tractor," another had interrupted, "they will be after you and before you know it, you have another three or four wives!"

Everybody had laughed then and the argument had degenerated into a series of anecdotes about what black people did when they made a bit of money.

Jonas looked at his fields again and thought how lucky he was to have a wife and an employer like he had.

But Jonas's thoughts of his employer and his wife brought him back to what had been bugging him. There was only one solution, he decided. He would ask his wife if what he had overheard his boss saying was true and if it was why she had never told him about it. He did not get the chance to ask.

"Jonas, is there another woman?" Sekai asked as he walked towards her.

Jonas stopped dead in his tracks. What on earth was the woman talking about?

"Another woman? What stupid question is that?"

"Don't tell me I am asking stupid questions. Is there another woman or isn't there?"

"Of course there isn't and you know it…"

"Don't tell me what I know or don't know. The Venters organised me for you, didn't they? Perhaps they have organised another woman for you."

"Don't be stupid! Do you think that I cannot find a woman for myself…?"

"So, you have found yourself another woman!" Sekai sounded triumphant, "I knew it?"

"Did you sleep with Mr Venter?"

Jonas spoke quietly, but Sekai stopped as though she had been pole-axed. She stared at her husband as though she were looking at a stranger. Her mind was racing. 'Who had told him? Who knew? Why had she not told him herself when she could? Did others at the farm know? They couldn't have! He only called for her when Mrs Venter was away and there was no one else in the house. How on earth had her husband found out?'

"Did you sleep with Mr Venter or not?" Her husband's voice sounded so far away – and so cold!

"Jonas, I…"

"Come on, woman. It's a simple question. You do remember if you slept with him. Did he take your virginity, or were there others?"

"Jonas, please don't do this. I can explain…"

"Explain? What is there to explain? You were fucked by a white man. You are nothing but a whore!" The words were said with such venom that Sekai flinched. She did not recognise the man in front of her. Then she suddenly felt very calm. It had to come out some time, she thought, and now is as good a time as any.

"Yes, Jonas," she said simply, "I slept with Mr Venter."

It was Jonas's turn to be stunned.

"You slept with him? Like how you and I sleep together?"

"Yes, Jonas, like man and women have slept together since creation, like men and women all over the world, all over this village sleep together."

Jonas hated his wife and it showed in his eyes. He picked up the axe that he had been sharpening earlier and went into the bush without saying another word.

In Harare, it was just before ten in the morning and the Cabinet Ministers were gathering, waiting to hear what the emergency Cabinet meeting was about. Itai Mugwazo was badly hung over, having spent longer than intended with Lillian, which meant that he had consumed more alcohol than he would otherwise have had, particularly on an evening when he knew that there would be a cabinet meeting on the next day. He sat in one corner holding his head while the conversations of his colleagues, most of whom had heard about the crazy chief in Hwedza and wondered why they had to have a full Cabinet meeting to discuss the breaking of the law by a chief, who really had no power and was only there to be used by politicians when it suited them. This was usually at election time when chiefs could be relied upon to mobilise their people for ZIPA. But this did not give them the right to disrupt the economy as Chief Juru clearly was.

"I hope this does not take too long, I've had to postpone my usual golf round to this afternoon!" Mike Banga, Minister without Portfolio in the Office of the President had just discovered golf and had a regular game with three friends every Saturday morning.

"I really cannot understand golf. Where is the fun in following a little white ball round a field?" Denis Mangwiro was totally mystified by a game that many of his colleagues now seemed totally enamoured by. "And why is it called a sport when you have to dress as if you are going to dinner in order to play?"

"I will invite you for nine holes one day," Mike retorted, "and I challenge you not to get hooked."

"I don't have time for such nonsense...,"

"What nonsense is that?" The president had come in unnoticed and interrupted the conversation between the two ministers.

"We were... Eh, we were talking about golf," Mike Banga stammered, "I have just started playing. Perhaps his excellency would like to join us...."

Mike had to cut whatever he wanted to say short because of the glare he got from the president.

"Golf! Golf? You want me to live important matters of government so that I can follow a little ball around and, and...," he paused and looked around the room, "what do they do with the ball after following it around? What is the purpose of the whole exercise?"

"I was just telling Mike here that it is nonsense your excellency. It's one of those games that we have convinced ourselves that we need to play in order to show that we have arrived."

The President went and sat at the head of the large table that stood on one side of the room adjacent to his office that served as the Cabinet meeting room. The rest took seats on the other chairs around the table jostling for the chairs that were nearest to the President. Only Itai Mugwazo deliberately sat as far away from the head of state as possible, afraid that his breath might give him away. As soon as the President saw that everyone was seated, he got straight to the point.

"You may have heard, comrades, of the happenings in Hwedza, where Chief Juru and his people have taken over a farm. I have instructed the police not to act because I think that we have to be very careful how we handle this situation. I called this meeting so that we can all be agreed on how to respond." He paused, looked around the table and noticed that Itai Mugwazo, who up to this point had looked totally lethargic, probably because of a night of heavy drinking, had sat up. He was very sensitive about what he thought of as his portfolio, which was a success. 'I'll have to move him from there', the President was thinking.

Itai had been surprised firstly because it had been a while since the President had addressed them as 'comrades', a term he had come to recognise as one that meant that his leader was in particularly bellig-erent mode, but he also could not understand why the Cabinet needed to agree on something that was so simple and clear. He wanted to say something, then decided to hold his tongue until he knew what the President had in mind.

"When the fearless, gallant sons and daughters of this land of ours, the land we call Zimbabwe," the President went on, his voice taking on the tone that said that he was going to make one of his favourite political orations, "when our gallant sons and daughters took up arms, having been forced to do so by the failure of our white oppressors to accept that we needed to be able to determine our own destiny; when our young people left the comfort of their homes, the warm embraces of their families, when they gave up on their education and went across our borders to train as freedom fighters; to live in primitive harsh conditions and to come back and engage a better trained, better equipped and better backed up enemy, it was not so that we could go and live in Borrowdale and Mount Pleasant and Glen Lorne, it was not so that we could go and play golf like the white man," he looked pointedly at Mike Banga at this point, "it was because we wanted our land back. The war, my friends, was about the land!"

He had the undivided, if confused attention of all his ministers.

"The houses that we clamour for in the Northern suburbs are built on our land; the mineral resources that they claim to have found, are in our land, the farms that they now say they own, are on our land, the Mighty Victoria Falls, which David Livingstone is supposed to have discovered, even though there were people already living next to it, is on our land. Their cricket fields, their golf courses, their exclusive clubs and their exclusive schools are all on our land.

The biggest mistake we made, and I will be the first to put my hand up and say I was part of it, was that when we had the enemy on the run, when victory was close, we allowed ourselves to be duped into negotiating. We went to Lancaster House to negotiate with a defeated enemy!"

The President looked around the table again. He saw three groups. There were those who got him. They understood what he was talking about and they were listening attentively and nodding their approval. These included Denis Mangwiro. Then there were those, like Itai Mugwazo, who were not getting it. These had forgotten the revolu-

153

tionary credentials of the Party and were content to enjoy the apparent success of the partial independence that, as far as the President was concerned, they had got out of the negotiations at Lancaster House. The third group, made up mainly of the members of the now defunct Zimbabwe National Alliance (ZINA), a party that had been bludgeoned into submission by ZIPA and whose members now held junior posts in government, looked on without commitment one way or the other. They would wait to see which way the wind blew.

"What did we get out of Lancaster House?" The question was rhetorical. "I will tell you what we got. We got a constitution that entrenched white privileges in independent Zimbabwe; we got a constitution that tied our hands as far as our ability to redistribute land fairly was concerned and we got an independence that gave us nominal political power yet left the real power, economic power, in the hands of an enemy that we congratulate ourselves for having defeated.

"For twenty years, our people have watched us fumble and flounder under the limitations imposed on us by a settlement we negotiated and signed. For twenty years, our people have waited patiently for us to deliver the land so cruelly taken from our forebearers, and for twenty years all we have achieved is to acquire a taste for golf." He noticed that Mike Banga was sitting very low in his chair.

"Enter Chief Juru," he continued triumphantly. "Little known Chief Juru has gone and started what we, in twenty years, have failed to do…"

"Surely you are not suggesting…" Itai Mugwazo started.

"Shut up!" The President was clearly in no mood to debate this point.

"As I was saying," he went on after a few minutes staring at Itai who wished the ground could open up and swallow him, "Chief Juru's actions have brought to the fore a subject that most of us around this table have been reluctant to face up to. He has, in one morning, forced us to take a good look at our policy on land. He has simply told the farmer," the President looked down at his notes, "Mr Nicholson, that the land he is on belongs to the Juru people, has done so for centuries, and he wants it back. Is he wrong? I don't think so. The whites came and forcibly removed our fathers and grandfathers from land that rightfully belonged to them. Why can we not do the same?"

For a few minutes, no one spoke, mostly because none of them wanted to be spoken to the way that Itai Mugwazo had been spoken to a few minutes earlier, but also because they were not quite sure if the President wanted an answer to the question he had just posed, and if he did, whether he would accept their honest opinions. Denis Mangwiro was the bravest.

"Your excellency," he started, "you have clearly enunciated a case that many of us have been grappling with. Many of us have had guilty consciences because we have been aware that our people are not benefitting fully from our independence. Yet we are also aware that we are part of a global community that expects certain standards of behaviour from nation states…"

"By 'global community' you mean the British?"

"No, Your Excellency. I mean that we are part of the United Nations, the African Union…"

"But we are also a sovereign state, with situations and problems that

155

are peculiarly Zimbabwean. The global community has no solutions that can fit these, surely?"

"We have signed multi-lateral and bi-lateral investment protection protocols," Itai felt emboldened, "and many of our farmers are covered by them. How do we get over these?"

"The global community that you are so concerned about also respects the sovereignty of independent states and does not interfere in the internal affairs of sovereign states. Yet the British are giving aid to the opposition in this country. Is that not meddling in the internal affairs of the sovereign state of Zimbabwe?" He swivelled in his chair and looked directly at Dr Ruth Moyo, a lawyer who was also Minister for Legal and Parliamentary Affairs.

"You have many lawyers in your office, Dr Ruth, what can we do about this?"

"Well, with a bit of time…"

"Time, Dr Ruth, is one thing we do not have. Can I have a report on my desk tomorrow morning outlining the options that we have. We need to know what we can or cannot do before we decide our next step at the Nicholson's. What we do here could have far reaching ramifications.."

Everyone seemed to have taken their cue from the President and the fact that the Nicholsons land was now occupied by Chief Juru and his people was no longer being debated. Slowly, almost imperceptibly, the discussion moved to how Chief Juru could be supported. Dr Ruth promised to have the requested report in the morning and even Itai Mugwazo was getting resigned to the fact that the Nicholsons would lose their farm. 'It's only one farm', he was thinking, 'I have to find a way of reassuring the others'.

"I believe," the President cut into Itai's thoughts, "that we need to show these farmers that we are serious; that this is not one isolated incident. I have therefore instructed the intelligence services to manage the occupation of other farms – just enough for them to realise that all Zimbabweans, not just Chief Juru and his people, are hungry for land."

Itai's spirits sank. Once people realised that they could break the law without consequences, where would it all end?

Across town in Hurudza House, the Head office of the opposition MFD, they were almost in party mood. How was ZIPA going to deal with the Juru situation. This was a Godsend. If ZIPA evicted the invaders, they could not claim to be the champions of land reform. On the other hand, if they did nothing, they would be seen as promoting lawlessness! The MFD would then come in as the voice of reason, hailing Chief Juru and his people as heroes who had been forced to act by the inactivity of ZIPA on land, yet condemning ZIPA for not doing enough to protect the investment of those that could create jobs for the many unemployed.

"They will not get out of this one," Golden Tsvarayi, president of the MFD was gleefully wiping his sweaty brow. "We can just sit back, watch them shoot themselves in their collective foot, and then present our own plan for land reform. I believe that it is nearly finished and from what I have seen of it, it is a very well thought out plan which will look at the interests of the various stakeholders and still leave us with a viable agricultural sector." He looked up at the roof of his office in mock prayer, "God is so good," he took a sip of his beer and visualised himself in State House.

"Let's not celebrate too quickly," Tonderai Bodo, the Party's Secretary General had seen ZIPA get out of many a tight situation using 'whatever means necessary' and still found it hard to believe that their fortunes could change so quickly and so easily.

"How, pray tell, do you see them getting out of this one?" The President was convinced.

"I don't know. I just don't believe that it can be this easy."

"How many times have I told you, Tonderai, that when the change comes, it will catch us all by surprise? ZIPA is finished. Period."

"What about the people?" Charles Dube was the Party's Finance Officer and never really got involved in political discussions.

"What people?" The President and Secretary General asked the question together, surprised.

"The people of Zimbabwe." Charles answered calmly.

"What about them?"

"Well, aren't we doing all this for the people? How do they feel about what Chief Juru has done? Would your parents not want more and better land? Would they reject it if it was given to them?"

"What are you getting at, Charles?"

"It's all very well to have a plan on paper. But ZIPA could very well take advantage of this situation. They don't have to give land to everyone who needs it. All they have to do is carve up the Nicholsons land and give it to a few people. That would be enough to convince the rest of us that more land will be made available. They can even invade a few more farms just to make it more convincing. Then they can just go and tell the people that if they are given another mandate at the next elections, they will carry on the good work!"

Peter Mlilo, the Party's chief security officer let out a long, low whistle.

"Now it makes sense," he said finally.

"What does?" President Tsvarayi was feeling uneasy.

"We sent our own boys to Hwedza last night, just for them to keep an eye on things and let us know what is happening there. We were surprised to learn that they found only two constables from the Police Public Relations department. They were not there to evict Chief Juru. Rather they were there just to keep an eye on things and make sure that there was no trouble. Then this morning, they reported that they had spotted some of our friends from Central Intelligence and they seemed to be directing operations!"

"Come on, Peter, you don't believe that ZIPA would do that," the President was less sure of himself.

"I am just reporting what I have been told. I didn't know what it could mean until Charles spoke just now. I think they want to take this situation and turn it to their advantage."

159

"They are real swine," Tonderai Bodo said as he kicked the chair in front of him, then spent the next few minutes nursing his aching toe.

Jonas was getting desperate. He had been walking around the bush for hours. When he walked away from Sekai, he was not sure where he was going. He just wanted to get away from the woman who had betrayed him all these years. After a few hours of aimless wondering in the bush, his mind seemed to clear. He was still angry with Sekai, but he also knew that he loved her deeply. He felt an inexplicable rage each time he visualised Sekai with his employer and as the day wore on, he felt disappointed with himself that he had failed her the night before. He could not do so again. He felt the need to prove to his wife that he was a better lover than Mr Venter. He could not fail again!

Then he remembered his cattle herding days. There had been a plant that the other boys used to dig up and there would be a lot of giggling which at first he did not understand. Gradually, he had learnt that it had something to do with sexual prowess. Some of the older boys, he had gathered, were already sexually active, something he had found quite disgusting that there were girls in the community willing to let boys do THAT to them! Not being sexually active himself at the time, he had not been interested because he believed strongly that it would only happen after he was married. What was it called again? More importantly, would he be able to identify it now? It was some sort of creeping plant, he remembered, but there were so many of them and any one of them could have been it.

For a while, he considered trying each one in turn, but how would he know when he got the right one? He had never asked how long it took to produce results so he could eat a whole lot of plants and still not know which one worked, or even if any one of them would work. What if the results were instantaneous? Would there be enough time to get home to Sekai? He laughed to himself as he imagined himself getting home and trying to convince an angry Sekai that they should go to bed immediately! 'And how do you walk through the village with a bulge in your trousers'? He started to dig up one of the creepers and then froze. What if the plant was poisonous?

Mugondorosi! The name came to him suddenly and he felt excited that he had remembered what the plant was called. However, knowing the name of the plant, he realised, would not make it any easier for him to identify it. Perhaps he could go and ask a neighbour. He started to walk back home then stopped once again. There really was no one he could ask. Most of the boys he had played with as a youngster had either died in the war or had moved to the towns and cities to look for work. He could not very well approach an older man with his problem. It would be like telling his own father about his sexual problems! In any case, how could he, at his age, be telling an older person that he needed something to boost his manhood! There was only one way he was not going to fail that night. The row with Sekai would continue until it was time for him to go back to work!

Sekai was getting worried at the length of time that her husband was away. She started to worry that he may have met with some danger-ous creature – a poisonous snake for example – in the bush. She even imagined him being swallowed by a python. Yet it was still daylight and she could not really ask for help from the other men in the village. It was not unusual for man to be gone all day – all night even. 'Perhaps he has gone to meet with his girlfriend', she thought and found herself

161

getting angry with him all over again.

She was relieved to see him walk back slowly, only carrying the axe that he had left with. He still looked angry, however, but she had decided that she was going to make peace and had cooked one of his favourite meals; millet *sadza* with meat from one of her free range chickens that she had slaughtered specially as a peace offering. She did not get the chance to offer it.

"So, did you enjoy it?" Jonas asked before he even sat down.

"The day? How could I enjoy it when I did not know where you had gone? I was getting worried…"

"Sex with Mr Venter. Did you enjoy sex with Mr Venter?"

"Jonas, please, can we not do this?"

"We are not doing anything. It's what you did with Mr Venter that I am asking about."

"It was not what you think.."

"Was it not? How different was it? Did he use his nose or something?"

"He did not use his nose…"

"Whatever he used, did you enjoy it? That is all I am asking."

Sekai found herself getting angry with her husband. She was sorry that she had not told him, but he was being childish about the whole thing. She wished for a minute that she had listened to her aunt who had advised her to tell him that she had been raped as a little girl.

"You know how men are," her aunt had advised when she confided in her what had happened with Mr Venter, "every man wants to feel that he was your first. He will never understand that what happened with Mr Venter was against your will. Come to think of it, I don't believe you myself. It will be better if you say that you were raped."

But then again, if she had taken that advice, he would now have caught her in a lie. She had waited for him to ask why she was not a virgin to decide whether to take her aunt's advice or confess the truth. He had not asked and she had not said anything, believing that as he was a virgin himself, he did not know what a virgin girl would be like!

"Well?" Jonas was looking quite irate.

"Yes, Jonas. I enjoyed it thoroughly," she said, her anger taking over.

Jonas walked out of the room and walked back in almost immediately.

"How can you tell me you enjoyed it? Are you not ashamed? In any case, I heard that whites are 'small'," he indicated with his thumb and forefinger. "You cannot have enjoyed it!"

"I don't know about their size. I wasn't looking. But you wanted to know if I enjoyed it and yes, I enjoyed it!"

Jonas sat down then and wept. He wept uncontrollably, the disappointment of confirming what he had suspected feeling worse than the suspicion. He did not know what to do. Just sat there with his face full of tears mixed with his nasal excrement. Sekai was sorry that she had spoken to her husband like that. She had wanted to explain to him, but he would not give her the chance. Now she was worried that they may have reached the point of no return. She sat down and put her arm

163

around him. He did not resist.

She did not know how long they sat like that but after a time, she felt like she had his full attention. She felt like she could speak to him.

"Jonas, my darling," she said softly, "I need you to know that I love you very much." He did not respond, just sat there holding his head but leaning against his wife.

"When I went to work for the Venters, I was very young and quite naïve. Mrs Venter had asked for a second maid because the older woman who worked for them was apparently not coping with the work. However, as soon as I was employed, she let me do all the work while she spent her days gossiping with the other women in the compound. After a while, Mrs Venter realised that I was doing all the work and the other woman lost her job." She spoke softly, but was not even sure that her husband heard anything she said.

"Anyway," she went on, "after she left, having threatened me with all kinds of black magic because I had got her fired, I moved into her old quarters, which were close to the main house. I was worried at first that she may have left something in there that might cause me damage, but Mrs Venter assured me that no harm would come to me. Trouble started when, one day, while I was taking a shower, Mr Venter walked in on me. I assumed it was accidental and thought nothing of it except that he seemed to spend a longer than necessary amount of time examining me." She chuckled humourlessly. "Do you know that I felt no embarrassment? My clothes were too far for me to reach and quite honestly, it had never occurred to me that a white man could look at me as a woman. The way he looked at me, he could have been looking at his horse or even his dog."

There was still no reaction from her husband so she carried on, wanting to unburden herself.

"After this incident, I thought I caught him staring at me a few times but every time I looked at him, he would look away quickly. I felt a little uncomfortable because I thought that maybe there was something I was doing wrong.

Then, one day when Madam was away in Marondera, he sent for me to bring him some tea. It was during my tea break but you know how they don't really respect our times and it was not the first time this had happened. But when I took the tea, I found out that I was not serving it in the dining room, but in one of the children's bedrooms – the children were in school at this time. Again I took the tea innocently, but when I got there he grabbed my arm and threw me onto the bed. I did not know what to do. Hc… Hc.." She broke down then and wept, so that both of them were sobbing in each other's arms. She seemed to recover quickly and went on.

"He was saying things in my ear, trying to push his tongue into my mouth and … as suddenly as it had started, it was over. Anyway, he got up suddenly, put his trousers back on, mumbling something about not realising that I had never known a man, then walked out without even a backwards glance. I was ashamed and felt dirty; his sticky mess mixed with blood made me feel like I would never be clean again. I don't know how long I spent in the shower afterwards and yet I still felt unclean!" I thought that that would be the end of it, especially when he totally ignored me in front of his wife and even started to criticise my work as though he was trying to get me fired!"

For a while, Sekai sat motionless as she remembered the pain of something she had suppressed for so long.

"But it didn't stop," she went on. "It became a regular ritual. Every time Mrs Venter went away, he would call for me. I knew what was coming and began to dread the times that the madam went away on her own. In the end, he was not forcing me; I would just take off the necessary clothing and lie on the bed wishing that his wife would walk in on us, but worrying that if that happened, she would probably accuse me of seducing her husband, and I would lose my job!"

She stood up and went outside to make sure that her chickens were closed in. She was not sure what her husband was making of what she had told him, but she felt a sense of relief. She had been carrying her guilt for so long and with the passage of time, she had begun to believe that this day would never come. She still wondered who had told her husband but decided that this was not the time to ask such questions.

When she went back into the hut that served as their kitchen, her husband was still sitting in the same position that she had left him in, his arms folded and legs stretched out before him. He did not look up when she walked in.

"Did I enjoy it?" She sat down next to her husband, "all I know is that during all those times with Mr Venter, I kept thinking how overrated sex was. I wondered why so many people talked about it as if it was something they could not live without; until I met you…"

"At the instigation of Mrs Venter," Jonas spoke for the first time in a while.

"Yes," she said quietly. "To be honest, I had never seen you as anything more than the garden boy who happened to work in the same

166

place I did. I am not sure how Mrs Venter found out. One morning, she called me into her sewing room and offered me a chair, something she had never done before.

'You've been sleeping with my husband', she said without any warning.

I was shocked, of course, but it seems that the embarrassment of her friends knowing that she had lost her man to the help was greater than the pain of her husband cheating on her! I don't even think she saw it as cheating!"

She took his hand and intertwined her fingers with his. He did not resist.

"Anyway, arrangements were made for me to see you and while I found the whole thing embarrassing and awkward at first, I soon got to like you, no, to love you and I have never regretted the fact that they compelled me to see you. They gave me the best husband that any woman would want and, Jonas Mangwende, I want you to know that I love you very, very much and I am sorry that I did not tell you this before."

He hugged his wife very tightly and for a long while, did not say anything. He felt so much anger towards his employer that he could not speak. But then, he felt something else. He was not going to fail her.

"Let's go to bed," he said suddenly.

"Now? You haven't had anything to eat," she protested feebly.

He picked her up, surprised that he could still lift her so easily, and carried her out of the kitchen into their main house.

Elderly Mrs Jekiseni, from the next homestead, stopped what she had been doing to watch the young couple. She missed her late husband.

Chapter 11

R oyal Harare Golf Club was in particularly pristine condition, the rains that were coming to the end of their season, having turned the whole course a lush green. In the dry season, only the fairways and the greens would be green from the constant watering out of the bore holes that the club had drilled for that purpose. The shadows of the tall pine trees that lined the fairways had lengthened onto the club house veranda as the sun was approaching the Western horizon. But for the constant humming of traffic on the nearby roads, one could have been at some country resort, away from the hum drum of city life. Yet Royal Harare – or The Royal – as its members liked to call it, was an easy five minutes or so drive from Harare's Central Business District. In fact, one could easily walk there from the city centre.

But the four men that were walking off the course, having just completed their round, did not have to walk to The Royal. They had come each in their own car even though three of them lived in quite close proximity to each other. They had played in the afternoon because the fourth member of their group, Minister Mike Banga, had been held up in an emergency Cabinet meeting all day. Having finally given up on their friend, they had roped in Ian Howard, a white businessman who had come in looking for a game. Having played the game from childhood and being of a much lower handicap than the others, Ian and his partner for the afternoon, David Chitende, Permanent Secretary for Education, had trounced the other two, Giles Kamba, Permanent Secretary for Agriculture, and Doctor Ivan Mbodza, Managing Director of Regal Foods, a diversified food processing company, who were now regretting the decision to invite the white man.

"Take it like men, guys," David was saying to them, "this is the first time in, how many weeks that I have taken any money off you? Thank God for emergency Cabinet meetings."

"Mike does struggle a bit…," Giles started.

"A bit? In truth, that guy should try something else, like fishing," David said to loud laughter from the others, "I don't know how I ended up with him as my regular partner…"

"It was your decision that we should have permanent partners," Dr Mbodza reminded him.

"I thought the guy would improve, but eish!" David threw up his arms in resignation.

"What is the meeting about anyway?" Ivan had been asking for a while without getting any straight answers from the civil servants.

"Don't you listen to the news? It's been all over the radio…"

"Quite honestly, I don't watch Dead TV (ZTV – Zimbabwe television). I have satellite television, but I only flew in from Joburg last night and haven't had a chance to watch any news."

"You should," said David, "the country will go to war and you will not know. Anyway, a chief in Hwedza has moved – with his people, onto a commercial farm and is asking the white farmer to leave because the farm, apparently, is on land that used to belong to his ancestors."

"Is he quite mad?" Dr Mbodza was incredulous.

"Who? The farmer?" David was mocking.

"No, you dope. This chief of yours. Does he know how important farming is to the economy of the country?"

"It's quite worrying, hey," Ian spoke for the first time since they left the course, "my parents farm in Marondera, not too far from where this happened."

"Oh," Ivan said, not quite knowing what else to say. The others were equally surprised and a little embarrassed, so there was a lengthy awkward silence.

"They are alright, though," Ian said finally, "I spoke to them just before I came here. They think that it is an isolated incident although I hear there have been copycat invasions in one or two farms in the area."

"I'm sure it is," said Giles, "isolated, I mean."

They sat around a table to drink Ian and David's obligatory winner's round, but the mood had changed. The civil servants were feeling uneasy about being in the company of one who had obviously been adversely affected by the thoughtless actions of one of their own. They realised, of course that land was a sensitive issue, but thought that there were better ways to address it, although none of them, except perhaps David, had any ideas on how this could be tackled. Ian was counting his blessings. The chance meeting with senior civil servants could be useful in the future, especially now that such connections might be the difference between his parents losing or keeping their farm. He had to cultivate his newly acquired friends, as he was already thinking of them as. He ordered snacks from the kitchen and bought another couple of rounds as, he explained, the victory had been so comprehensive. By the time he left, Ian had exchanged contact details with the civil servants and they had promised to 'do it again'.

"Nice man," Giles said after Ian left.

"Good golfer," David said, "do you think we could ask him to become part of our regular four-ball? He could always replace Mike, who clearly has more important matters of state to deal with!"

"That would be clear theft. You'd just be coming every Saturday to collect from us. We might as well pay you now!" Giles said to laughter.

"Do you think these land invasions could be serious?" Ivan Mbodza had been thinking about how disruptions to farming might affect his business.

"No," Giles was adamant, "there is no way that the government would allow such lawlessness to carry on."

"Yet so far, nothing has been done," David said thoughtfully. "You know what I think? ZIPA as a governing party has run out of ideas and this could just be the cue for them to do something drastic."

"Surely not," Giles was not convinced.

"Think about it," David went on, "the land question has not been addressed except in little skirmishes since independence. The MFD is gaining ground rapidly and saying things that people want to hear – engaging the West so investment can be attracted and people can get jobs, engaging the international community so that we can get support from such institutions as the World Bank and the International Monetary Fund, bringing more aid donors into the country (and you know how every man and his dog is looking for some donor or other to fund their sometimes dubious projects). What has ZIPA got to offer? Slogans, more slogans, air punching and stories about gaining a victory that, to many, brought misery. Imagine what they are thinking now. 'If one chief and his people can do it, why not the whole country'."

David's mobile phone rang at this point and he went off to answer it. When he came back, he was very excited.

"ZIPA has now adopted a new policy on land," he said, his eyes bright, "and I have been moved to the Ministry of Agriculture."

"I am Permanent Secretary for Agriculture," Giles said.

"Not anymore," David retorted, "I hear your man has been moved to the President's Office as Minister without Portfolio."

"Can they do that? I mean can they just move you like that? Without even consulting you first?" Ivan Mbodza was surprised.

"Well, these are not exactly normal circumstances. Things are moving fast. The actions of Chief Juru and his people have caught ZIPA completely by surprise. But the President sees advantages for his party in taking the initiative away from the chief and turning it into a ZIPA Policy that they have been planning all along. He feels that your Minister Mugwazo is not the right man to take this policy forward; too cosy with the white farmers and all that so he has moved Mangwiro from Home Affairs to Agriculture and, I suppose because I have been quite vocal in supporting radical land reform, he has moved me from Education to work with Mangwiro in formulating a new policy."

"It's a mistake," Giles's feeble protest was unconvincing even to himself.

"I agree," said Dr Mbodza putting on his Agricultural Economist hat, "agriculture is the backbone of this economy and I don't see how they can condone this kind of haphazard so-called policy for such an important sector. Imagine the knock-on effect on the rest of the economy: Agro industrial companies like mine will suffer, suppliers of agricultural inputs and equipment, we may even run out of bread because we will not produce enough wheat! Has ZIPA thought of all that? We may end up with riots when people are hungry."

"It's up to me and Minister Mangwiro to come up with a policy framework that will obviate such eventualities…"

"And how do you do that? You cannot train farmers overnight." Giles Kamba was quickly accepting his fate, but still could not see how his carefully thought out policy recommendations that he was about to present to his Minister could be replaced by a knee jerk reaction to some rural chief's whim.

"Giles, I have only just had the news so I don't really have answers to those sorts of questions now; but I have some ideas. First and foremost though, we would need to find a way to regularise the new farmers' tenure on the farms if we are to realise the dream of turning our agri-

174

culture from being controlled by a minority, to one where our people have a significant stake. Then of course we will have to find ways to finance them. It's all very new, but I am excited. I think I will spend a few hours on it tomorrow so that by Monday, I have something to present to Minister Mangwiro."

"I believe there have been other invasions. By Monday, you may not have an agriculture to talk about. Supposing people all over the country decide that this is a good idea and invade farms all over the place, how are you going to "regularise" things amid such chaos?" Ivan Mbodza remained sceptical.

"And once people see that they can benefit from such lawlessness, where does it stop? Can you stop people invading factories and other industrial and commercial installations? What about our homes? What happens if people take over your home in Borrowdale simply because they decide that they like it…?"

"Giles, I don't have all the answers now. All I know is that we are embarking on a new path which, I believe, will lead to a more equitable distribution of our most abundant resource, our land."

"It sounds to me," Giles said, his voice heavy with scepticism, "like we are hoping to create order out of complete chaos. Our 'plan' is to enunciate a policy that we hope will work itself out. Good luck to you in your new Ministry. I am sure you will need lots of it."

"I think that, Giles, you are not being fair to the people of Zimbabwe. The truth is, at no time in history have people in an advantageous position willingly given up their advantage simply because it is the right thing to do. They will fight tooth and nail to hold on to their advantage;

they will give all sorts of "good" reasons why their advantage should be maintained. It is a sad fact of life that the disadvantaged group will generally have to take what they need, by force if necessary. Majority rule is accepted by most of the world as the right thing, yet we had to take up arms in order to get that accepted by the whites who ran this country. For the last twenty years, they have laughed at us because they saw that our idea of independence did not include economic control of the country."

"Well, then, congratulations on your new appointment David. I hope it will make a difference for the better to the average Zimbabwean. Good night," Giles concluded tersely as he stood up, took his jacket from the back of his chair and walked out of the Royal bar, jingling the keys to his official Mercedes Benz absentmindedly. He was weighing up his options – to stay in government or try his luck in the private sector.

"I think you upset our friend, David," Dr Mbodza said after Giles left.

"I didn't mean to, but I feel very strongly that we have left our struggle unfinished and we are apologetic about taking back what is rightfully ours. Anyway, I think Giles was already upset about losing his apparently successful portfolio. He will get over it."

"Can it be done, though?"

"Can what be done?"

"Can we successfully build a new agricultural sector from the ashes of the destruction of this one?"

"I don't know," David answered honestly, "but I have some ideas. Look, in Zambia, and I think even Mozambique, all land belongs to the state and all tenure for farmers is leasehold – with ninety nine year leases, not freehold like we have. It would be interesting to know how they did it."

"Isn't that possibly why their agriculture is not thriving?"

"Perhaps," David was looking quite thoughtful in spite of the fact that he was a bit tipsy from the alcohol he had consumed, "we shall see. How would you like to be a farmer, Ivan?"

Dr Mbodza laughed heartily, "me? I don't think so. I can't afford the land anyway."

"But if you were given land, and maybe some start-up capital, would you be interested then?"

"I've never really thought about it. Are you suggesting that land can be taken away from the white farmers and given to blacks. That's not ethical surely."

"I am not suggesting anything. My mind is just wondering, considering various scenarios, and this is just one of them."

"I don't really know how I would react if I got that offer for real," Ivan Mbodza was now finding the proposition not quite so preposterous. Some of the farms were very well developed and one could live quite comfortably there. But would that be right? Whatever happened in the past, the current crop of farmers had probably bought their farms and had spent a lot of money developing them. Would it be right to take that away from them?

"It may come to nothing, but I do believe that if we are to successfully transform our agricultural sector, we need to take some bold steps, and we need people like you to lead the transformation."

In spite of his reservations, Ivan Mbodza found himself getting excited at the prospect of taking over a well-developed farm and, with his level of education – which many of the White farmers did not have, taking it up to the next level of development and mechanisation. It could be quite exciting, he thought.

"Well, David," he said out loud, "agriculture is in for some interesting times under your watch. Another beer?"

"Better not. I have decided that I will be in the office tomorrow. This, my friend, is the next stage of our struggle, and I have the opportunity to contribute significantly to it."

They walked together to the car park where they each got into their cars. David had the beginnings of a plan forming in his head. A plan that was to have a profound impact on the Zimbabwean agricultural sector and on the economy as a whole. Ivan Mbodza was imagining himself as a major landowner with a country mansion as a home. He also saw himself as a major supplier of agricultural raw materials to his current employers. He thought of the amounts of money that his company paid to some farmers and decided that he would live quite well on a fraction of that.

"Let's hope they can pull it off," he said aloud to himself as he drove out of the Royal and headed home.

In Hwedza, the Nicholsons had come home to a veritable party. Many scuds of the traditional brew produced by a transnational had found their way into their homestead and there was much alcohol-induced revelry. The rhythmic beating of traditional drums accompanied by the wild gyrations of the dancers would have made an amusing sight, in normal circumstances. But there was nothing normal about this. The mess they had left that morning looked worse and the Juru people looked to have made themselves quite comfortable in the outbuildings of the farmyard with some freshly laundered baby clothing and napkins hanging from Mrs Nicholson's clothes line and a big port of Sadza on the fire. They did not know it then, but one of their prize Bulls had been slaughtered to feed the mob.

"Ah, George, you are back!" The chief was clearly enjoying the party and was holding a bottle of what looked like a cheap brandy. "Perhaps you can join us."

"No thank you Changamire," George replied politely, "we are very tired and would rather turn in."

"Well, good night then. You don't mind us carrying on, do you?"

"No, Changamire. Don't mind us."

They went into the house and tried to sleep. Throughout the night, the drum beat reminded them again and again that their lives had just changed and would probably never be normal again. They finally fell into fitful sleep in the early hours of the morning when the drums finally fell silent, only to be woken by the resumption of the drumming at daybreak.

Chapter 12

S ome three kilometres North of Manhowe Township, linked to the township by a dirt track is the Ndlovu homestead, commonly known in the area as *paMundevere (*the home of the Ndebele man), so called because Mr Ndlovu from Matabeleland, where the Ndebele (or *Mandevere* as the Shonas of this area call them) live, had settled in the area and for many years, was the only one of his ethnic origin for miles. It was an unremarkable homestead, primarily because Mrs Ndlovu had died sometime during the war of liberation, heartbroken because her son Themba, had joined the war and she was convinced that she would never see him again. Mr Ndlovu had lived long enough to see his son return a hero, but also to see him turn into a drunken layabout who seemed to have no plan for his life. He died a disappointed man. The younger woman that Mr Ndlovu senior had taken up with after the death of his wife had stayed long enough to have a fling with Themba and had moved on.

With Themba's two sisters married and moving away to live with their husbands in Bulawayo and Mutare respectively, only Themba was left and the homestead, once a significant landmark with its layered thatch that was typical of Ndebele huts, had become derelict. The main 'hut', a rectangular structure that once had had glass windows and a metal doorframe, had holes where the windows and doors had been, Themba having sold them when he had fallen on hard times. Gone also were the asbestos roof sheets that Mr Ndlovu senior had worked so hard to procure, albeit at a cut price because they had been 'liberated' by those who worked in the factory in which they were made. But in the bad old days of colonialism, many people augmented their meagre incomes by taking what they could from their privileged white employers. The other two huts on either side of the rectangular one, which had served as the boys and girls bedrooms were also without roofs, one having caved in as it succumbed to the industry of termites, and the other having burnt when Themba came home drunk and went to bed with a lit cigarette. Only the quick actions of an observant neighbour had saved Themba's life.

The only structure left that was still more or less intact was what used to be the kitchen, but was now Themba's whole living space. Yet even that, to the casual observer, looked abandoned. To the neighbours though, there were signs of life which included smoke permeating through the roof on those rare occasions when Themba managed to organise himself well enough to cook a meal, or in winter when he needed the warmth of a fire.

This February Sunday morning, there was no sign of life even though Themba was there. As usual, he was hung over, but the severity of his hangover this morning was unusual. He felt as though he was having an out of body experience, his head seemingly operating independently from the rest of him. The taste in his mouth was foul even for a man whose encounters with toothbrushes had been terminated many years earlier. It took him a few minutes to realise that he was lying on his own floor, in his own hut. Groggily, he got up to relieve himself outside and found himself standing naked in bright sunlight, having not realised that it was daylight because his hut, it's only window now shut permanently with a piece of metal sheeting, did not let in any light at all. The girl from next door stopped her morning chores and watched the man who was possibly her teenage son's father relieve himself and go back into his hut. She was so happy that she had pointed at some-one else as the boy's father; someone with whom she had only had one sexual encounter. Even though he had refused to marry her, he at least supported the boy who had turned out to be his only child because his marriage was childless and he blamed his wife, pointing to the fact that he had a son as evidence that he was not the problem!

Themba stood inside his hut and looked around. On a small table, the only piece of furniture he owned, was a half empty bottle of whis-ky. He had no idea how it had got there; nor did he know where the unopened packet of expensive cigarettes had come from. His clothes lay in a heap on the side of his sleeping grass mat although he did not remember taking them off. He did remember how the previous day had started, but at some point, he must have blacked out, he thought.

He had been sitting outside the Mberi Trading Store waiting for some-one, anyone to come and rescue him from his hangover. There were still people in the community who remembered his status as a war hero and there was bound to be one of those coming round this Satur-day morning. It was unusually quiet for a Saturday morning although he did not notice this until a group of youths came round the corner singing loudly and looking very excited about what Themba could not imagine. They were being led by George Magaya, the ZIPA District Youth Chairman.

"Let's go, Themba," George shouted enthusiastically as they approached, "we are going to take over Mr Venter's farm."

"What do you mean take over Mr Venter's farm? Have you nothing better to do?"

"What is better than taking back our land? You went to war, Themba, surely you know that it was so that we could take back our land."

"A job would be nice," he replied without enthusiasm.

"Well, the whites are closing their factories because now there is a black government so there are no jobs. But if we take back our land, we can create our own jobs; we can be our own employers!"

Themba had not moved. He wished that George and his crowd would move on and leave him in peace.

"Well?" George was not giving up.

"What do you want from me? Go on and create your own jobs. I am too old to work anyway."

George was not going without Themba. The instructions had been very clear. War veterans were to be part of this stage of the struggle. They would make it more legitimate.

"Do you know how much booze these whites keep in their houses? Once we take over the farm, that will all be ours!"

"Perhaps you are right. We do need to take our land back," Themba had said, getting up.

Because no one was really sure of the boundaries of the commercial farms, they went to the wrong farm. They went to Jack van Breda's farm, which was probably just as well because the van Breda's had gone to another meeting at the Venter's. With only a skeleton staff in place, which included Smart, the house boy, there was no resistance at all. All they had to do was tell him they were from the youth wing of ZIPA and he was more than pleased to open the house for them, particularly because they carried sticks and spears and he thought that he saw a gun on one of the people whose face he did not recognise.

Themba had heard how opulently whites lived but nothing he had heard had prepared him for what he saw in Jack van Breda's house.

"How many people live here?" He asked Smart after doing a quick tour of the ground floor where there was a kitchen that could easily sleep five or six people, more if necessary, a lounge and dining room that looked big enough to hold a meeting of a hundred people. There were two toilets on the ground floor that could accommodate another two people!

"Just the boss, his wife and their two children, when they are not at boarding school."

Themba whistled softly. Four people lived here! What did they need all this furniture for?

"So why do they need all these chairs?" He asked, thinking how useful some of the furniture could be as fire wood!

"They get lots of visitors and they have lots of parties. Sometimes the chairs are not enough," Smart explained.

They went upstairs where George was jumping up and down on the biggest bed that Themba had ever seen. The room itself was enormous and had a very large curved window through which one could look out and down into the garden below. The curtains looked thick enough to be used as blankets if the need ever arose but clearly never did in this room whose cupboards were full of extra blankets and other linen. Themba opened a door that came off what Smart had explained was master and madam's bedroom and found himself in another large room.

"That is their bathroom," he added.

Not for the first time, Themba was amazed at the size of the room.

"Their bathroom being where they... do what exactly?" Themba was looking at a gaunt, dishevelled figure that looked back at him from the other side of the room. It took him a while to realise that he was staring at his own image in a full length mirror that ran the length of one wall of the room.

"They wash in here, in the bath over there and if they choose to, in the shower," Smart went across the room and turned on the shower which produced a fine spray of water. "They can turn on the hot water here and the cold water over here," he demonstrated. In no time, the room was filling with steam and although Themba had many more questions to ask, he felt that he had to leave the room, partly because he was not sure where the steam was coming from and how it would affect him, but mainly because he did not like the image of himself that he had seen in the mirror. He had not seen himself in a mirror for a long time – he in fact never seen himself in a full length mirror before and he did not like what he saw.

Outside, it was getting quite warm. Themba felt more comfortable in the open air than he did inside the house whose level of comfort seemed overdone somewhat. There was commotion on the other side of the house and Themba went round to investigate. The commotion was at the far end of the lawn where there was a large lake, and it was because someone had had the bright idea that they could drive a tractor and it (the tractor) had ended up in the lake. Frantic but fruitless efforts were being made to push the tractor back onto dry land – a task that was proving impossible mainly because the efforts were totally unco-ordinated in the excitement and everyone was pushing or pulling in different directions!

"You are Themba aren't you? Themba Ndlovu." The questioner was sitting on the lawn, somewhat removed from the others watching the scene in a detached manner but seemed amused by it all. Themba had seen him earlier without really paying attention to him.

"Yes, I am Themba. Who are you?"

"Sit," the other man patted the ground besides him on the lawn.

Themba hesitated. The man was dressed casually but his clothes looked very expensive and he smelt fresh and clean. Themba was keenly aware of his own unclean condition which had just been highlighted to him by the mirror in the bedroom he had just left. He sat down heavily, away from the stranger who knew his name.

"Have a drink," the stranger offered, "it's a Johnny Walker blue label."

Did the man think that Themba was so stupid that he could not see that the label was blue? And why did he speak to him with such arrogance, as if they knew each other? 'I may not be as smartly dressed as you, my friend, but I am a hero of the war of liberation' Themba thought to

186

himself although even he was not so sure that this was an important fact to most of his countrymen. He accepted the proffered drink and gulped it thirstily. The burning sensation that he felt all the way down his throat was unexpected and his face contorted as if he was in pain. The man had said that it was smooth! Was that some sort of trick he was playing on Themba?

"You don't recognise me, do you, Themba?"

"No," Themba replied honestly, "should I?"

"I am sorry that life does not seem to have been kind to you. Those of us who fought in the war should not end up like this…"

"You were in the war?" Themba was incredulous.

"Yes, but I suppose it would be too much to expect you to remember me. I was part of probably the last group of recruits to make it into Mozambique. We were still in basic training when the ceasefire was declared. Your exploits at the front were talked about in glowing terms. We all wanted to go to the front in order to be talked about like that. What happened?"

"The war finished," Themba said simply, "and I soon found out that being a good bush fighter was not a clever career choice."

"But I thought you would have stayed in the army! You were being talked about as officer material. How did you end up like this?" He felt an immediate guilt. This had been his hero, yet after the war ended and he joined the intelligence services, he had not ever thought about Themba. He never questioned why he never saw Themba's name in the officer ranks of the Zimbabwe National Army. Themba Ndlovu had just disappeared from Paul's consciousness.

"My name is Paul, by the way, Paul Kamera," he introduced himself, "it's an honour to meet you again," he shook Themba's hand, "have another whisky," he poured Themba another shot. It was just what the doctor ordered for the latter's hangover and he was already beginning to feel better even though he still found the taste of the whiskey unpalatable.

Side by side, they sat and watched the comic efforts to get the tractor out of the lake. They said nothing to each other although they felt a strange camaraderie between them that they could not explain. Their look, their attire, their demeanour could not have been more different, yet they sat together on Mr Van Breda's immaculate lawn and shared a bottle of the finest whiskey that Paul had managed to find in the farmer's not inconsiderable stock of imported liqueurs. It was Themba who broke the silence.

"So, why are we doing this?" He had asked.

"Well, I am not sure really, Chief Juru in Hwedza led his people onto a neighbouring farm and demanded that the farmer must leave because the land he is on was taken away from the Juru people many years ago. It seems that this has given our leaders an idea – the idea that we can take land away from the whites and redistribute it…"

"That is not a new idea," Themba interjected, "during the war, that is what we were told. That the farms, the houses, even the companies owned by whites would be taken away from them and given to us!"

"That was then, Themba. The reality of running a country, the wealth that some of our leaders have enjoyed since independence," Paul, stopped and looked pensive for a while. "Did you ever read George Orwell's 'Animal Farm'?" He asked suddenly.

"It was one of our "O" level English Literature set books, but we always read it with the view that the whites wanted us to believe that if we gained independence from them, what happened in Animal Farm would happen to us."

"And now?"

"To be honest, I haven't really thought about it since those days. We never finished it anyway. We went to war."

Paul looked into the distance and seemed in two minds about whether to carry on this conversation or not. Seeing Themba looking like this had not only shocked him, it had made him realise just how expendable people were. The Themba who, during the bush war, was being touted as a possible future Army General was now destitute. What happened?

"How come you, of all people, were demobilised?"

"I don't know. When the list of people who were to be demobilised was posted, I went to look really not expecting that my name would be there but curious to see whose names were on the list. I was disappointed, of course to see my name but the monies that they were promising to pay seemed like a lot and I saw myself putting my money into a business of some sort and living the rest of my life on the profits. It seemed to me that going to war had been worthwhile after all. How quickly that money ran out! I had my life all worked out, then, just like that," he clicked his fingers; "I had nothing."

189

"Have you ever thought about how your name ended up on that list?"

"I did at first, but what is the point? I lost the only profession that I knew anything about and, unlike some of our other colleagues, I have not been able to find another. I cannot even get a job as a house boy for these whites. They will not employ a former terrorist!"

Paul looked across at Themba. Had he been cleaner, Paul might have hugged him then. His sympathy did not go that far.

"It has been said," Themba went on, "that I had the wrong surname!!" He laughed then; a harsh, dry, Johnny Walker Blue Label-induced humourless laugh that had Paul leaning back away from Themba whose breath, a mixture of the said whiskey and years of little or no oral hygiene, could have fumigated a small room!

"I lived all my life among the Shona people; I don't even speak the language that my surname suggests that I should speak; I identify myself more as a Shona than anything else, but because I have a name that says I am something else…," he left the sentence hanging and stood up to go and relieve himself onto a nearby rose bush. It was the first time he had talked about this and he felt an anger welling up in him.

"There is a toilet right next to you," Paul said, not quite sure what else to say.

"Fuck their toilets. I am pissing on Zimbabwe; the land that I went to war and died for!"

"You are not dead, Themba…"

"I might as well be."

"Well, you are not and there is hope for you. I am not sure what these farm invasions mean, but there could be an opportunity here for you. Anyway, have you ever thought that you may have been demobilised because you were a threat to someone in the hierarchy? That someone thought, 'This Themba is being talked about so much he may be promoted ahead of me' and then set about reminding the powers that be of your tribal heritage?"

"Who cares? Who bloody cares?" The whiskey was beginning to take effect and this continued talk of something he had no control over; something that happened all those years ago was only taking him away from his newly found favourite drink.

The tractor had been abandoned where it stood, its wheels half submerged and an attempt was being made to start the boat. When this failed, as many as could get in piled into the boat and rowed by hand, but were making little progress. The lakeside was strewn with empty beer bottles with the odd brandy or wine bottle among them. Across the other side, some had found fishing tackle and were attempting to fish, without success as none of them had ever fished with 'machines' before.

"I want to go home," Themba had said suddenly, and passed out.

Now he stood just inside his hut, oblivious to the fact that the door was open behind him, unsuccessfully trying to remember what else had happened and how he had got home. He again noticed the packet of cigarettes on his bedside table, reached for it and took one out, then realised that he did not have any means to light it. He went back outside, remembering to put on his trousers which, he discovered, were wet. The smell soon told him that he must have pissed on himself in his drunkenness! He went across to his neighbours to light the cigarettes on their fire. Here, he came face to face with Dorothy, the girl with whom he had had a passionate love affair in the days when every girl for miles wanted Themba. He remembered how disappointed he had been when, after she got pregnant, she pointed at someone else as being responsible. How could she have cheated on him without his knowing – and none of her rivals for Themba's affections were aware of another man in her life? She did not treat him with her usual disdain, greeting him almost politely, which surprised Themba, who, after his encounter with Jack van Breda's mirror the day before, was aware just how unlovable he looked.

"What car brought you home last night?" Dorothy asked as she bent over to take a piece of wood out of the fire for Themba's cigarette.

"What car?" He was staring at her behind and wondering what chance he had with her after all these years. He decided that she would probably laugh at him if he even suggested that they…

"A very nice car brought you home last night," she interrupted his thoughts. "You, of course were totally out of it and the man was surprisingly kind. He was struggling to get you into your house and I had to come across to help him. I even helped him undress you," she said with a naughty glint in her eyes.

Themba was excited. She must have liked what she saw! After all, there did not seem to be a man in her life and she was probably remembering the good times that they had had. He was almost drooling just thinking about what a relationship with Dorothy would mean, remembering how passionate their love making had been…

"Can you introduce me to him?"

'The bitch'! He thought before saying, "I don't know that he would be interested. He told me about his family and how happily married he is," Themba lied, "he is an old comrade from the war, you know."

"That's the problem when you get to my age. All the nice ones are married."

'I'm not', Themba thought to himself.

"Anyway, how come, if he was in the war with you, he drives such a fancy car and you…," she did not quite know how to finish the sentence.

"it's not what a man owns," Themba tried to make a joke out of the situation, "he has a fancy car and I have land."

"What land, Themba?"

He pointed to his homestead, "that land," he said, "it is all mine…"

He was interrupted by Dorothy's laughter, "that piece of waste ground? What can you do with that?"

There could be an opportunity for you…', he remembered Paul, his friend from the day before, saying.

"Actually," he said, "I could soon be the proud owner of a large piece of land. Part of Mr Van Breda's farm. Have you seen his house? It will soon be mine!"

For the second time in a few minutes, Dorothy laughed at Themba's apparent fantasies. It was the first time in a long time that she had had a civil conversation with her former lover, and it had to be on this day, when he was particularly foul. She felt sorry for him because he had once been a popular young man whose prospects seemed bright. Now he had few friends, if any, and quite honestly was destitute. But even in her current situation, with no man in her life and little prospect of her getting married, Themba was not one she could think about as a prospect. She wondered what it was she had ever seen in him.

Themba was thinking how beautiful Dorothy still looked. She had a pleasant laugh and although she had obviously cheated on him once, at a time when he was cheating on her anyway, she was a good woman who seemed to have not followed other girls of her generation into prostitution or into having many babies whose fathers could only be guessed at. As far as he knew, she had not really had a serious relationship since they broke up. Yet when he looked at her face, she regarded him with pity, not affection or fondness. Would she still look at him like that when he became a land owner, as he now determined he would become?

"I better get going," he said quietly, "Paul will be here soon and I better be ready." He did not know for sure that Paul would come for him; he just hoped he would. And if he did not, he could always tell Dorothy that they were meeting at Manhowe Township.

"Is that his name? Please introduce me when he comes. You never know," she was teasing him although he did not get the joke.

"You never know," he repeated as he walked off towards his hut.

"Invite us to your new home," she shouted after him.

"New home?"

"Mr Van Breda's house, remember?"

"Oh yes. I will," he was now determined to live in that house, or at least one like it. What would Dorothy think of him then?

Chapter 13

P astor Jones's chapel was unusually full; so full in fact that he had had to bring chairs from his cottage to increase its sitting capacity. He looked at the congregation whose singing sounded heart-felt this morning as they sang an old and popular hymn – Abide with me. He saw faces in the congregation that he had not seen in many months; faces that, in fact, he only saw at funerals and probably at Easter and Christmas, usually because their wives would have insist-ed that they go to church on such occasions. Jack van Breda, who he had noticed never sang in church was at least mouthing the words this morning.

'Amazing how adversity brings people to God', Pastor Jones thought to himself.

He had heard what had happened in Hwedza and, more worryingly, what seemed to be happening throughout the country, although at this point, it seemed confined mainly to the East of the country. He had, for many years, been advocating for a fairer distribution of land, but had never envisaged it being done in such an unstructured manner. He wondered, as he had been wondering since the news first broke, if this was as spontaneous as the state media were making it. It seemed to him that the invasions were being co-ordinated from somewhere. Yet he could not believe that the government of Zimbabwe would allow such lawlessness to prevail.

"...I triumph still if thou abide with me."

The last strands of the hymn almost caught him by surprise as he had been so deep in thought. He asked the congregation to sit and scanned their worried faces. Jack van Breda, in an ill-fitting suit that he must have borrowed, was looking particularly flustered. He was bleary-eyed from lack of sleep and it looked as though he had been crying. His eyes looked pleadingly at the pastor, almost as though he expected the man of God to speak a miracle into existence. Even the Coloured man, Peter Lawrence was in church today – probably the first time he had seen him in this church. What could he say to them as a last word? He had had to change his sermon at the last minute to one that he thought would suit the circumstances. Had it given these people any hope? Had the story of Job, who kept faith in God in spite of great losses and trials inspired them in any way? Had the ending of the book of Job, with its tale of God restoring Job's losses given them any hope?

He could imagine what silent prayers were going on in their minds. Most were probably still praying that their farms be spared; a few, like Jack, were praying for restoration, but they were probably all praying that what had happened in the last couple of days was a collective nightmare that would soon pass. For a fleeting moment he wondered what prayers were being said in the other churches on this Sunday morning – the churches in which the majority of the population worshipped. But right now, at this moment, his responsibility was to this congregation and its palpable uncertainty.

"In closing," he put on his sombre, pastoral face and tone, "I shall

197

read from the book of Romans!" He quickly leafed through his Bible, "Romans Chapter eight verse twenty eight. I shall read in your hearing from the King James Version:

'And we know that ALL things work together for good to them that love God, to them who are the called according to His purpose'."

He looked up into his congregation again.

"Jack," he addressed Jack van Breda directly, "you will note that I deliberately emphasised the word ALL. The Bible is being very clear that whatever happens to us, even losing our livelihood and our homes, will bring some good if we love God because we are called to his purpose."

Jack was not sure what to think. He had not come expecting to be told that what happened to him was part of God's purpose. He had come to church expecting God to answer his prayer and restore his farm and his home. Involuntary tears ran down his cheeks as he thought about how the last forty eight hours had changed his and his family's lives. For the first time since this whole saga began, he realised that what the farmers had thought of as an isolated incident was probably more sustained and more organised; that he was not likely to be going home soon, if at all.

"Come on Jack, let's go home," he was startled by Jacques Venter's voice, which sounded concerned, but offered little comfort, "You know you are welcome to stay with us as long as you can."

Jack almost laughed at his friend's apparent naivety. Did he not see that this was possibly the end of their comfortable lives? What made him think that he was going to be spared the fate that had befallen

Jack; that had befallen a couple of dozen farmers that they had so far heard about, whose farms had also been invaded by marauding crowds of spear wielding ZIPA supporters? Slowly, he got up and followed his friend out of the chapel. He was in a sort of daze and was not aware of the many hands that shook his or patted him on the back; nor did he hear the words of encouragement and comfort from the other farmers. All he could think was, 'why me?'

The mood at the Venter homestead that afternoon was sombre. None of the farmers present could quite comprehend what had just happened in a couple of days. Their confidence in the "sacredness" of their sector – because it was successful and was important to the country's economy - had been almost totally eroded by the events of the last couple of days. They sat around Jacques Venter's bar but no one was drinking. Even the meals that had been placed in front of them were only half consumed as their normally large Sunday appetites seemed to have deserted them.

"Surely they cannot..."

"I don't see how..."

Dudley White and Jacques Venter's spoke at almost the same time then both went quiet as they either deferred to the other or were not quite sure how to finish their sentences. It was another ten minutes or so before anyone else spoke, and it was Dudley White who broke the silence.

"I suppose," he said haltingly, "we have to start thinking about life after farming..."

"Have you gone quite mad?" Jacques Venter, whose Afrikaans accent seemed more pronounced in his anger, was red in the face, "we cannot start to think so negatively now! We can still engage government; make them realise that what they are doing is foolish…"

"You're going to use the term foolish, are you?" Dudley White responded, quietly.

"No, but it is foolish what they are doing. Do they not realise that this sector is what is keeping the economy going. We provide thousands of jobs, we are second only to mining as an earner of foreign currency and we ensure food security for the country and the region. Why can they not see that?"

"Perhaps because they believe that they can do it themselves; or because they are worried about the gains that the MFD are making in electoral support, who knows?" Dudley was still speaking calmly.

"How can you be so calm?" Peter Johnstone was getting irritated by the other man's apparent indifference to a crisis in their lives, "do you know something we don't?"

"All I am saying is, these people had to go to war in order to gain their independence, because you lot refused to share with them, yet we still live in luxury while the majority of them continue to wallow in abject poverty…"

It was too much for Jack, who stood up and took a few steps towards Dudley.

"Abject poverty is all they have known," he jabbed his figure towards Dudley's face. "When we came here, this country was nothing but bush and they were wandering about in loin cloths, eking out a miserable living in their miserable lives. We brought them civilisation; clothes on their backs, education, we developed this bloody miserable country and now they think they can kick us out just like that…?"

"Did it not ever occur to you lot that at some point, they would see that they were being treated unfairly…?"

"What the bloody hell is the matter with you?" Jacques Venter was seething, "you Poms think that you have the answers to all the world's problems. We have an incompetent government that has run out of ideas – and things to loot – who are now targeting our very livelihood and you keep finding bloody excuses for them?"

"He came when we had turned this piece of dry wasteland into a veritable oasis in this, this bloody dark continent…," Peter Johnstone trailed off as the emotion of the moment got the better of him, "and now he wants to lecture us on what we should and should not have done?"

"I am not lecturing you on anything," Dudley was not giving up, "but, if the truth be told, we should have seen this coming and all I am saying is that now that it is here, what are we going to do about it? What can we do about it? This is what should be occupying our minds, not the past glories of a bye gone age. The world is different now and we have to accept the reality of this situation and deal with it accordingly."

"It's alright for you to talk;" Jack was almost in tears again, "you still have your home."

It had been a difficult twenty-four hours for Jack. They had met on the previous day to discuss what it was they needed to do as news of the spreading invasions continued to filter through, both on the national news and on the two way radio. For some reason, none of them gathered at Jacques Venter's home felt any vulnerability. They knew their Africans, as they liked to call them. They were a peaceful lot and would not consider emulating the actions of a few agitators and malcontents who had nothing better to do. The farmers were all agreed that this would not happen in their area.

"I think that we have pretty good relations with our neighbours," Peter Johnstone had said as the meeting started. "We need a strategy to ensure that they stay on our side."

"Yes," Jack had agreed, "I was talking to my houseboy Smart, who, like his name is rather smart," he stopped as the others smiled politely at his oft repeated joke. "He was very unhappy at what is going on. He does not want to own any land. The man is happy working for me!"

"They are all happy working for us," Jacques had agreed, "it's the unemployed layabouts, running about as the bloody ZIPA Youth Brigade who cause all the trouble!"

" And they are not well liked at all," Peter Lawrence, whose loyalties even he was not sure of, talked a lot with his mother's side of the family and believed that he had better information than the others, "I think that they will find little support among ordinary people who hate the fact that these so called youth brigades are always forcing them to go to meetings to chant meaningless slogans and punch the air on hungry stomachs."

"So, what you are saying, Peter, is that we really have nothing to worry about?" Dudley had asked, his voice sounding not convinced.

"I wouldn't go as far as that. We should be worried to an extent, but

I think that this whole thing will prove so unpopular that the government will have to do something about it."

"I hope you are right," Dudley said, still sceptical.

"Of course he is right! He has relatives on the other side," Jack said without remembering Peter's reaction when he first suggested that the latter had another side.

Peter let that one go this time. He had been accepted into the group of white farmers and he felt comfortable around them and almost felt like he was one of them.

"What have we here," Jacques had said as he stood up to look towards his farm gate where the figure of a lone black woman was half running, half walking towards them.

"She is in some hurry," Peter Johnstone had said.

"Hang on, that looks like Maria," Jack said without feeling any concern.

"Your house maid, why would she be in such a hurry?"

"Smart has probably set the house on fire," Jack said as he walked towards the gate to meet his servant.

She was breathless and having arrived safely, the panic that someone might have followed her subsided and she clutched at her knees as she tried to tell her master the errand that had got her running so hard.

"They came," she said pointing towards the gate before she had to take in gulps of breath.

"Who came?" Jack asked waiting for her to catch her breath. This was the first time she had had to run in many years and being a house maid meant that she ate well, as her ample girth clearly demonstrated.

"You have to be patient with these people," Jack said, turning to the others, "they panic over the smallest incident. It's probably a snake in the house or something."

"No!" Maria had got some of her breath back, "they came to take the farm!"

You could have heard a pin drop on sand.

Jack knew what Maria had just said, but did not understand it. Not his farm surely? Not the farm that his grandfather had worked so hard to hew out of virgin bush; not the farm that his father had spent so many years developing and modernising; not the farm that Jack himself had developed and mechanised to the point where it was recognised as one of the most productive in the area. He had plans for his farm; he was building greenhouses for the lucrative flower export market in Europe; he had ordered more dairy cows to increase his milking herd; he was getting out of tobacco but had a crop, his last, ready for market. What on earth were they doing taking his farm?

"No, no, no, Maria. You don't understand. They cannot take my farm. What will happen to you?"

She was calmer now. Her heaving bosom had subsided and her breath was less laboured although the sweat was still pouring down her face. She lifted her apron to wipe her face.

"They made Smart open the house for them and when I left, they were all inside the house…"

"In my bloody house? I am going to kill that Smart." He turned to the others, "come on, get your guns, we'll shoot the fuckers." He started to walk towards his car then stopped. The others were not following him; they stood on Jacques's lawn looking at him as if he was a ghost, a strange being who had somehow landed in their midst.

"I'm so sorry, Jack," Dudley was the first to speak, but he did not know what else to say. Even though he had been saying that they should be expecting this, it still had caught him by surprise. It was happening too quickly. He had been going to suggest that they send a delegation to the Commercial Farmers Association on Monday to demand that their representative organisation should engage government as a matter of urgency. He did not know this at the time, but the CFA had been trying to speak to the Minister of Agriculture since the news first broke, but he had not been taking their calls. Now they had just heard that their Minister, Itai Mugwazo, had been shuffled out of the Ministry of Agriculture and replaced with Minister Mangwiro from Home Affairs, a tough talking ideologue who seemed unlikely to be as sympathetic to the white farmer as Minister Mugwazo had been.

"Let us all sit down and consider our options," was all Dudley had managed to say.

Jack was sobbing uncontrollably now. Twenty four hours later, no viable option had been suggested. There was no comfort in the news that more farms were being invaded and it seemed that, for the first time, there was a polarisation in their community between those who still had their farms and still harboured hopes that they could keep them, and those whose farms had been invaded, and were looking for ways in which they could get them back. It seemed to Jack that in this group that was gathered at Jacques Venter's home, he was completely alone.

In Hwedza, George Nicholson was playing a game of drafts with Chief Juru who was now leading twenty to nil in their series. It was a popular game among black Zimbabweans who had become prolific at it because that was the only entertainment they had had as they queued for jobs at factories in Harare. George had been watching them play from inside his house and decided that he should try and engage the chief to see what information he could glean from such an engagement.

"Might as well try to find out where we are going from here," he had said to Mildred.

"Be careful, George, as we have seen over the last couple of days, these people can be unpredictable.." Mildred still could not believe that after forty years of living side by side with a people that seemed so placid and agreeable, they could turn as violently as they had without any warning. She was still mourning the valuable bull that they had slaughtered and could see some of the meat that had been hung out to dry; the gazebo, in which she had entertained lavishly, had been turned into a kitchen and the women were preparing what seemed to be the first of many helpings of sadza and beef that would be had at intervals during the day.

"Don't worry," her husband said with a wink, "if they try anything, come out with the rolling pin…"

He had had to duck as Mildred threw a cushion at him.

"*Mangwanani* Changamire," he had said in the traditional Shona greeting, "*marara Sei?*" (Good morning chief, how did you sleep?*).

The people around the chief gave way and George was able to watch the game for a while. It seemed that the game, played on a board similar to a chess board but, in this case, a crude home made one, had its own language.

"Punishment plus good move!" They would shout every time a player missed an opportunity to jump over the opponents bottle top (thus 'eating' the said bottle top), the idea of the game being to take all your opponent's bottle tops while you still had some left.

It also seemed like the game was communal. The spectators would take sides in advising one side or the other, sometimes switching sides, on the best move so that sometimes, after some argument between the spectators, moves would be made, not by the opposing players, but by the spectators.

"*Bhobho!*" They would shout excitedly every time one of the players breached the opponents defences to reach their base line and were rewarded with another bottle top placed on top of the victorious one – the bottle tops were either closed or upturned to show which players' were which. The bhobho or crown was an important piece because it had longer and more flexible moves and the player who got it first was likely to win the game.

"Can I also play," George had asked after a while. It was not the first time that he had seen the game, but he had never really taken it as seriously as this guys seemed to. They had been playing it almost continuously since the day before.

Twenty games later, with the support of the spectators who were happy to watch their chief beat the white man and thus did not insist on the normal rule that the losing player must give way to another, he had not won a single game although they were getting closer because he was getting the hang of it, but also because many of the spectators had come over to his side. He had wanted to try and beat the chief without their help, but clearly, spectator participation was very much part of this game.

"One more game, chief, then I have to go," George said.

"Oh? Where are you going today?"

"Back into the house…"

"Stay and have breakfast with us," it did not sound like a request.

"But my wife is making breakfast for me…"

"You can have that later. Join us for a real man's breakfast."

Several hours later, bellies full from the heaviest breakfast George had ever had, he sat side by side with the chief under the shade of a large Jacaranda tree that Mildred had planted many years earlier. The chief was taking bits of meat out of his teeth with a little twig while rubbing his stomach contentedly while George was still feeling a sense of guilt at having eaten part of his most valuable bull.

"So, chief," George said at length, "where do we go from here?"

"Hmmm?" The chief had dozed off.

"What happens now?"

"I don't know," the chief yawned loudly, "we have been told to just wait until government decides what to do, but as I said yesterday, you are free to come and go as you wish. You understand, of course that while we are here, we need to eat, so we will, from time to time go into your grain store, your vegetable garden and of course into your cattle pen."

Inside the house, George related his conversation with the chief to his wife. "So, I really don't know how long this could go on, but we can come and go as we please, until they decide to kick us out of our home, that is."

"You don't think that government wants to teach us whiteys a lesson or two? Surely they can't let this go on much longer... Talking of which, you seemed to eat the meat with particular relish there, didn't you?"

"Well I..." He had started to defend himself before he realised that Mildred was only teasing him, "he was well fed, you know! But seriously, that was not fun. Still, one has to do what one has to do to accommodate the neighbours hey."

"And you say that they are going to slaughter more?"

"The chief seemed to think that I, like any reasonable man, should understand that they need to eat while they are here. So if they are here for a year and slaughter our whole herd," George shrugged his shoulders, "what do we expect them to eat?"

"You are taking this rather well, George."

"It seems," George spoke carefully, " that on one of the other farms, I am not sure where, a farmer has been shot dead."

Mildred gasped, "Oh George, his poor family!"

"My Shona isn't what it should be, but I heard them say that he had come out with guns and had organised his workers to resist. When guns were produced on the other side, something the workers had not expected, they fled and left him alone."

"Surely the government must act now?"

George went across the spacious lounge into the passage and turned on the two way radio. They had switched it off the night before in order to try and sleep. What they kept hearing on the radio was quite depressing and they had decided that, for this one night, they would bury their heads in the sand. It was all the communication on the radio. The farmer, a Mr Jessop, was from Chinhoyi in Mashonaland West, some one hundred or so Kilometres North-West of Harare. George was relieved somewhat that it was not someone he knew and that it was a long way from them. But the fact remained that a white commercial farmer had been killed! This was getting out of hand. George was not even sure that the government was in control of this anymore and he said as much to Mildred.

"I don't know if our government has the capacity to act in this situation."

"Sure they have," Mildred insisted. "If there was the political will, they could send in the army and push the hooligans off the farms. But

210

there isn't the political will because ZIPA sees some advantage in the chaos. They can now seize the initiative from the MFD and tell our gullible black friends that this was what they planned all along!" She went across the room and switched on the radio and caught the President in mid-sentence.

"… our independence is meaningless without the land. There are those of our detractors who will say that we are being barbaric, yet when the British took our land from our ancestors, they did not so much as discuss it with them. As far as they were concerned, Africa was vacant land…" She switched it off and went and sat down, hands on her head. For a good few minutes, they did not speak; they just listened to the crackling of the two way radio and the many messages of condolences, outrage, despair that were going out from farmers depending on their situation. One game farmer was reporting that he had released his caged lions.

"There are just too many of them and they don't seem intimidated by the lions. The lions are now just lying in the shade watching them. Perhaps I should not have fed them yesterday!"

"The people or the lions?" Someone tried to make a joke out of it, but the farmers had a collective sense of humour failure this morning.

Jonas and Sekai had had a lie in that morning. They lay in bed listening to the sounds of a typical Rural Murewa Sunday morning; the singing of the birds, the laughter of children who would not be in school today; the shouting of mothers at their daughters to get up and start on their chores, the distant sound of a heavy duty truck making

211

its laboured way up the hill on the Harare/Nyamapanda highway on its way from Malawi; or was it to Malawi. All was well with Jonas.

"I could live here you know," he said to his wife turning to look at her and thinking again how lucky he was to have married such a beautiful, hardworking woman.

Sekai was feeling sad. It was always sad on Sunday morning whenever her husband came to visit. This was the day he was going to leave and go back to work and she had no idea how long he was going to be gone for. She regretted the fact that they had rowed and wasted most of Saturday not speaking to each other. She was sad, most of all because she felt that everything they had planned for was falling apart. Inflation was eating into their savings and Jonas's wages, although increased every year, were no longer enough to sustain them as they did in the past. She had to find some project to do in order to supplement his income.

"Yes, you could, my love," she was not convinced of that fact, "but you just might have to give up on certain luxuries – like tea and bread every morning for breakfast! You might even have to go hunting for meat…"

"Shut up!" Jonas tickled his wife to stop her talking. "Where could I go hunting here? All the trees have been cut and whatever game there was seems to have moved voluntarily into game parks. We would have to live on sadza and vegetables."

"As if you could," Sekai was looking thoughtful. "What about these farms that are being taken over. Can't we go and get our own piece of land there?"

"Where? Do you think that government will allow this kind of lawlessness to go on? I think that they have just been caught by surprise and are not quite sure what to do about it yet. I don't see this carrying on much beyond this week."

"I don't know," Sekai had spent most of the previous day, in Jonas's absence listening to the news on the radio and hearing that more and more farms were getting occupied. "It seems quite widespread and I heard a few people saying that they will go and get some free land. Even old Mrs Jekiseni is talking about moving!"

"They are all mad! Do you think that government will continue to allow this? We have a good home here and…"

"Just because we have a good home does not mean that we cannot do better. You spend most of your days at Mr Venters; drinking clean water that comes out of a tap – do you know how far we have to walk to get clean drinking water? In the dry season, we have to get up in the middle of the night to make sure we get water before the borehole dries out…"

"I could dig a well for you…"

"That is not the point, Jonas Mangwende! Anyway, in all these years, why have you not dug a well for me? The point is, we live in these arid, crowded and infertile lands while your employers have how much land? Surely there has to be fairer way of distributing the land…"

"And you think that by moving onto the White man's land, we are being fair? What about all the work that they have put in; the dams they have built, the boreholes they have sunk; the houses they have built? Is it fair to them that they should lose all that?"

"I don't know why I love this man," Sekai threw up her arms in mock exasperation, "do you know how many opportunities we have lost because of your belief in this fairness of yours? The world, my love, is not fair."

"I just believe in working for everything I get. It would not feel right to just end up with land that I have not earned."

"You could end up in Mr Venter's house, you know!"

"What would I do with such a big..." He stopped and looked at his wife. 'That would be some revenge', he thought to himself. "No." He said out loud. "Mr Venter has been good to me over the years, and I have seen him develop that farm..."

"With your help," Sekai interrupted, "with the help of the many workers that work for him. Look, if this land thing is going the way that I think it will, why not try and make a claim for ourselves. If it does not work, we can always come back to our good home, as you call it."

"I think you've been going to too many ZIPA meetings in my absence," Jonas said light heartedly, "you now think that all whites are bad. Look, the racists, the ones that did not want to mix with us have all left. The ones that are still here are Zimbabweans who have our country's interests at heart..."

"Or have nowhere to go where they could have the same lifestyle that they have here."

Jonas looked across at his wife. She had never seemed to take any interest in politics before. What was it that had changed? She seemed to read his mind.

"Life is a great teacher, you know. You have lived most of your adult life in the insular world of being Mr Venter's garden boy – fetch this, fetch that. You have not lived in the real world that most of us, black Zimbabweans live in."

"Being Mr Venter's garden boy has given us all we have..."

"And how much is that? Do you believe that in all the years that you have laboured, this is all that we deserve? An arid piece of ground with a couple of mud huts on it...?"

"We have a brick house," Jonas protested, but he was beginning to see her point, although he still found it difficult to agree with her.

Sekai looked at her husband and felt sorry for him. One of the reasons she was so in love with him was because of his principles, naïve though some of them were.

"I'll go and warm up your food for you. I had made chicken stew and sadza for you yesterday, but I think you had more important things on your mind last night," she said as she got out of bed smiling to herself.

Jonas was disappointed. He had wanted to make love to her one more time this morning but somehow, the mood didn't seem right.

Chapter 14

David Chitende was in his office bright and early this Sunday morning – for two reasons: he needed to start clearing his desk and packing in readiness for the move to Agriculture, and he needed to start putting down his thoughts on what he would recommend to the Minister on a way forward for land redistribution in the country, in view of the new reality. It had been a while since he had been in the office on a Sunday and the silence was almost eerie. He looked around his spacious office and thought about his first day there, some two years earlier and how large he thought it was when he was first promoted to Permanent Secretary level. He had liked the office because it was right in the Central Business District, close to all his favourite haunts. Now he was going to leave it to move to the Agriculture Ministry which was on the fringes of the centre of town.

He had very few personal belongings in the office and within a few hours, he was done and was ready for the movers who were due to arrive the next day. He had wanted to get the packing out of the way so that he could concentrate on the document he wanted to present to the Minister the next day. He had not slept very well since he had heard the news of his move. He had half hoped that he might get his chance to put in place ideas that he had, for a long time, with regards to what needed to be done with what he liked to call "the land question." Not many of his colleagues agreed with his ideas, but he was convinced that this was because they did not understand them and could not see the vision that he had for Zimbabwean agriculture.

David was in no doubt that however land was taken away from the minority white farmers and given to the majority, it was the right thing to do. His only problem was how it would be distributed once it was in government hands. He had been grappling with this problem for a couple of days and was beginning to formulate some ideas in his head. Now he could start to put them down on paper.

One of his major challenges was that of numbers. He had no idea how many people needed more land; how many people actually wanted to take up land. Then there was the problem of keeping the agricultural sector producing at current levels. Not everyone who wanted land would have the resources or the skill to farm it successfully. But even those would need to be catered for as there was need to release pressure on the overcrowded communal lands. To complicate his life further, those with the resources and skill were not particularly interested in farming, most of them associating farming with the poverty they were brought up in on their parents and grandparents' subsistence plots. They would need to be convinced that the economy needed their resources and skills.

The sudden shrill sound of the phone on his desk startled him in the silence. Who could be calling him in his office on a Sunday. He had told his wife that he did not wish to be disturbed unless there was an emergency.

"What is it?" He shouted into the phone.

"Touchy, touchy," it was Giles Kamba on the phone, "what's with your phone? I have been trying to call you all morning!"

David had a mobile phone, but was not quite used to having a phone that could reach him everywhere, so it generally was switched off.

"Oh, I forgot to switch it on this morning. Anyway, I didn't want to be disturbed today."

"I was desperate to get hold of you and eventually phoned your wife."

"Why?"

"To find out where you were, of course."

"I mean, why were you desperate to find me?"

"I have been thinking about our discussion on Friday, you know, about a new agricultural policy…"

"Why don't you come over to my office? We can talk here."

"OK. Shall I bring you lunch? I am told you've been gone since morning."

"Lunch?" David was surprised at how late it was. He had been so preoccupied that he had not realised how much time had lapsed since he had come into the office that morning. He was also relieved that Giles, who had left in something of a huff on Friday seemed to be back to his normal self. Perhaps he now realised that a new policy on agriculture was inevitable; that unless land was redistributed more equitably, there was likely to be trouble in the country, as developments in recent days had shown.

218

"Lunch would be good," he said, suddenly realising how hungry he was. "There is a place down the road from here that does amazing sadza and 'road runner' chicken. Why don't you get me some of that?"

"You surprise me Mr Perm. Sec. Chitende. I would have thought that you would want me to bring you something from one of the new up market take aways that are sprouting all over town."

"Just bring me sadza and road runner, these Western style take aways are responsible for that girth you have. It is not healthy!"

"It's called good living, my friend," Giles was aware that he was carrying a lot of excess weight, but could not be bothered to change his diet or lifestyle. "If I want sadza and road runner, I go and visit my mother. No one cooks sadza and road runner like my mother – and the chicken will be freshly slaughtered…"

"That's not good for you either," David liked to rile his friend, "it needs to 'cure' a bit."

"Do you want me to buy you lunch or not?"

In a few minutes, Giles arrived with two packed lunches: one in a plain polystyrene box, and the other, boldly emblazoned with the name of the take away from which it came. David had warned the security guards on the ground floor to let his friend in.

"No prizes for guessing which one is mine hey?" David said, accepting the plain box. He watched his friend greedily opening his box which had a much stronger aroma than his and almost wished he had asked for the same. But when he saw the oil and grease that was dripping from the flour encrusted chicken pieces, he was glad to have opted for the much simpler meal.

"So, what is it that you are so desperate to talk to me about, Giles," he asked casually after a few mouthfuls.

"You know, David, you know how to spoil a man's Sunday lunch. First you preach to me about what I should and should not eat with missionary zeal, and now you won't let me enjoy my meal in peace."

They both laughed, but David knew that he had little time.

"You are the one who came to disturb me in my madness, because, as you say, you are desperate to talk to me. I hope that you have changed your mind about getting yourself one of these farms."

Giles looked serious for the first time since he came in.

"I hope you understand that I am not against land reform and against the majority of our people getting more land."

"Nobody in their right mind would be," David agreed.

"What I am worried about is that we will do it in a way that may suit politicians, because it is expedient and has electoral advantage, but that will irreparably damage our economy." He stopped to try and gauge David's reaction.

"Go on," David said. "I'm all ears."

Giles stood up and went to the window. He wanted David to under-stand his position; to understand that they really were on the same side. He came back to his seat opposite David across the desk, reached for his briefcase and took out a thick file which he threw on the desk between them.

"This," he said, "is the blueprint of what we have been working on. It starts at the point where we recognise and acknowledge the contribution that the white farming community has made to this economy. It acknowledges that, for all sorts of historical reasons that I will not go into, white farmers are more experienced, more skilful, better organised and better equipped than we are; it accepts that – again for historical reasons – the black farmer in Zimbabwe, apart from a few notable exceptions, has only ever known subsistence farming, thus going into commercial farming would be a big leap. It therefore seeks to fill the gap that necessarily exists, thus looks for ways to reform the agricultural sector without disrupting what is, after all, the base of our economy."

As David said nothing, Giles went on, feeling emboldened.

"We think that much as we do not like it, this country still needs its white farmer. It is estimated that we have just over four thousand white farmers controlling an in-proportionately large percentage of our productive agricultural land. Many have unnecessarily large farms that do not take into account the hunger for land that is in the majority black population. Some have more than a farm each with a few having as many as six farms each. Clearly, this is an untenable situation that needs correction."

"Agreed," David concurred.

"Given that these farms are freehold, meaning that the farmers have documents that say that they own the land, how do you correct the situation? They can simply tell you that they are not selling; look David, since 1980, we have been working on the willing buyer, willing seller principle as agreed at Lancaster House. How many farms have we been able to acquire?" Giles was tapping his pencil on the desk, looking directly at David.

"Too few, and we have not really distributed them in the fairest and most efficient manner, and the process does need to be speeded up. But how do you do that, given the fact that there are no funds to buy more land and the British, who were going to provide the funding are now dragging their feet and, to be honest, the farmers are doing very well for themselves, thank you, thus have no incentive to sell anyway?"

"This is where we think government needs to use its authority. ZIPA has the more than two thirds majority that it needs in parliament in order to pass any laws. They can pass a law, for example, limiting farm ownership to one per farmer; then pass another law limiting farm sizes to, say, 500 hectares per farm. We estimate that this could free close to one million hectares of land for distribution to black farmers..."

"That is still not enough..."

"Hear me out," Giles put his hand up telling David not to interrupt, "this is only phase one. We can then work on a hub and spoke system where each white farmer is given a group of black farmers to mentor and pass on his experience to. If we give each white farmer, say, ten black farmers around him, we suddenly have forty thousand farmers who are reasonably skilful and our productivity will probably go up!"

"Forty thousand is a drop in the ocean, surely. We have millions of people wanting more land. Even if you double, no, quadruple that number, it would still be way short of our target."

"In order to keep our economy going, we need to move slowly and carefully. In any case, how many people do you know who want to go farming? As the world has industrialised, we have seen the number of farmers dwindle. I don't think Zimbabwe will be any different. Not everyone wants to be a farmer; most are quite content to be employed and not have to worry about where their next pay packet is coming from."

"You are beginning to sound like a white man, Giles. Most of us have farming backgrounds. We grew up with our parents in rural Zimbabwe and we have been growing things since we were this high," David stretched his hand to indicate the height he was talking about. "We just have to do what we have always done on a larger scale, that's all."

"Commercial farming is a whole different ball game from subsistence farming. It's running a business, which is not the same as growing your own food."

"And you think we cannot run businesses because...?"

"David," Giles was getting frustrated, "this is a plan that experts in the Ministry have spent many months working on. At least look at it in detail."

"I am asking you these questions because they are the sort of questions that our political masters will ask. Look at it from their point of view. They have, for the first time since independence, a viable opposition snapping at their heels and quite frankly, they don't have a plan! What would you do?"

"I'd step down and let someone else try," Giles said earnestly, "look, David, there is no doubt that ZIPA's role in the liberation of the coun-

223

try was pivotal to what we have become; an in dependant sovereign state. But good soldiers do not necessarily make good politicians. Why not let someone else try? They have been at it for twenty years. Are we any better off?"

"Don't let your bosses hear you say that, Giles. They might construe it as you biting the hand that feeds you. Anyway, I will look at your plan. There are parts of what you have told me that we may use."

Giles was not convinced. It sounded like David was being polite, but was not sold on Giles's ideas.

"That's all I ask," Giles said. "What's your plan?"

"I don't know yet," David was being honest. "I think that a lot depends on what the politicians decide to do with the current wave of invasions, which seem to be getting out of control. They can stop them, of course, if they wanted to, but I do not think that, right now, there is the political will to do so. I have the skeleton of a plan that says that if government are serious that this is the way they are going to take land from the white farmers, then we have to work on a plan to redistribute it, catering for both the commercial and the subsistence farmer."

"And if they decide to stop the invasions?"

"Come on, Giles, you don't expect me to think that hard on a Sunday, do you?" David was sure that the course of action that had been triggered by Chief Juru's actions a few days earlier was not going to be stopped. But he was not going to tell Giles that.

It was getting dark outside. Neither man had realised how long they had been having this conversation for.

"I'll need to get home," David said, "the Mrs will be wondering where I got to."

"Yes, I need to go home too," Giles agreed, getting out of his chair with some difficulty.

"You need to do something about that weight, Giles. Your family still needs you."

"I don't know, I think they will probably be better off with me dead, with all the insurances I have taken out!"

David tried to walk briskly to the elevators, but had to slow down for his friend to keep up.

Themba was drunk again and he was feeling good about himself. After his encounter with Dorothy, he had gone back to his hut and tried to clean himself up a bit, not for Dorothy's sake, but because he was expecting Paul who, according to Dorothy, drove a very fancy car and had promised to pick him up. He had a bath for the first time in many weeks, but when he tried to dress himself, there was not a single item of clothing that had no tear in it. For a while, he considered going to ask Dorothy to patch up one of his less tattered shirts, but decided that she would probably make fun of him. After some time, he had come up with a plan: he would wear two sets of clothes, one over the other. The tears would not exactly match thus he could look quite decent. He was in the middle of doing this when he heard the sound of a car approaching.

Not wanting his guest to see the inside of his quarters, he quickly went outside to meet his visitor. Even though the car had been described to him by Dorothy, he had still been surprised to see just how fancy it was; and even more surprised at Paul's attire. He looked down at what he had up to that point thought to be his best set of clothes and felt ashamed.

"I was just about to change when I heard your car," he lied unconvincingly.

Paul, who was dressed casually in jeans and a tee shirt still managed to look almost regal; to Themba's eyes at least. His shiny shoes looked like they were not meant to stand on such ground as they now stood; Paul himself looked odd surrounded by Themba's dilapidated homestead. He regarded Themba with some disgust although the latter could not see this as Paul had dark glasses on. He smiled at Themba although, if Themba had been able to see his visitor's eyes, he would have seen that the smile did not go beyond the lips.

"Don't worry," Paul took something out of the car, "I brought you these."

Themba could not believe it. The parcel that Paul brought out had two new pairs of shoes, three shirts, two pairs of jeans, a suit and even a tie. In a smaller packet were socks and underpants. Themba, Paul thought, behaved like a child who had just opened his Christmas presents. He kept picking up his new clothes, one at a time, measuring them against himself and putting them back down, all the time mumbling to himself, 'I'm back! Themba Ndlovu is back'!

"You better go and change," Paul said finally, "we need to get going."

Themba went into his hut and was so long in there that Paul had to follow him in. He was so spoilt for choice that he did not know which of his new acquisitions to wear first.

"Just put on some jeans and a tee shirt," Paul had said helpfully. "It may get rough where we are going."

"Where are we going."

"Back to the farm we took over yesterday, of course."

Themba dressed hurriedly, the excitement in him obvious to anyone who might have looked. But only Paul was there. Yet he knew that when he got to Mr Van Breda's farm, all those who had sneered at him, who had made fun of his appearance would be there to see the new look Themba. Of course there was the big mirror in which he was going to be able to see himself...

"We are going to have to do something about that hair. Is there anywhere near here where you can get a haircut?"

"There is a guy at Manhowe Township who sometimes comes with his scissors and cuts people's hair under the big tree..."

"Good. We will go there."

Themba smiled to himself as he regarded himself for the umpteenth time in the big mirror. He was swaying a little as the effects of the whisky – or was it brandy? – began to manifest themselves. He was still amused at the surprised looks of the others when they saw him arrive with Paul; and bemused by the sudden deference that everyone seemed to treat him with. The room was not as clean as it had been the day before and Themba felt some disappointment that the others had ransacked it and taken whatever valuables they could. What they had left was strewn all over the floor, in the bath and even inside the toilet bowl. He found himself trying to tidy up the room that he had decided was going to be his, but the effort was too much and he just threw the parcel with his new clothes on the unmade bed and went to join the others outside.

"There you are. I wondered where you got to." Paul was leaning casually against the big tree in the middle of the lawn, now almost invisible under the many bottles of beer, spirits, scuds and drunken youth who had just had a breakfast of meat – as much as they could eat – and sadza. Paul was worried. If the farmers decided to attack them now, there was no way that the invaders could hold out.

"Themba, I need you sober…"

"How can I be sober with all this free booze available…"

"I am being serious, Themba," Paul shook Themba a little, "we are not here to get drunk. This is the next phase of our struggle and we need to have our wits about us. For all we know, the farmers could be organising to attack us and drive us off this farm."

"They can't! There are too many of us…" Themba stopped as he looked around and saw the state of many of his comrades, "I see what you mean," he said finally, noting that there was a group that was sitting near the lake and appeared not to be drinking. They numbered about fifteen to twenty. His military mind had already begun to calculate. These were probably civilians who had never held a gun in their lives. Could they be relied upon to defend this place in the event of an attack by the farmers…?

"You were a good soldier once," Paul was saying to him, "do you think we could defend this place with the manpower available?"

"We have to," Themba's tone was defiant, confident. He had faced a well-trained army in the bush and was sure that he could take on a group of farmers with beer bellies.

Paul seemed to read his mind. "You know, of course that these are the same people that made up the Rhodesian army."

"If only we had guns…"

"We have," Paul said quietly. Themba was no longer surprised by anything Paul said. He seemed to have thought of everything. It was also becoming clear to Themba that the invasion had not been as spontaneous as he had first thought.

"Then we might be able to bluff them into believing that we can defend this place. We have to try and speak to everyone who is half sober and make sure that they understand what is going on. The ones that are completely out of it will have to be moved out of sight – I think I saw a barn at the back of the house, we can move them in there. The alcohol has to be removed as well. We cannot afford to lose more people to drink."

Paul was impressed. It was amazing what a little cleaning up and a change of clothing could do to a man's confidence. Themba had been a good leader of men and clearly, the years of hardship he had endured over the years had not taken that from him. A little toughening up and he could become an important part of this stage of the revolution as

229

the President had called it. He watched as Themba organised the sober group to move the drunks out of the way; he saw how he spoke to those that were still coherent and he saw how he strategically placed everyone in positions that they could make some noise if the need arose. He was impressed by the fact that Themba had not even asked where the guns were. He accepted Paul's word that they were available and would be produced when and if the need arose.

The attack never came as the farmers had decided that it was not prudent at this time to be confrontational. The invaders seemed to have the support of government and it had been decided that, through the Commercial Farmers Association, dialogue with the authorities was the best way forward.

But Themba had done enough to convince Paul that his decision to find him and recommend him as one of the leaders of the farm invasions was the right one. That evening, they discussed in detail what needed to be done going forward. They had taken one of the smaller bedrooms as their command centre, or the "officers mess," as the others soon called it.

"So, what is going on, Paul?" Themba asked with more than a little curiosity. "This seems to be more organised than I first thought."

"The situation is quite fluid at the moment. It seems that our leaders have decided that this is the only way we can get the land back from the whites. After all these years of independence, there has been no tangible movement on the land reform front. The whites are doing better now than they did before independence and they are feeling comfortable and will not willingly part with their farms."

"But why wait this long?" Themba was not convinced. "When we were in the bush, we were told that as soon as we won the war, we would chase the whites away and take over their homes and farms. Some of us have suffered all these years and now I see that the enemy we were fighting is living in the lap of luxury," Themba found himself getting quite angry, "while we, who keep hearing on the radio that we won the war, that we are the heroes of the armed struggle….," he could not finish the sentence as his anger overwhelmed him.

"Well," Paul had to choose his words carefully, "if the truth be told, we did not exactly win the war," he stood up and paced the floor. "Yes, it was getting uncomfortable for the whites and the war was getting unpopular with parents who were losing their children and, of course, many were leaving the country."

He came back to his chair opposite Themba, "The best that can be said, if you ask me, is that we forced the whites to come to the negotiating table, something that they had been unwilling to do for years," he paused to reflect. These thoughts were coming to him for the first time and he was surprised that he had not seen it like that before, having bought into the popular story that they had actually defeated the Rhodesians.

"So," he went on, "Lancaster House happened, and once you are negotiating, you are having to give and take and we agreed to leave things more or less as they were. Agriculture, it was reasoned, was the backbone of the economy and it was better not to do anything that might jeopardise it…"

"So what has changed now?" Themba interrupted.

"The MFD," Paul said simply. "We got complacent. We were the party that was loved by the people and we did not feel that we needed to do anything to retain their support. All we had to do was remind the people of our heroic struggle against imperialism and colonialism and they would support us out of gratitude. The MFD has changed all that. Now there is a party that can actually challenge us at the next elections and we need something tangible to give to them…"

"And the land is it?" Themba was beginning to understand.

"What else is there?" Paul stood up again and looked out of the window. It was hot and sticky. There was not even a breeze as the stillness of the trees could testify. Out in the distance the only movement he could see was the shimmering horizon and a lone eagle that circled high in the sky probably stalking some prey on the ground. Just as they were, he thought, waiting to pounce on some farmer who, like the prey on the ground, knew that an attack would come, but had no idea when or how it would come. Again he walked back to his chair and sat opposite Themba.

"Most of the people who are part of these invasions are layabouts with nothing better to do and this gives them a bit of excitement in their tedious lives. If we told them tomorrow that the invasions have ended and they are to go back to their homes, most of them would be quite happy to go back and do whatever it is they were doing before. You, Themba, are different. You are a military man; you fought in the liberation war and you understand what the struggle is about. We need men like you to lead and guide these people as we enter this phase that means our total emancipation from the yoke of colonialism. We are now taking back the reins of our economy from the foreigners that invaded us years ago and you are going to be spearheading it." He paused to see if this was having the desired effect on Themba, who was listening intently, his face betraying the excitement that he felt at being entrusted with such an important task.

"What is it you want me to do," Themba's voice took on a conspiratorial tone.

"Not much," Paul sounded casual, "I have to move on to other areas in a few days. You will be in charge of this base, and I will leave it up to you how you organise yourselves. From here, you can lead invasions onto the other farms around here. In fact, I understand that this was not the farm we had intended to occupy, but it will serve the purpose just as well. We had wanted to take over Mr Venter's farm, but we got lost and ended up here. That should be our next target."

For the first time, Paul saw some hesitation in Themba's eyes. He looked like he was going to protest, but thought better of it and was quiet for a few moments. Paul wondered about the hesitation. Mr Venter was not particularly liked in the black community in these parts. He had expected Themba to jump at the chance to harass one of the most hated farmers in the area. Why was he hesitating? Had he gone soft? The truth was that Themba was thinking about his friend, Jonas. In the years of hardship that Themba had gone through, Jonas was probably the only person who had retained some respect for Themba; always willing to share a drink with him while they discussed the politics of the country. Jonas seemed to have done well in Mr Venter's employ and always said that people hated his employer because they did not understand him.

'He shouts a lot and has been known to physically manhandle some of the workers in the fields' Jonas would say, 'but he has really looked after me and my family and hardly anyone gets fired from Mr Venter's farm'. Now Paul wanted him to go and get Jonas out of his job?

"Can we not start with one of the other farms?" He asked hopefully.

"Why?" Paul was puzzled. "He is probably the one farmer that the other white farmers look up to and if we can break him, the others will be easier."

"On the other hand," Themba was clutching at straws, "it seems that all the other farmers are gathered at Mr Venter's farm which makes it the best defended position. You have said yourself that the people on our side are not trained, and as we have seen, lack any sort of discipline. Can we trust them to be able to deal with a well-defended position?"

Although Themba's argument made some sense, Paul was still not convinced that that was the reason for Themba's reluctance. He was sure that there was something more to it, but could not think of any other reason for his friend's hesitation.

"As I said," he said at length, "it's your call, but I think you are making a mistake. If we do not break Jacques Venter, we may be giving them a chance to regroup and strategize."

The relief in Themba's eyes was quite obvious. "I am not suggesting that we leave Jacques Venter for too long. We just need enough time to be able to go in with a plan that will ensure our success. In the meantime, we can go for those farms whose owners are gathered at his farm. They will be as easy to take as this one was."

234

"Ok then, we go for Dudley White's Bristol Farm. I believe that he is relatively new in the area and is English, which means that he is not particularly well liked by the other white farmers who are of Afrikaans descent – and still remember the atrocities inflicted on them by the English during the Boer War a century ago!"

"I think that they will close ranks at this time and it will not matter what tribe anyone comes from. They will be united by the common threat to their race and their livelihood. But, yes, I think Bristol Farm would be a good target for now." Themba was happy to have bought some time. He had to get to Jonas and find out what his friend's position was on this. If they were going to invade his employer's farm, the least he could do was warn his friend and give him a chance to either get out or be part of the invasion so that he too could benefit from his employer's eviction.

Unaware of his reprieve, Jonas was having a strange conversation with his employer and his friends. Strange, not least because he was sitting on a chair with the white farmers surrounding him and hanging onto his every word. They had even offered him a glass of whiskey, but he had declined, preferring instead to drink the White man's Castle Larger, which he would normally only drink at month end when he got paid, as a wash down for his normal scud.

His journey back from Murewa had been uneventful although the roads were unusually quiet for a late Sunday afternoon when various people would normally be returning from visiting their rural homes – as he was - or returning from holidays and weekends away, for those that could afford such luxuries, and increasingly, they were many black

Zimbabweans that could. People were still talking about the invasions, mainly in hushed tones and, because many of them were farm labourers returning from an unexpected weekend away from work, rather sneeringly because they did not believe that these invasions were such a good idea; nor did they believe that they would be allowed to carry on for much longer.

"I think that the government knows that without the white farmers, there will be so much hunger in the country that they will lose even that little support that they still have," one of the passengers on the bus suggested, which started a heated debate on the pros and cons of the invasions, with most of them arguing that these actions would only help the MFD while a few diehard ZIPA supporters were talking about how this would mean that everybody would have more fertile land and be able to feed themselves. Jonas did not join in the conversation because he preferred to keep his thoughts to himself at times like this. In any case, he was preoccupied with thoughts of his wife, Sekai, reliving the weekend's highs and lows. He was slightly amused at her suggestion that they should try and grab some land for themselves and found himself smiling as he relived his afternoon in the bush and what now seemed like his childish anger at Sekai for something that happened a long time ago and over which she had little control.

For some reason, he had not expected the invasions to have affected his area of employment and the gathering at his employer's home did not suggest to him that anything was amiss. Even the fact that the mood of the Whites was not as boisterous as normal - in fact it was sombre, almost as if there was a funeral – did not ring any alarm bells in his head. He walked across to where his employer and his friends were to greet them in his customary deferential style, expecting some crude joke about what he had done with his wife after so many weeks apart. Instead, he had found himself being invited to sit with them and talk about what was happening out there. Reluctantly, he had sat down, tentatively accepting the bottle of beer that was proffered with a glass for him to drink from. Somehow, the beer did not taste quite as good from a glass as it did coming straight out of the bottle, but he could hardly refuse the offer to drink out of the glass like everyone else around him.

"How are your wife and children?" Mr Venter asked the rather unexpected question. He had never asked before, at least not the way he asked now, as if he actually cared for the answer. For a brief moment, Jonas visualised his employer's naked, flabby body on his naked wife, his hands pawing clumsily all over her and he felt his anger rising. But when he looked at the faces of the men around him, they all seemed interested in what he was going to say.

"They are very well," he replied, "well, my wife is. All the children are away at University and school..."

"You don't say!" Mr Venter's exclaimed, "even the little one, what's his name, is away from home?"

"Tapiwa," Jonas reminded his boss.

"Yes Tapiwa – Taps, we used to call him," he addressed the last remark to the other farmers, "how quickly children grow, hey."

In all the years that Jonas had worked for Mr Venter, a conversation such as this one had never taken place and the former was getting a little confused. What had got into his employer to actually remember that Jonas had a family?

"So, why did you come back here, Jonas?" The questioner was Jack van Breda, who, Jonas had noticed, was a lot quieter than usual.

"I came back to my job," he replied, a little surprised at the question.

"Why?" Jack persisted.

"Because Mr Venter said that we must come back today, sir…"

"What is the matter with you Jack?" Dudley White was getting irritated at Jack, who he had little respect for anyway, "the man has come back to his job. Does he need another reason?"

"He could be a spy, sent here to come and case this bloody joint!"

The others laughed nervously although some of them were wondering if Jack might be right after all.

"No, not Jonas," Jacques sought to allay their fears, "I have known Jonas for upwards of thirty years, he came here as a little boy and, well I would know if he was hiding something from us. Jonas is almost part of this family, you know."

Jonas, who had gulped the first beer thirstily after his lengthy walk from the bus stop was looking around at the farmers bemused by it all. He did not quite understand Mr Van Breda's comment about him being a spy; he could not fathom why his employer was being so complimentary of him and he certainly did not understand why they were all treating him like he was one of them, almost.

"So, what is the story out there, Jonas," Jacques Venter asked almost casually.

"Story?"

"I mean, what are they saying about these farm invasions?"

"Oh, that," Jonas said accepting another beer, "I don't think that many are supporting what these people are doing. They cannot just take people's farms like that," he snapped his fingers, "I think that the police will soon move in and remove them."

"They have not done anything so far, Jonas," Peter Johnstone cut in.

"It's because they caught them by surprise. I think you will see tomorrow that the police will have organised themselves and these people will be pushed out."

In his excitement, Jonas was drinking too quickly. He could not believe what was happening. His employer had never consulted him on anything before. Now, it was as if they were all wanting to know what he, Jonas Mangwende, thought! He stood up and helped himself to another beer, almost falling over as he tripped on one of the small tables in his way. Dudley White caught him as he fell.

"Sorry, sir," he said, slurring his words. "I was nearly falling." Jonas stood among the farmers swaying slightly as the beer took effect. He waved his bottle expansively in the air, as he had seen the whites do when they were having what he always assumed were important discussions. "This is all tempor…, tempol…, it will not happen for a long time."

"You reckon so, Jonas?" Jacques asked.

"I what, sir?"

"Do you think so? That it is temporary."

"Of course, of course." Jonas's confidence had grown by the bottle and he felt as though he was privy to information that his white 'friends' did not have.

Jack van Breda, sitting across the veranda, slightly removed from the others, was getting irritated with his friends who appeared to be taking the word of a garden boy with a seriousness it did not deserve.

"How the hell do you know this, Jonas? How do you know that it is temporary?" He asked impatiently.

"Well, everybody on the bus…" Jonas started.

"On the fucking bus! That's where the Cabinet met this week, was it? That is where government policy was discussed…?"

"Come on, Jack," Jacques interrupted his friend, "Jonas has just come from the community and all he is telling us is what people in that community are saying. What the mood is with regards to what is happening on the farms. We need all the information we can get."

"And the discussions of a few farm labourers on a rural bus are 'information' to you, Jacques?"

"These are the people who have voted ZIPA into power, election after election, because the rest of us have let them. The government is bound to listen to their voice because even the so called black 'intelligencia' does not bother to vote."

"Do you believe, Jacques, that the voice of these people will say 'no' to the land invasions. Have you seen how they live in their communal lands?"

"Yes, Jack. I think that these people value their jobs and…"

"Yea?" Jack stood up and took a step towards Jacques, pointing in the general direction of his farm, "then, how come, apart from Mary, those voters that we left on my farm for the weekend have not run away? How come, the little information we are getting from there suggests that they are looting my farm as much as the rest of them?"

"You don't know those ZIPA youth. They can force…," Jonas wanted to explain that he thought the workers were probably being forced to participate in the looting but Jack was not having any of it.

"They are not being forced! You cannot force someone to get drunk; to take furniture from my house…," he broke off and sat as his emotions overwhelmed him again. "They are using my furniture; my antique furniture as firewood!"

A heavy silence followed Jack's statement, which seemed to have made the farmers realise just how helpless they were. Up to that point, they had only been thinking about keeping their farms. They had, collectively, made the assumption that after a few days of lawlessness, government would step in and restore their land and life would go on as normal. Jack's statement had just made them realise that their lives would never return to normal. By the end of this, they would probably have lost a lot a valuable properties some of which meant something only to them and no one else. They also realised that the master-servant relationship that all white people thought they had with their black counterparts had been breached, probably irrevocably. For a good few minutes, no one said anything. Those who still had their

241

farms felt sorry for Jack, of course, but they were still hoping that all of this was temporary. But some were already beginning to think about what they would do if what had happened to Jack were to happen to them. Dudley, for example was thinking about how he had sunk all his British savings into his farm. What could he do? He wondered whether he could go back to Britain and live on his pension.

Jacques, on the other hand, was feeling very angry. 'How dare they'? He was thinking. This land had been in his family for three generations. Three generations!! He would die first before giving it up. He could barricade himself in his house. He started to make plans in his mind. If it was not too late, he would go to Marondera on the next day and get some supplies – tinned foods and other dry goods could last for months, by which time the whole circus would be over.

"This is the only country I have ever known, I am a citizen of this bloody country," Peter Johnstone said, almost to himself, "why can I not own a farm? I am not racist."

"Are you suggesting that the rest of us are?"

"No, Jack," Peter said, tersely, "all I am saying is that the racists have all left. We stayed because we love this country. We want to make positive contributions to the development of Zimbabwe."

Jonas found himself left out again as the whites got into a somewhat heated debate on what the best way forward was. They seemed to have forgotten about him – and the beer – so he helped himself to a few bottles and walked off the veranda to his quarters.

Chapter 15

*❙❙*I like it!" David Chitende had just finished outlining his thoughts on how they could go about redistributing the land once it had been acquired, and his new Minister was impressed.

"When do I get to see it in writing?" Minister Mangwiro was so impressed he could not wait to show the plan to the President.

"My secretary is typing the document now and it should be ready this afternoon." David was pleased, but a little disappointed that the Minister seemed to be swallowing his plan without any amendments or additions. There were parts of it that needed some refining and he had hoped that the Minister would have picked those up and, together, they would have made the necessary changes. He had also hoped that the minister would give him some direction on the legal ramifications of what he was suggesting.

"There are parts of the plan that worry me, though," he started, not quite sure how the minister would make of it. He was used to working with Itai Mugwazo, an academic who would wait until he had had a chance to study any suggestions before he made any comments.

"Those can be worked out, surely?" Minister Mangwiro sounded impatient.

"I think that they can, eventually, but…"

"No buts! We will find a way to overcome whatever obstacles you think there may be. Nothing is insurmountable! We fought a war against a very strong foe and prevailed. We can win this one too!"

'Here we go again', David thought to himself. Out loud he said, "our constitution and our legal system protects private property, and we have signed various international investment protection protocols. We can't just…"

"Of course we can," minister Mangwiro sounded almost flippant, "His Excellency, the President has already instructed Legal Affairs to look into it. Look, David, I am not interested in your excuses. I said that this is a good plan and it is a good plan. You do what you have to do to start the ball rolling and leave the relevant experts to deal with the legal side of things."

"Yes sir," David felt as though he was being attacked personally, "but at this moment, we have no idea how many people actually want land and what resources they have at their disposal to utilise that land once they have it."

"So?" Minister Mangwiro was beginning to wonder if this was the right person for the task.

"I'll get on it right away, sir," his taste for the job was waning rapidly.

His plan was quite simple. The majority of black Zimbabweans were subsistence farmers who were looking for better land in which to grow crops for their own consumption. These would be happy to continue working in the cities, mines and commercial farms while their wives and families worked the land, mainly in the rainy season. Little capital was required here. There was a need, however, for an element of commercial farming in order to continue the production of cash crops like tobacco, fruit, vegetables and flowers for the export market and the large scale production of what had become the main staple, maize, and some winter wheat. This was more specialised and required that the farmer not only have a better-than-working knowledge of farming and substantial resources, but also be willing to give up comfortable jobs in order to concentrate all their efforts on the farms.

He was quite comfortable that there would be enough land to accommodate the subsistence farmers who he expected would not be in large numbers as most people did not like the idea of staying on the land and would rather look for employment – there were still enough companies in the country and hopes were high that foreign investment could be attracted to Zimbabwe. It was in the commercial sector where he had doubts. Most people with resources had comfortable jobs or were running successful businesses and were thus unlikely to want to abandon these in order to go into agriculture, where the income could not be guaranteed as it could succumb to the vagaries of nature – droughts, frosts in winter, too much rain, hailstorms.

Further, the professionals with the prerequisite skills and resources had very little, if any, knowledge of farming. He had thus included in his plan, suggestions from Itai Mugwazo's document that there was need to leave some white commercial farmers in place. These could then be asked to mentor groups of the new black commercial farmers so that they could impart their knowledge and experience. He had not mentioned this part of the plan to Minister Mangwiro as he was not sure what the view of the politicians was on this. It seemed to him that, at that point, even the politicians were not sure how far they would go in taking farms away from the white farmers. The invasions seemed to have taken on a life of their own and stories were filtering through that there was large scale destruction of property on the farms – including the destruction of farming implements and equipment.

David sat up in his chair. How were the new farmers going to cope if the equipment was destroyed. It had taken the White farmers years to build up their equipment "portfolios" and if the equipment was destroyed, could it be replaced? Even if it was not destroyed, would the White farmers be in the mood to sell? 'They might just decide to destroy it themselves rather than leave it to people who would have taken away their homes and livelihoods'. Perhaps, he thought, if government were to make it clear that anything that was an improvement would be compensated for. Only the land was to be taken for free, just as they had done when they took it from the indigenous peoples a century or so earlier. He decided that the next time he met with Minister Mangwiro, he would recommend that the government should engage the farmers, through their representative organisation and let them know that although the farm invasions could not be reversed, there was need for both sides to start to work together on a viable way forward.

In spite of the fact that Minister Mangwiro had assured him that the Department of Legal Affairs was looking at how the government could 'legalise' the new land dispensation, David was still worried. The farmers had legal title to the land and if they clubbed together, had enough resources to challenge the government even in international courts. Some of the farms were owned by major multi-national corporations that could not only challenge government on their own, but could scuttle any new investment into Zimbabwe.

David stood up and went to the window to watch the traffic on Borrowdale road. This was more complicated than he first realised. They had signed bilateral and multi-lateral investment protection protocols with various governments and organisations. If they broke these, who would ever trust Zimbabwe with their investments again? His whole plan was predicated on the premise that more investment would come into the country, creating more jobs, thus limiting the numbers that would need land. Unemployment was already high in the country and if no more jobs were created…

Across Borrowdale Road, he watched the little boys playing cricket on the lush green lawns of the private school where his son attended. Although there were some black youngsters there, the school was still predominantly white. Strangely, he found himself thinking how privileged he was that his son could go to such a school – that he could afford the fees for the school. He thought about the very basic schools that he had attended during his time; that many black children still attended even now. He wondered how many of the white children were sons of farmers. How would they be affected by their parents loss of their land?

'David', he chided himself, 'you are not a politician. Go to lunch'.

"Praxedes," he called out to his new secretary wondering where parents got such names, "how far are you with that document? The minister wants to see it today."

Praxedes came into his office carrying some files which she put on his desk.

247

"I'm nearly finished, sir," she said smiling at him in an all too familiar manner, "I think you should take a look at these," she indicated the files she had just put on his desk and started to walk out of his office. She stopped at the door, turned round with a flourish and said, "by the way sir, most of my friends call me Pracky."

'I'm not your bloody friend', he thought to himself, but out loud he said, "I am going to lunch. Please have that document ready when I return."

"But, sir, I'm also going to lunch!"

"Praxedes," he was being patient with her, "as long as the document is ready when I get back, I don't care what you do."

She went back into her office feeling quite angry with her new boss. He had not even commented on her dress which she had bought especially for him over the weekend. She picked up her phone and dialled her friend Beauty's number. Beauty was the Personal assistant to the Deputy Minister for Agriculture. The two had been friends since their days in the typing pool at the Ministry of Education, although Beauty had gotten married and Pracky was still looking and getting desperate somewhat. Not that she had no suitors; she just was not getting the right kind of suitors! A girl needed a man who could change her status for the better in the shortest time possible – preferably with immediate effect. She could not stand these men who talked about 'building something together'! How long would that take?

"I don't believe that man," she said as soon as Beauty picked up the phone, "he expects me to work during my lunch hour!"

"What man… ? Oh, your new boss. I told you he is a no nonsense man. You'll only make a fool of yourself trying to flaunt yourself in front of that one. I believe he is devoted to his wife."

"We will see about that!" Pracky said and nearly hung up before realising that she would need some lunch. "By the way Bee," her voice softened, "now that I have to work, can you bring me something to eat - I'll give you the money when you get back."

"Whatshisname isn't bringing you lunch, then?"

"Tobias? No, I had to break if off with him. He started to talk as if he was my husband. 'You can't go to this or that party; I don't like your friends; as if he had paid *roora* for me!*"

"He seemed like a nice guy. But of course the prospect of working with a new 'prospect' was incentive enough for you to dump poor Tobias. I liked him."

"You marry him then. Bring me some lunch will you? Now let me get on with 'his highness's' document." She hung up and started typing.

Giles Kamba was there first, having had little to do in his new capacity as secretary to the Minister without Portfolio, Itai Mugwazo. He had spent the morning arranging and rearranging his new office while he waited for some direction from the minister. He had no idea what a minister without portfolio did! By twelve thirty, he had gotten tired of waiting and decided to take an early lunch break, taking a leisurely walk to the aptly named "The Usual Place," which was their usual lunch time meeting place. He ordered himself a gin and tonic and found a seat in the corner of an empty bar that would soon be filled with lunch time diners and tipplers. He was soon joined by Ivan Mbodza, who came earlier than usual because he was anxious to hear news from David on his meeting with the new Minister for Agriculture earlier that morning.

"Give me the same as Mr Kamba," he said to the waiter as he joined his friend, "Gin and talk shit, is it?"

He sat down next to Giles and they made small talk about their families and the weekend.

"I don't know what qualifies some people to be government ministers," David Chitende said, joining the others, "I spent the weekend cracking my head over what we are going to do with the farms that we are taking over, I outline my proposals to the minister and all he says is 'fine'. Can you believe that?"

"What did you expect him to say if the plan is, as he says, 'fine'?" Giles was still unhappy about losing the agriculture ministry.

"I expected some input from the man; some indication that he had given the matter some thought. It's as if he expects me to formulate the whole policy."

"I'm surprised you are complaining. I would have expected you to be happy to have the opportunity to put into place the ideas on land that you always bore us with! As for the minister's qualifications; do you not know that he fought in the war of liberation? What other qualification does he need?" Dr Mbodza was half joking.

"You think that government will go on with the land invasions? I'm still convinced that they will see how unsustainable the whole thing is and will do things differently…"

"I don't think that there is going to be a significant change of direction," David interrupted Giles, "it's too good an opportunity for ZIPA. You guys may not want to go farming but there are millions out there who will welcome the move…"

"I don't think so," Giles interrupted in turn, "most people just want to get paid at the end of the month without having to worry about where the money is coming from. Giving them land is asking them to run their own businesses! Not everyone is an entrepreneur you know!"

"We all know that! That is why my plan will work. There will be a certain element of commercial farming, where people with resources and skills will get bigger tracts of land so that they can continue to produce at current levels. The vast majority will get small subsistence plots where they can continue to farm at weekends while they keep their jobs in the cities."

"Who has the farming skills that the whites have?"

"Ivan," David was getting frustrated with his friends, "you don't need farming skills. What you need are management skills – like you and I have – and when we take over the farms, we also take over the workers who have the required farming skills, and we manage them…"

"But won't the farm workers be eligible to get their own pieces of land? They will take their skills to their own land, surely?" Giles was looking to pick holes in the whole plan.

"Guys, guys, this is still a work in progress. I am still to look at all the different angles – which is why it would have been nice to get the minister's input – can we have lunch now? I still have to refine the whole thing."

Over lunch, they talked some more about the land invasions, David still trying to convince his sceptical friends that this was probably the only way that land could effectively be redistributed. The others agreed with him on the need for land redistribution, but were advocating a more structured and planned method. Dr Mbodza, who was still not sure about the methodology, was softening towards David's position because the more he thought about having a country mansion, the more appealing the idea was to him.

"Have you never thought about owning a farm?" He asked Giles.

"To be honest, no. I just think that it's too much hard work. Anyway, even if I wanted one, the thing to do would be to save up and buy one, but as I don't want one…" He left the sentence hanging and shrugged his shoulders.

"The monies that my company pays some of the farmers is quite staggering," Ivan Mbodza could have been speaking to himself.

"Exactly my point!" David was quite animated, "you guys don't seem to realise how much money there is in farming."

"You can have it. I would not enjoy making the money on the back of someone else's suffering…"

"Who says they will suffer? These people have millions stashed away in foreign bank accounts…" David was stopped by laughter from the others.

"Are you sure you are not talking about our leaders?" Giles was almost choking with laughter.

David got back to his office to find the document that Praxedes had been typing on his desk. He quickly read through it and was impressed that there were very few mistakes. His hand writing was not particularly legible and very few people could read it as well as Praxedes seemed to have done. He made the few necessary corrections and gave it back to his PA thinking how much easier it had become to make corrections on documents since computers were introduced to government departments. He thought back to the days of typing pools where he had sometimes had to send documents back several times because they would have come back with new mistakes each time he took them back. He remembered the time when, in exasperation, he had gone to the typing pool to shout at whoever was responsible, only to find out that a different person had typed his document – a letter with no more than ten lines – each time he took it back! Their explanation that the mistakes were only because they were in conversation did nothing to lighten his anger and he had shouted at all of them because they seemed to think that having their private conversations was more important than getting their work right. They had stared back at him incredulously, as if what he was saying was the most ridiculous thing they had ever heard!

"Are we supposed to work in silence?" The typing pool supervisor had asked defiantly, "we are not slaves. We are in independent Zimbabwe, you know!"

David smiled to himself as he thought about how people seemed to believe that independence meant that they did not have to work as hard as before; that insisting on certain standards of work was considered a relic of colonial days! Little did they realise that their attitudes were the legacy of colonialism; because in segregated Rhodesia, black people were treated like children, who were not in any way involved in any decision making, thus most of them did not understand the relationship between the work they put in and the monies that they earned.

As he waited for Praxedes to finish with the corrections, he went through the plan he was going to present to the minister in his head. He was quite pleased with himself because the plan took care of the redistribution to the majority, who would only want small pieces of land, but also left a sizeable number of commercial farmers, including white farmers, in place. Most people, he reasoned, were quite happy to work in the cities and only farm for their own consumption. The commercial farms were to be given only to those who not only had the resources, but also showed a keen interest in farming. He was not sure yet how these could be identified but he was sure that by the time they called for applications, a plan would be in place. David was convinced his new minister would be impressed and if he could sell the plan to the president, David's own stock would rise in the eyes of the President!

"All done, sir," Praxedes interrupted his thoughts as she placed a well bound document in front of him. Her stock went up in his eyes. It seemed that she had initiative too – and looks. Not that that would matter to a happily married man like David.

"Thank you, Pracky. I'll go and see the minister now."

To his disappointment, the minister was not in the office.

"What do you mean he is gone for the day," David asked the minister's secretary, "he told me that he wanted this document today!"

"He probably forgot. Leave it with me; I'll make sure he gets it."

David stood there for a while, holding the document limply in his hands. He could not believe what Primrose had just said. Was this another one of those stunts that secretaries liked to pull just to show how important they were? Minister Mangwiro could not have forgotten! This was the most important document of the day, as the minister himself had put it.

"Please, stop playing games. I know that the minister wants this important document today."

"I am not playing games, sir. Minister Mangwiro has gone for the day and he did not say anything about any important document that he was expecting…"

"He told me this morning that he wanted it before the end of the day to present to the president."

"He said nothing to me about any document. He will be here in the morning and I'll make sure it's on his desk…"

"He might want to go through it tonight. Is there no way you can get it to him?"

Primrose, who had moved with Minister Mangwiro from the Department of Education knew her boss well and he was not the kind of man that took work home. By now, he was probably on his third double whiskey and was well on his way to tomorrow's hangover. Yet the man standing in front of her seemed genuinely desperate to get his document to his new boss, and she did not think that it was because he wanted to make an impression.

"Let me try his mobile phone although he normally switches it off when he leaves the office."

She tried a couple of times and got the same message to the effect that his phone was indeed off.

"It is switched off," she said, "what is the important document anyway?"

"It's my suggested land redistribution blue print!"

"Oh, that," she seemed to lose interest, "I'm sure it can wait till morning. Do you honestly think that government will go along with what is happening on the farms?"

"Well," David started, hesitantly, wondering why many people seemed to have forgotten that the same land had been taken from the indigenous people of Zimbabwe by force, "I think that the fact that the president has felt it necessary to effect a Cabinet reshuffle in order to deal with the matter is an indication of the government's seriousness on this. Would you not want some land for you and your husband?"

"We have some land already. My husband's father bought a small farm which we have inherited. You know, the old African Purchase Area farms. We have not really done anything with it and I don't think it would be right to want more land when we have not utilised what we have."

"Would you not like bigger land?" This had given David an idea. The people who had grown up in the African Purchase Areas would surely have some experience of farming, however limited it may have been. If he could encourage them to give up their farms in favour of the bigger, better equipped and more fertile land that the government were acquiring from white farmers, they would form the basis for the new commercial sector that he had in mind.

"What does your husband do," David asked hopefully.

"He is a lawyer, and I don't think he wants to leave that in favour of farming. He sees our plot as somewhere that we could retire to eventually, not as a source of income. We have plans to build a nice home there for our retirement."

"Talk to him, anyway," David thought that someone with a farming background could be persuaded, "he may change his mind. The farms we are talking about would have ready-made homes."

Primrose did not think that her husband could give up land on which he had title in favour of land that could eventually be taken away from them, but decided to keep that to herself.

"I will talk to him," she said as David left her office.

Minister Mangwiro was in Mbare. This was an unusual place for a government minister to be found, Mbare being one of the most densely populated and poorest parts of Harare. Formerly known as Harare African Township, Mbare had changed its name to Mbare High Density Suburb when Salisbury became Harare. It is one of the oldest black residential areas in the city, built next to the largest industrial area so that workers could easily get to work without having to look for transport. Most of the houses are small three and four roomed bungalows with toilets that are not much more than holes in the ground with plumbing so that they can flush. A section of it had what had been built as working men's hostels where men, who came to the city to work, leaving their wives in their rural homes, stayed. The hostels had, since independence, been turned into family accommodation and now housed many more people than originally intended, thus they are grossly overcrowded and the facilities cannot cope with the increased population. Not far from the hostels, is the biggest market and long distance bus terminus in Harare – in the whole of Zimbabwe in fact.

Minister Mangwiro was in the nicer part of Mbare – the Beatrice Road Cottages, so called because they were adjacent to the main road between Harare and Beatrice – a small farming town some fifty kilometres or so South of Harare. He had heard, although he had never bothered to confirm it, that the cottages had originally been built as a prisoner of war camp for Italian prisoners during the Second World War in which the Rhodesias – Northern and Southern – had fought as part of Great Britain. Minister Mangwiro had grown up in an area of Mbare that was called 'National', close to the Beatrice Road Cottages which, when he was a child, were referred to as *'kumatariana'* – where the Italians live. As a teenager, Minister Mangwiro had been a regular patron in 'The Blue Bar', probably the most upmarket drinking establishment in Mbare then.

He was sitting on a stool in the Blue Bar's cocktail lounge. Although he now resided in the formerly whites only Northern Suburbs of Harare, he still felt most comfortable here where most of his childhood friends still lived, and where the woman that was his extramarital affair, Regina, resided. She had given up on any notion that the Minister might leave his wife and marry her, but was quite happy to be seen with him by all her friends and with the financial security that that liaison brought for her and her family, which now included a ten year old son by the minister.

"I didn't expect you today," Regina was playing with his hair, "I thought that you would be busy with your new job." He liked that about her. She never questioned his movements and was only too pleased to accept whatever amounts of time he allocated to her.

"I got bored," he said casually, "my new permanent secretary is an academic who does not seem to understand the meaning of 'revolution'. We are taking farms away from the whites by force and he is presenting me with academic proposals of how we are to go forward!"

"How could he understand? He did not go to war like you did, my love…"

"He thinks that we should have a plan! A revolution does not work like that. Taking the farms is the first part of this stage of our revolution. When all the land belongs to the state, we will then decide on who gets what…"

"Will I get a farm?"

"Of course, of course," he answered quickly, even though Regina had asked the question as a joke, "how can you not get a farm when I am the Minister for Agriculture?"

"Really? My own farm?"

"I just said so, didn't I? Anyway, perm sec Chitende is working on some document that he expects me to read. I'll put my signature on it and present it to the president, but I don't think that even His Excellency is interested in academic arguments at this point!"

"Can I get a farm near Harare? I don't want to be right in the bush. I am not exactly a rural girl, you know."

"Are you even hearing what I am saying?" The minister liked to talk to Regina because she always paid attention to him without asking too many questions. But not today.

"I am listening, my darling, you said you will get me a farm. Now, let's go home before its time for you to go home to your wife. A girl has needs."

They rode in his official Mercedes Benz to her home, a simple cottage in a particularly crowded part of Mbare where the car was familiar to the boys playing football in the street. They ran after it shouting the name of the car – *"bheenzieeee"* – and calling Regina – who was something of a cult hero for bringing such a car into their neighbourhood, by her name.

Minister Mangwiro made his mind up at that point. It would be good to get his concubine out of this neighbourhood and put her on a farm. That way, his visits would be discreet and they could have some private time without the whole neighbourhood speculating about what they were doing. It struck him then that his wife would probably also want a farm.

Chapter 16

Within two weeks, a pattern of invasions was becoming apparent. Hordes of youths would invade a targeted farm and occupy it, ransacking it in the process and taking whatever they could, and asking the farmer to take what he could and leave. Very few farmers complied initially with some barricading themselves in their houses. In many cases, the workers would tend to support their employers in resisting the occupations, although there were cases where the workers were happy to see their bosses harassed for a change. Some of the farmers tried to negotiate or bribe their way out of being occupied and appeared to succeed for a while. State television newscasts were filled with white farmers attending ZIPA rallies in their numbers and being part of the song and dance that accompanied such occasions as well as being seen punching the air in the traditional ZIPA salute.

What also seemed apparent was that those farmers that had openly supported the MFD seemed to be targeted first, which meant that, very quickly, a significant portion of the opposition party's funding dried up. The opposition party themselves were taken by surprise at the speed with which the invasions had spread. Their earlier confidence that ZIPA had pressed the self-destruct button was waning.

"How are the people responding to this situation?" Party President Ts-

varayi asked as his 'shadow' cabinet met to discuss the rapidly changing situation.

"It's hard to say," Peter Mlilo answered cautiously. "It seems that the
prospect of getting more land is exciting most people even though, at
this stage, it is not clear how the land will be allocated."

"Do we have a plan of our own – one that would convince the people
that these invasions will ruin the country?" President Tsvarayi was a
worried man.

"It is obvious to anyone with half a brain that this is desperation on the
part of ZIPA…"

"Yet," Party Finance Officer Charles Dube interrupted the Secretary
General, "the invasions are continuing and appear to be gathering
pace and there are vast numbers of rural folk who have moved on to
those farms that have been occupied. All they want is more land. They
are not interested in the country's GDP, balance of payments or FDI.
Unless, in whatever response we have for this crisis, we address the
fact that the people want more land, we may become irrelevant to this
whole equation."

"Are you suggesting, Charles, that we support what ZIPA are doing?"
Secretary General Bodo was incredulous.

"Not tacitly," Charles responded calmly, "I am only suggesting that
perhaps we should not be opposing it as vociferously as we have done
thus far – unless we have a viable alternative. We should be express-
ing an understanding that out of frustration with the slow pace of land
reform, the people have taken matters into their own hands; that the
lawlessness that we are witnessing is a result of ZIPA's inaction. But

we need to put forward a viable plan that will convince the people that if they elect us, we can deliver a more structured, more sustainable land reform."

"What about getting our friends in the developed world to increase the pressure on ZIPA? Surely when the people see that the quality of their lives will suffer as a result of this chaos – increased joblessness as investors flee – they will want to come over to us!" President Tsvarayi thought that this was a good plan.

"And we can get our own people to get involved in the invasions, but with a view to disrupting them, or at least slowing them down," Security Officer George Mlilo supported his president.

"It could work," Charles Dube was still not convinced, "but remember ZIPA are already claiming, with some success, that the bulk of this country's problems emanate from the so called Developed Word, or, to put it more clearly, the West. If the economy worsens and ZIPA can point in that direction, most of our folk will happily accept that, especially now that there is the added incentive of more land for them."

"How about coming up with some solutions, Charles?" Golden Tsvarayi was getting irritated with the young man's continually shooting down any ideas.

"I don't have any ideas of my own, sir, but I can see flaws..."

"Then shut up!" George Mlilo shouted at the young man. But even though they carried on discussing for many more hours – without Charles's participation – they could not come up with a plan that could effectively counter the apparent groundswell of support for the land invasions.

"Who is Themba Ndlovu?" The President of the Republic of Zimbabwe asked as soon as he sat down to chair yet another Cabinet meeting. The name did not immediately register with any of the people round the table so no one ventured to answer the President's question.

"I hear that he is doing some sterling work leading the land reform programme in the Macheke area."

Itai Mugwazo was surprised. He could not understand what the President meant by 'sterling work'. Reports were coming through of some quite serious atrocities being committed not just against the white farmers, but against their workers as well. When the cabinet was called, Itai had hoped that it was to discuss the deteriorating situation on the farms and to stop the quite senseless destruction of property, the cruel beatings that were taking place – indeed there had been some loss of life! The last thing he had expected was to hear that there was some sterling work taking place there.

"I have not heard of Themba Ndlovu, but what work is he doing towards land reform?"

The President glared at Itai, who stared back blankly, unsure why his leader was looking so belligerent.

"I am disappointed in you, Comrade," the President said at length. "I thought that, as one of our cadres who fought in the war of liberation, you would have been taking more interest in this phase of our struggle," he said, turning to the rest of his cabinet, as if he needed their support. He did not. He had already decided on a course of action and that was what he was here to tell his colleagues that they were going to do.

"In 1980," the President started, his voice hardening, "after a protracted armed struggle, we won our independence from the British and their surrogates, the settler regime of Ian Smith and his cohorts. In order to keep within the spirit of the agreement we had signed at Lancaster house, we extended the hand of reconciliation to our erstwhile foes. I made a speech, which was praised as a good example of good statesmanship by the way, in which I asked the whites of this country to join hands with us to develop our country together. In so doing, we allowed our white friends to continue to enjoy the privileges that they had gained unfairly on the blood sweat and tears of the black majority. I sincerely expected that that gesture would be reciprocated in kind."

He paused and looked round the table to assess whether what he was saying was having any impact. A few of his colleagues nodded their heads in agreement, some looked incredulous while others – the majority, he thought, looked confused.

"What have we seen over the last twenty years?" He continued, "they live as though they are not part of this country; they continue to treat our people as second class citizens while they still own all the mines; all the companies, and all the fertile land. Our people have got poorer since independence, while the whites have got richer and fatter. Clearly, my expectations, our expectations of what reconciliation meant are different from theirs. To them, reconciliation means that they are allowed to keep their privileges and status as being above the rest of us. I expected, as I am sure the rest of you did, that they would have come to us with a plan on how the resources of the country could be distributed more evenly. Instead, they, with the aid of their British backers,

266

British controlled financial institutions and intelligence services, have continued to impose conditions on us that entrench their privileges and ensure that our people and our country remains dependant on them. Yet we claim to be an independent, sovereign state!"

In the silence that followed, the President looked round the table once more and took note of those who appeared disinterested. As no one made any contribution, he continued.

"To cap it all, they have now decided to challenge us politically. They have formed an opposition party that they control. The so called Movement for Democracy is nothing more than a puppet of the West and the Rhodesians who want to further their 'Regime Change' agenda. Once again, the British are interfering in the affairs of an independent, sovereign state and are positioning themselves to rule us by proxy!" He brought his fist down onto the table with a little too much force and had to wince and bite his lower lip as the pain shot up his arm. He was quiet for a while as he secretly nursed his aching arm under the table. The pain only increased his ire.

"I say these things because some of you," he paused and looked at his colleagues in turn, "some of you have forgotten the sacrifices that were made in order that this nation can take its place proudly in the international family of nations. Some of you appear to believe that the little scraps that you have received by virtue of being in government – or the bribes that you receive from the whites – are enough to betray those comrades who paid the ultimate price."

There was some uncomfortable shifting at the President's mention of bribes. Many of the ministers had thought that they were being discreet and that the president was unaware of the source of some of their now quite considerable wealth.

"I know that some of you believe that because you now play golf with the whites, you are now equal to them," he glanced briefly at Itai Mugwazo once again. "Nothing could be further from the truth," he shuffled his papers until he found the piece he was looking for.

"Fortunately, we have committed comrades like Themba Ndlovu, a man, who, after the end of the war took his place in civil society and has spent the last twenty years quietly tending his family lands in Macheke, not making any demands on the state, happy to live with his memories of the immense contribution he made towards the liberation of his homeland, but ready to make more sacrifices if his country ever needed his services. Indeed we are indebted to such men who remain true to the ideals of our revolution. In the last two weeks, Themba has been instrumental in the occupation of a large number of farms in the Macheke, Marondera, and Hwedza areas and has not asked for a cent from the government or from the party."

Suddenly, as if a light had come on in his head, Itai Mugwazo remembered. He remembered a tall handsome man, slightly older than him but with vastly superior battle experience. He remembered the man who had taken him under his wing when he first arrived at the ZIPA camp in Mozambique; how he had seemed to take particular interest in a scared little boy who missed his mother and wished he had not made the fateful decision to join the war effort. But he remembered something else. On his last visit to Manhowe Township where he had made the speech about taking land back from the whites, Themba had been there! Itai had felt an inexplicable discomfort at being regarded by a dirty, ragged layabout who nonetheless appeared to look down on him with a strange superiority and was apparently unmoved by the excitement that Itai's speech appeared to be generating. He had felt a strange affinity to the man but could not believe that he could have anything in common with one so dirty.

So, that was Themba. What was his part in all this? Itai wondered. Was that some sort of disguise or had he genuinely fallen on hard times. Itai could not believe that that *hobo,* could be any use to anyone, so why was the president speaking so glowingly about him?

"… he has almost single handedly delivered close to twenty farms in that area to us and, while the rest of us have gone soft because of the relative comfort in which we live, Themba remembers the revolutionary methods that we used to win the war, the methods that we should be using now!"

The President paused for a while, then picked up a thick document that had been in front of him from the beginning. He tossed it in the direction of Minister Mangwiro.

"What is that, Comrade Mangwiro?"

"It's the blueprint…"

"Ah! Now we have blue prints, do we? Did we win the war of liberation with blue prints? Need I remind you comrades that we are a revolutionary party? In a revolution, we do not have blue prints. We move! I don't need a theoretical document about what we need to do; I know what we need to do. Do you think that Chief Juru came up with a blue print before he moved onto the Nicholsons farm?"

"Your excellency, you asked for a document…" Minister Mangwiro started.

"I did no such thing. I asked you to tell me how you were going to go about redistributing the land. Our people need more land, period!" He turned to the Minister for Legal Affairs. "How can we legalise this whole process?"

"Well, Comrade President, under current law…"

"I know what the current law says. What I want you to tell me is how can we change it so that all land, and I mean ALL land, belongs to the state?"

"ALL land, sir?"

"Is there a problem?"

"Yes, sir. We could end up in endless court battles as most farmers have freehold title to their land – and we have quite a few black farmers who have bought land, not to mention the former African Purchase Areas where land has been held for several generations…"

"What about urban land?" Housing Minister, Thomas Chikonzo cut in. "Most people in the urban areas own the land on which their houses are built. If all land were to belong to the state, how would we deal with those?"

"Much of the farmland is owned by multinational corporations. The very investors that we are trying to convince that Zimbabwe is a safe destination for their investments. The little investment that we have would leave and there would be no new investment."

"Your excellency," Itai Mugwazo felt more confident, "I can, all of us can understand the very urgent need to share the resources of this country in a manner that reflects the goals of our independence. But the truth is, we are not isolated. We are part of a global community that expects certain behaviours from country States. We have signed investment protection protocols that guarantee that foreign investment will be safe in this country. There must be another way, surely?" Itai could not understand why this discussion was even being held. Zimbabwe had one of the best economies in the region because they upheld the rule of law and adhered to certain economic principles that were necessary for success.

"Comrades," the President spoke with an authority that silenced everyone. "We have slowed down our revolution because we have allowed ourselves to be sidetracked by the so called civilised principles of the British and their friends. As a result, we are the laughing stock of all the developing world. What did we go to war for if we cannot own the very land for which we fought? What is the meaning of our independence if our people continue to wallow in poverty while those who we defeated are getting richer?"

"There is no doubt, sir," Itai Mugwazo tried again, "that we do need to address the imbalances that are a result of our colonial history, but can we afford to destroy our agriculture to do so? In any case, if our white farmers are so bad, how come our brother African States are advertising in our own press that they will take them and give them incentives to go and farm for them?"

"Who is advertising in our press, South Africa?" The President was hearing this for the first time.

"Angola, Mozambique, Zambia..." Itai listed them.

"Even countries as far away as Nigeria and Congo are looking for our farmers."

"They can have them. We will not be held to ransom in our own country. If those countries need the racists to run their agriculture for them, let them have them. We have our own farmers here. We will show them that we can do this without the whites!"

It was clear then to all those round the table, who knew their president well, that no argument would convince their leader to change course. He was not a man to take what he saw as betrayal lightly. The British had betrayed him, and the white farmers had betrayed him. Both had taken his call for reconciliation as a weakness; as stupidity, in fact and he was going to show them who was in charge in this corner of the world.

"Mangwiro," he addressed the Minister for Agriculture, "I want you to start taking applications from farmers who want land. I want land surveyors to start surveying and sub dividing those farms that we have acquired. Legal, start working on a bill to make the acquisitions legal. We will see who has the last laugh on this!"

"Sir," Dr Ruth Moyo had been caught completely unawares, "our present constitution guarantees property rights…"

"Well, change it, Dr Ruth! Do we not have the necessary parliamentary majority? As I have said, I want all land to belong to the state!"

"That could get quite complicated."

"Uncomplicate it, Dr Ruth. When we were in the bush fighting to unseat the usurpers of our land – a task that most of our countrymen

272

thought was complicated, by the way – you were sittings in comfort in London learning the laws of the British. What did they teach you? Now is your chance to participate in the revolution that I keep talking about!"

"But, sir, these people hold title to the land and there are laws – even our own laws – that will support them!"

"Change the laws, change the judges if need be!" The President was almost shouting, "I will not be told by the British, or anyone else, how to run this country. Who tells them how to run Britain."

In this mood, no one dared contradict the President of the Republic.

Chapter 17

Themba was getting frustrated. What was it about this Mr George bloody O'Connor that made him so stubborn? All the other farms that he had invaded had been relatively easy. All he had had to do was come in with his mob, singing, chanting and generally looking menacing and the farmer would, after some minimal resistance and some attempt at negotiating, leave relatively peacefully. A few barricaded themselves inside their homes for a couple of days but not many could put up with drunken mobs playing the rhythmic African drum all night and most of the day. They would lock their homes and leave as if they would be coming back, making sure that all windows were closed and everything was secure. Themba smiled to himself. Little did they know that as soon as they left, he would give the signal for everything to be broken into and for the mobs to help themselves to whatever they could – alcohol, furniture, electrical gadgets (even though most of them had no access to electricity). This was part of the new instructions. The farmer's property had to be destroyed so completely that he would have little, if any desire to come back.

Themba was leaning against a Jacaranda tree just outside Mr O'Connor's rather formidable gate. They had been here for nearly a week and had not been able to break into what appeared a well-fortified homestead. Mr O'Connor's workers appeared well trained and it seemed that they were well prepared for an attack such as this. 'This man was obviously not as comfortable with the new Zimbabwe as the other farmers were', he thought to himself. The little resistance he had come up against thus far had been rather shambolic and the workers very quickly changed sides as they realised just how drastically power had shifted and when they saw that there might be some advantage in aligning themselves with the invaders. There had been the girls as well, of course. After many years of being sneered at by girls, Themba found himself in the unusual position of being able to have any girl he wanted, with or without her consent! By now it was mainly with the girls ascent as the new Themba, suitably clad in new clothes – mostly acquired from white farmers wardrobes – and clearly wielding the power, was a good catch for any girl.

There had been some violence, of course and some farm workers who had tried to defend their employers had had to be beaten up – quite severely in some cases – to get them to understand the importance of what Themba was doing. He thought about the one farmer, a Mr Smith, who had also been severely beaten because of his name. He must have been related to that arch coloniser, Ian Smith! They had even made him watch while they took turns to rape his daughter. Themba felt a huge sense of guilt. The man had cried like a little child! The picture of the man lying on his veranda covered in blood, cuddling his little girl would haunt Themba for a long time. It was all part of the revolution, he told himself.

But Mr O'Connor's farm had been different. They had arrived some six days earlier to find the main farm gate wide open and had rushed in expecting the farmer to have already fled. He was disappointed that they probably had taken everything valuable and there would be very little to loot. When they got to the gate into the main homestead, however, they found it locked and bolted. Themba, with his liberation war background, sensed rather than saw that the house was occupied. Some of his 'men', a collection of ZIPA Youth Brigade members with little or no military training, "converted" farm labourers who had decided, after their own places were invaded, to join what was now being loosely termed the third revolutionary struggle, had started to climb over the fence when he stopped them. Their response was slow and laboured until someone shouted,

"NYOKA!"

The response to the Shona word for Snake was almost comical. People scattered in all directions even before they saw where the snake was – except it was not one snake. Mr O'Connor was a snake collector and he had placed his snakes in a place where they could be released remotely in the event of an attack. Of course the snakes did not all move at the same time so it took a while for Themba to realise that this was Mr O'Connor's first line of defence, by which time most of his "troops" had fled, except for one that had jumped off the fence too hastily and was now struggling to push himself away from the snakes with a sprained ankle. His face was a study in terror. Themba knew that the snakes had not really been provoked and were probably as fearful of the intruders as his men were. He called frantically for them to come back.

"Let's not make any sudden moves," he advised his incapacitated comrade, "the snakes will not attack unless they feel threatened." He was not sure if the man understood as he was shaking so much that

Themba could not tell if the movements he was making were in response to Themba's reassurances or if he was just shaking with terror.

Then he heard the others coming back.

"The farm gate is locked and the fence is electrified," several of them said at the same time. It took Themba a while to get most of his men to calm down enough for him to give instructions, by which time he was facing another problem. It appeared that they were hemmed in with some of the O'Connor farm workers coming from behind his returning comrades. He could not tell how well armed they were but a quick assessment told him that he was probably outnumbered and was faced with a better trained foe than his rag tag collection of hung over wannabe troops. All the movement had scared the snakes and many of them were moving away, in the direction of the main farm house. Themba was pleased. The farm workers were probably as afraid of the snakes as his own troops were thus the threat from that direction would be curtailed for a while. But how was he going to deal with the enemy from behind?

"*Sekuru!*" One of his men appeared to have recognised someone from the other side, "what are you doing here?"

"I work here, remember?"

There were violent hugs and handshakes as the two cousins rejoiced at seeing each other. Themba saw an opportunity.

"You two know each other?" He asked rather unnecessarily.

"Oh, sorry *shefu,* this is my *sekuru.* His father and my mother are brother and sister."

277

"So, he is also my *sekuru,* hey?"

"Of course, of course," Garikai was pleased to be talking so closely to the man they had all come to respect as their leader and boss. He did not mind sharing a cousin with the man who had led them on so many adventures where they had had as much food as they wanted, as many girls as they could use and of course as much booze as they wanted.

"So, sekuru," Themba realised he did not have much time before Mr O'Connor realised what might be happening outside, "why are you fighting your *muzukuru?"*

Trust had worked for Mr O'Connor for only a few months and knew him to be a hard task master. He had joined in the plan to foil the invaders because he believed that he was safeguarding his job.

"You will have no jobs when these people take over," his employer had said on numerous occasions, "we are on the same side and we want to continue farming as we have always done?"

But now, 'these people' included his cousin! What was Garikai doing? Surely he realised that these farm invasions were going nowhere. No black man could farm as well as these whites could...

"Do you realise that we are only trying to take back what was taken from us many years ago?" Themba interrupted his thoughts.

"But Mr O'Connor says..."

"Of course Mr O'Connor would say that," Themba cut in, not wanting to waste much time, "look at his house, look just how well he lives compared to how you live. We want to take our land back so that we too can live like that."

"What do you want me to do?" Trust was nearly convinced.

"Come to our side," his cousin, Garikai cut in, "we are going to take over this farm and you can run it and make all the money that your Mr O'Connor makes now. This is the revor... Relov... This is part of the war of liberation that had remained unfinished! So now we can also call ourselves war vets."

"I'll talk to the others," Trust went over to the other farm workers.

"By the way, sekuru," Themba called after him, "do you know that Themba means Trust? So you and I have the same name really."

"Oh, yes," Trust responded gleefully, "I had not thought of that."

They had gained the trust of those workers that had been left outside the main compound, but here they were, six days later and they still could not get in. Two lions were roaming inside the compound since the second day meaning that they could not even risk a night incursion. There was no telling how many other wild animals Mr O'Connor had up his sleeve. And, of course, there were the snakes!

Themba was startled by an unfamiliar sound; and it seemed to be coming from him. It took him a good few seconds to remember that about a week earlier, Paul Kamera had given him a cellular telephone. It was a gadget he was proud to have but he was under strict instructions to switch it on every Tuesday.

"Only on Tuesday's," Paul had stressed, "I will call you every Tuesday and if I have not called you by two o'clock, switch it off. This is very

279

important so that we can preserve the battery. It is a long life battery but I don't want you fiddling with the phone when I am not going to call you. I am the only one who can call you on that line."

So he had switched it on today because it was Tuesday.

"Hello," he said timidly, still not convinced that he could communicate with someone far away through this thing.

"Themba," Paul's familiar voice came through although it was somewhat intermittent. "I have been trying to call you for a while; how are things your side?"

"Okay," he responded hesitantly, "everything is fine."

"Good, good. You were mentioned in Cabinet yesterday. The President is very impressed with the work you are doing."

"The President?" Themba was not sure what to say.

"Yes, the President. Anyway, how are you dealing with your problems with Mr O'Connor?"

'How does he know', Themba was surprised. He wondered whether it was the cell phone that was keeping tabs on him.

"Everything is okay," he answered, hoping that he was not giving away his concerns. "I understand that he had a plan to hold out until the police arrived, which means that things are probably getting desperate in there. I think that we will try and rush them later today."

"How are you going to deal with the lions?"

The man was surprisingly well informed, Themba thought. Out loud, he said, "there are quite a few of us now with the farm workers who have come to our side. We can find a way of distracting them, I'm sure. But why is the man so stubborn?"

"He is Irish," Paul said.

"Irish?" Themba had never heard that word.

"Yes, from Ireland. They are quite stubborn."

"Britain is an island, isn't it?"

"Yes, but this s another island called Ireland."

"An island called Island?" The pronunciation sounded the same to Themba. "I thought they were all British."

"They are the same people. Just think of them as one of the British tribes," Paul could not think of a better explanation. "Anyway, do what you have to do there. The President is counting on you." He hung up.

Themba called his "inner cabinet." His most trusted lieutenants which now included sekuru Trust. This siege had to end today.

Inside the house, George O'Connor was getting desperate. What had started as a bit of fun had turned into a full scale siege. A confirmed bachelor, George had bought the farm on arrival in Rhodesia some thirty-five years earlier and, like most white farmers, had immediately gone into tobacco farming with some maize grown mainly to feed his workers. He had quickly found the other white farmers around him not to his liking; the Afrikaans speaking ones were a closed group, while the rest, mostly English were, well, English. He had found the African maids – a necessary accessory in these parts – quite adequate for quenching his sexual appetites and had thus not found any reason to marry. His latest, a young twenty-two year old named Nomatter (or the lovely Nomatter, as he liked to refer to her as), had been with him for about two years and he had begun to think of her as his wife. Albeit one that did not argue or back chat and one that he was never seen in public with.

When the news of the invasions first broke, George had, like many others, thought that the police would soon get on top of things and life would return to normal. However, as the invasions appeared to be getting closer and closer to his farm, he had put in a defence plan that he thought would keep the invaders at bay until the police arrived. He had no radio and, unlike most other white farmers, he was not connected to the radio network that others considered so necessary. What he knew of what was happening on the other farms was what his workers told him.

The plan was simple. He had quickly noticed how terrified most Africans were of snakes – which he had started to collect and study soon after his arrival in Africa – and he had moved them, in their cages, to the fence that faced the main road into the farm, with a pulley that could open all the cages at once from inside the house, sure that the sight of so many snakes would be enough to deter the invaders. He had then instructed the other workers to be ready to take their positions in the bush at any sign of trouble, leaving the main gate wide open. They would let the invaders in, then come in from behind them once the invaders were on the farm. For extra insurance, two lions that he had found as Cubs after their mother had been killed by trophy hunters and had brought up as pets, were to be released to roam the yard and look menacing. He still could not understand why people flew thousands of miles just to hunt and kill these magnificent creatures. "Each to his own, Paddy. Each to his own," he had been telling himself over the years.

So confident was George of his plan that inside the house, he only had the lovely Nomatter, her brother, Never and his foreman, Tendai. As a man not too fond of firearms, he only had an old Second World War rifle that he kept on his wall as part of the decoration of his home. He had taken it down and cleaned it and found, after much rummaging, some ammunition for it, still not expecting to use it but thinking that if his other defences did not work, he might just have to point it at the invaders and even let off a round or two for effect.

His plan had sort of worked at first and he had had much fun watching the terrified faces of the invaders at the sight of the snakes and when the lions first appeared. However, six days later, they were still there, having slaughtered one of his cows and raided his grain store. They were in no hurry to go anywhere! He had not expected the siege to last this long, having assumed that the police would very quickly come to his rescue. They had not showed up yet and his hopes were fading that they would.

"Maybe we should just surrender," George verbalised what he had been thinking for a while.

"They'll beat us up!" Nomatter was worried more about being gang raped than any possible beatings but she was not going to say out loud what she dared not think about.

"We'll soon run out of food," George had not really prepared for a siege this long and even the tinned stuff was running out.

"Let me go out and try to talk to them," Tendai, the foreman offered.

"NO!" George and Nomatter said almost simultaneously.

"They already see you as a sell-out and you have heard what they have done to perceived sell outs. Let me go," George was not feeling as confident as he sounded but, somehow, this impasse had to be broken.

"I am not liking this, George," the lovely Nomatter was looking very lovely indeed, to George's eyes at least.

"I'll take a white bed sheet with me. Surely everyone understands the international symbol for surrender," he said feeling even less sure of what he was doing.

"I am still not liking it," Nomatter said resignedly, moving closer to her brother, Never, and holding his hand.

Outside, a decision had been made. They were going to raid the homestead that night, under cover of darkness. They had noted that the lions seemed to retire to their cages at the back of the house at night and as no snakes had been seen for a few days, it was assumed that they had slithered away into the bush from where they had originally come. Themba, who had the only loaded rifle, was to lead the assault in the early hours of the morning. The others would follow right behind him brandishing their empty firearms and making a lot of noise. None of them knew how to handle firearms and it had been Themba's idea that they be given unloaded ones to give the impression that they had more fire power than they actually had.

"Will you have to shoot him?" Sekuru Trust asked excitedly.

"Not unless he looks like he wants to fight. If we are quiet about it, we may catch them before they have time to react. We will just rough them up a bit and call the television and newspaper people to come and take their pictures in the morning."

"What about that Nomatter? She acts like she is a white madam."

"Well, if she is as beautiful as you say she is…" Themba left the sentence unfinished.

"Someone is coming out of the house!" The shout came from one of the men who had been assigned to watch the house. "It's the white man, and he is carrying a gun."

Everyone scrambled into their prearranged positions and watched as the lone white man slowly made his way out of the house. His red mop of unkempt hair and the beard that he had always kept because, as he put it, it made him look like a European explorer in Africa, made him look rather frightening. He held his rifle pointing upwards, with the white pillow case that he had picked up instead of the bed sheet covering its muzzle. The brightness of the sun surprised him a bit and it took him a while to make out the heads of the many man who were lying in the grass outside his home. Many of them appeared to be holding weapons that they were pointing in George's direction. He raised his arms higher, making sure that everyone could see the White cloth that he had at the end of his antiquated rifle. He took another step forward.

"Hey there!" He shouted with a bravado that he did not feel. "Can we talk about his. I am unarm…"

In the stillness of a hot tropical afternoon when even the birds seem to take a break from their constant chattering, a single shot rang out, repeating itself several times as it echoed through the bush. George O'Connor fell forward, his arms still in the raised position of surrender, a bright red spot appearing on his forehead. For a few minutes, the only sound that could be heard was that of a woman screaming. It came from inside the late George O'Connor's former residence.

It was all the news on the next day. Another white farmer who had tried to resist the onslaught of a people out to regain their lost lands had had to be shot. Photos of the gallant heroes who had carried out this act were all over the newspapers and footage of it was on the evening news.

"In our African culture," Chief television reporter Reason Garwe intoned, "the keeping of snakes is only done by witches and wizards. Yet this man, had dozens of deadly poisonous snakes that he kept and had released so that they could bite the invaders. How cruel are these white people?" He picked up a dead black snake' "this is a black mamba," he said holding it to the camera, "one bite from this and you can be dead in minutes." Of course a little research would have told him that the black mamba is not black, and that what he was holding was, In fact, a Cape cobra.

The picture then moved to a shot of two lions being taken away in a trailer towed by a truck from the department of National Parks.

"These ferocious beasts," the reporter went on, "were meant to *mawul* the farm invaders, but thanks to their courage, there has been a successful outcome and the farm is now back where it belongs."

There was also footage of the inside of the house where the farmer and his few trusted servants had resisted the invasion for almost a week.

In the untidy lounge sat the leader of the invasion, his arm around the shoulders of a beautiful young woman who looked like she would rather have been somewhere else. She had spent the night with the man who killed George O'Connor; her George O'Connor, the man who had taken her out of abject poverty and had treated her better than she had been treated by any man – by anyone – in her whole life. The lovely Nomatter could not envisage a future without George.

Chapter 18

David Chitende had had a particularly bad round of golf. It had been a while since he shot a score that was in three figures! It seemed that the harder he tried to correct his swing, the worse he got. As they walked off the course at The Royal, the others were making sympathetic noises but were inwardly laughing at their friend, whose game had been improving in leaps and bounds of late. But even Minister Mike Banga had shot better than David today!

"What's eating you today, partner?" Mike was probably the only one that felt genuinely sympathetic, "you played almost as badly as me."

"If the truth be told, I played worse than you did today; and this was supposed to be some relief from the madness that is my office these days. I should have stayed in the office! It's the land thing. I think that it is getting a bit out of hand."

"'A bit' is an understatement surely," Dr Mbodza joined in the conversation.

"I hear another farmer got killed yesterday," Giles Kamba said.

"That's worrying, and sad of course," David agreed, "but that is not what is bothering me."

They had just finished their regular Wednesday afternoon round and were sitting down to a few drinks before making their separate ways to their respective homes.

"It's the sheer volume of applications. I had no idea that so many of our people are interested in obtaining land; and I am not getting any direction from our political masters on the criteria to be used in allocating the land. All they are interested in is how much they can get for themselves and their families and there doesn't appear to be any thought on what it is we are trying to achieve for our agriculture. Would you believe that my minister has already made it clear that he wants a farm for himself, for his wife and for his mistress? If they all have these expectations, there just isn't enough land to go round."

"I'm sure the excitement will wear off and you will see that only those that have a genuine interest in farming will be left," Giles was sure that this would be the case.

"I don't think so," David was looking thoughtful. "There was a trickle to start with, but it seems that as people realised that the government is serious about this we've had a veritable deluge in the last week!"

"So, what is your problem?" Dr Ivan Mbodza asked as he hailed a waiter, "you've been saying that you need people to go farming and now you have them."

"Not the right kind though. I have had a chance to interview a few of them and they do not have the resources that it would take to get our agriculture going; not if we want to maintain our current levels of production anyway."

"But this is a revolution, David, is it not?" Giles was mocking, "the

289

people need land and land they will get!"

"Be serious, Giles," David chided gently, "there needs to be a way to correct the wrongs of the past and while this is not the best way, it may be the only option we have. Those white farmers have the resources to tie us up in litigation for years while our people get poorer…"

"Or Golden Tsvarayi gets in and puts in policies that will ensure a more sustainable economy and create jobs. I think the numbers that are applying for land are really because there are no jobs to be had, and people are thinking that perhaps getting a free piece of land might help their situations; but if, as you say, many have no resources, they will soon find out that farming is not as easy as they think." Dr Mbodza believed more in the policies enunciated by the MFD.

"Look," responded David, "I know where your sympathies lie, but even if the MFD do get in, they will still need to address the land question, because it will never go away."

"It will, if people have jobs," responded Ivan.

"You know what I think;" Giles came in, "farming in this country has gone way beyond subsistence. We have an agricultural sector that may not be as sophisticated as those in the developed world, but our farms are run as businesses which require not only capital, but the right skills as well. I bet you that most of the people applying have no idea which end of a tractor is which and about how you decide what crops to grow in what region. They will just go and grow maize in inappropriate areas and we will end up with no food!"

"I realise that there will be problems; there are bound to be in this situation. But I believe that we have enough people with the right academic qualifications to be able to learn and acquire the necessary skills quickly. In any case, I believe that there will still be room for subsistence farmers – who can grow enough to feed themselves and thus not want anything from the national grain store. But in order to keep our agricultural sector contributing to the economy as much as it does now, we need skilled commercial farmers. These will be a combination of those white farmers that will be left on their farms and the new black farmers that will have been identified as having the potential to bring the farms back to full production quickly..."

"Oh! Good!" Ivan said sneeringly. "A command economy! Of course you know what has happened to those countries that have tried this...?"

"You listen to too much western propaganda my friend. Other factors have come into play in countries like Russia and China – droughts, embargoes from the West and so on. It has not always been because the policies are wrong."

"But even here in Africa, there have been such policy aberrations. I was talking to an Algerian friend who tells me that the course we are embarking on has been tried in his country..."

"Really...?" Giles interrupted Ivan incredulously.

"Yes. He tells me that they chased away the French colonisers and very quickly turned the country's fortunes from one that exported wheat to Europe to one that is a net importer of the same commodity, even today!"

"It will never happen here," David said unconvincingly, "anyway, Algeria is not really Africa. Those people are almost white!"

"Now you're being racist," Ivan said with good humour, "and showing your ignorance to boot. The same Algerian friend tells me that most Algerians are not of Arabic descent, but come from genuine African tribes whose names he gave me but I cannot remember because it did not seem important at the time. They have tended to be classed as Arabs because they accepted Islam as a religion but they have their own African languages which are not Arabic! In fact, he tells me that there is a tribe that lives in the desert whose people are blacker than us. So black, in fact that they look blue; but have blue eyes."

"You know," Giles had been listening attentively, "I am amazed by Zimbabwean arrogance. How long are we going to go on saying that certain things will 'never happen here', as if we are a special brand of Africans. We said that corruption would never happen here – it did; we said that we would never have a one Party state – we very nearly had; we said that we had a very strong economy that we would look after and grow! Guess what? Our economy is in shambles. Now we are adding to that by trying out things that have failed elsewhere because what happened there will not happen here. Why? Because they did it wrong and we will do it right? Because they were stupid about it and we are so clever?" Giles was quite agitated.

"Perhaps," Mike Banga spoke for the first time in a while, "it is necessary that countries that have a history of being colonised should go through this phase. A phase in which, quite honestly, we are all learning."

As no one said anything for a while because the others were stunned at the admission of ignorance by a politician – they always seemed to have all the answers – Mike went on.

"Do you know that, when we took over the reins of this corporation called Zimbabwe, some of us had never even run a vegetable stall in the market, let alone any organisation that requires the kind of skills that one needs to run a country – at however small a scale?" He paused to look round the table at the others, who were looking bemused. "Look, when we were colonised, we were introduced to a whole new way of living, a whole new way of governance, a whole new system of economics; except we were not really introduced to these systems. The colonisers totally excluded us from everything and treated us like children who were only told what to do without being told why – in fact we were worse than children because if we dared ask why, we got beaten up - a reaction not unlike that of many African parents whose children ask too many questions!"

" Anyway," Minister Banga went on after a long pause, "when at some point we decided that the way we were being governed was wrong and we wanted more say in how our country was run; when we in fact showed our determination to get political emancipation by taking up arms and the whites realised that they would have to be prepared to die for their cause – and not many were – they jumped ship and left us afloat with a crew that had never been on the bridge of a ship before, let alone pilot one."

"Then as we started to flounder," David had immediately understood the analogy, "they stood ashore and laughed. 'Look at them', they said, 'we gave them a ship in good working order and they are headed for the rocks'!"

"And then they took away the life boats; the support systems that we needed in the form of financial support from such organisations as the

IMF, The World Bank and so on. When people are drowning, particularly people who have never learnt how to swim, they thrash about in the water and grab at anything in their bid to survive. If those who are ashore are not willing to assist, they will vent their desperate anger at them and call them all sorts of names, even as they are drowning because they have nothing to lose!"

"Are you suggesting that we have been put in this situation?" Giles asked, not quite believing what he was hearing from the politician. "They did try to assist. We got a lot of aid funds which we abused and when they tried to teach us how to pilot the ship by telling us how to run our economies, we accused them of interference and said we were going to do it our way. What did you expect them to do?"

Mike stood up and went to the bar to get another round of drinks without having to call a waiter. He needed time to think.

"Giles," he said when he came back, "if your child decides, after attaining a certain acceptable age, that he wants to leave home and be independent, would you let him?"

"Of course I would," Giles replied flippantly.

"If," Mike went on, "he begins to flounder, as young people will as they start to experience life outside their parents protection, if he makes mistakes along the rather steep learning curve of life, as most young people will, would you abandon him to the elements?"

"I would not, but I would expect him to listen to my advice."

"And if he does not listen to your advice? Would you abandon him then?"

"We are talking about a country, not a child," Giles was less sure of his position. "We have seen how other countries have floundered by wanting to take the helm before they are ready and we should have learnt from them, surely?"

"Yes," Minister Banga was being very patient, "but if the present Captain does not allow you anywhere near the helm, when are you ever going to be ready. Surely you understand that in such a situation, the only way you are going to learn is to forcibly remove him and teach yourself? And as for us learning from the experiences of others, it is a fact of life that, generally we do not. We only learn from our own experiences. For centuries, parents have been telling their teenage children, 'we've been down this road; we know that it will lead to grief'. Do they listen? Yet when they grow up, they give the same advice to their children who, in turn, ignore them but go on to advise their own progeny. It's the cycle of life."

"Giles," David felt that his point had been enunciated more clearly than he could have ever hoped to explain it himself, "that the farms are being taken is now a *fait accompli*. The farms will be redistributed with or without your consent. Yet, relatively, you have more resources than most of the people who are applying; you have the sort of education that will enable you to quickly grasp the principles of farming; you earn the kind of salary that would enable you to put substantial resources into whatever farming venture you decide to embark on. But you refuse to even consider applying because according to your principles, it is wrong. Think about it at least," David's tone was almost pleading.

"I'll give it some thought," Giles heard himself say, almost as if it was someone else saying it, "now can we have our absolute bloody final drink and go home. It's work in the morning."

As they went to their separate vehicles, Giles had a thought.

"Minister Banga!" He called out, " you do realise that we are not the colonisers biological children. We were sort of adopted without getting the full rights of adopted children; so they can very easily abandon us to our fate when we don't listen to their advice."

"All the more reason," Mike Banga retorted, "why we are thrashing about in desperation!"

They both laughed as they got into their respective cars.

By the next morning, a thought that had been playing in David's mind had begun to take shape. He was going to have to apply some sort of "means test" in the allocation of farms. Those that could show that they had the means would be allocated the bigger farms – which, he had decided, were to be no bigger than five hundred hectares. The rest, he had decided, were to be given small plots with an average size of twenty hectares. That way, as many people as the available land would allow would get some land.

He did not know it then, but Cabinet was, that very morning, going to make a decision that would have a profound effect on agriculture over the next few years.

"We will, through the land bank," the President said to his colleagues, "make money available to our new farmers at low interest rates. That will ensure that our production levels are not affected too much."

"But, Mr President," Itai Mugwazo was incredulous, "our government is very short of funds as it is. Where are we going to get the money to give to our inexperienced farmers?"

"Our Central Bank has a subsidiary that prints money do they not? We will print the money we need …"

"Mr President! Do you realise what that could do to our money supply? Inflation would skyrocket and…" Economic Planning Minister Sam Gumede was unable to complete his sentence as he wilted under the President's stare.

"Do not ever interrupt me like that again," the President pronounced every syllable, "I am not debating this point. I am tired of you people giving me theoretical bookish economics and telling me that this and that cannot be done! When our forefathers were dispossessed of this land, what economic theories were used? I do not want to ever remind you again, comrades, that we are in a revolutionary struggle and as such, we will do whatever it takes to make sure that we take back what belongs to us!"

The silence that followed was indication enough that the President had made his point. When he was in this mood, no one dared speak up; not even to agree with him.

Chapter 19

The next eighteen months saw a change in Zimbabwe's agriculture that no one would have foreseen, and very few would have even considered a possibility. By July, 2000, government appeared to have adopted the rather disorganised land redistribution programme as official policy; announcing that upwards of three thousand farms were to be acquired for resettlement. However, there seems to have been some confusions as the numbers of farms to be acquired kept changing as well as the stated objectives of the process. Retroactive legislation which appears to have been specifically designed to legalise processes that had been illegal was enacted and passed quickly.

In June 2001 for example, The Rural Land Occupiers (Protection from eviction) Act was passed and a few months later, the President, using his rather extensive but ill defined "Presidential Powers," amended the Land Acquisition Act, retroactively stating that any land that had been acquired by any government authority would have its ownership transferred immediately to the acquiring authority, regardless of any court challenges.

It was David Chitende's duty to keep up with the many changes and ensure that the resettlement process was orderly and fair – or so he thought. Unfortunately, they were many other players with an interest in the process and David was not only dealing with avaricious government Ministers and senior government officials who wanted the best farms for themselves and their friends and families, he had to satisfy the demands of veterans of the Zimbabwean independents struggle, various ruling party functionaries at all levels of the party, his own friends and family – who felt that they had certain rights as one of their own was in charge of the process. In reality, of course, David was not in sole charge of the programme. War veteran leaders and the ruling party militias who accompanied them who were leading the farm occupations felt that they had certain rights and in fact decided in some cases, that the land was theirs to allocate.

The forms, which David had so carefully designed for the purpose were being photocopied and distributed by everyone who felt they had the authority, which meant that sometimes the same piece of land was being allocated to different individuals; the disputes arising from such situations halting any operations that may have been on the farms. The confusion also meant that those who were given the land were unsure whether to start farming or not, especially when the government announced that resettled farmers should not erect any permanent structures on the land allocated to them.

The farmers themselves were in a difficult position. The goalposts for them kept shifting as government's intentions seemed to change every week. The changed legislation meant that, once a farmer got a letter advising them that their farm had been "gazetted," that is, published in the weekly government gazette, which meant that they were listed for resettlement, they had three months to vacate their land. As no one knew when their listing would come, the farmers were unable to plan long term thus operations on most farms came to a halt. The few that continued to farm were often disrupted by invaders who could appear at any time. The realisation that moving onto a white farmer's land was not illegal meant that even villagers could decide to invade the farmer next to them, disrupt his operations and allocate themselves pieces of land. But most of the invasions were being orchestrated by ZIPA functionaries with the apparent collusion of the Police and the army.

The Zimbabwe Commercial Farmers Association, which for many years had held sway over government policy on agriculture found themselves side-lined and completely irrelevant. Their initial response of challenging the government in the courts had been nullified by new legislation. Senior, mostly white, judges, who were perceived as being sympathetic to the farmers cause had mostly "retired" and replaced by younger black counterparts. Too late, the ZCFA tried to engage government with a view to voluntarily offering some land for resettlement. But the government and its sympathisers saw little value in that engagement as taking the farms forcibly showed the general population that ZIPA was a powerful force that could take land from white people! The electoral advantage of such a position was not lost on the ruling party's spin doctors.

"I don't understand why they are in such a hurry," David could have been speaking to himself.

"Who?" Dr Mbodza was just finishing his favourite lunch of sadza and steak and was looking around to see who was leaving in a hurry.

"The government, well, ZIPA in fact. They have completely disrupted agriculture and I am not sure how long it will take us to recover."

"I suppose their reasoning is that once the process is started, it should be completed as soon as possible so that things can get back to normal quickly," Dr Mbodza had recently been allocated a large piece of land complete with a beautiful modern farmhouse, a large dam and all the irrigation infrastructure he would need and he could not wait for the farmer to leave and for him to take over and start farming. The three months' notice that the farmer had been given meant that there would not be enough time for the farmer to harvest his wheat crop and Ivan could see himself inheriting the crop, selling it and having enough capital for the next crop.

"But at what cost?" Giles was still not sold on the idea of taking over farms in this manner. "Have you been out in the country lately? There is nothing in the fields! Areas which would now be preparing for the next rains are completely idle and if we have another bad rainy season..." He left the sentence unfinished.

"All temporary my dear fellow, all temporary," Ivan Mbodza was almost convinced of this. "In a few years, we will have taken over and will be producing as much, in fact more than the whites did. I have plans to double or even triple the production on my farm."

"I'm not so sure," David was looking worried, "farming is very capital intensive and I am not convinced that we have the capacity to..."

"The banks will lend us the money, surely. The whites were so successful because of the support they got from the banks."

"Yes," David responded, "but the whites had title deeds to their farms and the banks could take that as security. At the moment, none of the resettled farmers are sure how long they will be allowed to stay. Do you think that the banks will take your word; the word of an inexperienced farmer who is still learning the ropes?"

"Well, the farm workers will still be there and they have the experience and knowledge that they gained by working with the farmers."

"I don't believe you, Ivan," Giles was laughing, "you think that you will just walk in and the farm workers will accept you? Many of them have seen their employers of many years harassed and beaten up. Many have themselves been beaten up. Why would they want to work with you, the symbol of their harassment?"

"In any case," David added, "they too want to be allocated land. They'll be off working on their own plots."

"But if everyone gets land, who will do the work," Ivan could not believe this!

"Just kidding. There isn't enough land to go round anyway." David had seriously been thinking about this. It had seemed to him that the current process was going to end up with everyone a land owner; but he had only just realised that there could not possibly be enough land to give to everyone who wanted it.

"Anyway," he went on, addressing Giles directly, "good farms are running out fast, my friend. Are you sure you don't want one? I can give you an application form now and within days, I'm sure we can find a suitable piece of land for you."

"David," Giles felt uncomfortable about the whole thing, "much as I would want to try my hand at farming, I do not believe that it is morally right for us to take the land from the whites in this manner.

302

They have put their whole lives into developing those farms. How can anyone feel comfortable about just walking in and taking away their livelihood," he snapped his fingers, "just like that?"

"When you see what comes with the farm," Dr Mbodza said, picking at his teeth with a tooth pick, "you will not feel any remorse. After all, they came to us and forcibly took that land. How do you think our grandparents felt about that. These developments that they have made will go some way to compensating us for the years of virtual slavery in our own country!"

"Anyway, Giles," David said, producing a form from his briefcase, "just take a look at this form and, in your own time, fill it in. I'm sure we can still find you a decent piece of land with some infrastructure. Unfortunately, some of the farmers have found ways of removing their equipment from the farms so you may get one that is not as well equipped as the one that Ivan got."

Giles felt even more uncomfortable with this discussion, but took the form anyway. David was not going to let up until he did so he took it. Not even David could force him to fill it in, after all.

Jacques Venter was almost relieved to receive his letter advising him that his farm had been listed for resettlement. It had been a torrid few months for him. All his friend's farms had been invaded but, for some reason that he did not understand, he had been spared that fate. While this had pleased him initially because his home became the safe haven where the farmers could meet and discuss their collective fate, he had, of late, sensed a distancing from the other farmers. They had first started meeting at the Macheke Country Club until that too was invaded and taken over, after which they had taken to meeting at Dudley White's place. Jacques could not believe that his fiends of many years could abandon him for an English man!

The truth was that the other farmers had become suspicious. Why was Ventersberg Farm the only one that was left uninvaded in the area? What deals had Jacques struck with ZIPA? Some of his friends had even begun to question the many meetings that always seemed to be held at the Venters. The legendary hospitality of Mrs Venter had long been forgotten and they now believed that all along, he had been stringing them along while ZIPA were able to monitor their conversations and plans! Every day, he looked towards the farm gate hoping to see a singing, dancing crowd coming towards his home; every day, he ended the day in disappointment as nothing happened. He was lonely; it had been a long time since he had had to spend so much time alone with his wife and their conversations had become terser than usual, with long periods of silence during which he sat on the verandah drinking, and Cindy busied herself doing whatever she did inside the house. Her cheerful sounding humming was a source of constant irritation for Jacques.

His only "friend" at this time was Jonas, who he could talk at without much response. Jonas, of course was disappointed with the non-arrival of invaders for different reasons altogether. He had thought that the invasions would bring the revenge that he so wanted against his employer who had taken advantage of his wife all those years ago.

"So, Jonas," Jacques had asked a few afternoons earlier, "when is your friend coming?"

"My friend?"

"You do know Themba, don't you? Isn't he the main force behind the invasions."

"Yes, I know him, but I have not seen him for months…"

"Why don't you bloody find him and ask him. Ask him when he is bloody coming to take over my fucking farm." As was usual these days, Jacques was drunk.

Jonas almost felt sorry for his boss. He had heard from the other farm workers how the other white farmers had begun to believe that he was not being invaded because he had a deal with ZIPA. He had seen for himself how his employer was being shunned by people who for many years, had been frequent visitors to Ventersburg; people who had been lavishly entertained by his employer. But every time he looked directly at Jacques sagging stomach and alcohol reddened face, as he did now, Jonas felt an inexplicable rage well up inside him. Why were they not coming for this farm? Was there any truth in the rumours that he was a member of ZIPA? – they had even been suggestions that he was with the intelligence services!

"I brought some letters for you form the Post Office last night. Did you see them?" Jonas was keen to change the subject and to get away from his employer. It had been part of his duties for many years to collect mail from the Venters Post Box at Macheke Post Office and he knew that once his boss got stuck into his letters, Jonas could sneak away and take a rest where he could not be seen. Both Jacques and his wife were taking less and less interest in their home and Jonas had found out that he could get away with doing very little.

"YES!" Jonas heard his employer shout behind him. He continued to walk away wondering what could have so excited his boss. Perhaps he had just won the lottery; not that he needed it, Jonas thought.

"Cindy, CYNTHIA," Jacques shouted excitedly, "it's come!"

"What has?" Cindy showed little enthusiasm for her husband's excitement. 'Another drunken rant', she thought.

"The letter from the Ministry. We've been listed for acquisition!"

"Oh," she could have been talking to a stranger about the lateness of the rains, "is that a good thing, then?"

"Of course it's a good thing…"

"Why?"

"Because, because we can now show our friends that we are all in the same boat!"

"Your friends," she said coldly. "So now you think that YOUR friends, who believe that you are a disgraceful sell out to our race will now see that you are not because you have received a letter from your friends in government. Why were you not invaded? No, Jacques, you are not in the same boat."

"But Cindy, you know that that is not true…"

"Do I? How do I know that?"

Jacques sat down on the bed. Surely his wife knew that he had done nothing wrong? Why was she being so difficult?

"Cindy," he tried again, "you know how I feel about ZIPA and what they have done to this country. You know that there is no way that I could do a deal with those people. I have no idea why my farm has never been invaded; for all I know, they have no idea that we are here."

"I don't know. People do the strangest things when the pressure is on," she believed her husband but just wanted to be sure as she had begun to have her own doubts. There was a certain childish honesty in what he had just said.

"They can't not know that we are here," Cindy went on. "They must have their reasons for not invading us. Perhaps you unknowingly did that Themba a good turn and he decided to pay you back!"

"I have not done these people too many good turns and I would know if I had. I think God has, 'in his infinite wisdom' as Pastor Jones would say, decided to spare us the trouble of finding somewhere else to live. We might have had to go and stay with you parents!"

"Well," Cindy was in good humour, "we have three months to find somewhere and my parents house is still an option."

"I'd rather go to bloody Mozambique," he said as they both laughed together for the first time in many weeks.

"Why not?"

"Why not what?" Jacques had mentioned Mozambique without really thinking and now wondered what his wife was on about.

"Why not Mozambique. I believe that they are very welcoming to us unwanted Zimbabwean whiteys. We could just go and make a fresh start." She was feeling quite excited with the thought of her husband without his other friends. They might even be able to make a fresh start in their marriage!

"I don't know," Jacques was wondering why he had not had the thought himself. Everyone around was talking about relocating somewhere. Why not Mozambique indeed?

"But they don't even speak English in Mozambique…"

"Neither do you," she could not resist teasing him about his Afrikaans brand of English.

"We've got used to the good life here," he said throwing a pillow playfully at her, "you particularly."

"Me?" She stood in front of the mirror and did a twirl to show off her petite figure. "If a stranger were to walk in here, who would they say was having the good life; you or me?"

Jacques looked down at his stomach, which now sat on his knees. How had he let himself get like that? He asked himself, if it was not the good life he had enjoyed in Zimbabwe? He slapped his stomach a couple of times as he got up.

"Time to get rid of this," he said although he was not sure how.

"What about poor Jonas?" Cindy was very fond of her garden boy in spite of appearances to the contrary, "he's been with us for ever!"

"I'm not sure that he'd be interested in relocating. He has his home in Murewa and his wife… Eh.. What's her name again?"

"Sekai," Cynthia said calmly, "and don't you go pretending you don't remember her name. You bedded her enough times."

Jacques was stunned. When he had been caught, he had sworn to her that it had only been the once and in all these years, he had been convinced that she had believed him. His mind was racing. How much did she really know? Why was she bringing that up now when they were about to embark on a new adventure? It was only when he saw that Cindy was smiling that he realised that she had been teasing him. But his moment of hesitation had confirmed to Cindy what she had suspected but had not been able to prove and, quite honestly, would rather not have known.

"So, it was more than the once, then?"

"Cindy, she meant absolutely nothing to me. I was young and curious, yes, curious about what they were like…"

"And once did not satisfy your curiosity?"

"Yes… I mean no I was… I'm sorry Cindy, I should never have done that!"

"Now, let me think about this." Cindy was enjoying herself, "the first time was to satisfy your curiosity, the second time was to confirm that it was indeed as good as you felt the first time, the third time was…?"

"It was not like that Cindy…"

"Tell me what it was like, then, Jacques. I believe that they give quite a ride…"

"She was a virgin and…"

"You deflowered her even! Does Jonas know this? Perhaps we should get him in here and get the poor man out of his misery. He must have wondered all these years why his new bride was not a virgin."

"Cindy please, I am begging you. I have never done anything like that since…"

"How do I know when you hardly touch me. There are plenty other Sekais in the compound…" She stopped and looked at her husband. He looked like a child that had just been caught stealing. In spite of his size, he looked small and shrivelled. "I don't suppose you are capable of much these days," she said sneeringly, "you can't even find it in all that fat!" Cynthia walked out of their bedroom and slammed the door behind her. She went into one of the other bedrooms, slammed the door loudly and locked it behind her. For a good ten minutes, she laughed. She had to be careful not to be heard but she had not had such a good laugh in years. Jacques Venter, former schoolboy rugby captain, son of one of the most prominent Afrikaner families in Zimbabwe – the Venters - custodians of racial purity, had had sex with the help and had enjoyed it! To think that they had been upset that he had married outside the tribe! The swine! "I would never…!" She stopped herself as she felt herself blush. There had been the one time… "aargh but nothing happened," she said out loud to herself. She had been down with the flu and had thus not gone to Marondera on that Wednesday. She had been woken up by loud music, she remembered, and had wondered what had happened. On investigation, she had walked in on Antonio in her kitchen, clad in nothing but his boxer shorts. His back turned, he was completely unaware of her presence and he had continued his gyrations to the loud African music that the staff seemed to love so much. Mesmerised, she had watched his lithe black body move in time with the music and thought how lean and muscular he was – there was no sign of any fat!

Then he had turned round, completely lost in the music, his eyes closed, she had found her eyes drawn to his crotch, which pulsated as though there was a live creature trying to find its way out of there; was he even wearing underwear?

"I am so sorry madam. I thought you had gone out with the boss. I've never done this before. I'll never do it again…" Antonio was kneeling on the floor, hands clasped in front of him as though he was praying.

She had felt her blush deepen. Had he seen where she had been looking?

"Get out of my kitchen!" She had retreated and run upstairs to her bedroom suddenly wishing that Jacques was home; but for a few minutes, she had continued to visualise that body, wondering what it would be like….

"But NOTHING happened," she said in the present.

Jacques was slumped on their bed, almost in tears. He had learnt his lesson with Sekai and had never ever looked at another African girl. Why was this happening to him now? He had lost all his friends and now, he was convinced, he was about to lose Cindy.

"You say it never happened again?" Jacques looked up to see his wife standing by the door just inside their bedroom. She still looked quite angry but also looked as though she had just washed her face, which made him assume that she had been crying.

"No! Never!" He was almost shouting.

"If I find out that you lied to me again…"

"Cindy, I love you, only you." He had not said those words to her in many years and she felt herself melting. But she was not going to let him off that easy.

"Jacques," she said quietly, "this happened many years ago, but if we are to get over it, I need to know the truth. The whole truth. How many times did you sleep, with Sekai?"

"I don't remember…"

"YOU DON'T REMEMBER? Surely you have an idea. Was it a dozen times? A couple of dozen times?"

"Not as many as that."

"Not as many as which? A dozen or a couple of dozen?"

He tried to remember but could not. At the same time he knew that he had to give a realistic figure even if it was not necessarily the correct one.

"I think it was eight times…"

"Eight times! Not nine, not six not ten but eight. Did you keep a diary? Do you have the dates as well?"

"Cindy, this is stupid…"

"Are you calling me stupid?"

Jacques was getting angry. "I slept with Sekai more than twenty years ago, Cindy. It was wrong, it was stupid. I have regretted it ever since. But you wanting me to recall how many times I did what I have already agreed was wrong all those years ago is stupid. What will it achieve except open old wounds?"

Cynthia could see that her husband was getting angry. For a moment, she wondered how he would have reacted if she had been tempted by Antonio's body and he had found out. She felt herself blushing again.

"You're right, it can only open old wounds."

Chapter 20

George Nicholson stood on his veranda and looked across what had once been his farm. He felt sad, yet he felt a certain gratitude. He had developed a very good rapport with Chief Juru over the two years that his farm had been occupied. In turn, the chief had put in a good word for the Nicholsons and while the bulk of their farm had been carved up and given to a few dozen small scale farmers, the Nicholsons had been allowed to keep their homestead and the surrounding ten hectares. It was not ideal, but he was sure that they could do something with it. They had discussed the idea of relocating as so many other farmers were but had decided that they were too old to try to go and start somewhere else. The idea of them asking to be allowed to keep their homestead had been suggested first by Mildred.

"The chief did say, did he not," she said suddenly one afternoon as they sat across each other over a scrabble board, neither of them able to find new words as the game was drawing to a close, "that they were not interested in our home? Do you think they would let us keep it if we asked?"

"I don't know that the chief has a say in what happens now. This is now being controlled by the President's office and they will decide; and if some minister or other decides that they like our house, they will take it."

"I don't think that our ministers will want only ten hectares of land. They will want more substantial land, surely."

"Of course they will. But you know that these new settlers have no security of tenure either. The government has made it clear that they are not to build any permanent structures, which means that they can still be moved on if someone more important wants this land. And now that chief Juru has been allocated another farm and is no longer on this farm, who knows what the authorities might do?"

"YER," Mildred said excitedly putting down her last two letters.

"There is no such word, Mildred," George said, taking them off.

"Look it up in the dictionary," she insisted.

"There is no such word!"

"Look it up."

George had no choice but to get up and go to fetch the dictionary. As he sat back down, Mildred said quietly,

"There's no harm in trying, is there?"

"Not with non-existent words."

"No, I mean trying to speak to the chief. He has not yet moved and you have a good relationship with him. He can only say no."

The next morning, George visited the chief at his "home," the former farm foreman's four roomed cottage. The chief was about to go out to his new farm but was pleased to see George, who he offered a cup of black tea – as there was no longer any milk on the farm, some of the cows that produced the milk having been slaughtered for meat – and a game of draughts. After a few games, all won by the chief although the contests were a lot closer, the chief wanted to leave.

"What brings you to my house so early, George?"

"Well," George started hesitantly, "I believe that you will soon be leaving us, Changamire."

"Yes. They have given me a six hundred hectare farm with a house that is much bigger than yours, so I am moving. But I will not be far away. These people are still under my jurisdiction and you will continue to see me from time to time – until, of course you have to vacate the house."

"About that chief. Mildred and I were wondering whether consideration might be given to us, you know, being allowed to remain in the house."

"I've already said…" The chief started then realised what George was requesting, "oh, you mean being allowed to stay here for good? I don't know, George. Our people can be quite difficult and you may not like them as neighbours."

"We've already had them as neighbours for the last two years and we think we can leave with that, as long as we get some sort of demarcation that says that this space – a couple of hectares around the house maybe – belongs to us."

"You know, of course that I have little say in these things, but I will try.

I will tell them how co-operative you have been and request that you be given ten hectares around the house. It's better than two, isn't it?"

So now George stood on his veranda and surveyed his new estate. The initial elation at being allowed to stay had soon given way to doubt. What could they do with ten hectares. Once again, Mildred had come up trumps.

"Fish ponds," she had said one evening as they were clearing up after supper.

"What about fish ponds?" Gorge inquired not following his wife's line of thought.

"We can build fish ponds in the space we've been allocated."

"And do what exactly with fish ponds?"

"Well, a lot of the dams on the farms are being overfished and soon there will be no fish for the market in the cities. Also, there will still be a significant white population in Zimbabwe even after all this. They need somewhere to go and fish. We can be that somewhere."

"You, Mildred Nicholson, are an amazing woman!" George exclaimed his appreciation. "Why did I not think of that!"

"You know what they say about women being behind successful men."

"So," George went and hugged his wife, "if I want more success, I should have more women, then?"

"That's not even funny, George. The poor women will be starved of sex. You are having trouble satisfying one!"

317

George smiled to himself as he remembered; but his mind as already planning the fish ponds and how they were to be made, stocked with fish and marketed. He could just see their lawn regaining its lost glory under Mildred's careful stewardship; the flowers, children's playgrounds and, of course, families – of all races coming from the city with their picnic baskets to enjoy an afternoon's fishing and family togetherness. They could even put in a couple of lodges, he thought.

George Nicholson was feeling really alive for the first time in two years.

"What do you mean, 'it makes sense'? It cannot make sense! For the last two years, we have been campaigning on the premise that what ZIPA is doing is all wrong!" Golden Tsvarayi was shaking with indignation. His Secretary General had just told him that he had applied for a farm under the fast track land resettlement programme and he had been allocated one thousand hectares in the fertile North East of the country where he was already making plans to grow a large hectarage of tobacco.

"Well," Tonderai Bodo was unrepentant, "the way I see it, the land redistribution is going ahead whether we like it or not. I am a citizen of Zimbabwe and am entitled to benefit from the redistribution as much as the next man. Why should I not apply...?"

"Because, as a party, we have agreed that we will not support ZIPA on this one. You have just provided them with a huge propaganda coup and believe me, they will take advantage of it!"

"Look, Golden," Tonderai had a habit of calling his president by his

318

first name just to remind him that he did not really feel like he was his superior, "it is very clear that the majority of the people in our country want more land and ZIPA are giving it to them. Perhaps we should be rethinking our strategy somewhat."

"And recant on everything we have been saying for two years?"

"Not necessarily," George Mlilo had been quiet for a while, afraid to speak up because he too had applied for land although he was still waiting for a response, "we don't have to say anything. If anyone finds out that we have applied, we can always say that we wanted to see if ZIPA would give land to the opposition; that we wanted to prove that the whole exercise was partisan and favoured ZIPA."

"What are you going to say now that they have given it to you? Refuse to take it? Don't tell me you also applied, George?"

"Well, yes," George looked almost embarrassed, "I just thought that it was too good an opportunity to miss."

"Don't worry about anyone 'finding out' that you guys have applied for land. ZIPA will make sure that you get the land, then they will have it all over the newspapers! 'EVEN THE MFD SUPPORTS LAND REFORM'; I can just see the headline. I cannot believe that you guys can be so naïve and stupid!"

"Now, now, Golden," Tonderai Bodo was getting annoyed, "don't you go all righteous on us. Land is a national resource and in our private capacities, we are entitled to get some. Why is that so difficult for you to understand, Golden?"

"We, Tonderai, have become public property. If we hope to take over

319

the reins of government at the next election, we have to show that we are better than ZIPA; that we have a genuine concern for the people of this country. Do you think that you got allocated that land fairly? Many of our members are being denied land simply because they support us. How will it look to those people when they find out that the leaders of the party whose name has caused them to lose out are themselves benefitting from a process from which they are excluded for the simple reason that they happen to agree with the policies enunciated by that party?"

"I can go and withdraw my application," said George Mlilo.

"They will not accept that! This is too good an opportunity for ZIPA. I can see them even beginning to suggest divisions within the MFD, with me cast as the isolated ideologue who cannot see the national vision that my colleagues are seeing."

"So, what do we do?" Tonderai was beginning to see his leader's point.

"Damage control," the Party President was not sure how this could be achieved, "call James Mambara. He is the PR guru and should be able to figure something out. He will have to do some work for the money we pay him for a change. He's had it too easy over the last few months because ZIPA have been on the back foot somewhat."

James Mambara was called in and after many hours of deliberations, a statement was released from Hurudza House.

"The Movement for Democracy condemns, in the strongest possible terms, the current haphazard so called 'fast track' land reform process. Once again, ZIPA have shown their complete disregard for the law and for the aspirations of the people of Zimbabwe. We, as the party that champions the strengthening of our democratic institutions, the growth of our economy, and the creation of more jobs for our people are totally against the current process.

However, we do understand that our people have become impatient with the slow pace of land reform under ZIPA; hence the occupation of the Nicholson's' farm in Hwedza by Chief Juru and his people. They could no longer wait for ZIPA to make their minds up whether they wanted land reform or not. Unfortunately, the actions of the Juru people, driven by their genuine desire to reclaim their ancestral lands and to relieve pressure on their overcrowded Communal Land, have been used by ZIPA, as an excuse to embark on the disastrous course that they have taken and are calling the fast track land reform process. It is a process that will destroy our most successful sector to date and will lead to wholesale starvation in the country. We have seen over the last two years, how our agricultural production has plummeted and we are now having to look to import maize from countries to which we used to export.

A major concern for us is the partisan nature of the land allocation system. Many of our members are being denied access to land for the simple reason that they support a political party of their choice as enshrined in our constitution. In many places, particularly in those places where the allocations are being controlled by the so called war veterans – many of whom are clearly not old enough to have participated in the war of liberation (and certainly not in the Second World War) – the holding of a ZIPA party card is what determines whether one gets land or not. Yet we know that a significant section of our population, judging by the results of the last election – which we still believe was rigged – support the Movement For Democracy, the party that has the interests of The whole of Zimbabwe as their guiding light.

It has been decided, therefore, that in order to protect our people, we will participate in the current process, not because we agree with it, but because we believe that there should be some land that is not in the hands of ZIPA, whose stewardship of our country over the last twenty-two years testifies to their incompetence! After all, the land belongs to all Zimbabweans and, in the interest of future generations, we need to guard it jealously as it is a finite resource."

The next day, the statement appeared in all the independent newspapers in the country – but the state run papers and the sate run radio and television stations, the only ones in the country, refused to run it.

The statement from the MFD made his mind up for Giles Kamba. For weeks he had struggled with his conscience. He felt that it was not right for people to take land away from those who had invested in it and developed it over many years; yet the more he listened to his friends, the more he thought that perhaps there was some justification to what was happening. David Chitende particularly would argue passionately about how this process was only reversing injustices of the past – when land was taken from the indigenous people of Zimbabwe forcibly! But more and more, Ivan Mbodza made some sensible academic arguments about how Zimbabwe's independence would be meaningless without the ownership of the most valuable resource, land, which after all was the basis for agriculture, the storage for Zimbabwe's considerable mineral wealth and it was the one piece of earth that gave them all the right to be called Zimbabweans.

"We are called Zimbabweans because there is a small section of God's earth that is called Zimbabwe. It belongs to those of us whose ances-

322

try and heritage are inextricably linked to this piece of the earth," he would argue.

Further, on the previous weekend, Giles had had the opportunity to visit Ivan's newly acquired farm. It was most impressive and Giles could almost imagine himself in a farmhouse like the one Ivan now owned – although he was still not quite convinced that any of the settlers on the "new" farms could really be said to own them. Even his wife, Charity, who to this point had not expressed an opinion on the land question, preferring to go with her husband's position of being against the methods being used to resettle people, expressed a view after the visit to the Mbodza's farm.

"I feel so refreshed after that," she said as they prepared for bed. "I didn't realise that life in the country could be so, so comfortable. It's like living in Borrowdale with a bigger yard   a much bigger yard – and fresher air to breathe."

"Ummm," Giles said, non committally. He too had been thinking just how impressive the Mbodza's farm was, except where his wife was talking about the farmhouse, he had been thinking about the rest of the farm and how well equipped it was. With a good farm manager, he thought, he could have a good go at farming.

"…but Mrs Mbodza could have done better with the house," he heard his wife say, "it looks as though they are in transit. What I could do with a house like that!"

"Perhaps they are in transit," he said, thinking about Ventersburg, the farm that David had shown them on the way back from the Mbodza's. In spite of his well-known reservations, Giles found himself dreaming about living in the Venters' impressive home.

"This one is not yet allocated," David had said, "and if you put in an application quickly, I could make sure that you get it."

"You'll have your chance at Ventersburg," he said to his wife.

Charity could not contain herself. She hugged her husband, jumped up and down on the bed like a child, then sat next to her husband, breathlessly.

"You mean you WILL apply for it? Oh, Giles, you would make me sooo happy," she so wanted to make love to the man.

"Let us just say," Giles, whose reservations still gnawed at his conscience, was still unsure what he was going to do, "that I am thinking about it."

Now, as he sat at his desk, the application form duly completed, his reservations came back again. He had seen the Venters when they visited Ventersburg. They seemed like a nice couple and even welcomed them into their home and offered them a cup of tea. Yet as he recalled their faces, it seemed to Giles that they had been going through the motions, more resigned to their fate over which they had lost control. The care with which their home had been kept clearly showed how committed they had been to it. What was going to happen to them? He kept asking himself without getting a satisfactory answer. Could he move into their home and enjoy it knowing that the people who had built this from scratch had had to vacate it because they were forced to?

Giles hesitated. He had been going to take his form to David that afternoon. Instead, he put it in his desk drawer, which he locked, and decided to sleep over it one more night.

On the following afternoon, after another evening of debating with his wife, who was, by now, completely sold on the idea and could not believe that her husband was still hesitating, he took the form in to David.

"I was expecting you yesterday, my friend," David said as he stood to greet Giles.

"I got busy and before I knew it, it was five o'clock and I thought it was a bit late to come to you..."

"You could have telephoned, even in the evening," David chided gently as he went over his friend's form, "but this looks fine, we should be able to allocate you a farm soon."

"Ventersburg, right," Giles was confident.

"Well," David could see how eager his friend was on Ventersburg, which he really had wanted for Giles, but they both had been overtaken by events, "it seems that yesterday morning, our Minister Mangwiro visited Ventersburg and has decided that he wants it."

"I thought Mangwiro had already been allocated a farm!"

"Yes, but apparently, Ventersburg is better and he wants it."

"Can he do that?" Giles was incredulous.

"Don't act like you don't understand our political masters, Giles. They make the rules along the way and if he decides that he wants a farm, he will get it."

Giles was disappointed, of course. He had already been seeing himself as the new 'Lord of Ventersburg'. Charity would be devastated! The previous evening, she had even been thinking up names for what she already considered their new farm and had finally settled on *"Pamuzinda pa G & C."* How was he going to tell her that they had lost their dream farm? Then he had an idea.

"So, we can take over the one that Minister Mangwiro is vacating, then?"

"Not quite," David looked uncomfortable, "he is not vacating the other farm…"

"I thought it's supposed to be one man, one farm!" Giles was almost shouting, "how can he keep two farms?"

"He is not. He is keeping the other one for his teenage son."

"I don't believe this!" Giles was nearly frothing at the mouth, "I am a senior civil servant who needs land but I cannot get it because a minister's teenage son takes precedence over me?"

"You did hesitate somewhat Giles and land has been going fast. I think I may have found something for you, though," David took out a map of the area which he spread over his ample desk.

"As you can see, right next to Ventersburg is another farm that is just as big. The same river that runs through Ventersburg, runs through this farm and, as you can see, just as is the case with Ventersburg, the river that runs past the homestead has been dammed so that it creates a quite

326

scenic view from the house across the *vlei*."

Giles was getting quite excited again.

"I'll take it," he said.

"Unfortunately," David said quietly, "this is one of the farms that were occupied very early when this phase of the land reform programme started. In other words, it has been occupied by invaders and war veterans for two years and is, as a result quite run down. The potential is great, though."

"How bad can it be? I'll take it anyway."

A couple of days later, Giles and a very excited Charity, accompanied by David Chitende, visited what was once Jack van Breda's farm. But nothing they had heard had prepared them for the level of destruction they found on this once thriving commercial farm. Charity was almost in tears.

Most of the Windows on the double storey hours were broken, the lawn, which looked like it had once been well cared for was overgrown, flower pots that Charity would have 'killed' for were either broken or discarded all over the grounds. Giles looked around with utter disbelief. How was it possible that a home that looked like it had once been the pride and joy of its owners be destroyed so thoroughly? And what was the tractor doing in the middle of the lake? That was just the outside.

Inside, they were met by a mixture of strong smells - human waste, cooking, smoke, tobacco – and it was a hive of activity. Pregnant mothers, nursing mothers, mothers with little toddlers all busied themselves preparing meals for their families on open fires which seemed every-where, no withstanding the fact that the floors were all parquet! There was no furniture whatsoever, apart from a few cardboard boxes that served as tables, storage cupboards and so on. It seemed that they had decided that the large lounge and dining room would be the communal kitchen where each family had its own piece of floor that served as a kitchen. The other rooms had been allocated to the different families as bedrooms come living rooms, the size of each family's living space indicative of their status in the communal household.

Charity made the mistake of opening the door to one of the toilets. She immediately went outside to vomit and refused to come back into the house. There had been no running water for months, but the residents – some of them at least – had continued to use the toilets! The rest, of course had resorted to using the surrounding bush. Thankfully, Charity did not venture out any further that their car, into which she retired in desperate disappointment. Giles and David went on upstairs which was an elevated version of what was on the ground floor.

Charity could thus not believe it when her husband, on returning to the car announced:

"We'll take it."

That evening, they had a heated discussion on the subject..

"I don't believe you, Giles. How could you accept that, that, rubbish pit as our new home. Surely they will be other, better farms which David can allocate to you?"

"They might be," Giles responded calmly, aware of his wife's deep disappointment, "but David tells me that most of the good ones are taken and any really great ones are wanted by the politicians, who, by the way now include those from the opposition MFD..."

"NOOOO!" Charity found this hard to believe, "the MFD are opposed to this method of land reform..."

"So were we," Giles reminded his wife. "I think that, once again, ZIPA has found a way of getting people behind them even against their wills! Who does not want free land, which promises so much?"

"But, Giles, that place is worse that a pig sty. Who is going to clean those toilets? Certainly not me and I do not see you doing that particular chore."

"I think that you should try and look beyond the dirt. Try and imagine that house cleaned up and painted with all the damage repaired. It is a solid structure that will not only last well beyond our lifetimes, but will look majestic once it is finished. At the moment, we will have little competition for it because most people will react to it with the revulsion that you felt. It means that we are unlikely to be competing with the big guns who can have any farm they want."

"Still, those toilets..."

"We will hire people to clean those. It will be great, you will see. In any case, it gives me a certain comfort to think that I have taken over a rundown farm and fixed it up. Surely you can see that that is not as bad as walking into somewhere like Ventersburg and literally sleeping in the White man's bed linen – more or less."

"What about those people? I heard them talking when I was in the car and they believe that the farm belongs to them because they invaded it. They will resist, I'm sure."

"Well, this is where being uneducated can be a problem. They do not realise that there is a process by which their occupation of the farm needs to be legalised. The people in the Ministry are only working with maps and documents. They have no way of knowing which farm is or is not occupied. I have the offer letter, which for now at least, means that I have the legal right to be on the farm. They have nothing. Anyway, David assures me that they will be offered other, smaller and less developed land for them to go and practice their subsistence farming. That farm is too valuable to be left to peasants."

"And if they resist?" Charity was still not convinced that this was the farm for them.

"Then the police will go in and throw them out. It's as simple as that."

Themba Ndlovu was tired. He had been on the go for nearly two years and, while his earlier exploits had been exciting, not least because of the girls, he was getting bored. He wanted to go back to his new home – his new Home at the van Breda farm which he and his comrades had first occupied. He had visited it periodically and he knew that, while the rest of the house had deteriorated, his room, which he kept locked, was clean and comfortable. One of his girls had the key and made sure that it was swept once a week. When Themba was home, of course, she stayed in the room with him but was not allowed in any other time, except to sweep and tidy up, once a week. He was really looking forward to getting home this time, and he hoped it would be for the final time. He had some ideas on how he was going to reorganise the farm and move some of the people out of the main house – which, quite frankly, they had turned into a pig sty. He would keep two or three families in the main house with him – it was too big for one man after all.

It was a pity about the lovely Nomatter, he thought as he made his way back to Macheke. She was a really pretty girl and that white man had had himself a good woman. But in spite of all his efforts, he had failed to convince her that he could replace her George O'Connor. For weeks, he had stayed with her, had sex with her and showed her off like some sort of trophy. But it had been clear for a long time that she was with him because it was, she felt, necessary for her survival. That she loathed him was clear for anyone to see and while at first this excited Themba because it gave him a sense of power over her, he soon realised that what he wanted most was for her to want him and love him as much as she had wanted and loved George O'Conner. He could never coerce that out of her, he soon realised. So he had given up and let her go. He was caught between wishing her the best and hoping that life without him would be so difficult that she would come looking for him!

He was met at the gate by the rather drab looking Consolata, his almost live in girlfriend, who was saying something about some 'shefu' coming to take their farm.

"What nonsense is this woman? We took over this farm. It's ours!"

"But he had a letter from the government saying that he has been given this farm."

"There must be some mistake," Themba was unworried, "we will sort it out."

"I knew you would," she said linking arms with him, "I bathed today hoping you might come. And I cleaned our room."

He thought about the lovely Nomatter who would have insisted on bathing every day, and even had Themba doing the same. He was finding it difficult to be as enthused with this reunion as Consolata seemed to be.

"I'll join you in the room just now," he said, "let me see what the others have to say."

'The others' included George Magaya, the ZIPA District Youth Chairman who, after a few farm invasions had seemed to lose the appetite for the violence that was a necessary part of evicting white farmers and had gone back to their base at the van Breda farm and was now the de facto leader of the group there.

"Good to see you, Themba," he said insincerely. He hated the fact that Themba was back to take charge of what had become his personal fiefdom over the preceding months, but he was not going to tell Themba that!

"Good to see you too, George," Themba disliked the man who he saw as an opportunist who did everything only for his own good, "what's this I hear about some government big wig wanting to take over our farm?"

"Well, I did not see him myself as I was at Ventersburg trying to concientise the people there about the new land policies, but, yes I believe he had some letter from the Ministry of Lands stating that he had been offered this farm, but the people who were here don't think that he will accept it. His wife did not seem to like it, they said."

Themba knew that George would have gone to Ventersburg for a beer drink – the people there were still employed and would have had some money that he could extort, letting them know that they were beholden to him for their continued employment – but this was not the time to deal with that.

"So, what have we done about it?"

"What can we do? They say that he looks like he has a lot of money. Maybe he can employ us."

"Employ us? We took over the farm so that we can use it ourselves. We don't want some fancy government officer taking it away from us, surely?"

"But if the people at the top have decided that this is the best way, who are we to argue with that? Actually, things are quite tough here. The white man's grain store ran out some months ago and most have been surviving by selling things that we have got from the farm; roof sheets from some of the workers' houses, Window frames, door frames and so on..."

"But, how can you guys do that? We took over this farm so that we can use it. If we start to destroy the property on it, it will soon be unusable. Where is everyone going to live if the workers houses are being destroyed?"

"As I said, things got tough," George was wringing his hands nervously, "some people used to go and do piece work at places like Ventersburg, and a few other farms that are still operating, but now Mr Venter is no more farming. I hear that he has got his eviction letter and is planning to go to Mozambique. We were running out of food!"

"How about growing your own?" Themba was finding this conversation quite depressing.

"With what? We have no seed, no fertiliser, no draught power…"

"There is a tractor still sitting in the lake! With all the manpower you have here, you couldn't retrieve that? And instead of eating all the grain from Mr Van Breda's stores, you could have used some of it for seed. I cannot believe that you guys could have been so thoughtless!"

"We thought that the government was going to give us inputs. In fact they promised to, but we have not seen any yet…"

"Do you know how many people are hoping to get those inputs? They may get to us yet but in the meantime we starve because we cannot do the simplest things. What else have you sold?"

"A few other items that were of no use, but the electricity has been vandalised so now we have no power. I tried to speak to the electricity people but they want thousands of dollars to fix it!"

"What things were of no use on a farm?"

"There were some tyres in the store room at the back. We sold them to that Coloured man, Mr Lawrence, but I understand that he too has received his letter."

Themba sat down feeling very tired. He did not want to ask any more questions because he could see that there was a lot more missing from the farm and George was going to have some stupid explanation for why they had had to sell. He knew that a lot of the stuff would probably have been exchanged for a few mugs of beer or something stupid like that. But how could electricity be vandalised without the resident knowing about it? He asked George.

"We did not know that we had to pay for the electricity and we got disconnected. Anyway, some of the bills were from Mr Van Breda's time. I think the whites took advantage of that and came at night to take away some of the electrical equipment."

"Did you expect Mr Van Breda to come back and pay the electricity bill for a farm from which he was forcibly removed?"

"He used the electricity…"

Themba walked out then. Was it possible that a man with such little common sense could be elected to a powerful party position? What was it that George Magaya had that made his peers feel that he was the right man to lead them? Surely they were youth out there who could have done a better job. It occurred to him then that there was something seriously wrong with the way the ruling party was being run. Why were so many competent people shunning it, leaving the likes of this particular district youth chairman to run things?

As he walked around the farm, he saw that the destruction was a lot worse than he had feared. The plastics had been taken off the greenhouses that Mr van Breda had been building for the export market and some had been used to roof the houses from which roof sheets had been taken; the main tobacco curing shed had been vandalised, although it looked like someone was using it as a bar; virtually every building within sight had no roof – including a brand new storage shed that looked like it had never been used. And then there was the tree cutting. With no electricity, everything was done with firewood and there were clear signs that the once thick forest of msasa trees was getting depleted.

"One thing we are not short of is firewood," Themba had not realised that George Magaya had been following him. "We have so much wood that we do not even miss the electricity!"

Themba just shook his head in despair.

There were women carrying buckets of water and Themba asked them where they were coming from.

"Hello Mr Ndlovu," they all said cheerfully, "it's so good to see you."

"Good to see you too, ladies," he responded, "but where are you coming from with the water?"

"Ventersburg," one of them said, "we steal water from one of the boreholes that they use to water their cattle." She said it like it was the most normal thing to do.

It was not the home coming that he had so looked forward to; and it got worse when he felt his shoe sink into something soft and sticky, and then noticed that the area he was standing in appeared to be some sort of toilet space! Carefully, he walked out of there, avoiding any more close encounters with human faeces and wiping his soiled shoe on the few tufts of grass he could find.

His room at least was clean and he went back there to try and get away from all the destruction around him. But even here, Consolata had decided to create a kitchen in one corner meaning that the walls were all darkened with smoke and all the blankets smelled of smoke. She clearly had ignored his instructions to not use the room in his absence.

"Why did you decide to cook in here?" The question was asked with an even voice but there was no mistaking the anger in it.

"It got so crowded downstairs and people were stealing food whenever you were not in the house. I thought that here I would be able to keep my things safe."

He slapped her hard across the face and then caught her as she fell. He sat her on the bed and walked out to try and find a quiet place to think. He felt sorry that he had slapped her but said nothing to her. She had just been the one person he could hit out at in all the frustration he felt over what the farm had become. He could not understand why some senior government official would want this. No wonder his wife had not appeared too keen!

He needed to speak to Paul Kamera, but the battery on his mobile phone had died several days earlier. He had hoped that when he got 'home', he would have been able to recharge it! But now there was no electricity! Then he thought about his friend, Jonas. If he could get to him, he would not only be able to recharge his phone battery, he could also catch up on what had been happening in his absence.

Jonas was clearly very happy to see his friend, running across the drying lawn as soon as he recognised who the visitor was and enthusiastically pumping Themba's hand up and down several times.

"It is so good to see you my friend. How are you? I heard so much about your exploits with the farm invasions. How come you never invaded this one? Have you got a farm for yourself now and did you find yourself a wife on these white farms? There are some nice women you know…"

Jonas was so excited at seeing Themba that all the questions were coming out in what sounded like one long sentence. He only became quiet when Themba put his hand up as if in protest.

"I am well, my friend, how are you? How are your wife and family?"

"Sekai is well, though getting old," Jonas said laughter in his voice. He really had missed Themba and was happy to see that his friend was clad in very nice clothes, unlike the rags that he was used to seeing him in when they drank together at Manhowe Township. Themba really looked the part of a liberation war hero.

"My children are alright," he went on, "Chenjerai finished his degree but jobs are getting harder and harder to come by. He now has some idea that he wants to go to Agriculture College so that he can take over a farm for himself. Children. You spend all your money educating them and then they have their own minds. I expected him to get a fancy office job where he could wear a tie every day and drive a fancy car, but no, he wants to work the land."

"Perhaps we need people like your son to take over these farms, Judging by what has happened there," he indicated with his thumb over his shoulder, "I don't think that what we have done with these farms is going to end well." Themba was quiet for a few minutes as he looked around the Venter homestead across the lake. He had never been this

338

close before, so he had never seen it in its prime. Still, it looked very neat and well organised.

"I hear your Mr Venter is leaving. Are you guys taking over?"

"Not a chance. Mr Venter himself had said that we could, after he received his letter. He called us all and told us the news. 'Jeremiah', he said to the foreman, 'you have run things here for many years. You have a good team around you. Perhaps you should apply for this farm yourself and continue to work it. I can help you with the application before I leave'." Jonas paused and looked thoughtful for a while. "Of course, no sooner had Mr Venter said that than others began to challenge Jeremiah. 'What was so special about him? What was it he could do that they could not? And before we knew it, meetings were being held with that ZIPA Youth Chairman…'"

"George Magaya," Themba interrupted.

"Yes, him. And suddenly Jeremiah was a sell out who was colluding with the white man and was only being left in charge until Mr Venter could come back!"

"That is also possible, of course," Themba said quietly, "these people can be devious, although I would not put too much faith in anything that George Magaya says. He is a real opportunist who will try to use any situation to his advantage. Anyway, you guys should be grateful that we did not invade you. Have you seen what has happened to van Breda's place?"

"No, I have not seen it first-hand but I have heard many accounts of how the place has been destroyed. Mr Venter is even being very kind to the people there although they don't know it. They come to fetch water from our boreholes and think they are stealing, but Mr Venter actually instructed us to let them. You know, pretend that we do not see them even though they form long queues and there are many loud arguments about queue jumping and so on. 'They have no power', he said, 'where are they going to get water from'?"

"I thought he was supposed to be a hard man, your Mr Venter."

"Well," Jonas had to pick his words carefully. He did not want to let on about what happen between his erstwhile employer and Sekai, "he was quite good to me and my family but, yes, he was, is quite a tough employer, although I did hear that he sometimes took advantage of the black women on the farm."

"You mean sexually take advantage of them? I don't believe it. These white men don't like us very much you know. Although I did come across one Irishman who seems to have been in love with one of our women. Actually lived with her as man and wife, although the other whites apparently did not approve. He was a bit strange, but Mr Venter taking sexual favours from our women? That sounds unlikely."

"Believe me, it was more like forcing himself on them…"

"Raping them, you mean? Why would he do that?"

"I don't know. Curiosity, perhaps." Themba noticed that Jonas seemed to be getting angrier as they spoke on the subject and decided to let it go.

"Anyway, I hear that you may have a new employer coming?"

"Yes," Jonas was glad to move away from the subject of Jacques Venter's sexual exploits, "a government Minister who has already made it clear that he does not want any of the people who worked for Mr Venter to stay because, according to him, we are contaminated by the White man's ways. He has even instructed us to stop the women from your place coming to fetch water, but we will wait until he actually moves onto the farm."

"Many of them are not moving onto the farms. At best, he will put in a competent manager to run this for him, but like most of them, he will probably find a relative, who may or may not have any relevant experience to come and run things. What are you going to do?"

"Well, we still have our home in Murewa. Sekai had some idea that we could also take advantage of this situation and get bigger, better land but the chaos that she found on the farm that she tried to move onto cured her of that notion and she went back home. Now I'm under pressure to dig a well for her."

"You mean in all these years you have not dug a well for you wife. What did she do for water?"

"She walked for many miles to fetch water from the nearest borehole – sunk by some aid organisation – and, do you know that I just accepted it as normal. It did not occur to me that there could be an alternative until she mentioned it as one of the reasons she would want to move? Living here, at the Venter's home where I could get water by simply opening a tap had really spoilt me…"

"No, Jonas, you are just bone lazy!"

They both laughed as they walked arm in arm into Jonas's quarters where Themba could recharge his mobile phone battery.

Chapter 21

Occupation of what had been Jack van Breda's farm ended suddenly one Sunday morning. Themba was still in bed, having got Consolata to clean up his room thoroughly over the previous two weeks and thus was in a relatively clean and comfortable environment. Talk of the government official who was apparently planning to take over the farm had faded as nothing seemed to happen and no one else was showing any interest. Consolata was busying herself in the next room, which Themba had commandeered as a kitchen, making breakfast for Themba although she was starting to worry that the provisions that her man had brought were depleting fast and there seemed no way that they could be replenished.

Themba was thinking about his telephone conversation with Paul Kamera, a few days earlier. The latter had been promising Themba that he was sure land would be made available for the man recognised as the main force behind the land invasions in this area; but now he seemed to have changed his tune.

"Did you apply for land, Themba?"

"What do you mean, 'did I apply'? I was busy chasing the whites off our land and no one told me I needed to apply!"

"Well, it seems that the people in the Ministry only deal with people who applied. I can get a form to you in the next day or two so that we can get your application in."

Themba could not believe what he was hearing. He had been instrumental in getting a significant portion of the land that was being allocated, in this area at least, and he had not been allocated anything! He was even being threatened with eviction on this farm that he had considered his home when he was busy getting land for other people, some of whom had openly opposed the land invasions when they first started!

"Are you saying to me, that there is a chance that I may not get land for myself?"

"Of course not, Themba. But these things have to be done in an orderly fashion and…"

"Why did we not wait for the land to be occupied in an orderly fashion? We faced many days and nights out in the open; we were threatened with guns, with snakes and even wild animals in order that the land that you say belongs to us is returned to its rightful owners! And now you tell me that we have to wait for some orderly process being done by people in air conditioned offices in Harare, who drive air conditioned cars to their air conditioned homes in in Borrow bloody dale in order to get a share of what we were so instrumental in facilitating?"

"This is just a formality, Themba. You, of all people, should get the best land available…"

"This land that I am on now is very good. Why is it being given to someone else?"

Paul himself was feeling quite let down with the way that civil servants in Harare were handling the land redistribution process. Those who occupied the farms that they were now allocating were being treated like they were some sort of malcontents who did not deserve land on the grounds that they neither had the skills nor the resources to do anything meaningful with it. Yet history had shown that even those with resources – apparently – had done very little with the land that they had been allocated over the years. In any case, the President had made an announcement to the effect that money and inputs would be made available to those to whom land had been allocated.

"Themba, I promise you that, once you have filled the form in, I will personally take it to the Ministry and make sure that you get allocated a good piece of land with water and good infrastructure."

"I hear that there are not many of those left as most are being allocated to the top brass; and those that are not yet allocated have been vandalised like this one here. Where are you going to get a good piece of land for me?"

"There is a lot more land than you realise, Themba. We are talking about the whole country…"

"I don't want land in the whole country," Themba was quite emphatic, "I have lived all my life in this area and this is where I want to remain, close to my parents graves."

"I believe that there is still a lot of land in Matebeleland and I'm sure I can organise for you to…"

"I don't even speak that language! In any case, I hear that it's a drought prone area. What am I going to do with land in Matebeleland?"

Paul nearly laughed at the irony. Themba's surname gave him away as one who must have originally come from Matebeleland. Surely he should want to return to his roots; to where his parents must have come from.

"With a name like Ndlovu, you should fit right in. Your father must have left his parents' graves to come and settle in these parts because he saw an opportunity for himself. Now there is an opportunity for you to go back to where your ancestors lived for centuries. Your children will learn the language of your ancestors and things will have been restored to where we were before the white man came."

Now as he lay languidly in his bed, he smiled to himself as he thought about this conversation, and the thought that he might have children. He wondered who it might be that could mother his children. He was not so sure that Consolata was the right woman for him – not as a wife to live with for the rest of his life. His thoughts drifted to the lovely Nomatter. He could just see himself with that woman, building a home on their new piece of land in Matebeleland. But she had sophisticated tastes, that one, he thought. She had been spoiled by that white man and he could not see her agreeing to go and start afresh on what he hoped would be virgin land with few amenities and far away from any shops – most whites had lived in very remote places because they had cars and could drive to wherever they needed to go. He had heard many stories of resettled farmers having to walk distances of up to twenty and thirty kilometres to get to a bus stop – or at least to where they could thumb a lift. No, he could not see the lovely Nomatter agreeing to live like that. In any case, where was she?

Suddenly his thoughts turned to Dorothy, his neighbour in Manhowe.

Had she found someone while he was away? She was a very good home maker and she had been without a man for many years, as far as he could tell. But why was he thinking of her now. They had lived side by side for many years since their relationship had broken up and she had never shown any interest in reviving it. Anyway she had cheated on him, had she not. Or maybe she had lied to the other guy.

"Well," he said to himself as he turned over to try and sleep again, "I will never know."

He was dreaming about a farm invasion where he was leading a group that was attacking farm workers that were trying to resist in defence of their place of employment. The screams of the women were so vivid and sounded so close to his ear... He woke up with a start. There were people screaming indeed and he heard some commotion from outside. Quickly he dressed and went to the window.

Baton wielding policemen were everywhere, swinging their weapons with some abandon and not worried if the victim was a woman – pregnant or not – a child or even the elderly, of which there were quite a few. The younger men, like George Magaya were fleeing the scene and very few of them were being attacked. Themba dressed quickly and ran down the stairs, having checked for Consolata and found her cowering in their kitchen.

Outside he looked around and quickly identified the man who seemed to be in charge – a pot bellied sergeant who appeared to be amused by the mayhem before him.

"What is going on?" Themba asked desperately.

"You people have to move from here. The new owner of this farm wants to move in." The sergeant replied without even turning round.

"But why are you beating the people up?"

"Because we know that you were going to resist. You think that just because you moved illegally onto this farm, it belongs to you. There are people who have been given offer letters and they want to move in and start preparing their farms."

Themba could not believe the viciousness of the police attacks. These were the people that were supposed to uphold the law! Briefly, he thought about the irony that when he and his boys were attacking the white farmers who, according to the law, were the rightful owners of the farms, the police were nowhere to be seen. And for months there had been no talk of any law on the farms; as if the law had been suspended. He ran across the lawn to pick up a little boy that appeared abandoned and was wailing loudly and he came back to the sergeant, holding the baby.

"Do you think that he understands what is going on?" He asked the sergeant.

"Is he your child?" The sergeant asked without so much as a glance towards the child.

"No," Themba could not believe this man, "but he is a child, and they need our protection, they need your protection."

"Our instructions," the sergeant said, "are to remove everybody from this farm by whatever means. We were not told that children have to be treated differently; after all, everybody includes children, does it not."

"But you should be using your common sense, surely." Themba was thinking about how his own crew operated when they were invading farms and realised that his men too had not really been selective, although he himself had tried to avoid beating up little children.

"Who are you to be asking me all these questions," the sergeant turned round to see a well built, smartly dressed man who looked back at him with a quiet authority. He had been about to tell him to start packing and leave, but there was something about this man that scared the sergeant.

"My name is Themba Ndlovu."

The name obviously meant something to the sergeant because his demeanour changed at the mention of Themba Ndlovu.

"Comrade Themba, I did not realise it was you. STOP!" He bellowed at his men.

Almost immediately, the mayhem stopped and calm was restored, except for a few sobs and the cry of little babies.

"Sergeant," Themba approached the law man, "what were your instructions about where these people would go after you have chased them from here?"

"We were never given any such instructions. All I know is that we should remove the people from this farm."

"And what happens to them is none of your business, I suppose? Notwithstanding the fact that these are the people that enabled the new

349

owner to be able to come and take over this farm?"

"I know nothing about that," the sergeant seemed less sure of his position, "I suppose they can always go back to wherever it is that they came from to come here."

So, Themba thought to himself, after two years in which he was instrumental in getting many farms in the area taken away from the whites so that the indigenous people of this country had more land, he was to end up back at Manhowe while those in power, including some who had opposed the land invasions, got themselves bigger and better land! He felt a rush of blood to his head and could have strangled the sergeant had it not been for the baby he was holding. He felt a sense of *déjà vu*. Had he not fought in the war of liberation with everything he had, prepared to die in the belief that his sacrifice was going to be remembered for generations to come? Yet he had ended up in Manhowe Communal lands with nothing and his contribution to the liberation of the country hardly remembered except for a few blanket mentions of "our gallant sons and daughters who fought in the war of liberation" at various times in the year and particularly when elections were imminent.

Was he going back to Manhowe again? Was he going to end up with nothing again?

He could see the bloodied faces of those that had been attacked. They all looked at him with pleading eyes, willing Themba Ndlovu, their leader, to do something; to say something that could secure their future on this farm. Many of them had destroyed their Communal Land huts in the belief that they were moving to better accommodation built with brick and mortar, with cement floors and asbestos sheet roofs.

How could they be expected to go back to the communal lands where they would have to rebuild their miserable lives!

"Let's all move to Ventersburg," George Magaya, the ZIPA District Youth chairman had found his voice after returning from wherever it was he had gone to hide when the attack came. There were a few murmurs that sounded like agreement from a few of the other men.

"We can take over Ventersburg and make sure that we will be ready next time the police come," George was feeling bolder.

"No," Themba said quietly although there was no mistaking the authority in his voice. "A government minister has already been allocated Ventersburg. They will just send more police, the army even, to make sure that we move. I think we have to accept that we have lost. The best we can do is to move back to our homes and I will try to speak to the authorities to see if we can be given other land. George," he turned to the District Youth chairman who recoiled in anticipation of a rollicking, "why don't you take down everyone's details and we can try to make a blanket application for all of us. Sergeant, may I ask that you go to whoever sent you, tell them that we will be out of here within a week, but that they must let us collect whatever we have and go back to our homes in peace."

The sergeant gave the order and he and his men left. The crowd cheered Themba, relieved that he had saved them from further beatings and had at least bought them some time to put their meagre loot from their time on the farm and take it with them. It was something, at least.

Themba looked on, feeling a creeping desperation. Could he deliver on what he had promised these people? Would anyone in government listen to him when he went to plead his case? Would Paul Kamera be willing to help? He felt his desperation waning. He had a new purpose. He was going to make sure that he and the people here with him got some decent land.

Chapter 22

Pastor Jones scanned his congregation. Every week, it seemed to get smaller as more and more farmers lost their land and either moved into the cities or left the country altogether. Those who were left had a collective look of resignation, waiting for the time when their letters would come, advising them that they had three months to vacate their land; places that for years, they had considered their homes and their legacy for their children and their children's children. What could he say to them that would soothe their pain, that would give them some hope of what was to come after their days of farming were over.

Peter Lawrence, Pastor Jones noticed, was sitting on his own, looking particularly desperate. His was in an unenviable position. For years, he had lived in the shadow of his unknown white father, hoping that the fact that he had some white blood in him would make him acceptable to the other white farmers. Now, he was banking on his black heritage and had hoped that his "uncles" would have accepted him as one of their own. Clearly they did not because his farm had been designated for resettlement, which meant that, as far as the government was concerned, he was white. He did not realise at the time, that in fact there had been some black farmers who had lost farms which they had bought.

Pastor Jones continued his visual journey around his congregation. Those who had already received their letters, like Jacques Venter, looked less desperate, resigned to their fates. He had heard that the Venter's had decided to move to Mozambique and had already made contact with the government of that country, who were more than willing to welcome the famed skills of Zimbabwe's white farming community. Those who had not yet received their letters, like Dudley White and a few others still looked hopeful but with a palpable desperation.

The pastor knew that whatever message he had this morning, had to cater for the different expectations of all his congregants.

"Today," he started, "we are going to talk about ownership," he paused and scanned his audience again, unsure how what he was about to say would be received, "of land."

There was some uncomfortable shifting and shuffling as the audience was not sure where this was going.

"Most of us here are feeling desperate because we have lost, or think we are about to lose, our land. Yet those who are taking it away, the Africans of this country, believe that they are only taking back what was theirs and was taken away from them by the colonisers."

Pastor Jones paused and, again, studied his audience. There were looks of incredulity and disbelief. How could a white man be talking like this?

"But if we go back further into history," he went on, "we see that even those who claim historical ownership of this land were not always here; they migrated South from lands further to the North and pushed

354

out the Sun people, popularly known as the Bushmen, who were at that time occupying this land. If one were to ask them where they got that land from, they would probably answer that they found it here!"

Pastor Jones paused as he opened his bible to the relevant page.

"In Genesis one verse one, the bible starts by saying, "In the beginning, God…". In other words, before everything else, there was God. The chapter that I am reading from is, for us who are of this faith, what defines the Genesis – the beginning – of humankind. It goes on to describe how, in six days, God created everything that we see – and sometimes don't see – feel and touch. He created light; He created the sun and the moon and the stars; He created the land by separating the water from the dry land; He created the sky; He created the trees and the grass; He created the animals and the birds and all other living organisms, seen and unseen, and finally, He created Man in his own image." Pastor Jones paused once more and studied his audience. Most of their faces were still blank, but seemed less hostile.

"In other words," he went on, "when the first man, Adam, opened his eyes, the first thing he saw was the face of God, and then, when he looked around, the land. That is why God declares, through his servant, David," Pastor Jones paused again as he looked for the relevant page in his bible, "He declares in Psalms twenty four, verse one:

'The earth is the Lord's, and the fullness thereof; the world and they that dwell therein'.

I am reading from the King James Version. In verse two, it goes on to say;

'For He has founded it upon the seas, and established it upon the

355

floods'."

Pastor Jones looked up again. If what he had just read was making an impression, none of the faces in the audience showed it.

"What am I saying?" He went on, "all this land that we see was created by God before any of us were here. It has been here for centuries and will still be here long after all of us are no more. God only gave us dominion over it so that we can use it and leave it for the generations that follow. We cannot, we should not claim ownership of land; it belongs to God, the creator as we have just read from the bible.

Many of you are moving from this land that I know you love. You are going to other countries as defined by man and you have already been given, or will be given land to use. All of it, here in Zimbabwe, in South Africa, in Zambia, wherever, still belongs to God and we will do well to never forget that fact."

He paged through the bible again.

"Now, I know that there are some here who are in no man's land. You do not know what is going to happen; whether you will be allowed to keep your land or whether like many, you will be asked to leave. Let us remember that God has a promise for us too.

"*Therefore I tell you, do not worry about your life, as to what you will eat or drink',*" he read from Matthew chapter seven of his New International Version of the bible, "'*look at the birds of the air',*" he went on, "'*they do not sow or reap or store away in barns, and yet your Heavenly Father feeds them. Are you not much more valuable than they'?*"

356

He looked directly at Peter Lawrence, as if he was reading the next verse for him exclusively,

"*'Therefore do not worry about tomorrow for tomorrow will worry about itself. Each day has enough trouble of its own',*" he concluded his sermon.

Afterwards, Pastor Jones was standing outside the chapel shaking the hands of his congregation members and saying whatever encouraging words he felt were appropriate for each member, ending each brief conversation with the words "God bless you," when he noticed a group of youths approaching. Leading them was George Magaya, well known ZIPA District Youth Chairman.

"George," he said cheerfully, "you are a bit late, we have just finished our service. But you and your friend are welcome to come and share…"

"We have come to take over this church," George Magaya said simply.

"What do you mean, 'take over' the church?"

"It belongs to us now. It is no longer for whites."

"George, it's a church for God's sake. Everyone is welcome to come and worship here."

"Only whites worship in this church so now we are taking it over and blacks will worship here from now on."

"We have never said that blacks cannot worship here!" Pastor Jones's exasperation was very apparent in his voice.

357

"I don't know that," George sounded defiant, "but I know that only whites ever worship here."

"It belongs to God," Dudley White whispered to the Pastor.

"Another thing, can you prepare to move out of the house you are living in. It's ours now," George said triumphantly.

"Where am I going to go?" Pastor Jones asked the first question that came to his mind.

"I don't know," George's tone was also saying that he didn't care what happened to the Pastor. "Don't you have friends or relatives in Harare who can take you in? In fact, you whites always have more than one home. I'm sure you have another house that you can move to!"

"I don't have another house, George. This is the only home I know!"

"Then you were very stupid, Pastor. How could you not buy a house for yourself? If I had the kind of money that you whites have, I would have bought myself a lot of houses!"

Pastor Jones looked around for support from his congregation members, but there were none left, many of them having decided that they needed to get back to their farms before something like this happened to them. If George and his group were now coming for the church, who knows how many other groups were out there looking for some place to loot. It was becoming clear that not everyone who wanted land was going to get it – and of course there were those whose only interest was to loot what they could from whatever farm they found unoccupied! The only person left, standing some distance away under a large tree, was Peter Lawrence. Pastor Jones turned back to George.

"I suppose, like everyone else, I have three months…"

"One month," George interrupted.

"The government is giving people three months, George!"

"Well, we are not the government and we want to start worshiping at this church one month from today. We will bring in our own pastor!" George had no intention of doing any such thing. He wanted the cottage for himself but if he said that in front of the others, they would all want to move in with him!

Pastor Jones was not sure whether to keep this argument with George going or not. He could not believe that this youngster, one of many that he had helped to finish their schooling by finding donors to help pay their fees – he had in fact paid some of George's fees before a donor was found – could be serious in now wanting to take his home. Because of what he had hitherto thought to be a very strong relationship with many black communities in this area, he had not ever considered that his church might be at risk. He was apolitical; whatever he thought of the various players in the Zimbabwean political arena, Pastor Jones had always kept his opinions to himself, only addressing needs as he saw them without asking any questions as to the political leanings or affiliation of the recipient! So why was he being targeted?

He decided against continuing the conversation with George. He had one month within which to find out if the invasion of his church had been sanctioned by the government or if it was the independent action of a small faction of disgruntled youth. He had met many youths in his travels, who were becoming frustrated because what they had participated in, believing it to be process that would leave them in better positions than they had been, was now being used to reward friends, families and indeed cronies of the powerful while the youth were being left out!

"Alright, George," he said at length, "in exactly one month, the church and the cottage will be empty and you can take it over."

"Good, *M'fundisi,*" George Magaya felt that he had done a reasonable day's work, "now tell me, is there any food in your house? We are hungry."

Pastor Jones could not believe this man. First he comes to tell him that he (the pastor) must vacate his home and now he is asking for food! But it was not in the pastor's nature to fight or argue, so he went into his cottage and brought back leftovers from the night before that he had kept back for his lunch. He did not get many Sunday lunch invitations these days. He also brought some bread, a cordial and a few tins of baked beans that he had in his cupboard.

"Here you are, George," he said with a cheerfulness he did not feel, "you guys go for it."

He then went across to Peter Lawrence who was still waiting in the shade under the big tree.

"What's on your mind, Peter," his voice sounded genuinely concerned.

"I don't know, pastor. At the moment, I feel like the whole world is against me and I really have no one to talk to. Can you spare a few moments for me? I know you've got problems of your own right now and will understand if you are not able..."

"Of course, Peter, come inside my home, well for the moment at least, and we can talk there."

Peter followed the pastor into his cottage, passing George and his crew who were busy trying to open the baked beans cans with a knife that someone had. They walked through the front garden which was full of colour as the pastor generally relaxed by tending his lawn and flower garden, with the occasional help of one or two of the farmers' workers who would have been 'volunteered' for the task by their employers. The cottage was relatively neat although last night's dishes remained unwashed in the sink.

"Excuse the mess," Pastor Jones said as he led the way into a sparsely but tastefully furnished lounge. "Can I get you something to drink?"

"No, thank you, Pastor, I need to get back."

"Okay then. Shoot." The Pastor sat in a more upright chair opposite Peter.

"Do you know that I never knew my father, pastor?"

"No, I didn't," the pastor answered honestly, "but I do know that many coloured folk were the result of 'illegal' liaisons between white man and black women – usually their employees – many of whom had no real choice in the matter."

"I have never really asked because it seems that I was something of an embarrassment to the family so no one was willing to talk about it. The only name that I knew for my father was 'Chikwepa', a nick name he was given by his workers because he always had a pipe in his mouth which he smoked endlessly. A Chikwepa is…"

"I know what a Chikwepa is," Pastor Jones interrupted, "but go on."

"Well, over the years, I have been curious as to whether my father had any other children. I have half-brothers on my mother's side but, as you know, they tend to treat me, not as their brother, but as a more privileged member, well, half member, of the family to whom they can turn for any help. I have always been willing to help, of course, but in my current circumstances, I feel as though they are now distancing themselves from me and are almost celebrating the fact that I have lost my farm."

"It is an unfortunate legacy of our history as a nation that people were compartmentalised to such an extent that those who came from the same womb could not live as brothers and sisters because, according to our laws, they were of different races. Your siblings would have known all their lives, that you were a class above them and while this may have been a source of pride in the community, they still felt that you had been given an unfair advantage over them. Most blacks in the country believe – with some justification – that whites and coloureds have resources, because of the advantages they got before independence, way beyond anything that they can master. So, although you feel your loss, it is possible that your black side of the family believe that you have a fortune stashed away somewhere and you can always fall back on that. After all, whenever there have been financial problems in the family, I suspect that you were the one that came to the rescue."

"Yes of course, but a lot of the time, I helped with money that I did not really have but because I felt that I was in a much better position than they, it was incumbent on me to find the money…"

"So, when there was a funeral in the family, you paid most of the expenses…"

"Yes I did, and when my brothers needed money for *lobola,* I was the one they came to. They also came to me when they had no money to pay for their children's school fees."

"Endless supply of money," the pastor said. "You will get no sympathy from that side of the family because, as far as they are concerned, you must have a lot of money somewhere!"

"Anyway, Pastor," Peter wanted to get back to the reason he wanted to speak with the pastor. "I have done some research and I found out that the man that was known as 'Chikwepa' was, in fact a Mr Maguire who died many years ago but was buried on the farm. I visited his grave some time ago – the farm has since been sold to another white man, a Mr Palmer – and I found out that his first name was Francis. It seems, from talking to people who have been on the farm for many years, some having worked there for several generations, that Mr Maguire had been widowed and his wife's family had taken the children from that marriage as it was felt that a man on his own could not cope with running a farm and looking after children. I would like to find my half siblings and see if I can connect with that side of my family."

Pastor Jones did not say anything for a while. He could see that Lawrence was hurting; had probably only recently had the courage to ask questions that he had not dared ask for many years. But knowing the history of the country, would his half siblings from his father's side accept him as one of their own or was he just setting himself up for more disappointment?

"It will depend," he was choosing his words carefully, "on whether your half siblings were aware of your existence or not. If they did know about you, there is a chance that they may accept you. If not, you may come as a complete shock and they may even wonder why you are only coming forward now."

"I did not know until a few months ago that I had another family. I had always been under the impression that Chikwepa was a bachelor who sired me with the maid and lost interest."

"That is possible too, but he is not here to confirm that he had fathered a younger sibling to his other children. Was he even made aware of your existence?"

"I don't know," Peter was painfully aware that this was one question he should have asked his mother while she was alive, "I honestly don't believe that he was told."

"That makes it even more complicated. Anyway, what is your interest in looking for your other family? They may feel that you probably believe that there is a large inheritance and that you want part of it."

"I have never, ever thought about that. I had nothing to start with and whatever I have achieved, I have worked damn hard for! Why would I want a share of the inheritance of a father I never met? I am just curious about who they are and whether there would be any chemistry that comes from the fact that we shared a father."

"They may believe you," Pastor Jones was not sure what to say.

"I suppose" Peter went on after a while, "I am looking for some sort of inheritance from my father."

"Oh?" Pastor Jones was startled.

"Well, I believe that I can claim British citizenship through ancestry. If I can prove that this Mr Maguire was my father, I could apply for British citizenship and leave this Godforsaken country for ever."

"At your age, Peter, what would you go and do in Britain? I don't know that they want retirees who will be a burden on the state's social security system."

"I am good with my hands, pastor. I can do anything that I put my mind to and I'm sure there would be opportunities for me, even in Britain."

"Are you that disappointed with the land of your birth?"

"Do you know how hard I had to work to get to a point where I could buy a farm? Even then I struggled to buy one because I was neither African, nor European. My black family cannot sympathise with me because I am coloured and therefore are in a better position than they are, and now it seems that my white family does not want to know me either."

"We don't know that they will reject you, but given the history of this country, I would not hold out much hope that you will be accepted just like that."

"Would you return to the country of your birth, Pastor?"

The question took Pastor Jones completely by surprise. This was one proposition he had never even considered. He had always told himself that he would retire in Zimbabwe and live out the rest of his years and be buried in Zimbabwe. The political events of the last two years and George Magaya' actions of that morning had got Pastor Jones rethinking his future.

"Wales? For years I told myself that I would never return to that cold and damp climate. Most of the coal mining towns in South Wales that I grew up in are now ghost towns following the demise of the coal mining industry in the area. What would I go and do?"

"What are you going to do here?" Peter was asking the same question of himself.

"Well," Pastor Jones had not made up his mind but he could see Peter's point, "good luck with finding your family. I just may have to try finding my own family."

"Then maybe we can see each other in Britain. You can carry on as a Pastor, and I can be your handyman."

They both laughed as Peter stood to go. But the seeds had been sown for a relationship that was to carry on beyond Zimbabwe's borders.

At The Royal, another round of golf had just finished. The usual Sunday four ball combination of David Chitende partnering Minister Mike Banga playing against Giles Kamba and Ivan Mbodza were just going to have a couple of drinks before going off earlier than they used to; they had farms to attend to now.

"Just a quick shot of whiskey for me," Giles was thinking about the amount of work he had to do on the farm he had just acquired, "I have a longish drive ahead of me."

"You're taking the farm, then?" David Chitende had thought that his friend might decline because of the poor state that the farm was in.

"Of course I'm taking the farm. It's got great potential," Giles was sounding quite excited.

"Pity about the invaders. I'm afraid that some of them were a bit over enthusiastic and did not really understand what we were trying to do."

"Did anyone explain it to them?" Ivan Mbodza had just paid the waiter, "they probably thought that whatever they invaded would belong to them!"

"I don't mind the state of the farm," Giles said enthusiastically, "at least now I can say I've had to work for the land I have. But it will take a while. I don't really have the kind of money that it will take to bring that farm up to speed. I'll have to take it slowly."

"You might not have to, there is talk that government will make some finance available to new farmers to help them with their initial Capital and working capital requirements," David was feeling quite proud because this was one of the major recommendations he had made, "I'm sure that your farm will qualify for such funding."

"I wouldn't be quite so sure," Minister Banga knew exactly how ZIPA were hoping to capitalise on this funding, "we are looking to finance the new farmers without means. They need it more than you guys who are on fat government salaries…"

"And, of course there is no real political gains from funding us," Giles said sarcastically.

"Exactly! You guys will take our money and then go and vote for the MFD anyway," Mike Banga retorted.

"It's not your money, Mike. That money belongs to the tax payers of the country…"

"Good afternoon gentlemen, did you have a good round?" Ian Howard had just come back in from his own round.

"Yes, thank you Ian. I always have a good round when you are not in our four ball to rob us," Ivan Mbodza said to laughter.

"Well, enjoy gentlemen," Ian said giving a thumbs up to David Chitende, "thanks for the advice, by the way," he said as he walked off.

"What advice was that?" Giles was curious.

"I advised him to apply for a lease on his parents farm…"

"They already hold title to it," said Giles, "why would they want to apply for a lease on something they already own?"

"Because if they don't, they will lose it anyway," Mike Banga said quietly. "But can they do that?" He addressed the question to David.

"Why not? They are Zimbabweans…"

"Yes but we are taking land from them to give to the majority of our people."

"The majority, Mike, will not produce at the levels that these guys can. I think there is room for them to continue farming on land that now belongs to the state. The problem is, most of them are refusing to take up that offer because they say that we have taken the land from them illegally and they are still hoping to get it back," David explained.

"They may be right, of course," Giles came in, "I hear that they are planning to take their case to the International Court of Justice…"

"Good luck to them. I think that if they do that, it will only harden the President's stance. And you know how he is if he feels that he is being snubbed," Minister Banga already knew what the President's response had been to the news that the farmers were going to take that route.

"Ian is a practical young man," David went on, "he has no interest in farming, his parents are old and have no one to leave the farm to – his only other sibling, a sister, has married into one of the richest families in England and is not going to come back here! So, why not secure the farm for as long as his parents live and not worry about what happens after."

"Government policy might change in the meantime and if they are still on the land…," Giles left the statement unfinished. He was still not convinced that what had been done with the land was sustainable and thought that government might have a rethink when they realised just how disastrous their actions had been.

"I don't see that happening," said Mike Banga, "not while the old man is in charge, anyway."

"The MFD might have something to say about that." Like many other people, Giles believed that ZIPA would lose the next election to the MFD, at which time government policy would change. He had no way of knowing just how the move on land had polarised opinions even among the people who would have routinely voted for the opposition.

"I hear that you've had a run in with that Themba *Nshlovu*," Ian Howard said as he passed on his way to the toilet.

"Who is Themba Ndlovu?" Like most black Zimbabweans, there was a tolerance for the way the whites mispronounced African names and Giles immediately knew what Ian was trying to say.

"You have not heard of Themba Nshlovu? He is only the nightmare of every white farmer, I mean every decent farmer in the Marondera, Macheke, Hwedza area."

"I have not heard of him, and no, I have not had a run in with him." Giles had no idea what Ian was talking about.

"I thought he had taken over your farm," Ian insisted.

"There were some malcontents on my farm – vandalised the place badly – but I hear that the police dealt with them and they promised to leave. In fact, I am going there now because I hear that they are leaving and that they should be gone by the time I get there."

"That's alright, then," Ian said walking off.

Giles and his friends left soon afterwards to go to their respective farms.

Chapter 23

Themba Ndlovu stood outside the fence of the Macheke Country Club. It had been a week since the police had come to remove them from the van Breda farm and, true to his word, he had made sure that everyone had moved off the farm. Most had moved back to their original homes having accepted Themba's assurance that he would use his influence to get them resettled officially somewhere else. He was not sure what George Magaya had in mind but whatever it was, he was up to no good. Themba had seen George leave with a group of other youths and he had had the impression that they were on some sort of mission.

Fleetingly, he thought about Consolata, who had reluctantly agreed to go back to her parents' home. She had begun to behave like she was his wife even though there had never been any kind of discussion about their relationship, which had started as a casual physical relationship and, to Themba's mind, was convenient for both of them. He had never regarded her as someone he might one day want to marry. So when the time came for them to leave, he had separated their things, making sure that she had some provisions to take home with her and casually but firmly letting her know that she was going back to her parents.

"But, Themba, I thought you and I were going to be together even after this," her voice was pleading.

"I will send for you as soon as I am settled," he had no intention of doing any such thing but he had felt the need to let her down gently. "I'm not sure what the state of my home is and I may have to live rough for a while…"

"I can live rough with you," she interrupted.

"No!" Themba's voice had hardened, "I will send for you as soon as I can." He had seen her off as she got onto a bus that would take her to Marondera and then on to Goromonzi, where her parents lived. Over the past week, Themba had been moving some of his possessions in small manageable tranches from the van Breda farm to Peter Mberi's store. From there, it would be easy to get someone with an ox-drawn cart to take the stuff to his home in the Nhowe Communal Lands. It was not much; one easy chair, a couple of dining room chairs, a cupboard and some cooking utensils. The bed had proved too heavy so he had taken off the mattress which he had folded and carried by borrowed bicycle to the Mberi Trading Store. Now all he had with him was a flimsy suitcase that he had found in one of the van Breda bedrooms, into which he had crammed as many of the clothes he had acquired as could fit into it, with both him and Consolata having to sit on it to get it closed.

He had stopped outside the Macheke Country Club partly because the suitcase was quite heavy and he needed to rest, but mostly because he had been shocked at the state of the club. Themba had never been inside the club before, but over the years, it was one of the facilities in his hometown of Macheke that he was very proud of. It had always been well tended, it's lawn watered and its colourful flowers that changed with each season always looking, well, colourful. Now as he stood there, he saw a facility in ruins. The cricket ground, where he had sometimes stopped to watch the, mainly white, members of the club playing something that looked quite boring to him, had been turned into a rudimentary soccer pitch with goal posts that did not look like they were the same width and whose crossbars sagged so much in the middle that many a legitimate goal would be disallowed for being over. The club house buildings looked like they were in need of paint – he did not remember ever seeing them in that state.

Themba almost went in to take a closer look but the noise that came from within – a combination of a radio that was playing too loud and conversations that were necessarily loud as the people tried to be heard over the sound of the radio and got louder as the alcohol that they must have been consuming took effect – discouraged him. He decided to walk on.

Had he gone inside, he would have found a club house bereft of any furniture as that had been shared by the leaders of the invasion that took over the club. He would have seen a clubhouse that looked like it never got swept and people in various states of drunkenness sitting on the floor or on paint tins and other improvisations that served as stools, with empty scuds littering the floor. He would have found that one of the invaders had taken over the kitchen and turned it into a bar with the serving hatch as the counter where people could come and buy beer, cigarettes, condoms and some other such accessories that were a necessary part of the entertainment available. He would also have found a clubhouse that only functioned during the day time as all the electrical fittings had been removed and sold off to any willing buyer.

But Themba did not go in. Instead, he picked up his suitcase and started again on the long trudge that would eventually take him to the Mberi Trading Store.

In the late afternoon, Themba finally arrived at his destination only to be greeted by an eerie silence. Had the Mberi Trading Store closed in his absence? He had been so looking forward to meeting some of the characters that frequented this particular establishment but, clearly they had moved elsewhere.

"Is that you, Themba?" the voice startled Themba who had begun to believe that he was the only one there.

"You gave me such a fright," Themba said, clutching his chest, "I thought the place was abandoned."

"Abandoned," Peter said, his voice sounding amused, "how dare you suggest that such a fine establishment could be abandoned? We even have one of our regulars, well, the only regular in fact, inside enjoying a cold beer – it would be cold if our fridge had not packed up last week because of the constant power cuts and attendant power surges that seem to go with the cuts."

"It's a good thing I only drink scuds these days," Jonas had come outside when he heard voices, "there is nothing worse than a warm larger!"

"Jonas, my friend!" Themba was really happy to see Jonas, who seemed to be the only thing in his life that had not changed. "But, Mr Mberi," he addressed the businessman, "what happened? This place used to be busy; everyone from miles around came here for their entertainment, to catch up on local gossip…"

"To attend ZIPA rallies…" Jonas cut in.

"Yes, that. But this is where everyone used to come. Where have they all gone?"

"To the Macheke Country Club," Peter Mberi said. "It's where the whites used to drink and everybody now wants to drink at the smarter establishments to which they could not go to before."

"Have you seen what the Macheke Country Club is looking like now. I passed it on my way here and it is in a really sorry state."

"But it is a symbol; it's our way of saying 'we have taken over your farms, we have taken over your club and we will do with it what we want."

"This is what I don't understand about this whole process. We have taken over working farms and vandalised them, so that now, we cannot use them as the whites did; that club provided somewhere for people to go and relax after a hard day's work. Why can we not keep it for the same purpose?"

"Themba, Themba, Themba," Peter Mberi put his arm round Themba's shoulders, "for someone who fought in the war of liberation, you seem pretty uninformed about the nature of revolutions. Whatever symbolises the privilege that our erstwhile rulers enjoyed must be destroyed thoroughly. We need a fresh start. We will build our own country clubs; we will put in our own electricity which has nothing to do with the colonialists, we will make everything new!"

It was only when Themba looked up into Peter Mberi's face that he saw the amusement in the latter's eyes.

"For a moment there I thought you were serious," he said, laughing.

"You look very well, by the way. These farm invasions agree with you; but what are you doing here? I thought that you of all people would have been given the biggest farm in this area."

"It seems," Themba was getting into the spirit of the conversation, "that while I was busy reclaiming our land from the whites without any restrictions, others were putting together applications to the Ministry of Lands so that they could get offer letters to enable them to occupy those farms that we had liberated. We, on the other hand were so busy liberating that we did not have the time to make applications; in fact no one told us that we needed to apply! We assumed that whatever we liberated was ours. We thought we were spoilt for choice! So now we are putting in our applications and hoping that the farms will not have run out by the time they get to us."

"So, what are you going to do in the meantime?" Jonas wanted to know.

"I don't really know. I suppose I will go back to my home and see what state it is in; do whatever repair work I need to do and wait to hear from Paul Kamera who has promised to make sure that I get a good piece of land. I have also promised my comrades that I will make representations on their behalf to make sure that they too are looked after. I am not really sure how I'm going to do that, though."

"Can I offer you a warm beer; sort of welcome home token?" Peter Mberi went behind the counter to find the beer.

"I have a better idea," Themba said as he reached into one of his pockets, producing a small bottle of cheap brandy – popularly known in these parts as a quarter, because it was a quarter of one litre. He placed the bottle on the counter and invited the others to join him. Peter Mberi quickly brought out a couple of enamel cups and a glass tumbler which he kept for his own use. This time, he offered the tumbler to Themba who, after all was some sort of special guest.

"Whatever happened to that young lady you were seen on television with? I thought she was quite a catch for you." Jonas was only half joking.

"The lovely Nomatter. She is very beautiful. Too good for the likes of you and I." Themba was quiet for a few moments and looked rather pensive. "I think she hung around for some time because she was afraid."

"Afraid of what?" Peter Mberi had not seen that particular news item.

"Afraid of me," Themba said without any show of emotion, "she had just witnessed the killing of her white live in boyfriend and she had good reason to believe that the same fate would befall her if she did not co-operate. But I think that she was afraid most of all of the future. The white man, by all accounts, had looked after her well and she must have wondered what would happen to her without him. But she clearly hated me and I watched her begin to get stronger emotionally, so I decided to let her go. The kind of hatred she had for me could drive her to do something crazy; like poison my food or pour boiling water on me while I slept!"

"Why do you always refer to her as 'the lovely Nomatter'?" Jonas had noticed this from their first meeting at Ventersburg.

"Do I? It must be just a habit I developed subconsciously. Apparently that is what her white boyfriend used to call her; she is lovely anyway."

A second 'quarter' of brandy appeared, having been retrieved from Peter's private stash and they carried on their banter without any interruption except for one customer who came in to buy a box of matches. Themba thought that business must have been very bad and he expressed that thought to Peter Mberi.

"I've had better days," the businessman and District Chairman of ZIPA said, resignedly. "Sometimes I get as many as five customers in a single afternoon." The sarcasm did nothing to cheer him up, though and he carried on in a much more serious voice, "Things have really changed you know. The farm workers were my main customers because they were really the only people in the area with regular incomes. Very few are left in employment now; and as I said earlier, most people now prefer to go and drink at the Country Club."

"The Country Club," Themba said with a sigh, "is not what it used to be."

"Are you ever going to get married, Themba?" Jonas asked suddenly. He had worried about his friend for some time.

"I suppose if the right woman comes along…"

"The right woman is not just going to 'come along', Themba. You have to be actively looking." Jonas was going to give Themba more gems of wisdom then remembered that his Sekai had, in fact, 'come along' while he was not looking.

"What about that neighbour of yours? She comes in here regularly and, as far as I can tell, she remains unattached. You two made a very good couple, once." Peter Mberi had always liked Dorothy and had been disappointed that she and Themba had not got married.

"We were young and innocent..." Themba started then seemed at a loss for words.

"Now you are older and wiser," Jonas was looking directly at Themba and could see that his friend's face got quite animated at the mention of Dorothy.

"I don't know," Themba was not quite sure what, if anything, he felt for Dorothy, "it was a long time ago, and she cheated on me."

"She was young, Themba and you were not exactly the model of faithfulness yourself, were you?" Having raised a subject he had been meaning to raise for some time, Peter was not going to let it go.

"So what do you want me to do?" Themba had just realised that he quite liked Dorothy, but he was a proud man and the thought that she had cheated on him still did not sit comfortably with him.

"Ask her!!" Peter and Jonas spoke at the same time.

"Or I can ask her for you," Jonas offered, timidly.

"No!" Themba said emphatically, "I'll ask her myself."

"Good man!" The effects of the alcohol and the excitement of the moment were evident in Peter's voice and he was slurring his words.

"When are you going to do that?" He asked, pouring himself another drink – or at least trying to; but the second quarter was empty. "Oh, look," he said turning the bottle upside down, "you guys have finished my night cap for the next week!"

"Give us another quarter," Themba offered, producing some coins.

"I don't stock these anymore," replied the entrepreneur, "no one can afford this kind of stuff these days. But I can still offer you some warm larger," he said, placing three bottles on the counter.

"Why not?" Themba opened his bottle with his teeth and took a swig. "It's not too bad, you know," he was also having difficulty pronouncing his words.

Some three hours later, Themba approached his homestead. It had taken him longer than usual because he was very drunk by the time he had left the other two. Peter, who had a room behind his shop, had the shortest distance to go and although he had offered that Themba could stay the night, the later had refused on the grounds that he needed to talk to Dorothy as soon as he could.

"Besides," he said trying to balance himself, "what would our president say if he heard that one of his most gallant fighters was sleeping with another man?" All three had laughed and Themba and Jonas had taken, rather, staggered off in different directions.

It was full moon on a clear sky and he could see his homestead from some distance away. Was he that drunk or had his kitchen, the only room he could use, disappeared? It had. He walked around his derelict homestead and wondered what he was going to do. He had left his suitcase at the Mberi Store because it was too heavy and he had reasoned that the night was warm enough for him to be able to sleep without any blankets; but he had not considered that he might have had to sleep out in the open.

"I know," he said out loud to himself, "I'll go wake Dorothy. She will not let her former lover sleep out in the open, surely."

With the courage of drunkenness, he strode confidently to Dorothy's bedroom hut and knocked on the door.

"Who is it?" A deep, sleepy man's voice enquired from within.

"Shhhh," Themba was saying to himself as he ran off to hide behind a tree. After a few minute, the door opened and a tall, well-built man came out of Dorothy's hut. He yawned and stretched himself, looked around for a little bit and went back into the hut, closing the door behind him.

"She's cheated on me again," Themba said to himself over and over again until he fell into a deep drunken sleep from which he never awoke.

Next morning, local children on their way to school made fun of the drunken man who had obviously sat down with his back against a tree and must have fallen asleep in an awkward position. But, when on their way home after school they found the man still in the same position, they alerted the adults, having realised that he was not responding to anything. Not even when they threw stones at him.

"He's dead," one of them said.

"No, he's not dead, he is just drunk," another said, "dead people don't look like that."

"Yeah?" A third said, "what do they look like, have you seen a dead person before?"

At this point, Tonderai, who had run off to alert the adults came back with a few of them in tow.

"He obviously had one too many," one of the new arrivals said.

"More than one, I'd say," another said, "and I don't think it was ordinary beer. He must have been drinking *kachasu,*" he said referring to an illicit distilled alcohol that seemed to have become more available since independence and was a source of income for the brave as the economy of the country continued to offer little in employment opportunities.

There was a gasp from behind the growing crowd. "It's Themba!" Dorothy said to no one in particular, "Themba Ndlovu. What is he doing here?"

"No. He is too small to be Themba Ndlovu. I've seen Themba on television. He is a lot bigger." A teacher who had come to see what the commotion was about said.

"I know Themba!" Dorothy insisted. "I've been his neighbour for years."

"THE Themba?" A deep man's voice asked, "I thought you said that he was a bum. He is not so bad looking – I mean was not so bad looking. He is not at his best now, but clean him up a little…"

"I never said any such thing *sekuru!* I just said that he had fallen on hard times and life had been difficult for him, but that I hoped that things would improve for him now that he had become a hero again."

"Is that what you said, *muzukuru?* I must have misunderstood," the deep voice said, sounding amused.

"Well, he is dead now. What does it matter what I said?" Dorothy was sounding like she wanted to weep. She did.

The police were called and many hours later, they came to collect Themba's remains, which they placed in a metal coffin and took away in an open truck.

"Amazing," Dorothy said to her uncle as she watched the police vehicle's rear lights disappear into the dusk, "how we say we respect the dead, and yet our police can just throw the body about like a piece of junk."

"It's a difficult job they do," her uncle replied, "and they have to act as if they are unaffected by it. But dealing with death is never easy. It's probably their way of coping with it."

Dorothy looked across at Themba's old homestead and felt a sense of regret. 'If only he had been different; if only...' "But then, he would not have been Themba Ndlovu," she said out loud.

"You really liked him, didn't you?" Her uncle asked.

"Once, perhaps," she said with a chuckle. "Look at his homestead. Even in its derelict state, it was a constant reminder that we had a neighbour called Themba Ndlovu."

"What happened to it? It looks like it was a good home once," her uncle commented.

"What happened to his home is what happened to Themba. Both were neglected." She looked across at the kitchen hut – where it had stood – and wondered what Themba had made of the fact that the only building on his homestead that he had left intact had all but disappeared, having been struck by lightning in a tropical thunderstorm.

"Houses tend to fall apart when they are unoccupied." She said. "My father tried to keep his one hut intact but," she looked down at the ground, "after he died last year; the hut seemed to give up too."

"He was a good man your father," her uncle could see that she was heartbroken, "I'm very sorry that he died so young."

"Yes, well it comes to all of us in the end, and he wasn't that young anyway, he was over sixty!" She took one last glance at what used to be Themba's home. "I think that my father's one big disappointment was that," she hesitated, "that Themba did not come home to tell him about his exploits this time round. He had really enjoyed Themba's stories about the war of liberation; and he was always listening to the news just to hear his name mentioned." She was thinking about one of their last conversations.

'You lost a good man there, my girl', he had said after listening to the news and hearing about the white man who had been killed trying to resist Themba's invaders.

'Father that was a long time ago.'

'I know. But he is still a good man.' He had been quiet for a few minutes and then suddenly sat up and said, 'that boy of yours…'

'What about him?' She had asked.

'Never mind', he had said lying back again.

She had, for some time, wondered whether the time would come when she could tell her son who his real father was. That was never going to happen now.

"It's getting late," her uncle interrupted her thoughts, "I can't really get back tonight. I think I'll stay one more night."

"Won't aunty be worried?" Dorothy liked her uncle and could do with the company that night.

"Well, I think I'll give them one more evening to gossip about me with her sister in law."

The autopsy report when it came, said that Themba had choked on his own vomit, ending speculation that had spread in the village that he had been killed by the authorities because he was taking up the cause of those who had facilitated the land invasions but had ended up without land.

He was buried in a simple ceremony attended by very few people who included Dorothy, Peter Mberi, Jonas Mangwende, George Magaya, his two sisters – who came without their husbands and seemed in something of a hurry to get back – a few others from his time at the van Breda farm, and Themba's neighbours. To the surprise of everyone who knew her, the lovely Nomatter also attended. She seemed unsure what to do and just stood around making the right noises whenever she was spoken to. She stayed long enough to view Themba's remains and left soon after; leading to speculation that she had only come to make sure that indeed it was Themba who had died. Paul Kamera sent his apologies for not attending but bought enough food for what he had expected to be a big funeral. Peter Mberi gave a moving eulogy making all the good points that he knew about Themba.

"In conclusion," he said as he ended, "I think I can say that Jonas and I gave him his last farewell the night before he died. He was happy and really looking forward to the rest of his life. He did not, at the time, realise just how short that would be. We have lost a friend, a brother, and a true hero of Zimbabwe." Peter stood back and scanned the small crowd again. No one of any significance in the Party or government had bothered to attend the funeral of one of the real heroes of the country. It was so sad, he thought.

Apart from a lot of air punching and fist waving, George Magaya had nothing to say, although his speech took a lot longer than Peter's.

"The revolution will go on," he said in conclusion, "despite the loss of such dedicated comrades as Comrade Themba Ndlovu. His contribution will never be forgotten!"

'It's already forgotten', Peter thought to himself.

Dorothy watched as the simple plywood coffin, hastily put together by a local carpenter that morning, was carefully lowered into the grave besides Themba's parents' graves – they had to be careful; when they tried to lift the coffin from the house after it had been loaded with Themba's body, the bottom – with the body on it – had stayed on the ground while the rest of the coffin came up, surprising the pall bearers with its lightness! They had had to tie some barbed wire round it to hold together what the rusty nails could not. As Pastor Jones read the appropriate bits of scripture, Dorothy thought about just how the last two years had changed the face of the Zimbabwe she had always known. Peter Mberi had announced that he was closing the Mberi Trading Store because business was so bad; Pastor Jones, a fixture in this area for many years was leaving the country, his home at the church having been taken over by George Magaya; Jonas Mangwende was going back to Murewa to finally live with his wife after many years apart, his employers having decided to move to Mozambique; and Themba…

"At least Themba has claimed his own piece of Zimbabwe that no one can take away from him," she said out loud.

"That is so true," Peter Mberi said, "although I think in a few years, with the pressure of population growth, people will be ploughing over these graves."

"Yes, but Themba will still be down there."

That evening, with all the food and drink provided by Paul Kamera, the people of Manhowe had the biggest party of their lives. There was not going to be another party like it for years. It was, Peter Mberi thought, a fitting send off for a real hero.

Whose Land is it Anyway?

www.ingramcontent.com/pod-product-compliance
Lightning Source LLC
Chambersburg PA
CBHW070619260626
47161CB00007B/2501